Wives at War

If she hadn't been deaf he might have been tempted to forget himself and give her a telling off. He had been brought up to respect women, though, and under the layers of annoyance and anxiety, he was grieving too, grieving at last for Rosie and the lost infant.

When he'd tried to put his arm about her in the taxi, she'd pushed him roughly away.

He'd hesitated, then told her, 'I've arranged for your mother to come over and take care of you.'

'Where will you be?'

'Rosie, I'm sorry but I do have to go to work.'

'*Work?*' she'd shouted. 'You don't cuh-care about me, do you?'

'That's not true.'

'You don't cuh-care about the baby.'

'Rosie, I didn't know about the baby.'

'Well, I don't care about the baby. I'm glad it's gone . . .'

About the Author

Born in Glasgow, Jessica Stirling is the author of more
than twenty heartwarming novels, many with Scottish
backgrounds.

JESSICA STIRLING

Wives at War

St. Martin's Press ♏ New York

www.stmartins.com

Library of Congress Cataloging-in-Publication Data

Stirling, Jessica.
    Wives at war / Jessica Stirling
        p. cm.
    ISBN 0-312-34024-9
    EAN 978-0312-34024-7
    1. World War, 1939–1945—Scotland—Glasgow—Fiction. 2. Married women—Fiction. 3. Sisters—Fiction. 4. Glasgow (Scotland)—Fiction.

PR6069.T497 W57 2005
823'.914—dc22   2004060016

First published in Great Britain by Hodder and Stoughton
A Division of Hodder Headline

First U.S. Edition: April 2005

10 9 8 7 6 5 4 3 2 1

November

I

Babs had always suspected that industry and commerce were built around a wide margin of inefficiency but it wasn't until she went to work for the Ministry of Labour in the early autumn of 1940 that she learned just how wide that margin could be and how damaging to a nation at war.

'War,' Mr Harding informed her on her first day at the office, 'war is, by its very nature, the quintessence of insecurity. Our problem is how to strike a balance between security, which can easily bracket off into apathy or all-consuming self-interest, and insecurity, which leads to irritation, disunity and stress. Are you with me on that, Mrs Hallop?'

'Yes, sir, I do believe I am.'

He gave her the eye, not the sort of eye Babs was used to receiving from men but a deep, dour sort of scrutiny so magnified by his inch-thick lenses that she felt as if he were peering right through her. Without his glasses, she thought, his eyes would probably vanish altogether, like those of a hedgehog or a vole. He was, at a guess, not a day over twenty-five.

'Twenty-six per cent labour wastage in the third quarter of last year, according to government figures,' Archie Harding went on. 'My God, how the Germans must be laughing up their sleeves. My job, my role in this mighty conflict is to ensure that production quotients are increased by the simple expedient of redistributing the work force into areas where it will do most good. Only by winning the production war can we hope to stop Adolf in his tracks. And we're just the lads to do it, are we not, Mrs Hallop?'

'Absolutely,' Babs, laddishly, agreed.

'You're a qualified typist, I take it?'

'Secretary.'

'Where were you previously employed?'

'Manone's.'

'Manone's!'

She couldn't tell if he was dismayed or impressed by mention of the name. If he'd known even half of what had gone on in her brother-in-law's warehouse before the war, however, the patriotic Mr Harding would surely have run her out of the office there and then. Dominic Manone was gone, of course. In the autumn of '39 he had gathered up his ill-gotten gains, and his children, and escaped to America before the forces of law and order could muster a case against him for his part in a counterfeiting operation.

The fact that Dominic had left Polly, her sister, high and dry in Glasgow did not endear him to Babs. As far as she was concerned every Johnny Foreigner should be locked up. She kept the opinion to herself, though, for her sisters were outraged by the Government's cavalier treatment of foreign nationals.

'Yes,' said Babs, exaggerating somewhat, 'I was Mr Manone's personal assistant before I got married.'

'Ah, of course, you're one of the marrieds, aren't you?'

Babs held up her hand and displayed a tarnished wedding ring.

'Sure am,' she said.

'Do you have children?'

'Four.'

Mr Harding's brows rose. 'Four!'

'Three girls,' said Babs, 'and a boy.'

'Who's looking after them?'

'The wee one,' Babs answered, 'lives at home with me. The others are boarded out.'

'Evacuated, you mean?'

'Yes,' said Babs. 'Went off, came back, went off again.'

'Are they far away?'

'Not really. They're on a farm at Blackstone.'

'Where's that?'

'Across the river, near Breslin.'

'Very posh,' said Mr Harding. 'Staying with relatives, are they?'

'With friends of my sister, actually,' said Babs.

'Well, they're better out of the way, I suppose.'

Babs missed her children more than she cared to admit. She gave a haughty little toss of the head. 'I take it *you* don't have children, Mr Harding?'

'Not I.'

'Well then . . .'

'I do not wish to imply that there's no emotional distress involved in being parted from one's offspring,' said Archie Harding, hastily. 'It's simply that women can adjust better and put their shoulders to the wheel with more – erm – enthusiasm if they know their little ones are being well cared for.'

'Of course,' said Babs.

In fact May, June and Angus were thriving at Blackstone Farm, where they were cared for by Douglas Giffard and Miss Dawlish, Polly's housekeeper; an odd arrangement that seemed to be working well.

'Husband on active service?' Mr Harding enquired.

'He's in the army, somewhere in Devon.'

'You won't see much of him then?'

'Don't see him at all,' said Babs.

'He's safe, though,' said Mr Harding, 'in Devon.'

'As safe as any of us these days,' Babs said.

Jackie was a corporal in the Royal Army Ordnance Corps and repaired tanks and armoured cars on the manoeuvring grounds near Yelverton where he'd been stationed for the last ten months. Babs had a strong suspicion that he was having the time of his life but she couldn't be sure, for his letters were few and far between. She fretted more about her brother-in-law Dennis, who had transferred into the air branch of the Royal Navy and was presently pitching about on an aircraft carrier somewhere in the North Atlantic.

Back in 1939, when the older children had first been evacuated, Babs had experienced a sense of freedom the like of which she hadn't known since she'd been a girl growing up in the Gorbals.

Along with millions of others, she'd been lulled into a false sense of security by what they were now calling 'the phoney war', those weeks and months when nothing much seemed to be happening and air raids and gas attacks had failed to materialise. Then things had turned nasty, very nasty; British ships were being sunk ten-a-penny by German U-boats, the army had only just escaped from Dunkirk, London had been bombed, Italy had entered the fray, France had fallen and the war had spread into parts of the world that Babs had barely heard of.

'Know what worries me?' Archie Harding said.

'No, what?'

'The probability that when this war is over women will imagine they're entitled to all these perks and benefits.'

'What perks and benefits?' Babs said.

'Big pay envelopes, responsible posts, pensions. Parity, in a word,' said Mr Harding. 'Equality.'

'I wouldn't worry about it,' Babs said.

'Why not?'

'The trade union machine will grind us up and spit us out again just as soon as peace is declared.'

'Ah, but will women stand for it?'

'Women always do,' said Babs.

Archie Harding sniffed and gave her another dour, deep stare. He came round from behind the desk and perched on it, facing her. His office was hardly bigger than a closet and much smaller than the reception area at the front of the building where she, Babs, would work.

Cyprus Street Recruitment and Welfare Centre, a sub-branch of a branch of the Ministry of Labour, was situated in the middle of nowhere. Only one bus served the area and trams turned at the little depot behind St Jerome's church at the head of the disused ferry ramp that sloped steeply into the river. Bleak wasn't the word for Cyprus Street. All around were shipyards and graving docks; across the river, more of the same. A row of steel fencing, four long sandbagged warehouses and a brick wall separated the street from the oily brown waters of the Clyde along which ships of war and trade, identically daubed in Admiralty grey, slid past like the scenery in a puppet play.

The shops that hugged the corners at St Jerome's Cross had boarded windows and were already selling unrationed goods only to regular customers. Babs was registered with her local Co-op miles away on the Holloway Road, near where she lived. Shopping, she realised, would be a major problem, not one that the loquacious Mr Harding would be likely to take into account when he required her to work late into the evening.

'What,' Babs said, 'will I be expected to do here, Mr Harding?'

'Bit of this, bit of that. Adaptability will be your watchword, as it is mine.'

'Could you maybe be a wee tad more specific?' Babs suggested.

'Our job, boiled down, is to fit square pegs into round

holes,' Archie Harding told her. 'Too many tool setters in one factory, not enough in another – we fix it. Twenty skilled artisans conscripted *en bloc* from a single plant – we replace them. You'll soon become proficient in the ignoble art of filling in forms, and will, I don't doubt, groan at the weight of paperwork required to satisfy government regulations. You'll encounter tinpot tyrants from the Department of National Service and squander vital man-hours in pointless arguments with middle managers and personnel officers. But under my tutelage you'll learn to weed out the slackers and shirkers who slouch through that door with the sole intention of sponging off the state.'

Babs hadn't taken off her hat or overcoat, hadn't yet revealed her figure in a tight black skirt and one of Jackie's white shirts that she'd modified, on the make-do-and-mend principle, with several extra buttons. Even so, Mr Archie Harding was already breathing hard, his eyes reduced and multiplied in the curve of the lenses. It wasn't the proximity of a buxom young woman that excited him, though, so much as the volume of his own rhetoric.

'I tell you this, Mrs Hallop,' he went on, 'I can spot a slacker at a thousand paces and smell a shirker as soon as he steps off the tram. They are our enemies, our foes in the production war. Together we must stamp them out.'

'We will, Mr Harding,' said Babs staunchly. 'I'm sure we will.'

'Well, Mrs Hallop – Barbara – I reckon we're going to get along famously and I'm sure you'll find your work here rewarding.' He placed a hand lightly near her shoulder. 'Now, tell me, do you know how to make tea?'

'Pardon?'

'Tea,' said Mr Harding. 'Can you brew up a nice strong cuppa?'

'Of course I can.'

'Make me a fresh pot then, dear,' Mr Harding said. 'There's a good girl.'

Then he slid behind his desk and flopped down in his chair while Babs, sighing, removed her hat and coat and went in search of the kettle upon which, she would soon learn, the efficiency of the department depended.

Babs was obliged to rise so early that it still seemed like the middle of the night on cold November mornings. Before the war a network of lights had illuminated the valley of the Clyde but now the city and its suburbs were submerged in darkness. She did her best to cheer the dawn patrol by focusing her attention on her three-year-old daughter, April, who was her dear, her darling and the light of her life.

The morning ritual of rising, washing, shivering, dressing, was followed by a hasty retreat into the kitchen with April in her arms. The kitchen door was shut tight, all four gas rings lit and purring away. April would sit quietly while Mum finished dressing, then she would perch on Mum's knee and they would eat thin milky porridge sweetened with golden syrup while Babs wove a little story about the lion – 'Out of the Strong Came Forth Sweetness' – that was depicted on the syrup tin; no mean feat for an unimaginative young woman whose teachers had marked her down as a flighty wee trollop who would probably come to a bad end.

When the porridge and story were finished Babs would pour a spoonful of Scott's Emulsion from the bottle with the fisherman on the label. April would make a face and swallow the nasty stuff and Babs would give her a fruit pastille to take away the taste, then, downing a last mouthful of tea, would open the kitchen door and admit chill air from the hallway.

Slippers, stockings, knickers – little accidents do happen – handkerchiefs, a clean facecloth and towel were stuffed into a small canvas satchel, the gas-mask container secured on its green cord and April, equipped like a soldier of the line, was ready for the road at last. Hat, overcoat, scarf, gloves. Fags and matches popped into the floppy shoulder bag that had replaced Babs's neat little pre-war purse. Straighten stockings, cram on flat-heeled shoes. Switch off the fire. Turn off the gas and unlock the front door. Then, hand in hand, mother and daughter went down the steps to the pavement.

When the cold knuckled her nose and lips, April uttered her only words of complaint. 'Dark, Mummy,' she said dolefully, glancing up at the sky. 'Cold.'

'Yes, dear,' Babs told her, 'but it won't be for long now.'

Babs knew it was selfish of her to keep April here, that the little girl would be safer and more comfortable boarded out at Blackstone with her sisters and brother. In September, soon after she'd started work, guilt had prompted her to leave the baby at the farm for a long weekend, but fond imaginings of wild nights on the town, of drinking cocktails and dancing until dawn had swiftly evaporated and she'd been back at Blackstone by Sunday lunch time and home again before sundown with April safe in her arms.

She loved all her children, of course, but not equally. There was something rather sinister about May and June, who had a feline habit of not being around when chores were being allotted or mischief uncovered. Dougie Giffard had their measure, however, and his subtle tactics had added a degree of uncertainty to the girls' self-assurance, which, Babs thought, was no bad thing. She missed Angus more than she missed the girls, but her pining, such as it was, was tempered by the fact that being around Angus for any length of time exhausted both her patience and her energy.

She had to admit, though, that Blackstone and Angus were made for each other. The farm offered space, freedom and plenty of interesting things to do. Her son could still be as noisy as a cage full of monkeys, could trumpet like an elephant, or roar like a lion when something displeased him but he had also learned how to be quiet, like an Indian scout or a jungle explorer, and let the wonders of wood, moor and hillside soak into him, along with all the wonders of fringe warfare that buzzed about the country roads and the streets of Breslin, the posh little community where he and his sisters schooled.

Babs groped her way along Raines Drive into Holloway Road. She had tried using a shielded pocket torch but had found it so ineffectual that carrying the thing was more trouble than it was worth. Fortunately April was capable of navigating the route without bumping into hedges or lampposts and it was she, not Babs, who led them to the door of the Millses' house.

The Hallops were usually last to arrive. Five or six children would already be ensconced in Mrs Mills' front room, drinking piping hot cocoa and looking, rather sleepily, at the tinted photographs of Mount Fuji and Mount Etna that decorated the walls. On the piano top were a stuffed blowfish and a big conch shell. On the mantel above the gas fire were a row of Chinese figurines carved out of soapstone and a strange, spindly clock with a painted face that played waltz tunes when Mr Mills remembered to wind it.

Mr Mills was a retired ship's engineer. He was bald now and his legs were so bowed that he needed two sticks to walk with. Mrs Mills, on the other hand, was a tall upright woman with a mane of silvery hair and a vigorous manner. The war had roused the couple from retirement and six days each week they looked after seven very young children whose mothers were on early shift.

Rain, hale or shine at eight bells precisely the little band would be herded out into Holloway Road, old Mr Mills chugging in front and stately Mrs Mills sailing behind, and off they would go to the nursery school in the church hall in

Bonniewell Street. In the evening, light or dark, Mrs M. would collect those who needed collecting and keep them snug in her parlour, listening to the wireless or playing games, until their mums came to pick them up.

It was all very organised, all very civilised, but when a child fell ill – 'Scarlet fever? Don't tell me it's scarlet fever?' – or when, as happened, Mrs M. had one of her turns and was carted off to hospital, the pattern broke down. If there was one thing Babs feared more than bombs or gas attacks or, God help us, Jackie being run over by a tank, it was a breakdown in routine.

The double-decker tram that carried her on the first leg of her journey to the office was packed with shipwrights and factory hands. Strap hanging, she fumbled in her bag, fished out fags and matches, lit a cigarette and hung there, smoking, while the men listlessly ignored her.

She wondered if they ever wondered what she did, what she was. She hoped that the black skirt and swagger overcoat gave the impression that she was a woman of authority but if any of the men were taken in they gave no sign of it and huddled disconsolately in their boiler suits and greasy overcoats, smoking and scanning the early editions of the *Daily Record* for the latest football scores and news about the war.

Babs changed trams, waited, then boarded a little single-decker for the long haul down to St Jerome's Cross. By the time the tram reached Aerodrome Road she was usually the only passenger left on board.

Grey daylight seeped through the cloud. The flat horizon bristled with isolated farmsteads and the cranes and derricks of the shipyards. She smoked another cigarette, picked lint from her skirt, and felt as desolate as the not-quite-rural landscape through which she travelled. Then with a shriek of brakes the tram shuddered to a halt and a solitary passenger climbed on to the platform from the roadside.

He fumbled with coins, frowned, asked the conductor a

question, shook his head, paid his fare, moved inside and seated himself on the long bench as far away from Babs as possible. The tram started up and, gathering speed, rattled along the edge of the old aerodrome between the melancholy potato fields.

Babs glanced along the aisle and gave the stranger a tentative smile. He did not respond. He stared down at his shoes, not shoes but thick-soled rubberised half-boots laced up to the ankle. His trousers, corduroys, were tucked into the top of his boots. A folded newspaper was stuck down against his calf like a splint. He wore a heavy reefer jacket of navy-blue flannel and a thick roll-collar pepper-and-salt sweater, no cap or hat. He was short in stature, sallow, with a mop of curly black hair. Babs thought he looked vaguely Italian.

The tram didn't stop again and the man didn't look up until the tram reached St Jerome's Cross.

'End o' the line, Jim,' the conductor shouted.

The man leapt to his feet and got off.

Babs stepped down to the cobbles by the side of the tracks and glanced right and left. Something about the guy disturbed her, something odd, something alien. In spite of his haste to leave the tram, he seemed to be in no hurry now. He wandered to the pavement in front of the greengrocer's and looked about him with an air of bewilderment.

Babs was tempted to go over and ask if he were lost but she was already five minutes late and didn't want to give Archie a stick to beat her with.

She turned on her heel and set off for the corner of Cyprus Street.

When she glanced round again the man had gone.

It was an exceptionally busy spell in Cyprus Street and three days slid past before Babs had an opportunity to put the question to Archie Harding.

Changes to the schedule of reserve occupations had thrown several spanners into several works and Archie had been glued to the telephone all morning trying to placate an assistant labour supply officer from Clydebank, who had somehow got it into his head that the south shore of the river was lined with highly trained, able-bodied men that Archie was keeping to himself.

Shortly after two o'clock Babs heard the telephone slam down and the long, wolf-like cry that Archie emitted when he'd had enough of bureaucracy. A moment later he came trotting out of the office and went into the toilet.

Babs filled the kettle and put it on the gas ring. She unwrapped the sandwiches that Archie's mother had made for his lunch, very genteel sandwiches with soft brown crusts. Archie's Mama was proud of her one-and-only, for he was the first Harding ever to obtain a university degree. He had been two years into a teaching career at Paisley Grammar when war had broken out and because of his bad eyesight he had been conscripted into the civil service instead of the army.

Drying his hands on a damp towel, Archie appeared from the toilet, glasses hanging from one ear. He peered in her general direction, groped about his cheek, found his glasses, resettled them on the bridge of his nose, glowered at her and said, 'Is there no tea?'

'There will be in a minute,' Babs said. 'Go on, sit down. I'll bring it in when it's ready – and your sandwiches.'

'Corned beef,' Archie sighed. 'Ah well, better than nothing, I suppose.'

He returned to the inner office but left the door ajar.

Babs made tea, placed the sandwiches on a plate and carried the lot into the office on a tin tray. Archie had taken the telephone off the hook and was sprawled in the chair with his hands behind his head. Babs slid the tray carefully on to the desk, poured tea into the cup.

Archie watched her warily.

'What?' he said.

'Eat,' Babs instructed him.

He lifted the teacup in both hands, blew on the surface of the liquid, steaming his glasses. He sipped, then said again, 'What?'

'May I ask you a question?'

He grunted. 'I knew you'd something on your mind. You've been hovering all day just waiting to catch me unawares. Out with it.'

Babs seated herself on the interview chair and tugged her skirt over her knees. She watched him lift a sandwich, sniff it, bite into it.

'Archie,' she said, 'do you believe in spies?'

'Spies?' He chewed reflectively then said, 'Might as well ask if I believe in fairies. Spies, do I believe in spies?'

'How about an answer?' Babs said.

'Yes certainly, assuredly, I do believe in spies. The enemy is everywhere. That Belfast woman who came in the other day, the one with the moustache, she was probably a spy. The old bloke with the limp and the glass eye – one of the Gestapo's finest. And I'll swear Hermann Goering was seated behind me on the bus this morning, peering over my shoulder at my *Times Educational Supplement.*'

'Be serious.'

Archie filled his cheeks with bread and beef. 'All right, it's been a long morning and I could do with a good laugh. Tell me, dear, where did you run into this spy of yours?'

'On the tram, on the Aerodrome Road.'

'It isn't called that now. It's been renamed to confuse Jerry pilots.'

'Damn it, Archie!'

'Go on, go on.'

'I've seen him every day this week,' Babs said. 'He gets on

at a stop in the back of beyond and gets off at the Cross. He doesn't appear to be *doing* anything. He rides the tram to the Cross then just sort of hangs around.'

'Perhaps he's starting a queue for bananas.'

'Arch—'

'What's suspicious about him?'

'I'm sure he isn't British.'

'Italian?'

'Possible but hardly likely.'

'He could be a Greek,' Archie suggested.

'I wouldn't know what a Greek looks like,' said Babs.

'Well, lots of foreign seamen are hanging round the port these days,' said Archie. 'I wouldn't worry about it.'

'He has a camera.'

'Ah!' Archie sat up. 'Now that's different.'

'I only noticed it this morning. He keeps it hidden under his jacket. It's a tiny wee thing, the camera. Never seen one like it before.'

'How small?'

Babs squared a postage stamp of air with her fingertips. ''Bout this size.'

'God, that is small,' said Archie.

'Secret weapon?' Babs said.

'Could be,' Archie admitted. 'Could just be. When you noticed the camera – I mean, did he see you?'

'Yep.'

'How did he react?'

'Sort of . . .' Babs shrugged.

'Furtively?'

'That's it – furtively,' said Babs. 'He stuck it up his jumper real quick. What could he possibly be photographing round here? There's nothing round here but shipyards.'

'And an aerodrome. And an ordnance factory. And the fuel dump.'

'Fuel dump?'

'In the warehouses over the wall.'

'You're kiddin' me,' said Babs.

'Packed to the roof with emergency fuel. Didn't you know?'

'No.'

'What did you think those big lorries were delivering – ginger beer?'

'What if there's a daylight raid and a bomb falls on—'

Archie cut her off. 'Don't be morbid.'

'But if it happened, if it did, what would become of us?'

'They'd be sweeping us up with a dustpan,' Archie said. 'However, just so long as your spy doesn't have a detonator stuffed up his jumper at least he can't do us much harm – if he's a spy at all, that is.'

'What should we do?'

'Tell you what,' Archie said, 'tomorrow morning, you challenge him.'

'Challenge?' said Babs. 'Like, "Halt, who goes there?"'

'Not precisely the phrase I had in mind,' said Archie. 'More like "Fine morning, is it not, kind sir?"'

'What if it's raining?'

'Barbara, please, do not be obtuse,' said Archie. 'What we need to ascertain is whether he is or is not a foreigner. When he answers, you should be able to tell, A: if he speakada English; B: if he has a sound grasp of colloquialisms.'

'Of what?'

'Never mind,' said Archie. 'Just tell me what he says, how he responds.'

'Like – furtively?'

'Precisely.'

'An' if he does?'

'I'll contact the proper authorities.'

'Who are the proper authorities?'

Archie looked blank for a moment. 'The cops, I suppose.'

'My sister Rosie's husband – he's a copper. He'd know what to do.'

'What beat's he on?'

'He isn't on a beat. He's with the CID.'

'Really!' Archie was impressed. 'You never told me that.'

'You never asked.'

'Friends in high places,' said Archie. 'Well, well! Might come in handy if this chap on the tramcar does turn out to be a wrong 'un.'

'So you don't think I'm making a fuss over nothing?'

'Absolutely not,' said Archie.

As a rule Babs was untroubled by the sort of deep-seated anxieties that tormented her sister Rosie, but that Friday morning she was so nervous that it was all she could do not to snap at poor April during breakfast. She'd been awake half the night rehearsing how she would approach the stranger and lure him into revealing his intentions, and by the time she boarded the single-decker she'd smoked four cigarettes and her throat hurt.

The interior of the tramcar was dank, the windows dripping with condensation. The smell of stale smoke and unwashed bodies clung like sticky tendrils to the worn upholstery. The driver had a streaming head cold, the conductor a hacking cough. Fat lot of use they'd be, Babs thought, if she happened to need protection.

The tram hurtled towards Aerodrome Road. Familiar land-marks whizzed past – a derelict farmhouse, potato sheds, a wrecked and rusting tractor – then the tram began its grinding descent and finally jerked to a halt. Her handsome stranger, her spy, her Johnny Foreigner, neat and self-contained, hopped aboard and seated himself on the long bench.

The camera was well hidden. Babs could see nothing of it. He glanced down the aisle, gave her the ghost of a smile then fished in his jacket pocket and produced a packet of cigarettes, an odd-looking packet, all soft and crinkly. He flicked his wrist, knocked out a single cigarette, put the pack into his pocket and brought out a big metal lighter.

Babs found herself stumbling down the aisle.

He glanced up, the soft yellow flame of the lighter flickering under his nose, the tip of the cigarette dabbing about in space. His eyes were dark, not like Dominic Manone's or Angus's, but liquid black, like engine oil. The skin around his eyes crinkled a little as she lurched towards him and, shaken by the motion of the tram, toppled into his lap.

'Hey, lady,' he said, 'take care now.'

Babs thrust herself away, legs wide apart, shoulders sliding against the window glass then, raw and breathless, cheeks scarlet, plonked herself down on the seat beside him and growled in unabashed Glaswegian, ''Scuse me. Huv youse gotta light?'

'Pardon me?'

'A light, a light, for God's sake. Don't you speak English?'

'Sure I do' he said. 'Would you care for a cigarette too?'

'I've got my own cigarettes,' Babs said. 'What are those anyway?'

He brought out the packet and held it up between finger and thumb. 'Lucky Strike,' he said. 'I guess you don't have them over here.'

'American?'

'Sure. American,' he said. 'Take one. Take a couple if you want.'

'You're an American.'

'That I am.'

The Americans were our allies and an American wouldn't lie; it didn't cross Babs's mind that he might be a German or an Italian pretending to be an American. Engulfed by a wave of relief, she snuggled closer.

'My brother-in-law lives on Staten Island. Do you know where that is?'

He laughed. 'Every New Yorker's been to Staten Island.'

'New York!' said Babs. 'I've always wanted to see New York.'

He tapped out a cigarette and offered it to her. She took it. He lit it, cautiously holding the big scarf-like flame of the lighter at a safe angle. She inhaled deeply, smothered a cough, and blew out smoke in a breathy cloud.

'Maybe you know my brother-in-law. His name's Dominic Manone.'

'I don't think I do.'

'He took the kids away when the war started.'

'Because he's Italian?'

It dawned on Babs that perhaps she'd been a little too generous with the personal stuff and that mentioning Dominic's name had not been a good idea.

She said, 'Are you an Italian?'

'You're not the first person to ask that.'

'You *look* Italian,' said Babs, adding lamely, 'or Greek.'

'Believe it or not,' the man said, 'I'm almost as Scottish as you are. My old man was born in Greenock, my ma in Helensburgh. They emigrated soon after they got married.'

'So where were you born?'

'Milwaukee, me and my brother both.'

'Before you moved to New York?'

'Yeah.'

'And,' said Babs, as casually as possible, 'how long ago was that?'

'I'm thirty-five,' he said. 'You work it out.'

She was too caught up in the conversation to suspect that he might be trying to give her the brush-off. He had a little gold cap on one of his front teeth. She had never met anyone with a gold-capped tooth before. It seemed to fit with his liquid black eyes and curly hair and the faint, rich smell of American cigarettes that clung to his reefer jacket. It was the smile, though, particularly the smile about the eyes that really deceived her.

'Huh!' Babs said. 'An' I thought you were a spy.'

'Really! What made you think that?'

'The camera.'

'Aw yeah, the camera.'

'An' because you got on where you did. What are you doing here? Are you a sailor?'

Before he could answer, the conductor lurched back from the platform and bawled, 'End o' the line. All off, all off,' and coughed in staccato fashion, filling the damp air with germs.

Babs dropped her cigarette and made to rise. Her new-found friend offered his arm like one of the gentlemen at a ball in a Bette Davis film. Babs let him squire her on to the platform and down on to the cobbles.

Reluctantly she lifted her hand from his arm and stepped back. There were a dozen questions she hadn't asked yet, a hundred things she wanted to know, but Archie would be standing in the office doorway, champing at the bit. He had a nine o'clock appointment with a Labour Supply Board investigator over at Ostler's Engineering and required her to man the office. He would also, no doubt, be keen to learn if she had really unmasked a spy and if there would be glory in it for both of them.

'I – I have to go,' Babs said. 'Thank you for the – the cigarette.'

'My pleasure,' the American said.

'Tomorrow – maybe see you tomorrow.'

'Sure.'

He didn't turn away, didn't head for the pavement.

The tram trundled on, the conductor walking ahead with a long iron key to change the points. Babs felt space behind her, the moist sky bearing down on cranes and scaffolding and half-built ships, felt too the tug of Cyprus Street and Archie's impatience.

'I really do have to go,' she said.

'Sure,' he said again and, without moving, watched her leave.

She trotted across the cobbles to the corner of Cyprus Street before she checked and turned. She expected to find that he had vanished – but he hadn't. He was squatting on his heels in the middle of the road, pointing the camera at her. Babs opened her mouth to protest, then, on impulse, flung up an arm, flared her fingers and gave him the long haughty over-the-shoulder look that Jackie said made her look like a tart.

The delicate cocking of the photographer's middle finger was too discreet to be visible. He went on snapping, shot after shot, until Babs, suddenly and unexpectedly shy, dismantled her pose and darted round the corner out of sight.

Archie *was* hopping mad. He paused only long enough to enquire, 'Well, what is he? Is he a Greek or Italian? What did he have to say for himself?'

'He's American.'

'Oh, is he? What's he doing over here then?'

'Visiting relatives in Greenock,' said Babs, 'I think.'

'Huh!' Archie snorted. 'Is that all?' then grabbing his gas mask from the hook behind the front door, sprinted off to catch the tram.

It wasn't the first time that Archie had left her in sole command and she was much more assured than she had been a couple of months ago. The telephone was already ringing in Archie's office. Babs answered it. Shaken by her encounter with the American and puzzled as to why he had taken her photograph, she listened with only half an ear to the complaints that sizzled down the line, complaints about the inappropriateness of three young women whom Archie had sent over to the Riverside Bolt, Rivet & Nut Company yesterday, young women who didn't fancy working on a packing line and wanted a job that wouldn't damage their fingernails.

She remembered the girls vividly, three sisters, a bit like Polly, Rosie and she had been at eighteen, nineteen, unwilling to conform, unwilling to compromise and always on the look out for the easy option. There had been few easy options in the Gorbals, though, which was why Polly had given in to Dominic Manone and she had surrendered to Jackie Hallop.

She held the receiver away from her ear and let Riverside's personnel officer rant on for a while before she informed him that Archie would be out all day but would attend to the matter as soon as possible tomorrow.

She hung up the telephone, which immediately began to ring again. Ignoring it, she went to unearth the files on the three girls from the tall metal cabinet in the outer office.

Her American friend was leaning in the doorway, camera in hand.

'I shouldn't have done that,' he said. 'I'm sorry.'

'Done what?' said Babs.

'Photographed you without permission.'

'Why did you then?'

'You looked good,' he said. 'You looked right.'

'Right for what?' said Babs.

The phone was still ringing next door and she wished, sort of, that Archie hadn't gone out and left her alone.

'I'll send you prints,' he said.

'How can you send me prints when you don't know where I live?'

'I'm hoping you'll tell me,' he said.

'I'm not in the habit of giving my address to strangers.'

'Isn't this a welfare office?'

'Yes, but what does that have to do with you?'

'I'm looking for welfare,' he said.

'Welfare?' said Babs. 'What sort of welfare?'

'A place to stay. Digs.'

'For – for how long?'

'Couple of months. Maybe three.'

Babs closed the door to Archie's office, muffling the sound of the telephone. She seated herself at her desk, extracted a form from the drawer and uncapped a fountain pen. The form was an application for maternity leave, but the photographer didn't know that.

'Name?'

'Is this necessary?' he said.

'Of course it's necessary. We're a government department. Name?'

'Cameron. Christopher Ewan Cameron. Everyone calls me Christy.'

'Date of birth.'

'November tenth, nineteen-nought-five.'

'Nature of current occupation?'

'I'm a professional photographer,' he said.

'It isn't just a hobby then?'

'Nope, I'm in Scotland to cover the war for *Brockway's* magazine. When my security clearance comes through I'll be shipping out to do a series about the hazards of the North Atlantic crossing.'

'*Brockway's* magazine?'

'You've heard of it?'

'Yes,' said Babs. 'It's not as good as the *Picture Post*.'

'I've sold stuff to the *Post* too, and *Life*, and even *Ce Soir*.'

'Really!' said Babs. 'Current address, please?'

'I'm billeted with a unit of the Civil Defence in a concrete bunker with no running water and no cooking stove.'

'Who dumped you there?'

'Brockway's London office. Their idea of a joke, I guess.'

'What sort of accommodation are you looking for?'

'A clean bed and a bathroom where the taps work.'

'You'll have to pay through the nose for a place like that.'

'I'm sure I will.'

Babs scribbled away with the fountain pen, filling boxes at random on the useless form. When she glanced up she thought how forlorn he looked, how far from home. 'Well, Mr Cameron,' she heard herself say, 'I've a spare room at the moment and I'm prepared to take in a lodger on a temporary basis. You can come home with me if you like.'

'Oh yeah,' said Christy Cameron. 'I definitely like.'

'Five o'clock at the depot? Is that a problem?'

'No problem, Miss . . . ?'

'Babs,' Babs told him. 'You'd better just call me Babs.'

2

'Well,' Rosie said, 'I think it's a scandal and someone should put a stop to it.'

'I hope you don't mean me,' Kenny said.

'You?' said Rosie. 'Oh no, dear me no. You're far too busy.'

'For God's sake, Rosie, there's a—'

'A war on – yes, I huh-have noticed.'

She had been deaf since childhood and had never mastered sign language. Her talent for lip-reading was almost uncanny, however. Her sisters, mother and stepfather, Bernard, had learned to shape their vowels without effort but Kenny still had to apply a degree of concentration that Rosie regarded as unnecessary and, in the worst of her moods, insulting.

It had been different in the early months of their marriage when his sister, Fiona, had shared the flat with them or, more correctly, they with her.

As soon as war was declared, however, Fiona had enlisted in the WAAF. She was currently attached to a Fighter Command sector station at Kenley and had manned the communications system during the worst of the German air attacks in August and September. Kenny had been sick with worry. He had said a prayer for her every night, a gesture that Rosie had regarded as pure superstition, bordering on the unhealthy.

Rosie leaned across the kitchen table, soup spoon dripping.

'My sister is living with another man, a man who isn't her husband and you're not the slightest concerned.'

Kenny said, 'She's taken in a lodger, that's all.'

'Who told you that?'

'You did,' said Kenny, 'not ten minutes ago.'

He was tired. He was perpetually tired these days. He was still several years short of forty but felt like an old man.

Frayed nerves, overwork and worry, magnified by her handicap, had changed Rosie too. She was no longer the girl he had fallen in love with, and in spite of the fact that he loved her still there were times when he wished he'd heeded Fiona's advice and remained a bachelor.

'Who told you about Babs and her lodger?' he asked.

'Polly.'

'How did Polly find out?'

'Babs couldn't wait to run round to Manor Park Avenue to impart the news that she'd ditched Jackie and found another man.'

'Whoa,' said Kenny. 'A lodger isn't the same thing as another man.'

'As good as.' Rosie paddled her spoon in her soup. 'You know what Babs is like. She'll have this chap in her bed before he knows what's hit him.'

'Thousands of women are taking in lodgers,' Kenny said.

'Americans?'

'If he's American he probably won't stay long.'

'Just long enough to nin-knock her up.'

'Oh, Rosie!'

'I don't know what Mammy will have to say about it.'

'Doesn't your mother know yet?' said Kenny.

'No, and I am not going to be the one to tell her.'

When war had broken out he had assumed that his clever little wife would continue to work in Shelby's bookshop but within weeks she had gone out to find – to demand – her share of highly paid war work. Now this silly squabble, this storm in the family teacup had blown up and Rosie was off again, blaming him for her sister's indiscretion just as she blamed him for everything else that displeased her.

A precious hour, that's all the time they would have together this evening; Rosie seemed determined to squander it fretting about her sister's moral welfare. He had dragged himself home after a twelve-hour shift and would have to go out soon to fire-watch; ten until two, perched, freezing, on the roof of the CID building in St Andrew's Street. The canteen at police HQ would have supplied him with an unrationed supper and congenial company. He wished now that he hadn't bothered coming home at all.

'Where,' he said, 'did Babs meet this chap?'

'At the Welfare Centre, I think.'

'Not the Sweethearts Club?'

'I don't think she's ever been to the Sweethearts Club.'

Rosie broke bread into her soup and mopped it up with her spoon. She looked deathly pale and there were panda-like circles around her eyes. Eleven hours a day assembling tiny components in an ill-lit cubicle in Merryweather's electrical factory was ruining her health. Soon, Kenny thought sadly, Rosie would look as old as he felt.

'Perhaps he's an old chap, this lodger,' Kenny heard himself say.

'He is not an old chap,' Rosie retorted. 'He's young. Take my word for it – Babs is doing the duh-dirty on poor Jackie.'

Kenny wondered where Rosie had heard such a coarse expression and, come to think of it, *how* she had heard it. Probably at Merryweather's where the girls were more worldly-wise than his wife even though she'd been raised in one of Glasgow's toughest neighbourhoods and had had a gangster for a father.

He pushed away his plate. 'This American chap, what's he doing here?'

'Working for a newspaper, I think.'

'What? Like a journalist?'

'Photographer.'

'Really!' Kenny said.

'I don't know much about him,' Rosie said, 'only what Babs told Polly and Polly told me. I don't think Polly was interested, to tell you the truth.'

'I wonder,' Kenny said, 'why Babs told Polly in the first place.'

'To impress her,' Rosie said. 'It's always been Babs's ambition to go one better than Polly.'

'Taking in a lodger is hardly going one better.'

'Nuh, but taking on a lover is.'

Rosie lifted away the soup plates and put them on the draining board beneath the blackout curtains at the sink. She opened the oven door and brought out two small meat pastries. On top of the stove was a pot, a pot that gave off no steam or smell. She opened the pot lid, spooned luke-warm peas on to the plate with the pastries and put it down before her husband.

Kenny studied his supper without comment.

'What are you having?' he asked, at length.

'I'm not hungry.'

'Did you have lunch?'

'I bought something off the trolley.'

'You should eat something, Rose,' he said mildly.

'I *told* you, I'm nuh-not hungry. This business with Babs has ruined my appetite.'

Kenny cut into one of the pastries, more onion than meat within.

'What do you want me to do about it?' he said.

'Go see her,' Rosie said.

'I can't just barge in out of the blue and ask Babs if she's sleeping with her lodger.'

Rosie frowned, eyes darker than ever, the circles around them like huge blue bruises. 'Tell her you're checking his visa?'

'Checking visas isn't my department.'

'If Dominic were still here, he'd take care of it. He'd sort Babs out.'

Kenny knew better than anyone that Dominic Manone had been fortunate to escape imprisonment for his crimes. He was stung by the unfair comparison with his brother-in-law. 'Do you really want me to talk to Babs?'

'Yuh, I really want you to.'

'I can't go tonight. I'm fire-watching in half an hour.'

Rosie's frown deepened. 'You're not wriggling out of it?'

'I'll go tomorrow as soon as I finish my shift.'

'Is that a promise, Kenneth?'

'Yes, dearest,' he said, 'that's a promise.'

Hallop's Motoring Salon, once Jackie's pride and joy, had been taken over by the Civil Defence. The plate-glass windows behind which a selection of desirable second-hand motorcars had once reposed were crisscrossed with sticky tape. A water supply tank had been erected in the forecourt and only the pumps and repair pit behind the main building remained functional, reserved, Kenny guessed, for servicing emergency vehicles.

It was here on the forecourt of the salon during an investigation into Manone's shady dealings that he had first encountered Jackie Hallop and Babs and had become involved with Rosie and the rest of the Conway clan. If anyone had told him then that he would fall head over heels in love with the sister-in-law of a notorious Glasgow criminal and wind up married to her he would have called them crazy.

Kenny hadn't clapped eyes on Babs since early summer. He had been far too busy. The Special Protection Unit was no longer the paltry wee sideshow it had been under the late Inspector Winstock.

Kenny had spent that afternoon with a liaison officer from Naval Intelligence at the old Greenock Prison, interrogating two so-called 'businessmen' who had been arrested for running shipments of British-made arms to neutral ports in Portugal in contravention of about three dozen laws, at least four of which might see them hanged. The liaison officer had invited him to dine at the Royal Greenock Yacht Club – now a naval establishment – but mindful of his promise to Rosie, he had politely declined.

Instead he had hitched a ride in an RN gharry as far as Paisley, had caught a tram from there to Holloway Road and trudged the last half-mile to Raines Drive. By right he should be back at HQ, or with Rosie in the flat in Cowcaddens. He had rigged up red light bulbs in the flat's kitchen and bedroom and Mr McVicar, the local warden, had been instructed to press the button on the landing door the instant the siren sounded, for Rosie, being deaf, couldn't hear the warnings of air attack and he emphatically didn't want to have to rake among the rubble in search of his wife's broken body, thank you very much.

He stood on the doorstep of Babs's bungalow and listened to a wireless set playing dance music for a moment, then he rang the bell.

The door opened. Babs peered out at him.

'If it's the blackout again—' she began.

'No, it's me,' said Kenny.

'Who?'

'Kenny. Rosie's husband.'

'Blimey!' said Babs. 'What a surprise.'

'May I come in?'

There was a faint sheen of light under the door of the living room but the hallway, sensibly, was in darkness. The sound of the radio orchestra was louder now and Kenny recognised the tune – 'Only Make Believe'.

Babs frowned. 'What is it? Is Rosie ill?'

'Everyone's fine. I just happened to be in the neighbourhood . . .'

She stood back and admitted him to the hallway. In the darkness he could smell her perfume, her warmth, and sense, he thought, her agitation.

'I'm not disturbing you, am I?'

'Course not. Come in.'

She stepped ahead of him into the cosy, lamp-lit living room. There was even a fire in the grate, though the room was hardly what you would call warm. The wireless set, one of several that Jackie had collected over the years, was on a stand by the window. Babs switched it off.

The chap in the armchair by the hearth wore a heavy pepper-and-salt sweater, thick corduroy trousers and a pair of well-darned woollen stockings. A newspaper was folded across his chest and Kenny guessed that he had been catching up on his shut-eye.

'Where's your daughter? Where's April?'

'In bed, fast asleep,' Babs told him. 'Drink? We have Scotch.'

'No. No thanks,' said Kenny.

He thrust his hands deep into his overcoat pockets and tipped his hat back, his blue eyes watchful and assessing, not hard.

The man in the armchair rose and offered his hand. 'Hi,' he said, 'I'm Christy Cameron. I guess we haven't met.'

Kenny shook the chap's hand.

'This is my sister Rosie's husband,' Babs said. 'He's a copper and I think he's here to give you the once-over.'

Christy Cameron spread his hands. 'Well, here I am, in all my glory. You sure you don't want a drink, Mr . . . ?'

'MacGregor. Kenny.'

'Inspector Kenny?'

'Just Kenny will do.'

Babs brushed his shoulder as she passed out of the room into the hallway to check on the blackout curtain or to make sure that April was asleep.

'*Have* you come to give me the once-over?' Christy said.

'More or less.'

Christy laughed and seated himself in the armchair again. He nodded towards the sofa that faced the fireplace. 'Best make yourself comfortable if I'm gonna regale you with the story of my life.'

Obediently Kenny unbuttoned his overcoat, took off his hat and seated himself on the sofa

'I guess you're wondering what I'm doing here?'

'I assume you're a lodger,' Kenny said.

'Yeah,' Christy said. 'It wasn't my idea, but when Barbara offered me room and board – would you have turned it down?'

'I imagine not,' said Kenny.

'You get sick of hotels in my game.'

'What exactly is your game, Christy?'

'Nobody told you? I'm a photographer.'

'What do you photograph?'

'Anything and everything.'

'For instance?' Kenny said.

'If you wanna check my credentials call the London office of *Brockway's Illustrated Weekly*.'

'Where's your head office? New York?'

'Yeah, in Plaza Center,' Christy said.

'Are you on staff or do you work on contract?'

'Boy, you sure do come to the point, don't you?'

'Usually,' Kenny said.

'I'm not . . .' he glanced at the door again. 'It's not—'

'Staff or contract?' Kenny said.

The rhythm of the afternoon's interrogation was still with him but quizzing an innocent civilian wasn't part of his brief. What did it matter if Babs was having a fling? The Yank would be gone long before Jackie got out of uniform. The only danger, Kenny supposed, was that Jackie might arrive home unexpectedly on embarkation leave.

'Contract. I work for other magazines as well.'

Babs returned with April in her arms. The little girl, wide-eyed and not at all sleepy, was dressed in pink flannelette pyjamas and a pair of fluffy white socks. A dressing gown was draped about her shoulders.

'Hi, kid,' Christy said, winking. 'Too rowdy for you, are we?'

'She wants a drink of milk.' Babs put April down on Kenny's lap. 'Hold her for a minute, Ken, will you?'

Awkwardly he slid an arm about his niece's waist. He was unused to small children for he had no younger brothers or sisters, only Fiona, and the idea of Fiona ever sitting on his lap was ludicrous. April leaned back and stared up at him for several seconds, then glanced at Christy Cameron, who said, 'It's okay, honey. He's your uncle.'

The child nodded, and Kenny said, 'Aunt Rosie's my wife.'

'Uh-huh,' April said.

She squared herself on his lap, steadied herself with a hand on his arm and gave a comfortable little wriggle as if to say that she was prepared to let him amuse her and, if required, amuse him in turn.

Kenny sighed.

Uncle Kenny, not Inspector MacGregor.

Babs, he realised, had effectively spiked his guns.

After ten it seemed that the city really came to life. Pubs

emptied, buses and trams were packed and the streets bustled with wardens and special constables. It was ten thirty before Kenny reached Cowcaddens. Mr McVicar was already patrolling the pavement outside the tenement and a group of four or five elderly gentlemen from the neighbourhood, only two of them completely sober, were gathered in the close mouth, endeavouring to assemble a stirrup pump by the light of a hand torch. There had also been a delivery of sand that afternoon and two young women and a boy, armed with coal shovels, were filling fire buckets at the entrance to the backcourt.

'Have you seen Rosie?' Kenny asked the warden.

'She's fine,' Mr McVicar replied. 'Been home all evening.'

'I don't care for the weather. It's too clear for my liking.'

'Aye, one of these nights we'll be in for a pasting.'

'No doubt about it,' Kenny said, and wearily climbed the darkened stairs and let himself into the flat with his latchkey.

To his surprise Rosie hadn't waited up for him.

A 40-watt bulb burned wanly above the kitchen table, spotlighting his supper: three slices of Spam, some diced carrots and two cold potatoes dribbled over with salad cream. He felt uncharacteristic annoyance then, but reminded himself that Rosie had also had a long day of it, patiently took off his coat, washed his hands, sat down at the table and, in a matter of minutes, finished his meagre supper. He took the plate to the sink and rinsed it under the tap, then, with a cup of Bantam coffee and a cigarette, seated himself at the table again and bleakly contemplated the blackout curtains.

'Aren't you guh-going out tonight?'

He hadn't heard her enter the kitchen. She was so thin these days that she seemed to waft about the flat like a ghost. In lieu of a dressing gown she wore an old trench coat, pyjama legs flapping beneath the hem, and a pair of his old socks. Her hair was unwashed and she wore no make-up.

He turned to face her. 'No, I have to be up early tomorrow.' She didn't ask why he had to be up early. He lifted his cup. 'Want some coffee?'

'Nuh.' He glimpsed her breasts beneath the pyjama top before she tugged the lapels of the overcoat across her chest. 'You didn't go to Babs's, did you?'

'Matter of fact,' he said, 'I did.'

She hauled out a chair and seated herself at the table, facing him. 'What happened?' she said loudly. 'Tell me.'

'There isn't much to tell,' said Kenny.

'Did you meet him?

'Yes. He is what he says he is, a photographer from New York.'

'Name, what is his name?'

'Cameron.'

'Is she sleeping with him?'

'I doubt it,' Kenny said. 'In fact, no.' He repeated the word, shaping it emphatically. '*No*, he is not sleeping with her.'

Rosie threw herself back. 'Nuh-not yet.'

She folded her arms and seemed to be sulking. He longed to touch her but knew that she would only rebuff him.

'Nice chap. Christy. His first name's Christy.'

She frowned, and experimented. 'Cuh . . . Cus . . .'

'Kuh-riss-tee.'

'Christy?'

'That's it.'

'How old?'

'Thirty-five, thirty-six.'

'He spoke to you?'

'Yes, we had a long chat. Told me a lot about his job. He was in Spain covering the Civil War, Finland during the Russian invasion and in Warsaw throughout the siege.'

'If he is such a bloody great photographer what's he doing here?'

'Roosevelt wants to send more aid to Britain so the owners of national magazines have been asked to send chaps over here to take inspiring pictures to persuade the American public that we're worth helping.'

'Prop-a-ganda.'

'Yes.'

'Why did Babs take him in?'

'Because she felt sorry for him, I imagine.'

'Sorry for an American! They are all stinking rich, aren't they?'

'Only some of them,' said Kenny.

'Is he paying her for the room?'

'I expect so.'

'How much?'

'I didn't ask.'

Rosie's eyes were distant, focused on Kenny knew not what.

He had taken to the American, had found him honest and straightforward, but there was something sad about him too, a certain vulnerability. Kenny didn't really want to talk about Babs or the American any more and was bored by the gossip on which Rosie seemed to thrive. He wanted to tell her that he had lunched with Sir Charles Huserall, one of Naval Intelligence's chief liaison officers, and that Sir Charles had told him he was 'doing a grand job' and had congratulated him on the SPU's arrest record – but he knew that Rosie wouldn't be impressed.

'You must be tired,' he said.

'What?'

'Tired, you must be—'

'I heard you the first time.'

'Sorry.'

'I think someone should write to Jackie. Tell him what's going on.'

'Tell him what? That Babs is helping the war effort?'

'She is making a fortune in the process.'

'You're not doing too badly yourself, Rosie.'

'What do you mean?'

'You're earning good money at Merryweather's.'

'Don't you think I deserve it?'

Kenny sighed. 'Of course you deserve it.'

'It is not a job any Tom, Dick or Harry can do. I was picked, vetted and specially trained.'

'Of course, of course you were.'

He reached across the table and tapped his forefinger against her wrist.

'Let's go to bed.'

She glanced at him scornfully. He felt a spurt of temper at the realisation that she was more interested in Babs's affairs than his needs, and wondered if the sex side of things was about to be swallowed up by anxiety too. He rubbed his forefinger against her wrist then up under the sleeve of the overcoat to stroke the soft flesh of her forearm.

'I'm not tired,' Rosie said.

'Good,' Kenny said. 'I'm not tired either.'

She slid her arm away.

'I thought you had an early start tomorrow.'

'I do,' Kenny said. 'I have to be up at six.'

'There you are then,' Rosie said.

Pushing herself from the table, she scooped up his coffee cup and carried it to the sink. In the shabby trench coat and goblin socks, she reminded him of one of the ragamuffins that roamed the streets of the Gorbals. If he hadn't known better, he might have suspected that Rosie was reverting to type. He was no longer inclined to make love to her. What he really wanted to do was put his arms about her, kiss her and tell her that she had nothing to worry about, that he would take care of her and that everything would be all right – but he wasn't that much of a hypocrite. He stepped to one side so that she could read his lips.

'Good night, Rosie,' he said. 'Don't sit up too late.'

'I won't,' she said, addressing the blackout curtain.

And Kenny, hiding his disappointment, took himself off to bed.

Back in the good old days when he'd been coining money from selling stolen motorcars Jackie had brought her the pale peach housecoat.

Jackie was forever buying her things – jewellery, clothes, perfume, daft little ornaments for her dressing table. He was nothing if not spendthrift, her Jackie. All that had stopped when Dominic Manone had overreached himself, and the coppers, Rosie's husband among them, had come snapping at his heels. Jackie had never been mixed up in the big-money rackets, however, and whatever deal Dominic had done with the forces of law and order, Jackie and his brothers had escaped without a stain on their characters. Lucky? Oh yes, Babs thought, very lucky. Bad enough having a husband away in the army, far worse having him banged up in Barlinne Prison; explaining *that* to the children would have been no fun at all.

As it was, she was doing all right – well, moderately all right. She received a slice of Jackie's army pay every week and civil service wages weren't bad, even for a woman. She paid a shilling a day for April's nursery school. Polly had volunteered to meet the cost of keeping the other three at Blackstone. Babs had accepted her sister's offer with alacrity for, war or no war, Polly, being Polly, was doing more than all right for herself.

She knew bloody well that Polly had told Rosie about

the lodger, though, and Rosie had nagged poor Kenny into 'dropping in' to see what was what, and that the whole damned lot of them disapproved of her taking a stranger into her house. And, she thought, what about the soldier boys out there in the great unknown? What the heck do you think they're doing, half of them? Sitting about the NAAFI every night sipping tea and playing ping pong? I'll bloody bet they're not. Besides, she told herself, as she parked herself on the toilet seat to shave her legs, this is nothing, a cheap thrill, if you like, that won't get out of hand.

'Hi,' Babs said.

'Hi yourself.'

He was over by the wireless at the window, twiddling the knobs, a glass of whisky – Scotch, she must learn to call it Scotch – in one hand, a cigarette dangling from the corner of his lips. The wireless whined and whistled and then, responding to Christy's delicate manipulations, released a voice jabbering in a foreign language, a voice that almost instantly melted into Monte Rey crooning 'South of the Border'.

'I thought you'd gone to your room,' Christy said.

He was wearing the cable-knit sweater; so far she hadn't seen him in anything else. He had rolled up the woollen sleeves, though, and she noted how muscular his forearms were, and how hairy.

'Not without my nightcap,' she heard herself say.

The bottle on the coffee table was half empty. Christy had a puffy heaviness about the eyelids that suggested he'd been tippling steadily since she'd left the living room a half-hour ago. It was late now, coming up for eleven. After Monte wandered off down Mexico way there would be a news bulletin and that curious beeping that signalled the end of broadcasting for the night.

'We could both use a snort, I guess?' Christy said.

'Pardon?'

'Neat, or with ginger ale?'

'Oh – eh – neat.'

He poured a shot of whisky into a chunky glass and carried it across the living room. He walked with a rolling gait, like a seaman, toes turned in. She wondered what it would be like to dance with him. He gave her the glass, took the ciggie from his lips and held out his glass for a toast.

'Here's to family,' he said. 'Here's to Kenny.'

'What d' you mean?' said Babs.

'You didn't expect him tonight, did you?'

'Well, no, I didn't,' Babs admitted.

Glasses touched, clinking. He lingered close for a moment, looking directly into her eyes and not down the neck of the housecoat, which is what most men would have done under the circumstances.

Babs drew in a deep breath and, retreating, seated herself in one of the armchairs that flanked the fireplace. She sat back, crossed her bare legs, and modestly adjusted the folds of the housecoat.

'Nice guy,' Christy said.

'For a copper, you mean.'

'I've nothing against coppers.'

'I told my sister about you,' Babs said. 'That was a mistake.'

'Which sister would that be?' Christy asked. 'Polly, or Rosie?'

'Polly.'

'Manone's wife?'

'You've a good memory, haven't you?' Babs said.

'Pays off in my business.'

'Kenny's married to Rosie. She's the deaf one.'

'Children?'

'Not yet.'

He nodded, approached the armchair, looked down at her. She waited for him to brush her hair with his fingertips or tip up her chin and kiss her with all the courteous aplomb of a William Powell or a George Sanders. He took the cigarette from his mouth, coughed into his fist, and backed off.

Babs sat up. 'You okay?'

'Fine. Frog in my throat, is all.'

The whisky seeped warmly into Babs's chest. She had bathed in four inches of water, sponged herself down using the last bar of scented soap from her store. She could smell the fragrance rising from her body, the tang of Jackie's shaving soap too, and realised that even in the cooling air of the living room, she was beginning to perspire.

'How come she married a cop?' Christy said.

'Why shouldn't she marry a cop?' Babs said.

'It must've been awkward if Polly was already married to somebody from the other side of the street.'

'Did I tell you that?'

'Guess you did.'

'I don't remember telling you that. Still, you're right. It fair put the cat among the pigeons, our Rosie falling for a police officer. He was on Dom's case, you see, that's how he met Rosie. It's a long, boring story.'

'I like long boring stories.'

'I don't,' said Babs, 'not at this time of night, anyway.'

'You don't much care for your sisters, do you?'

Babs hesitated. 'How did you figure that out?'

He shrugged. 'Shot in the dark.'

Babs had never discussed what the family meant to her, had never told anyone that she longed to turn back the years and share again the closeness of the slum tenement when Polly had been her chum, not her rival.

'We were dragged up the hard way,' she said. 'My old man

bailed out when we were really young. My mammy worked her fingers to the bone to keep us fed and clothed. There was more to it, a lot more, but – yeah, you're right; Polly an' I don't see eye to eye. Since her husband took the children off to New York, she's changed a lot.'

'Changed? How?'

'You can't really talk to her any more. It's the war. It's always the war, isn't it? Anyway, that's my excuse for falling out with Polly.'

'You still see her, though?'

'We go over the river to visit Mammy whenever we can find time. We pretend everything's all right for Mammy's sake.'

'This farm where your kids stay, isn't that Polly's property?'

'Dominic signed it over to someone else.'

'Why did he do that?'

'I can't imagine.'

'Polly looks after it, though?' he asked.

'Polly looks after a lot of things,' Babs answered, 'mainly herself.'

He waited, watching her from the side of his eyes, then after a moment or two got up and uncapped the bottle. 'More?'

Babs shook her head.

She finished the whisky in her glass and got to her feet.

'Time I was off.'

'Stay,' Christy said. 'Talk some more.'

'I need my beauty sleep,' Babs said.

'No you don't.'

'Thanks for the compliment,' Babs said. 'But I really can't burn the candle like you can. Don't let me rush you, though. Stay up as long as you like.'

He put down the bottle and glass and waited.

Babs crossed the room and offered her cheek.

''Night, Mr Cameron,' she said.

He kissed her, his lips dry against her moist cheek. She

leaned into him for a moment, pressing her breasts against his arm. He did not draw back but what she detected in his eyes was not desire.

''Night, Babs,' he said, and returned to fiddling with the wireless set, seeking, so Babs imagined, not the soothing strains of a late-night orchestra but the voice that filtered through the static, ranting in a foreign tongue.

3

Polly could see nothing of Fin Hughes except his legs and feet. The legs were clad in immaculately pressed lightweight worsted trousers, the feet in hand-lasted brown brogans. His stockings were a pale brown colour, so fine that they seemed more like skin than lambswool. The right trouser leg had ridden up, however, and she could make out the clip of his suspenders and a section of white calf bulging above it, muscular enough but already stippled with the faint blue veins of middle age.

'Do you have a spanner there, Polly?'

She had several spanners, a whole battery of spanners. Fin had personally selected them from the rack in the garage, brought them into the kitchen and arranged them on a newspaper on the draining board above the sink.

For all his meticulous preparations Fin was no handyman and Polly took a certain malicious satisfaction in putting him into situations that exposed his lack of competence. She was, she knew, being entirely unfair, but in a society when a man's ability to use his hands effectively counted for more than his ability to use his brain, it was easy enough to make Fin feel small.

Small he was not, not in any way at all. He was tall, elegant, polished, and a good deal less effete with his clothes off than with his clothes on.

'Which one do you want?' Polly said. 'Tell me the gauge number.'

'Gauge num— Ah, the second smallest.'

His voice echoed from the hollow stone chamber beneath the sink. He had a fine courtroom voice, a rich, tawny drawl, and it was unusual for him to 'ah' or 'erm'. Fin, of course, knew no more about gauge numbers than she did but he was too vain to admit it.

She took a spanner from the row and passed it down to him. He groped for the tool with a long lean-fingered hand. His shirt cuff was stained and there was dirt under his fingernails, and Carfin Hughes, scion of the legal profession, certainly didn't like getting his hands dirty.

Polly smiled to herself and yielded up the spanner.

'Can't you fix it, darling?' she asked.

'Of course I can fix it. It's the flange nut on the stopcock.'

'Is it really?'

'I'll have pressure restored very shortly, I assure you.'

'Jolly good!' said Polly.

There was nothing seriously wrong with the plumbing. Falling water pressure was general throughout Manor Park, for an inexperienced crew from the Auxiliary Fire Service had ruptured a main pipe. A chap in a damp blue uniform had called round a couple of days ago to inform householders that full pressure would be restored as soon as possible which, these days, meant next month or the month after, or possibly not at all. Somehow, though, Polly had neglected to inform Fin of the fireman's visit.

'God, but it's stiff.' Metal scraped on metal. 'Damn and blast it!'

'If you can't manage—'

'I can manage. I can manage. Whoever installed this antiquated system should be shot, though. Why hasn't the stopcock been greased? Didn't your husband ever do it?'

'He had a man come in to do it for him.'

'Are you being sarcastic?'

'Of course not,' said Polly.

She watched the trouser leg lift in a spasm of effort, saw his hips twist and jerk on the carpet of newspaper that he had spread beneath the sink.

The useful little dribble of water from the tap dried up completely.

Panting, Fin said, 'How's that?'

'Not good.'

'Christ!'

'Oh, do come out,' Polly said. 'You'll only lose your temper.'

He had lost his temper before now, once with the lawn mower and twice with the cistern in the upstairs bathroom. His legs straightened and relaxed. Polly guessed that he would be staring up at the knot of lead and copper piping on the underside of the sink and plotting some face-saving excuse.

'Is anything happening, anything at all?'

'It's stopped,' said Polly.

'Oh!'

'Might I suggest you turn the flange of the wing nut on the stopcock in a clockwise direction.'

He said nothing. The long leg in the worsted trousers bent again and, a moment or so later, the cold water tap released a gush that settled into a weak barley-sugar-shaped coil.

'Is that better?'

'Somewhat better,' Polly said. 'Awfully clever of you. Do come out now.'

He emerged cautiously, piece by piece. She relieved him of the spanner and offered her hand. He pulled himself to his feet, brushed his trouser legs and scowled at the cold-water tap.

'That *is* better, isn't it?'

'A little bit,' Polly conceded.

'Well, it's the best I can do without proper tools.'

He washed his hands with a thoroughness that would have put a surgeon to shame and dried them on a towel that Polly gave him.

She didn't thank him for his efforts with a kiss. Except in the bedroom upstairs or more rarely in Fin's flat, they never kissed. She did not love Carfin Hughes and he did not love her. He did, however, appreciate her and that, in the midst of a miserly war, was quite enough for Polly.

He took the newspapers from under the sink and the collection of spanners and went out through the back door. She heard the rattle of the garage door and the clang of the bin lid and felt dank air from the garden seep into the kitchen. She shivered. She was cold. She was seldom anything but cold these days for the house in Manor Park Avenue was far too large now that Dominic and the children were gone, and in an unusual fit of altruism she had persuaded Margaret Dawlish, her housekeeper, to move to Blackstone Farm.

Fin returned. He washed his hands again, dried them carefully, ran a comb through his thinning hair, took his jacket from the back of a kitchen chair, slipped into it and glanced at his wristwatch.

'Art thou ready, my Polly?' he said.

It was precisely one o'clock. It was always precisely some time as far as Fin was concerned. He lived his life by the clock, which Polly assumed was a lawyer's habit and not something for which he could be blamed. She shared office space with him on the fifth floor of the Baltic Chambers in Glasgow and had witnessed first-hand the volume of business that flowed through the practice.

'We should really be moving,' Fin said.

'Yes, yes, I heard you.'

'Don't forget the eggs.'

She'd made up a small packet of shell eggs, precious as gold these days, that she had bought from Dougie Giffard to give to her mother. She carried the packet out into the hallway and placed it on a chair by the door while she put on her coat, hat and scarf and unhooked her gas mask from the hallstand.

The dark, cloud-ridden day made the house seem even more empty than usual. She would be glad to be out even if it was just to visit Mammy and Bernard for a couple of hours. Fin would pick her up again round the corner from the Peabodys' terraced cottage at half-past four. By then he would have made his weekly pilgrimage to check on his elderly parents and before they went their separate ways he would take Polly to tea in a tiny café tucked into a side street off Byres Road.

Polly enjoyed the hour they spent together in the café, sipping weak tea and eating toast. Many Italians had returned to Italy to fight for the Fascists or had been interned. Some had been shipped to the Isle of Man, others to Canada to sit out the war. She wondered what would have become of her last lover, Tony Lombard, if he'd stayed in Britain; what would have become of Dominic too; what might become of them yet if America entered the war.

She followed Fin down the drive to the motorcar parked behind the hedge. The big black Vauxhall Cadet looked suitably 'official'. Fin had picked it for that reason. The Cadet was hardly economical but Fin always seemed to have a tankful of petrol when he needed it.

Polly slid into the passenger seat and closed the door. Fin fired the engine, rolled the car out into Manor Park Avenue and turned left, heading for the city and the Clyde bridges.

Polly sat back, knees together, coat collar, fur trimmed, pulled up to warm her cheeks and ears. She watched the park glide past. The iron railings had been removed and the flowerbeds converted into vegetable allotments. Without railings to protect them the trees seemed larger and figures in the distance – young boys, old men – smaller, as if war had altered the scale of one's perception.

'I hear your sister has taken a lodger,' Fin said.

He drove with great authority, almost dashingly, like a man more used to sports cars than ten-year-old saloons.

'Who told you that?'

He tapped the side of his nose with a gloved finger. 'Little bird.'

'Rosie?'

'Lord no. Little bird. Enough said.'

'Well yes, it's true. Some fellow she met at the Recruitment Centre.'

'Why didn't you tell me?' Fin said.

'I didn't think it was important.'

'Have you met him yet?'

'Why would I want to meet him?' Polly said.

The streets were quiet, even the thoroughfare. Trams were few and far between and no other cars were visible down the long straight stretch that led past Ibrox. Fin gave the accelerator a firm tap and brought the speed up to forty.

'Curiosity,' Fin said. 'Have the billeting officers not been on at you again to open your house to strangers?'

'I think they've given up.'

'They never give up,' said Fin. 'It'll be a requisition order next.'

'And you'll deal with it.'

'I will.'

They drove in silence for a quarter of a mile.

Then Polly said, 'Did your little bird tell you Babs's lodger is American?'

'My little bird did.'

'Is that why you're so interested in him?' Polly said.

'Am I interested in him?'

'Of course you are. If you hadn't been interested you'd have brought up the subject last night.'

'I had more on my mind last night than your sister's lodger.'

'Be that as it may, darling, you're fishing, aren't you?' Polly said. 'You think I'm holding something back.'

'Are you?'

'No.'

Tenements closed around them and the road narrowed. Sunday shift at the shipyards filled the air with a secular racket and the outskirts of Govan, Dominic's old stamping ground, were almost as busy as a weekday.

'Are you fishing because he's an American?' Polly said, at length.

Fin changed gear and gave most of his attention to the road.

There were no traffic lights, no policemen on points duty but the threatening rumble of an army convoy in the vicinity rendered him extra vigilant.

Fin said, 'What part of the United States does he call home, I wonder.'

'Didn't your little bird—'

'Could it be Philadelphia, do you suppose? Or New York?'

Polly pressed her knees together and tucked her elbows into her sides. 'It did occur to me that this chap might be connected with Dominic,' she said, 'but no, it's pure coincidence that he's turned up here.'

'I'm not so sure I believe in coincidence these days.'

'Perhaps I should make a point of meeting him.'

'No,' Fin said. 'Wait and see if he comes to you.'

'Do you think he will?' said Polly.

'I think he might,' said Fin, and, spotting the army convoy up ahead, fisted the wheel of the Vauxhall and drove down into the docklands in search of a back route to the bridges.

★   ★   ★

Sunday afternoon in the Alba Hotel in Greenock: Christy
was waiting for a guy codenamed 'Marzipan'. Marzipan
and the owner of the Alba obviously had some kind of
arrangement for when he'd first arrived in Scotland he'd been
condemned to spend a week in the fleabag hotel before they'd
shipped him out to the bunker in the disused aerodrome near
Paisley.

He stood in the bay window looking down on the streets
where his old man had run wild as a kid. You didn't have to
be a genius to see why the Clyde was an important waterway.
Try as they might, German U-boat captains had failed to
penetrate its boom defences, even on explicit orders from
Hitler, a guy, so Christy'd heard, who got seasick just crossing
the Rhine. There's sweet irony for you, Marzipan had said,
if you happen to be a *Bootsmann* lying on the seabed in a
punctured tin fish, gasping for air. Christy didn't want to
think about anyone drowning, even a German. He hated the
sea. He hated Europe and longed to be back in Manhattan
with his fellow photo creatures.

Gloomily he contemplated the wave-streaked waters of the
estuary. His father had been born and raised on one side of
this river, his mother on the other. His brother, Jamie, an
ambitious son of a bitch, had used the Scottish connection
to persuade him to accept the assignment.

The array of ships was impressive, though: Clyde-built
corvettes, MTBs and destroyers were tucked into every cove
behind the boom defences, a gigantic steel net that stretched
between the Cloch lighthouse and the weed-strewn rocks of
the Gantocks hard by the little town of Dunoon.

The door of the lounge creaked open.

Figuring it would be Marzipan at last, Christy turned.

It was only a girl, very young, very nervous. She brought
in a tray with two bottles of light ale, two glasses, and a
plate of what looked like ship's biscuits. She put the tray

on a knee-high table in the window bay, bobbed a curtsy, and went out again.

No sooner had the girl left than Marzipan entered.

He closed the door, and said, 'Refreshment?'

'No thanks,' Christy said.

'What's the matter? Don't you like our Scottish beer?'

'Not much.'

Marzipan lifted one of the brown bottles and fiddled with the cap, then, changing his mind, put it down on the tray again. 'I hear you've left the aerodrome, struck out on your own, sort of thing,'

'Yep.'

'Have you made contact yet?'

'Not with the target,' Christy said. 'With her sister.'

'The one who works in recruitment?'

'Yeah, I'm lodging with her.'

'My, my! You are a fast worker.'

Marzipan was a beanpole with sunken cheeks, a hawk nose and a little sand-coloured moustache. His hair was set in tight curls, sand-coloured too. He wore no topcoat and his tweed jacket had seen better days. His shirt was spotless, though, the knot in his tie as small and tight as a peanut. Christy wondered if he was a naval officer like Jamie, and struggled to recall what he'd heard about navy regulations; no moustaches, no moustaches without beards, something like that. He knew better than to ask.

'Do I have a codename yet?' Christy asked.

'Would you like a codename?'

'Not especially.'

'You don't need one.'

'But you do?'

Marzipan smiled. He had small, foxy teeth.

Christy figured him to be about forty, maybe a weathered thirty-five. He spoke in a clipped Scottish accent, snipping the words into sentences as if he were used to dictating to a secretary.

'I do, alas,' said Marzipan. 'Tell me about the sister.'

'What's to tell,' said Christy. 'She's not important.'

'Are you sleeping with her?'

'Nope.'

'It doesn't matter to me if you are.'

'I'm not,' said Christy. 'I'm just approaching from the rear . . .'

'Really!'

'. . . like you told me to.'

'What about the husband?'

'In the army. Tanks. In Devon.'

Marzipan nodded. He knew that already, of course.

Christy said, 'Did he work with Manone?'

'He did, but he was small fry, very small fry.'

'There's a brother-in-law too – Dennis.'

'He's at sea,' Marzipan said, 'serving on an aircraft carrier.'

'If you already have all the answers, what do you need from me?'

Marzipan seated himself on the arm of a broken-down sofa. He said, 'Unfortunately we *don't* have all the answers. Even more unfortunately we aren't calling the tune. After you make contact with Manone's wife, we should have a clearer picture of what's going on.'

'Just what is going on?' Christy said.

'That's what you're here to find out.'

'When do I get my clearance to sail with a convoy?'

'All in good time,' Marzipan told him. 'Meanwhile, is there anything we can do for you? Anything you need? Money?'

'I'm fine.'

'The London office is coming through then?'

'Like clockwork,' said Christy.

'Where do you deposit the cheques?'

'No cheques. Postal orders.'

'Good.'

'Is that it?'

'For the time being.'

'You brought me down here just to pat me on the head?'

'Progress report,' Marzipan said. 'Candidly, I had hoped for a little more. Do you still have the number I gave you?'

'Yeah.'

'I'll be gone for a week or two,' Marzipan said. 'But the person at the other end can be trusted to take messages. I'll be in touch as soon as I get back.'

'From where?'

Marzipan laughed. His blue-grey eyes became wet. He wiped them with a knuckle as if Christy had just told him the funniest joke in the world.

'The States?' said Christy.

'Not the States, no.'

'If you happen to bump into my brother—'

'It's highly unlikely.'

'Yeah, well, if you do,' Christy said, 'tell him to go shoot himself.'

'I'm sure you don't mean that,' said Marzipan, still laughing.

'I'm goddamned sure I do,' said Christy.

Lizzie should have been pleased to see her daughters but she had become so set in her ways that she was quite disconcerted when all three turned up at once.

They were no longer bright young things. They had husbands, children and worries of their own, and sometimes seemed to converse in a language she could not now understand. The war had snapped the natural chain of events by which women her age anchored themselves to the past.

She was confused by what was happening in the world, and Bernard and the girls tried to protect her from its harsher realities, which made her feel even more stupid.

Babs breezed in about a quarter past one o'clock, April and a litter of bags and boxes in her arms. Puffing, she dumped the lot on a chair in the living room, stood April on the dining table and began to undo the layers of wool and flannel in which the little girl was wrapped.

'Let me do that,' Lizzie offered.

'It's okay,' said Babs brusquely. 'I've got it.'

'Mum's got it,' April said.

Leaning placidly on her mother's shoulders, she gave Granny a careful scrutiny that may, or may not, have ended with a smile.

'Have you had your dinner?' Lizzie asked.

'Nope,' said Babs. 'I've brought stuff. It's in the brown bag, that one.'

'You don't have to bring food,' Lizzie said. 'I've enough to go round.'

April said, 'We never went to see Angus an' the pig today.'

'Did you not, darlin'?' said Lizzie.

'We comed here instead.'

'Hold still, honey.' Babs avoided her mother's eye. 'You're gettin' too big for this old coat. Arms up, please.'

Stripped of her scarf, balaclava and overcoat, April allowed herself to be lifted from the table and placed in one of the fireside armchairs. She sat back against the cushions, legs sticking out. She wore long stockings, crimped with elasticised garters, and patent leather shoes. When she was April's age, Lizzie thought, Babs would have killed for a pair of shoes like that.

'Where's Grandpa?'

'Yes,' Babs said, 'where is Bernard?'

'Out.'

'I can see that, Mammy, but where?'

Lizzie shrugged.

Bernard had pitched himself into the war effort with energy and enthusiasm. He was some years younger than Lizzie. He had fought in the last war and was irked at not being able to fight in this one. Lizzie couldn't shake off the conviction that if the war lasted long enough, however, she would lose Bernard on the battlefield as she had 'lost' her first husband, Frank Conway. Frank hadn't died for king and country, though; he had deserted the army, abandoned her and the children without a qualm, and fled to America to work for Carlo Manone's outfit in Philadelphia.

'He's gone to church,' Lizzie said.

'Shouldn't he be back by now?' said Babs.

'Red Cross meeting.'

'Bernard isn't in the Red Cross, is he?'

'Ambulance class, I mean,' said Lizzie.

She really had no idea which of her husband's activities had delayed him after morning service. Between his job as a billeting officer for Breslin town council and his volunteer work she saw very little of him these days.

'He is a busy bee, our Bernie,' said Babs.

'Busy bee, busy bee,' April repeated, and giggled.

It was good to have a child in the house again, Lizzie thought. She missed Stuart and Ishbel, Polly's children, missed May and June too, and Angus most of all. She hadn't been invited to visit Blackstone Farm; Babs had somehow never got around to taking her, not even in summer when the days were long.

She was on the point of picking up her granddaughter and carrying her off into the kitchen to 'help' make lunch when the front door opened and Rosie stuck her head into the living room.

'Uh-anyone at home?'

April was out of the chair and across the room like a shot. She threw herself against her aunt and hugged her.

Rosie firmly disengaged herself and in a voice too loud for the small room, shouted, 'Oh, you're here, are you?'

'Why shouldn't I be here?' said Babs.

'I wanted to talk to Mammy.'

April tried again, hugging Rosie's arm.

Rosie shook her off.

'Oi,' said Babs, 'take it easy on the kid, okay?'

'She didn't hear you,' Lizzie said.

'She did an' all.' Babs faced her sister. 'What the heck's wrong with you, Rosie? If you want to talk privately to Mammy then go into the kitchen.'

April, near to tears, leaned disconsolately against the table. Babs picked her up.

'Have you had your lunch, dearest?' Lizzie said.

'I'm not hungry,' said Rosie.

'There's soup in the pot,' said Lizzie.

'I don't want anything,' said Rosie. 'I didn't know she'd be here.'

'"She" has a name, you know,' said Babs. 'An' why shouldn't I be here, for God's sake? I've as much right to be here as you have.'

'I thought you went to the farm every Sunday.'

'Well, I didn't, not today.' Babs put April back in the armchair.

Rosie's fingers trembled as she worked open the buttons of her overcoat.

'Where is he then?' she said.

'Where's who?' said Babs.

'Your fancy man, your Yuh-yankee doodle?'

'Oh, so that's it,' said Babs. 'You came to snitch on me, did you?'

'I thought you might have brought him along to show him how the other half lives,' said Rosie.

'Other half? What's that supposed to mean?'

'Fancy man?' said Lizzie, frowning. 'Who's got a fancy man?'

'She has,' said Rosie, with a cheap little smirk. 'Couldn't manage without a bit of the how's-your-fuh-father so she's found a man to move in with her.'

'If you weren't my sister,' Babs said, 'an' if you weren't such a pathetic little bitch, I'd smash your face in, so I would. Can't you get it into that nasty wee head of yours that Christy's a paying guest.'

'Uh-huh, but what's he paying for?' said Rosie.

'Christy,' April put in, 'is nice.'

'See,' Rosie said. 'He has even got to the kid.'

'Got to the . . . got to . . .'

Babs slapped her palm on the table, making the boxes jump.

Lizzie was not so naïve as all that. She was prepared to accept that, in spite of Babs's denial, there might be some truth in Rosie's accusation. Sensing trouble, she plucked April from the armchair and carried her through the kitchen, out the back door and into the communal garden that ran behind the terraced cottages.

'What's wrong, Granny?' said April. 'Why's Mummy shouting?'

'Because Aunt Rosie doesn't hear very well.'

'She's deaf.'

'Aye, deaf. Do you see what Grandpa has done with the shelter?'

April was not particularly interested in the border of broken roof tiles with which Bernard had decorated the mouth of the air-raid shelter. Eight identical shelters were humped along the length of the communal garden, all uniformly quilted

with turf but individually ornamented, for it was in the nature
of Knightswood folk to embellish conformity whenever they
possibly could.

'Mummy's angry,' said April.

'I think we'll go for a walk,' said Lizzie. 'Would you like
to see Mrs Grainger's cats?'

'Cats.' April nodded approval. 'How many?'

'Two,' said Lizzie. 'A daddy an' a mammy.'

'Do they like each other?' April asked.

'I'm sure they do,' said Lizzie, and, taking her grand-
child by the hand, led her away from the shouting match
indoors.

'Dear God!' Polly snapped. 'What's got into the pair of you?
You're going at it like fishwives. I heard you halfway down
the street.'

Polly had arrived unannounced at the height of the argument. Babs rounded on her older sister. 'None of your
damned business. It's all your fault, anyway. I should never
have told you about Christy.'

'I didn't know it was supposed to be a secret.'

'This way. Face me, both of you,' Rosie yelled.

Obedient to habit they turned to face Rosie.

Polly wore a mannish-cut jacket with padded shoulders and
a skirt with a front pleat. Her heavy fur-trimmed coat was
draped over her shoulders like a cloak and she seemed, Babs
thought, bone-brittle, her voice steely.

'All this fuss,' Polly said, 'over nothing.'

'It isn't nothing,' said Rosie. 'It's morally wrong.'

'Morally what? Are you accusin' me of cheatin' on Jackie?'

'Stop it. Stop it this instant.' Polly glanced round. 'Where's
Mammy? Don't tell me you've chased her out of her own
house with your squabbling?'

'She's taken April for a walk,' said Babs, somewhat chastened.

'Anyway, what are you doin' here? Have you come to tell me I'm a dirty trollop too?'

'I come every Sunday, as it happens,' said Polly. 'I had no idea you'd be here, either of you.'

'What's in the parcel?' Rosie asked.

'Eggs.'

'Did you buy them from Dougie?' said Babs.

'Yes, I was out at Blackstone on Wednesday,' Polly replied.

'Did you see the kids?'

'Yes.'

'How are they?'

'Perfectly fine.'

'I should have been there today but I haven't seen Mammy for weeks so I thought I'd better come here instead.'

'You don't have to apologise to me, Babs,' Polly said.

'I'm not apologisin'. I'm explainin'.'

'Explain him while you're at it then,' said Rosie.

Polly stripped off her gloves and placed them on the table beside the eggs. She took a silver cigarette case from her handbag, lit a cigarette and blew smoke towards the ceiling.

'Doesn't your husband talk to you, Rosie?' Babs said. 'He had a good poke about my house last week an' even met the mystery man. I thought he'd have given you a full report.'

'What if he duh-did?' said Rosie, sulkily.

'You're here to cry on Mammy's shoulder an' tell her what a bad girl I am, aren't you?' Babs said.

'Stop it,' Polly said again. 'First time we've been together in months, so I suggest we try to behave like civilised human beings and not alarm Mother any more than we have done already. Rosie, light the gas under the soup pot, then go outside and see if you can find Mammy and April and bring them in. It's far too cold to be wandering about outside.'

'Try next door,' said Babs. 'She's got cats next door. April loves cats.'

Polly nodded. 'Rosie, did you hear me?'

'I heard you.'

'Then do it. Please.'

Reluctantly Rosie pushed herself out of the armchair and drew the coat about her thin frame. She looked ghastly, Polly thought, unkempt and underfed, like a refugee. She watched Rosie go out into the kitchen.

Babs whispered, 'She's looks terrible, doesn't she?'

'Dreadful.'

'What's wrong with her? Is it the job?'

'I don't know.'

'Well, she's certainly got it in for me,' Babs said. 'She sent Kenny round to our house to interrogate my lodger.'

'I'm not surprised,' said Polly. 'What puzzles me is why you bothered to tell me in the first place.'

'I thought it was somethin' you should know.'

'Why?'

'Because . . .' Babs shrugged.

'Because your friend's American and you thought he might have been sent here by Dominic?'

'It did cross my mind,' Babs admitted.

'Has he said anything about Dominic?'

'Claims he never heard of him.'

'And me, what about me?' said Polly.

'What about you?'

'Has he suggested we might meet?'

'Not so far.'

'Do you see why I'm concerned?' said Polly.

'Kind of,' Babs said.

'It has nothing to do with morality.'

'Be a hoot if it did, comin' from you. You an' your lawyer boyfriend.'

'Well, Fin's hardly a boy,' said Polly, 'but you do have a point.' She glanced towards the kitchen. 'Look, if I calm Rosie down will you do me a favour in return?'

'Dependin' on what it is – sure.'

'If your lodger ever suggests that he and I meet, telephone me at home.'

'Not at the office?'

'No, at home.'

'Will do,' said Babs.

Babs left her mother's house later than she had intended to and April feel asleep on the tram. She carried her daughter piggyback from Paisley Road to Raines Drive, April's head bobbing gently against her shoulder. Fortunately the cloud had blown off, moonlight gave shape to rooftops and hedges and there were still plenty of folk out and about for it was only a little after nine o'clock.

Babs was relieved that she had made peace with her sisters, for it seemed that the hatchet had been buried, at least for the time being, and all in all Babs felt that the visit had been profitable in all sorts of ways.

She toiled up the steps of the bungalow and rang the bell.

Christy opened the door. He detached April from Babs's back, carried her through to the bedroom and laid her gently on top of her bed.

The bungalow was filled with delicious smells. Christy had made doughnuts. April wakened up enough to eat one and drink a glass of warm milk while Babs popped her into her pyjamas. With the child settled Babs returned to the lounge. Christy had made chips and fried up thick slices of Spam. They ate at the coffee table, while Jackie's big wireless set droned in the background.

'So,' he said, casually, 'you got together with your sisters?'

'Yeah,' said Babs. 'All three of us.'

'What did you all talk about? Old times?'

'We talked about you, actually.'

'Really!'

'My sisters are worried in case I've strayed from the straight an' narrow.'

'Both of them?'

'Rosie, Kenny's wife, in particular. Polly, less so,' Babs said. 'Polly's pretty much a woman of the world.'

'I'd like to meet up with your sister Polly,' Christy Cameron said. 'Think that could be arranged?'

'I don't see why not,' said Babs.

Polly lay awake in the big double bed and listened to the silence. The bed was the only warm spot in the house. She spent as much time there as possible. She had no children to pack off to school, no husband to get off to work, no real job to go to, no one to cook for except herself. She even resented having to share her bed with Fin on Saturday nights for he would be up with the lark, baying for breakfast long before she was inclined to face the day.

The threat of air raids didn't trouble her much. The big larder in the basement had been strengthened with wooden beams and was equipped with a cot, candles and a supply of ginger beer, even an ambulance kit and a policeman's whistle. So far there had been no raids, only false alarms.

She was barely awake when the telephone rang that Monday morning.

She reached for the alarm clock, saw that it was four minutes after nine and, throwing back the covers, leaped out of bed and dashed downstairs.

The telephone rested on a carved chest in the hallway.

She snatched up the receiver. 'Babs?'

'Yep, it's me. Were you still in bed?'

'As a matter of fact, I was.'

'Lucky bloody you,' Babs said.

'Where are you?'

'Where do you think I am? I'm at work.'

'Is there a point to this phone call?'

'Nope, just thought I'd give you a—'

'Babs!'

'You're standing there freezin' in your nightie, aren't you?'

Polly had almost forgotten how irritating Babs could be.

'Is he coming, or is he not?'

'If you mean Christy Cameron, yep, you were spot on, Poll. He *is* interested in you. No doubt about it. I wish he was as interested in me, I can tell you. No, I don't really mean that. It's all very well to have opportunity handed you on a plate but . . .'

'Where is he now?'

'Haven't a clue.'

Polly had no idea why the prospect of meeting the American excited her. But it did. If he'd hailed from Sheffield or Shrewsbury she would have had no interest in him whatsoever. The fact that he came from New York rendered him intriguing, for, like Fin, she no longer believed in coincidence.

'Why don't you drop by this evening?'

'Can't,' Babs said. 'I've nobody to sit with April an' I'm not draggin' her over to your place after blackout. Why don't you come here?'

Polly hesitated; a split second only. 'Look, if Cameron does have some connection with Dominic there's a fair-to-middling chance he's up to something shifty and the sooner we find out what it is the better for all of us. Tell him to come on his own.'

'What if he won't?'

'He will,' Polly said. 'At least make the offer.'

'All right,' Babs said. 'I just hope you know what you're doin', Poll.'

'I always know what I'm doing,' Polly said. 'Shall we say eight o'clock?'

'Will you feed him?'

'Of course I will,' said Polly, and hung up.

4

From the outset Rosie had been determined not to let her handicap stand in her way. When she'd learned that Merryweather's electrical engineering company was recruiting staff, she had immediately applied for a job.

Merryweather's had won a navy contract to manufacture ultra-sensitive sounding devices for submarine destroyers and a special assembly line had been set up in a converted church in Little Street, close to Glasgow University. All applicants were required to pass tests in dexterity, intelligence and reliability but deafness was not considered an impediment to efficiency and Rosie was duly accepted for training.

Thirty cubicles furnished with straight-backed chairs and swivel lamps had replaced the church pews. The work consisted of fitting forty-seven tiny components into a stainless-steel drum the size of a jam jar. There was no piped music in Little Street church and no intrusive Tannoy announcements to disturb concentration. Rosie, of course, couldn't hear the rumble of traffic in the avenue or the vague sparrow-chatter of schools letting out. She had no indicators to tell her whether the day was passing swiftly or slowly, and even the rhythms of her body seemed to be on hold for the four parts of the eleven-hour shift. Tea was served from a trolley in the corridor; one break midmorning, a half-hour for lunch and a second short break in the afternoon. Rosie coped well with the finger-numbing labour, much less well with the tea breaks.

It was Rosie's first experience of working with women

and her co-workers weren't at all like the loud-mouthed, soft-hearted, working-class women among whom she had grown up. They were doctors' wives, dentists' wives, the daughters of lawyers and teachers, middle-class ladies who, on the surface, epitomised respectability and decorum.

Individually they were pleasant enough but collectively they soon revealed a snobbish, almost vicious dislike of anyone who wasn't as perfect as they perceived themselves to be, and as weeks passed into months and they shed their inhibitions all their coarse prejudices came to the surface. A mild young wife with a brace on her leg was teased unmercifully about her limp; a tow-haired girl with a nervous stutter was frequently reduced to tears. In October, in the midst of an afternoon tea break, a good-looking girl in her twenties suddenly shouted out that *she* was Jewish and that if *this lot* was typical of the British Empire then perhaps it *was* time Hitler's storm troopers came marching up University Avenue. Then she stalked out. The women, unrepentant, brushed aside her accusations as pure hysteria.

They teased Rosie too, teased her unmercifully.

They mouthed words she couldn't interpret. They pretended to be deaf. They ostracised her by covering their lips with their fingers when they spoke. They enquired about her husband, asked what she would do when babies came, hinted that it might be better not to have babies since her babies would surely turn out to be defective and impose a further burden on society.

Rosie hated the women and was afraid of them. Rosie admired the women and aspired to be as perfect as they were. Rosie swallowed their insults and insinuations and wept in the lavatory at the realisation that in Shelby's bookshop she had been pampered and praised for her cleverness only because of her affliction.

She took her anger out on Kenny and on Babs.

She had always been jealous of Babs, bouncing, indefatigable Babs.

She had supposed that when she had a husband of her own things would improve. Things hadn't improved. Things had got worse.

She no longer liked the things Kenny did in bed. Didn't *he* realise what would happen if they made a baby together? Didn't *he* know how the baby might turn out? She tried to use Babs to tell Kenny that something was wrong, to make him read her mind as accurately as she read his lips. But Kenny was too tied up in his career to spare any thought for her. The only time he gave her any real attention was when he wanted her to open her legs. Perhaps the women in Merryweather's were right. Perhaps all men were just selfish creatures at heart and no woman, however saintly, could ever change their basic nature.

By the end of November the prospect of going to work in the morning was making her physically sick. Isolated in the glare of the lamp, she picked up the tiny components with tweezers and nudged them into place with a miniature screwdriver. She no longer had to think about what she was doing, the surgically precise process of assembly had become habit, had become drudgery. She didn't know what time it was, hardly knew what day it was. She felt permanently queasy, stomach knotted, bladder pressing against her pelvis.

It had been clear and cold and sunny that morning.

The glare of the winter sun on the tram window had made Rosie shiver. Now, in the afternoon, she was shivering again. The gurgling palpitation in her lap had reached up into her stomach. The meat paste sandwich that she'd eaten at lunch time burned in her throat. Her back ached. Her forehead was clammy. She raised her head. The checkers were coming down the line with collecting trays to take away the finished units. The foreman stood on the steps of what had once been a pulpit, whistle in hand.

Rosie shook her head again. She watched the foreman put the whistle to his lips, saw the women push back their chairs.

She rose and ran for the door that led to the lavatory.

A dentist's wife got there first.

A slender woman with a heart-shaped face, even in a white cotton overall and mobcap she exuded a delicate sort of arrogance. She smiled, raised her brows and deliberately blocked the doorway. Rosie pushed her to one side, stumbled into the corridor, tripped and fell on all fours.

The cramp in her stomach became violent and expulsive. She felt blood on her thighs, a great warm, oddly soothing splash. The dentist's wife stepped up to her and eight, ten, a dozen women stared down at her from a great height. She couldn't see their faces, only their stockings and shoes.

She rocked on her elbows and knees in a puddle of watery blood.

She cried out, '*Muh-Muh-Maaa-maaay!*'

She was still crying for her mammy when the ambulance arrived.

The telephone rang on and off all afternoon. Polly ignored it. It would only be Fin calling to remind her that correspondence was piling up on her desk and that as his diary was full for the rest of the week perhaps it would be advisable to put in an appearance before the end of the day.

As a rule Polly answered her letters personally, typing replies on an Underwood at the old roll-top desk that filled the niche beneath the window on the fifth floor of the Baltic Chambers. Fin liked to think that he was indispensable, however, and on that score at least she did not dare disillusion him. She wasn't entirely convinced that she needed an office at all but Fin had pointed out that even in wartime tax inspectors, bank managers and government agencies were invariably impressed by a city centre address and that given the level of income her investments generated she could certainly afford premises up town.

Making money in troubled times wasn't easy, however. Financial controls were tight. Currency restrictions necessitated the setting up of special accounts to handle payments in US dollars or Argentine pesos, but the hard currency markets of America and Canada remained open and it was still possible to arrange credit facilities for particular transactions, loopholes that Polly, with Fin's assistance, had learned to use to advantage.

She wasn't thinking of money that Monday evening, however. She was thinking of Dominic, Dominic and the intrusive American.

She'd heard nothing from her husband for months. The children wrote her every so often, dutiful little letters filled with news about their progress at school and Stuart's triumphs on a local softball team; Polly didn't even know what softball was. She'd requested photographs, more out of curiosity than anything else, but so far none had been forthcoming. Given the state of North Atlantic shipping, it was possible that a letter or two had wound up on the bottom of the ocean; Polly consoled herself with that thought when, in the wee small hours, guilt and loneliness took too firm a hold on her heart.

At first she'd considered breaking out the silver and setting the long table in the dining room. But the big basement kitchen was cosier and in the end she settled for a red-check tablecloth, matching napkins and the thick painted plates that Dominic had once imported by the crateload from Italy.

At half-past seven, with everything on hold in the kitchen,

she rushed upstairs to bathe and change. She put on under-wear that Fin had given her, filmy knickers, flawless silk stockings, a black lace-edged half-slip and matching brassiere, then an informal ready-to-wear dress that had never been out of the wardrobe before. She arranged her hair, applied make-up and perfume, then, seated before the mirror at her dressing table, realised that for the first time in many months she felt like herself again – quite like the old Polly, in fact.

At eight precisely the doorbell rang.

Polly ran downstairs.

She switched off the overhead light, opened the door and looked out into the clear night air. He was standing in the driveway. He wore a black reefer jacket, baggy corduroy trousers and ankle-high boots. He looked, she thought, like a tradesman, his only concession to formality a check-patterned shirt and a florid necktie.

'Hi,' he said. 'Mrs Manone?'

'You're Christy, are you?' Polly said. 'Please, do come in.'

He wore no gloves, no scarf or muffler. His hands were small, almost pudgy. He held a small parcel cupped like a football in one hand. He stepped into the hallway and carefully closed the door behind him.

He turned and offered her the parcel.

'What's this?'

'Cigarettes. Churchman's.'

'How – how nice.'

'Your sister told me you prefer that brand.'

'I do,' said Polly. 'Where did you find them?'

'Had them sent up from our London office.'

'Your London office?'

'Brockway's.'

'Ah yes, of course.'

Polly placed the parcel, unopened, on the hallstand and led her guest towards the front parlour. She had lighted a fire there and laid out drinks, but the room remained gloomy.

He looked around, swivelling his head.

'Some room!'

'Don't you like it?'

'Not much.'

'Nor I,' said Polly. 'It used to be my husband's lair and it's too clubby for my taste. Why don't you grab a bottle of anything you fancy and we'll go downstairs. We're eating in the kitchen anyway. I hope you don't mind?'

'Why would I mind?'

'I – I don't know. Honoured guest and all that.'

'I'll just be glad to have somewhere to rest my weary butt – I mean bones.'

Polly laughed. She waited by the door while he selected a bottle of malt whisky and another of gin from the trolley and carrying a bottle in each hand, followed her out of the parlour and downstairs.

He entered the kitchen, sniffing.

'Now this,' he said, 'I do like. What's that wonderful smell?'

'Meatloaf.'

'Hey,' he said. 'Haven't had a decent slice of meatloaf since I left home.'

'You may not be having one tonight either,' Polly said, 'if I don't leave you to your own devices for a moment or two. Do the honours, will you?'

'Honours again?'

'Drinkies,' Polly said.

She felt relaxed with him already and could readily understand why Babs had been instantly smitten. His dark eyes reminded her of Dominic's but Christy Cameron was a good deal less polished than her husband. She put on an apron and watched him slip out of the reefer jacket. He unbuttoned his shirt cuffs and rolled them a little way up his forearms, hairy forearms, knotted with muscle. What, she wondered, had built muscle like that? Surely not just fiddling with cameras and light meters?

He looked around the kitchen, found two glasses on the dresser shelf and brought them down. 'How,' he said, 'and what?'

'Gin, tonic. I've no ice, I'm afraid, and no fresh lemons.'

She kneeled before the oven. She knew he was studying her with the same relaxed curiosity as she had studied him. She hoped he liked what he saw. She was glad now that she'd decided to serve supper in the kitchen. Christy Cameron did *not* remind her of Dominic or of Tony Lombard. Christy Cameron was nobody's stand-in. She attended to the loaf and the potatoes. The cabbage could take care of itself. She got to her feet. He handed her the glass. He poured himself a whisky. She looked at him directly for the first time and, standing there in the kitchen in her ready-made dress and floral apron, realised that she was happier than she had been in many months; that, for good or ill, Mr Christy Cameron had already given her something to look forward to.

'Chin-chin,' she said.

He touched his glass to hers.

'To absent friends,' he said.

'Friends across the water, do you mean?' Polly said.

'Just so,' said Christy Cameron, and winked.

It was very peaceful in Redlands Hospital. The maternity wards were never quiet, of course, and the fretful wails of the newborn echoed faintly in the polished corridors. Rosie couldn't hear the infant sounds but even in antiseptic solitude behind the white muslin curtain that surrounded her bed she thought she could smell their milky odours.

Mammy patted her hand.

'Didn't you know you were carryin'?'

'Nuh-no,' Rosie answered.

She was dry-eyed now, dry through and through.

She had been ten minutes on a table in a delivery room with one elderly male and one younger female doctor bent over her. A sheet had been stretched up into a sort of tent so that she couldn't see what they were doing and they had worn gauze masks that hid their mouths.

There had been surprisingly little pain. She'd expected more pain, would have welcomed more pain, some astonishing reminder of or punishment for her neglect. It simply hadn't occurred to her that the absence of periods might signal the presence of a foetus. She'd assumed that her periods, like everything else, had gone into hibernation to suit the demands of war.

'Well,' Mammy said, 'it's just as well it happened early.'

'How old was it?'

Mammy hesitated. She was seated by the bed, her big, ungainly body perched on a little steel-framed chair. 'Only seven weeks.'

'What have they done to me?'

'Tidied you up, that's all.'

'I don't feel much different.'

Mammy patted her hand again.

Mammy smelled like pea soup and new-washed clothes. There was a faint trace of peppermint on her breath too and Rosie realised that she was sucking an Imperial sweet, a little Sunday comforter.

'Well,' Mammy said, 'I lost two . . .'

'Pardon?'

'I lost two myself.'

Rosie raised herself from the pillows.

'I had no idea . . .'

'I never said anythin' to any o' you about it,' Mammy

said. 'I lost one before Polly was born an' another a year after.'

'Duh-dear God!'

'Nobody's fault. The first was hardly anythin',' Mammy said, with a sigh. 'Six or seven weeks formed. Shed it while I was scrubbin' stairs.'

'Did you know you were expecting?'

'Aye.'

'And the other one?'

'Ten weeks or thereabouts. I was sick for a while afterwards.'

Rosie lay back. She had lived with this woman all her life and had never once suspected that there had been sisters or brothers who had failed to form and that there should have been five little Conways instead of only three.

'What was it?' Rosie said. 'Boy or girl?'

Mammy shook her head. 'I don't think they know at that age.'

'Perhaps they just don't want to tell us.'

'Poor soul,' Mammy said, 'poor wee soul,' and began, quietly, to weep.

Christy sat back from the table and watched her clear the pudding plates. He had helped her finish a whole bottle of Chianti before he went back to whisky. He had, Polly thought, as much if not more of a capacity for alcohol as she had, and a better head for it.

He lifted the gin bottle and offered to pour.

'Not for me,' Polly said.

'I'll help you wash up.'

'Certainly not.'

'I am house-trained, you know.'

'Who trained you – a wife?'

'My old ma. She wouldn't let us off with anything.'

'Do you wash up for Babs?'

'Sure.'

'Do you ply her with strong drink too?'

'Nightcaps, that's all. She isn't much of a drinker, your sister.'

'I know,' said Polly. 'It goes straight to her head. Do you like her?'

'What's not to like?' Christy said.

'Why did you make contact with Babs, not directly with me?'

'Make contact? I don't know what you mean.'

Polly took off her apron and put it on the rail by the stove. She poured a cup of coffee and carried it to the table. She seated herself across the chequered cloth from him, holding the cup in both hands.

She hadn't mentioned Dominic during supper and had avoided the question of what he, Christy Cameron, wanted with her. He had warmed quickly to the game of double entendre, of giving a little but not a lot. It was, she thought, like old-time country dancing with its flirtatious advances, passes, touches and retreats, and she was surprised that the American knew how to play the game.

It was late now, well after ten. Christy would have to leave by eleven if he hoped to catch the last tramcar along Paisley Road. Before the war she would have rolled the Wolseley from the garage to drive him back to Raines Drive but blackout and petrol shortages had confined the car to the garage.

'My husband sent you, didn't he?'

'Nope.'

'You do know Dominic, though?'

'We've never met.'

'Didn't he send you here?'

'Nope.'

'Who did?' Polly frowned. 'Not Tony?'

'Who's Tony?'

'Look, either you tell me what you want with me or—'

'Or what?' Christy said.

He wore a military-style watch on a chewed leather strap. She waited for him to glance at it, tell her that time was up and that he'd best be leaving.

She didn't want him to leave. She was intrigued and unsatisfied, burning with a combination of curiosity and something she didn't care to put a name to. She was not naïve and neither, apparently, was Christy Cameron. He had charmed Babs and now he was in process of charming her but, Polly reminded herself, she wasn't made of the same generous stuff as her sister.

'Babs thinks you're attractive.'

'I know she does.'

'Are you seducing her?'

'Maybe it's the other way around.'

'You do have a wife, don't you?'

'I told you – no wife.'

'And you've never met my husband?'

'Persistent lady, aren't you?'

'Very persistent,' Polly said. 'If Dominic didn't send you then someone else did. Are you with the FBI?'

'Hell, no.'

She put down the coffee cup, tapped a cigarette from his packet, let him light it for her. She fanned away smoke with the back of her hand. 'Whoever you're working for,' she said, 'your cover is jolly good. I read the address label on the cigarettes you brought me: *Brockway's Illustrated Weekly*, Orange Street, London. Are you really a photographer?'

'The genuine article. Straight A.'

'Spain, Finland, Poland; you've certainly been around.'

'No denying it,' Christy Cameron said.

'Trouble spots.'

'Yep.'

'Are you always this laconic?'

'Yep,' he said, grinning.

'So,' Polly said, 'you expect me to guess what you want from me? What is it? Some sort of test?'

'What makes you think I want anything from you?'

'Intuition.'

'I'm a great believer in intuition.'

'Well, Mr Cameron,' said Polly, 'my intuition tells me you're up to no good and will bring nothing but trouble. I'm going to allow you one more snifter from my fast-diminishing stock of whisky then politely show you the door. In other words, if you don't make your pitch within the next five minutes, your opportunity will be lost and gone for ever.'

'How much do you know about your husband's affairs?'

'A lot.'

'But not everything?'

'No, probably not everything.'

'He's made an offer to the United States Government,' Christy said. 'It's a generous offer, too goddamned generous.'

'What sort of an offer?' Polly asked.

'To finance a network of double agents.'

'Where? In Italy?'

'Yeah.'

'And you need to find out if the offer is genuine?'

'More or less, yeah.'

'Dominic still has relatives around Genoa, I think—'

'He also has relatives in Philadelphia,' Christy interrupted.

'Ah, yes,' said Polly, 'I see your problem.'

'His old man and his brother are criminal racketeers.'

'I know what his father is,' said Polly.

'Do you still pay dues to Carlo Manone?'

'No.'

'When did you stop?'

'When Dominic left Scotland.'

'What happens to the money now?'

'I'm not sure I want to answer that question,' said Polly.

'But you know, don't you?'

'Of course I do.'

'You and the lawyer, Hughes, you run the organisation.'

'Oh come now,' said Polly. 'It's hardly an organisation and it certainly isn't – what do you call it? – a racket. I look after my husband's business interests on his behalf, all legal and above board. The company's in my name so there's no question of either your government or mine being able to confiscate our profits or freeze our assets just because Dominic's an alien.'

'I don't know what the hell you're talking about.'

'I thought . . .'

'I'm only a messenger,' Christy said.

'From whom?'

'New US federal agency; Roosevelt sanctioned and approved.'

'Does this agency have a name?'

'Not yet.'

'In other words you're a spy.'

'No, I'm a photographer,' Christy said.

'And I'm the Queen of the May,' said Polly.

Babs had put the peach housecoat back in the closet once and for all. She was no longer inclined to tempt Christy Cameron into taking her to bed. Something about him made her wary, something within herself too. If it hadn't been for her loyalty to Archie and her job she might even have handed Mr Cameron his marching orders and decamped to Blackstone for a week or two just to steer clear of whatever scheme Christy and Polly were hatching between them.

She went into the back bedroom to check on April and found her daughter deep in the Land of Nod, cheeks slightly flushed, thumb in her mouth, a trickle of saliva glistening on her lower lip. Babs returned to the hallway. She had been wrestling with her conscience all afternoon. What she contemplated doing wasn't right but, by gum, it was tempting.

She stood before the door of Christy's room.

She knew where he was tonight and that the chances of him returning before midnight were slim. Even so, she paused for all of sixty seconds before she turned the knob and pushed open the door.

She was in and out of the room every day, of course, making the bed, changing sheets, emptying ashtrays, hoovering and dusting. She had put him into Angus's room and Angus's spoor was all over the place. Her son had taken his favourite toys with him but books, games and jigsaw puzzles, toy soldiers, a dismembered old teddy bear and a rubber Pinocchio doll with the nose bitten off remained. A glass and a half-bottle of Talisker on the bedside table were the only signs of the room's current occupant, for Christy lived out of two big, brown canvas duffel bags that he kept hidden on top of the wardrobe.

'Mr Cameron?' Babs whispered. 'Christy, are you there?'

He wasn't there, of course. He was round in Manor Park Avenue with Polly, plotting God knew what.

Babs switched on the light, pulled out a chair, climbed on to it and lifted down the duffel bags. They were heavier than she'd anticipated. The canvas had a gritty feel to it and one shoulder strap had been torn from its leather housing and neatly repaired with cord. All the travel labels had been washed off, leaving nothing but indecipherable scraps. She put one of the bags on the bed.

It wasn't padlocked but a hank of cord was knotted round the carry-handle. She picked at the complicated knot, worked it loose, unthreaded the cord and under a ridge of canvas, found four metal fasteners.

She popped them one by one.

Then, drawing in a deep breath, she opened up the bag.

Polly said, 'Look, whatever you want me to do for this mythi-
cal agency of yours, first you're going to have to come clean. I
was married to Dominic Manone for too many years still to be
gullible. Even the US Government, profligate though it may
be, doesn't send freelance photographers chasing across the
Atlantic just to chat with the wife of an Italian importer. What
exactly are you, Mr Christy Cameron? State Department,
military intelligence, or just a freebooter with an eye to the
main chance?'

'I told you,' Christy said, 'I'm a photo journalist.'

'Why then are you working for a government agency?'

'My brother dragged me into it.'

'Ah! Ah-hah!' said Polly. 'So your brother's to blame, is
he?'

'He *is* in military intelligence. US Naval Intelligence to be
exact. I really can't tell you who he's working with because I
don't know. You think I play it close to the chest – try getting
information out of Jamie.'

'More,' Polly gestured, curling her fingers. 'Give me a
little more.'

'All right, I'll tell what I do know,' Christy said, 'some of it
anyway. Franklin D. has established a whole new alphabet of
bureaucratic offices. Franklin D. is well aware that sooner or
later the United States will have to enter the war or the whole
of Europe will go up in flames. The fall of France was a real
blow. France cracked morally, you know what I mean?'

Polly nodded. 'Yes.'

'When that happened Roosevelt sent an unofficial envoy
– a journalist, as it happens – to London to compile a
first-hand report on the German victory. This journalist
creamed up information from lots of his journalist friends,

guys and women who'd seen the stuff happen and who knew the inside score in eight, ten European countries.'

'Were you included in this select group of information-gatherers?'

'He talked to me too, yeah.'

'If you and your newspaper friends have contacts in the occupied territories, I assume you're still useful to this unofficial envoy?'

'Not dumb, are you?' Christy said.

'Unlike my sister – no, I don't bury my head in the sand.'

'The United States maintains diplomatic relations with the Vichy Government,' Christy went on, 'so we have agents and double agents planted all over France. Right now, though, we're more interested in Italy. The journalist who's cosy with Roosevelt has been appointed co-ordinator of a bunch of writers, actors and photographers, just useless Jewish scribblers according to some Washington high brass, and for my sins I'm part of that team.'

'You're not Jewish.'

'No, I told you I'm out of the same can as you are.'

'What does all this Roosevelt stuff have to do with me?'

'So far military intelligence selects the agents, though that situation will change quite soon, I guess. My brother more-or-less blackmailed me into taking the job and I couldn't turn the son of a bitch down.'

'What do you get out of it?'

'I get to sail with a convoy and take all the photographs I want with minimum restriction. Brockway's is my employer. Brockway's is also my cover. I'm "serviced", for want of a better word, by Brockway's London office.'

'You still haven't explained how I fit into all this?' Polly said.

'For years Mussolini's secret police have been beating up the opponents of Italian Fascism into terrorised silence. But the opponents haven't gone away. They're hiding out in Rome, Turin, Milan, Genoa, all over the north. What you have in Italy, like what you have in France, is really a class war raging right under the Nazi guns.'

'Resistance,' said Polly.

'Lots of it,' said Christy. 'It isn't a recognised movement like the Fighting French and there's no up-front leader like De Gaulle – but it's there okay, stoked by smouldering fury at what the Duce's done to the country. When the time comes to mount offensives on Italian-held territories—'

'Like North Africa?'

'Like North Africa – we'll need inside help.'

'An active Fifth Column.'

'You got it,' Christy said.

'To overthrow the Duce.'

'Eventually maybe. One step at a time, though. First we need to set up organised grass-roots resistance groups – and we need to pay them.'

'Are you telling me my husband has offered to finance the anti-Fascist cause in Italy?'

'He has.'

'But you don't trust him?'

'Nope, apparently we don't.'

'Because his father and brother are criminals?'

'Because,' Christy said, 'it's all too good to be true.'

First out of the bag came two bath towels, then the camera cases and umpteen rolls of film. The cameras were nothing like the old box Brownie with which Jackie had recorded the growth and progress of the children. They were sleek objects in compact leather cases, a Rolleiflex and a Contax, plus the tiny two-and-a-quarter-inch miniature that Babs had seen on the tram. Beneath the cameras was a collection of lenses and light meters wrapped in chamois leather; beneath the lenses, three notebooks.

Babs placed the items on the bedspread in the order in which she took them from the bag. She was nervous now, scared almost.

She handled the notebooks gingerly.

The first was a log or journal, each page – and there were many pages – packed with coded records of delivered film. The record bristled with the names of foreign towns and cities – Madrid, Helsinki, Warsaw, Berlin. Babs didn't like the sense of smallness that those names gave her or the thought that a man who had been to all those places was sleeping in her son's bed.

Hastily, she closed the log and dropped it back in the bag.

The second book listed claims for expenses, most of which seemed to have been paid. The pages of the last notebook were almost blank but a word – 'Marzipan' – appeared on page one, together with a telephone number. Printed in the same dark blue ink in the same crabbed hand, her name appeared on the second page, 'Barbara Hallop', followed by the address of the Cyprus Street Recruitment and Welfare Centre, which suggested that her meeting with Christy had not been accidental after all.

She glanced at her watch: after eleven.

Carefully she repacked the bag and put it on the floor.

The smaller bag was less securely sealed than the first. It contained clothing: woollens, stockings, pyjamas, underwear, two shirts, one necktie, six or eight handkerchiefs, a shaving wallet and a fat packet of contraceptives. Six dozen contraceptives. Why was the man carrying seventy-two French letters in his luggage? Did he have women in every port and was he out in the streets of Glasgow looking for women when he wasn't with her or – Babs blew out her cheeks and cleared her throat – did he intend to use the entire consignment before he left

Scotland and if so who would be the lucky – or unlucky – lady on the receiving end?

Cheeks burning, she stuffed the packet back into the bag.

She was on the point of closing the bag when she noticed an envelope sticking out from between two cotton undershirts.

She slid it out, a plump brown 9 x 6 manila envelope all scuffed and stained and, fortunately, unsealed. She spilled the contents on to the bedspread. Photographs, not glossy professional photographs but family snaps similar to those Jackie used to take with the Brownie. Ma and Pa and the kids; Coney Island, 1928. Girls, three of them, in summer dresses, with a young boy in short trousers sitting cross-legged on a pavement at their feet. Another girl with a shawl over her head, raindrops beaded on the fringe of the shawl, a tear, or a raindrop, clinging to her cheek.

Two kids, boy and girl, posed informally with a tall guy in navy uniform.

Two kids whom she recognised.

Stuart and Ishbel: Polly's children.

Babs held the picture to the light, scanning it for clues as to where and when it had been taken. Nothing in the background but a white picket fence and a wall of shrubs. A bright day, the children squinting into the light. Older than she remembered them, more casually dressed: Americanised. She wondered about the naval officer, who might, she thought, be Christy's brother. She riffled through the rest of the photographs, found a shot of men and women laughing in the doorway of a tall building; three men in baggy suits leaning on the rail of a ferryboat; another girl, white-blonde and leggy in a torn dress, standing at a field gate with a dog lying at her feet; then one of six or eight people at a table in a nightclub; then a solitary shot of Christy in the reefer jacket and familiar sweater seated on a bollard against a background of misty skyscrapers. There were no more pictures of Polly's children, though.

Tucked into a corner of the envelope was a letter pencilled on a page torn from a notebook in a language Babs could not decipher. It wasn't French or Italian but it might, she thought, be German.

It was signed by someone called 'Ewa'.

Christy Cameron was not what Babs had imagined him to be. What she had mistaken for charm was in fact character, far too much character for her to cope with. The snapshots and the letter, to say nothing of six dozen French letters, gave him substance, a shape that she could not define. She wondered what he was doing here; not his purpose, which might be explained in due course, but his proximity. How could she possibly be attracted to a man who had so much more substance than she had?

She put all the stuff back into the bag, returned the bags to the top of the wardrobe then went into the living room and poured herself a drink.

Seated in Jackie's armchair before the embers of the fire, her plump, competent fingers trembled slightly as she brought the glass to her lips. At that moment she was afraid of her Yankee lodger and the wealth of suffering and experience that he had brought into her life, a wealth of suffering and experience that she had no wish to share.

At midnight she went to bed.

It was after midnight before Kenny got home. One of the 'businessmen' under lock and key in Greenock Prison had shown signs of cracking under interrogation and he had stayed on to press his advantage.

Mr McVicar was waiting for him at the close mouth to tell him that Rosie had collapsed at work and had been taken to Redlands Hospital. Panic and annoyance took possession of Kenny's reason. How could he possibly juggle a sick wife and the demands of the job? If Fiona had been home there wouldn't have been a problem, but Fiona was far away. He would have to rely on his mother-in-law. He ran out into the street and flagged down a taxi.

He reached Redlands at one o'clock in the morning.

Two soon-to-be fathers, one of them a soldier, were pacing up and down the corridor, smoking furiously. There was a commotion outside the delivery room where some sort of crisis demanded the full attention of midwives and doctors. He heard a woman scream, shrill as a copper's whistle, as he climbed the staircase to Rosie's ward.

The ward sister was manifestly reluctant to let him enter but, in view of his occupation, granted him five minutes at his wife's bedside.

Rosie was asleep.

He spoke to her very softly.

He touched her hand. He brushed hair from her damp brow. He straightened the sheet. He spoke to her again, less softly.

Rosie did not waken.

He felt little or nothing when the sister gave him the news about the baby. He asked a couple of questions, was given answers of a sort. He looked at Rosie, who had colour in her cheeks and seemed to be breathing evenly, who even snorted a little when he kissed her brow.

'When may I take her home?'

'Tomorrow.'

'Early tomorrow? First thing in the morning?'

'You can't stay here overnight.'

'I know. Say six o'clock tomorrow morning?'

'Half-past, not before.'

'She is well enough to go home, I take it?'

'Of course,' the sister said. 'I assume there will be a female person on hand to care for her if she should require nursing for a day or two?'

'I'll make sure of it,' said Kenny.

He went by cab to Knightwood, told the cabbie to wait.

Bernard answered the door.

Kenny did not go into the house.

An arrangement was quickly reached; Lizzie would come to Cowcaddens tomorrow morning and look after Rosie while he went to work.

He rode the cab back to St Andrew's Street, scrounged a meal in the all-night canteen and went to his office to try to snatch some sleep. His eyes were slitted with exhaustion and his limbs lead-heavy, but his brain just wouldn't stop whirring. At length he put on his overcoat and climbed the narrow staircase to the roof.

It was a fine night, without much moon. He could see stars, though, and the faint effervescent glow that the city gave off even under blackout. They would be working in armaments factories, steel mills, shipyards, in all the manufactories, small and large, that supplied materials for the war effort. He was no longer sure what his contribution to the war effort added up to, especially when he thought of the two stubborn, whey-faced men in the cell at Greenock prison, self-important provincial tycoons who had traded with the enemy.

'Mr MacGregor, sir. Is that you?'

'It is.'

'Didn't think you were on tonight, sir.'

'I'm not. I'm just taking a breath of air. How is it? Quiet?'

'Quiet as the grave, sir, quiet as the grave.'

Kenny leaned on the stone parapet, looking down at the river, a cigarette cupped in the palm of his hand. He had lost a son yesterday, or a daughter, a child he hadn't known existed. If he had known, if he'd lived with the knowledge for a week or two he might have felt more than he did. He was upset by the fact that he could feel no grief for the child who had never been.

At ten past six he left St Andrew's Street in a taxicab to pick up Rosie, who, he reckoned – rightly, as it happened – would blame him for the miscarriage just as she blamed him for everything else.

5

Every weekday morning Dougie escorted the children to school at Breslin Cross. May and June strutted along in their Wellingtons and little green overcoats while Angus loped by Dougie's side, prattling about the weather, the pig, barrage balloons, and the possibility that one of these days his dad would come back from repairing tanks and take him out for a ride on his motorcycle. When the children were safe inside the gates Dougie would buy a newspaper and ten Woodbine and stroll back to the farm, free until half-past three, when he would pick the little blighters up again.

On Sundays Babs came visiting but left again in midafternoon to be home before dark. Polly came midweek, usually on a Wednesday afternoon. Polly thought nothing of picking her way down the farm track long after nightfall to catch the last train from Breslin railway station and more often than not, Dougie would walk a piece with her, for since he'd – almost – stopped drinking his legs had regained their youthful spring and being cooped up indoors even in winter made him restless.

He was startled to see Polly in Breslin main street at nine o'clock on Tuesday morning, however. She stood under the faded canopy of the newsagent's shop wearing a Rodex overcoat, a tweed hat and calf-length boots that made her look more aristocratic than half the titled landowners in the county. He sallied up to her, feigning nonchalance.

'You're up early. What happened? Fall out o' bed this mornin'?'

'I need to talk to you,' Polly said.

'Are you comin' up to the farm?'

'No. I have to get back to Glasgow.'

'Serious stuff then, is it?'

'Probably,' Polly said. 'Is there somewhere we can take tea?'

'At this hour?' Dougie said. 'I doubt it.' At least it was dry, and since the sun had come up there was a hint of warmth in the dank November air. 'Tearoom at the railway station might be open. We'll walk down that way on the off chance.'

Polly fell into step beside him. 'I've had a message from Dominic.'

'Telephone or letter?' Dougie asked.

'Neither – a messenger boy.'

'Surely not old Tony Lombard?'

'No,' said Polly curtly. 'A man I've never met before. An American.'

'What does he want?'

'My money,' said Polly.

'How much?'

'All of it.'

'Uh-huh,' said Dougie. 'For what?'

'To send abroad.'

'To New York?'

'No,' Polly said. 'To Italy.'

'Why are you talkin' to me?' Dougie said. 'Why not ask your friend Mr Hughes for advice? Is that not what y' pay him for?'

'You've known Dominic longer than any of us.'

Dougie said, 'Has this got anythin' to do with dud bank-notes?'

'Not a thing.'

'Thank God for that,' said Dougie, and led her down the steep wooden steps to the railway tearoom, which had just thrown open its doors.

Kenny had never felt so trapped. Lizzie Peabody hadn't shown up yet, the clock was ticking away like a time bomb, and he was stuck in the kitchen of the flat in Cowcaddens with dirty dishes piled in the sink, the bed unmade and little or no food in the larder. Perhaps he should have come home last night and tidied up but he'd been so weary and had so much on his mind that he'd selfishly sought refuge in the office. What he found most depressing, though, was that Rosie had been on his back since the moment he'd picked her up at Redlands. If she hadn't been deaf he might have been tempted to forget himself and give her a telling off. He had been brought up to respect women, though, and under the layers of annoyance and anxiety, he was grieving too, grieving at last for Rosie and the lost infant.

When he'd tried to put his arm about her in the taxi, she'd pushed him roughly away. He'd hesitated, then told her, 'I've arranged for your mother to come over and take care of you.'

'Where will you be?'

'Rosie, I'm sorry but I do have to go to work.'

'*Work!*' she'd shouted. 'You don't cuh-care about me, do you?'

'That's not true.'

'You don't cuh-care about the baby.'

'Rosie, I didn't know about the baby.'

'Well, I don't care about the baby. I'm glad it's gone.'

'Oh, Rosie, for God's sake don't say that.'

'No place for babies in this world.'

'We can try again, when you're feeling better.'

'Better! I never felt better in my life.'

'You'll have to rest for a day or two. Your mother—'

'I am going back to work tomorrow.'

'No.' He'd shaped the words firmly. 'No, you are not.'

'No work, no pay.'

Bolt upright, she had turned her head away and stared out at the streets and he had no means of reaching her. He had thought of the hollow place where the foetus had lain and for a split second had felt tears swell under his eyelids. Perhaps that's what she wanted from him. Perhaps she wanted to reduce him to tears, to make him mourn in her stead.

Rosie had elbowed him hard in the ribs. 'Who else have you told?'

'Nobody, just your mother and Bernard.'

'Why didn't you tell Polly?'

'I couldn't get in touch with her.'

'What about Babs?'

'I – I didn't have time. I'll telephone her at her office.'

'Nuh-nuh.'

'She'll need to be told, Rosie.'

'She nuh-needs to be told nothing of the sort.'

'Rosie—'

'Over. Done with.'

She'd sunk back on the leather bench, shaking with the irregular rhythm of the wheels on the cobbles and had smiled a twisted little smile.

'Back to work tomorrow,' she'd said. 'No rest for the wuh-wicked.'

He'd no longer had the strength to argue with her.

While he'd settled the fare with the cabbie, Rosie had run upstairs and before he'd reached the door, had let herself into the flat and was dumping a kettleful of water on to the stove.

She lit the gas ring with a match.

'I'll do that,' Kenny said.

'I can do it myself.'

'What do you want, tea?'

'Hot water. To wash away the hospital stink.'

'Look,' he said, 'let me do it. It's freezing in here. I'll make the bed and put in a hot-water bottle and you can—'

'Why didn't you come to see me?'

'I did,' Kenny said. 'I told you, I did. You were sound asleep.'

'You should have been there sooner.'

'I couldn't . . . I mean, the hospital couldn't get in touch with me. I was in Greenock all day and half the night.' She was at the sink, paddling her hands in tap water. He leaned on the board to make sure that she could read his lips. 'I came to the hospital as soon as I heard. Didn't the nurses tell you? Of course they told you. If they hadn't told you, you wouldn't have been ready to leave with me this morning.' She pursed her lips. Water trickled through her fingers into the sink. 'Rosie, I'm sorry. I'm sorry about the baby, really and truly sorry.'

'I'm not.' She tried to mimic his voice but it came out as a quack. 'I'm glad. I don't want to bring a baby into this horrible world and if you think you're going to have fun trying for another one, you can thuh-think again, Kenny MacGregor.'

'I'll make the bed.'

'And you can bloody well lie on it,' Rosie said and, quite violently, tugged at the blackout curtain and let milky daylight flood the room.

In the tearoom, talking:

'Now hold on,' Dougie said. 'See if I've got this right. This man, this Yank, turns up out o' the blue, worms his way into Babs's good books an' camps in her house. When he meets you, he immediately claims he's workin' for the American Government an' Dominic's offered money to the partisans in Italy an' expects you just t' hand it over. When did he tell you all this?'

'I met him for the first time last night.'

'What's his name again?'

'Cameron.'

'Did he show his papers?'

'No, but then I didn't ask to see them.'

'Is he a chancer, d'you think?'

'I don't know what to think,' said Polly, 'that's why I'm here.'

'What you're askin' me,' Dougie said, 'is whether or not your hubby is committed enough to the Communists to send all his dough to Italy.'

'Communists? Nobody mentioned Communists. Dominic supported all sorts of political groups but he was never a member of any particular party.'

'Aye,' said Dougie, 'he was a great one for sittin' on the fence, your Dom. Maybe now he's made up his mind which way to jump.'

'By declaring himself a Communist?'

'Naw, naw,' said Dougie. 'By settlin' in America.'

'I don't understand.'

'Old Dom's not offerin' t' help the US Government out the goodness of his heart,' Dougie said. 'There must be somethin' in it for him. If you ask me the G-men are puttin' pressure on Dominic an' his family.'

'His family?'

'Carlo, the old man, the Philadelphia mob.'

'Do you think Dominic's trying to buy his way out of trouble?'

'He's done it before. Done it right here, didn't he?'

'I suppose you could say that,' Polly agreed reluctantly. 'It could, of course, be simple patriotism.'

'Hah-hah!' Dougie said sarcastically. 'Anyway, patriotism's

never that simple. It'll be some sort o' deal, a deal so fishy the Yanks aren't bitin' yet.'

'Is that why they've sent someone to spy on me?'

'Hardly spy, Mrs Manone,' Dougie said. 'This guy might've come in by the back door, but he's been direct enough in tellin' you what he's here for.'

'I wonder if he has,' said Polly.

'Easy enough to find out,' said Dougie. 'Telephone Dominic. Do you have his number in New York?'

'As a matter of fact,' Polly said, 'no.'

'Send him a cable then.'

'Kenny MacGregor's already quizzed Mr Cameron,' Polly said. 'Rosie thought he might have designs on Babs.'

Dougie shook his head. 'Typical.'

'Typical of what?' said Polly.

'Women,' Dougie said. 'The world's crashin' down around our ears an' all you can think about is who's goin' to go to bed wi' who. I take it our lovely inspector boy doesn't know the whole story?'

'No.'

'Why not tell him? Ask his advice, instead o' mine.'

'You're not being much of a help, Dougie.'

'Bloody right, I'm not,' Dougie said. 'I'm havin' a fine time feedin' chickens an' lookin' after your sister's bairns – keepin' my head down, so to speak. Remember what I told you a wee while back? Dig in, I said, dig in. Well, I've heeded my own advice. I'm well an' truly dug in an' I don't want t' be undug, thank you very much.' He paused, then asked, 'How much money are we talkin' about here?'

'I haven't done my sums yet,' Polly said.

'Round figures.'

'Fifty thousand pounds, give or take.'

'Jeeze!' said Dougie. 'If you hand over fifty grand to this joker where will that leave you financially?'

'Broke,' said Polly.

'Didn't your hubby transfer his holdin's into your name?'

'Most of them,' said Polly.

'So he's got no claim on any of it?'

'Legally,' Polly said, 'no, I don't suppose he has.'

'Well, now we know why Mr Roosevelt shipped somebody across the Atlantic to size you up,' Dougie told her. 'Supposin' you decide it's all above board an' that bringin' down the Duce is worth fifty grand then how do you get the money out o' the country? Stuff it into a suitcase an' hand it over to this Yank? Nah nah, Polly, you're not that daft.'

'There are lots of channels for transferring large sums of money from one country to another,' Polly said. 'Lisbon, for example. Hard cash can still be shipped through Lisbon.'

'Is that what your American friend told you?'

'Yes.'

'Hard cash in what currency?'

'I don't know. I haven't agreed to co-operate yet so naturally he's cagey. In addition to which,' Polly said, 'I've a strong suspicion that Christy Cameron doesn't really know what he's doing.'

'You mean he's an amateur?'

'In a nutshell, yes.'

'Somebody must be givin' him orders.'

'Who?' Polly said.

'Aye,' Dougie said, 'there's the rub. Who?'

'If I knew that,' Polly said, 'I'd know how to proceed.'

Dougie said, 'Why haven't you confided in Hughes? Is it because you know he'll be dead set against it?'

'Probably,' Polly said. 'Look, Dougie, my husband trusted you. I admit I never understood what sterling virtues he saw in you, but trust you he did, and for that reason I'm willing to trust you too.'

'You're makin' me blush,' said Dougie. 'Listen, if the Yank

is just an amateur somebody must be pullin' his strings. Bring him out to Blackstone. Let me talk to him.'

'Why?'

'Because,' Dougie said, carefully, 'he may have the impression there's a fortune in counterfeit banknotes still buried on the property.'

'Which there isn't, of course.'

'You know what's buried there, Polly, an' it isn't banknotes.' Dougie moved on quickly. 'Bring him out on Thursday when the kiddies are at school. Do you still have the motorcar?'

'It's stored in the garage.'

'Can you scrounge some petrol?'

'I expect so.'

'Then drive over about lunch time.'

'Why wait until Thursday?'

'To give him time t' contact his bosses.'

'What a clever idea,' said Polly.

When she returned home from Cowcaddens that evening, Lizzie was dismayed to find her husband crouched on the hearthrug with one knee over Irene Milligan. From the doorway she watched Bernard loosen the top button of the girl's blouse then, sliding down a little, undo the fastening at the side of her skirt.

The girl lay passively beneath him, eyes closed.

'Now,' Bernard said, 'the next bit's tricky.'

'I'll bet it is,' said Mr Grainger.

'I'm not going to do it,' Bernard said, 'I'm just going to pretend. Could you open your mouth a wee bit wider, please, Irene?'

Obediently Irene displayed white teeth and healthy pink gums.

Bernard said, 'Once the victim's clothing has been loosened then the mouth is opened and the tongue held to one side while any obstruction in the throat is cleared away. Shock can often cause vomiting so it's crucial that the airways are cleared.'

'What do you use,' said Mr Heron, 'one o' them stick things?'

Bernard swivelled round. 'Highly unlikely you'll be running about with a pocketful of tongue depressors, Gordon,' he said, 'so, as I've told you many times before, improvise, improvise, improvise. Use the blunt end of a pencil or a fountain pen if you have one, failing which, the finger, the good old-fashioned finger will do the job quite nicely.'

'Infection?' said Irene's mum. 'Germs?'

'If the victim's choking to death,' said Bernard, 'you haven't time to worry about infection. Meet each crisis as it comes. And remember,' he climbed off the girl and got to his feet, 'if there's any sign of bleeding or immobilising injury do not, repeat *do not* attempt to move the subject.'

'Why's that then?' said old Mr Heron.

Irene sighed, opened her eyes and answered, 'Because the end of a broken bone can puncture a vital organ and ex— exabertate the injury.'

'Well done, young lady.' Bernard helped the girl up. 'A round of applause for our victim, please.'

Lizzie caught her husband's eye.

He raised his brows in greeting.

Bernard's fortnightly ambulance class was popular and ten or a dozen neighbours from the cottage row were crammed into Lizzie's living room. Some, like old Mr Heron, came only to see women lying on the floor on the off chance he'd catch a glimpse of knickers. Most of the others were there because the risk of injury from a bombing attack had not gone away and they hadn't much faith in the ambulance service. The class was one of several that bolstered the community's sense of self-sufficiency and fostered the hope that, come what may, the good citizens of Knightswood would survive the ravages of war.

'Our thanks to Bernard too,' said Mr Grainger. 'Always instructive, always informative. Monday night, stirrup pump drill, half-past seven in the shed behind the bus garage.'

Lizzie usually served tea and biscuits at this juncture but tonight the neighbours dispersed quickly, squeezing past her to the front door. They dabbed her arm, asked after Rosie and nodded sympathetically, even though they had no idea what was really wrong with Bernard's stepdaughter.

Lizzie did her bit by murmuring platitudes.

She had no affinity with her neighbours, no authority over them. It wasn't like the old days in the Gorbals when everybody had looked up to her and treated her with respect. She wondered what had happened to the fierce, fiery woman who would stand no nonsense from anyone, and just when she had shrivelled into meekness and apathy, lost in Bernard's shadow.

'He's a grand man, a grand man, Lizzie,' Ella Grainger said. 'I don't know what we'd do without him.'

Lizzie watched her husband help young Miss Milligan into her coat, though the Milligans lived only four doors down and the night was mild. He stood close to the girl and tucked in her scarf. It popped into Lizzie's head that for all his uprightness, her husband was several years younger than she was and that these past few anxious months he seemed to have lost his enthusiasm for hugging, kissing and the other thing; that perhaps he, like so many others, was taking advantage of the war to help himself to a bit of excitement.

Irene Milligan was just Bernard's sort: young, lively and impressionable. Her father was off fighting in the desert and there had been rumours about Mrs Milligan and Mr Grainger; nothing definite, nothing you could really put your finger on. Lizzie hated herself for heeding such gossip but she couldn't help but wonder if the neighbours were gossiping about Bernard too and if anyone else had noticed how Irene looked at him and blushed when he spoke to her. She wondered what they would say about Rosie if they knew the truth – miscarriages were always news – and if they would blame her for not telling her daughter all about the dangers that faced a new young wife.

'Night-night, Mrs Peabody,' said Irene, and with a final coy glance in Bernard's direction, sauntered out into the street.

As soon as the room had cleared, Bernard came over to Lizzie and put a hand on her shoulder. She was taking off her hat, sliding out the pin, and flinched when he touched her. A whole day in the flat in Cowcaddens listening to her daughter belittle Kenny, her husband, had strained even Lizzie's patience. She had sympathy for Rosie but had fallen out of the habit of donating her love without question and had more than a little sympathy for Kenny too.

'How is she?'

'She'll be all right,' Lizzie said.

'Is Kenny back?'

'He came in about seven. I made him his dinner.'

'Is Rosie laid up – in bed, I mean?'

Bernard's concern was genuine. When he had married Lizzie Conway he had taken on her girls without a qualm. But Babs and Polly were grown up, or nearly so, by that time and it was poor deaf Rosie who needed him most. He still thought of her as his poor deaf Rosie but Lizzie was beginning to realise that Rosie was not so poor as all that. She had a good regular income and a kind, caring husband to whom she must give some kindness and consideration in return, even at a sad and difficult time like this.

'No, she's not in bed,' Lizzie said. 'She's up and about. She says she's goin' back to work tomorrow.'

'It's too soon, isn't it?'

'I talked to the lady doctor last night at the hospital.'

'And?'

'Rosie can still have babies.'

'That's not what I meant,' Bernard said.

'I know what you meant,' Lizzie said. 'I don't know whether it's too soon or not. Maybe goin' back to work will take her mind off things.'

'Is she brooding?'

'Aye, but not about the baby.'

'What, about the war?'

'She's not happy,' Lizzie said. 'She talked nineteen t' the dozen all blessed day, trailin' me about the flat like a puppy, never lettin' me out o' her sight – an' I still don't know what really ails her. It's more than just losin' the baby.'

'It's the uncertainty principle.'

'You've a pat explanation for everythin', Bernard, haven't you?'

'Well, it is.' He began to set the table for supper. 'I've a shepherd's pie in the oven an' stewed prunes for afters. Will that do you?'

'That'll do me fine,' said Lizzie.

She seated herself by the fire. There were rolls of bandage on the mantelpiece and on the rug a big wooden box filled with splints and dressings. Bernard's toys, Bernard's weapons; he loved all the paraphernalia and the status that went with it. He, like Kenny, had a lot of 'pull' because of his job, and a lot of responsibility too. He even had the use of a Breslin Council motorcar, though he never brought the vehicle home.

'I'll have to have a talk with her,' Bernard said.

'She's not in the mood for talkin',' Lizzie said.

'I thought you said—'

'Not in the mood for listenin' is what I mean.'

'Oh, she'll listen to me,' said Bernard. 'She always listens to me.'

Lizzie didn't have the heart to contradict him.

She nodded wearily and while her husband made ready to serve the supper, closed her eyes and snatched forty dreamless winks in her battered old armchair by the fire.

6

Christmas seemed a long way off. Babs had bought a little box of cards and two or three trinkets to put in the children's stockings, but with Jackie away she could work up little enthusiasm for the festive season.

She hadn't yet decided if she would take April over to the farm for the holidays or bring the other three home. Boxing Day, Thursday, she would have to be back in the office. Polly might look after them, or Christy, but she had a feeling that Polly and Christy would have other fish to fry. Lying in the cold bedroom in the bungalow in Raines Drive, she worried more about Christmas than the progress of the war.

She had been in bed for less than an hour when the air-raid siren wailed. She barely had time to sit up before the bedroom door flew open and Christy appeared with April, wrapped in a quilt, in his arms.

'Grab what you can,' he said, 'and let's get out of here.'

'Why, what's wrong, what is it?'

'Air raid,' he said. 'A real one this time.'

'Wait, I need to—'

'No,' he said. 'Now.'

Babs heard the drone of aeroplanes and the crump of bombs in the distance. There had been two brief incendiary raids back in September but she hadn't heard bombs before.

Christy steered her through the kitchen into the back garden. She stared at the sky over Glasgow, saw the shapes of aeroplanes in the searchlights across the river and the hills bleached by fire glow. Carrying April, Christy dived down the steps into the Anderson shelter.

Jackie had been gone before the shelter had been delivered. Bernard had come over from Knightswood one Sunday and dug out the pit and bolted the pieces together. Next afternoon Babs had covered the plates with earth and had installed two rough wooden benches and an old cot from the attic.

The tetchy old warden who had come along to inspect her handiwork had warned her that the shelter would flood unless she dug drains, but Babs had ignored his advice. She had done nothing to make the Anderson more habitable except stick in a smoke vent and an ancient iron stove.

Christy stepped into three or four inches of muddy water.

'For Chrissake!' he exclaimed. 'It's a goddamned swamp down here.'

'Sorry,' Babs said. 'Sorry, sorry, sorry.'

From the hills west of Raines Drive ack-ack guns were pounding away. Puffs of white smoke, like artificial snow, powdered the skyline. She heard whistling, felt the sudden blast of an explosion from the direction of Holloway Road and, reaching for Christy's hand, slithered down the steps into the icy water. He had already put April into the high-sided cot. He pushed Babs to one side, hauled on the rope that served as a handle and closed the door only seconds before a great trembling blast shook the earth around them.

'Jesus, that was too close for comfort,' Christy said.

He switched on a pocket torch.

April kneeled on the damp mattress inside the cot, the quilt cowled over her head. Babs paddled towards her. 'Darlin', oh darlin', are you okay?'

'More bombs,' April said. 'Daddy's fightin' again.'

'So he is, so he is,' said Babs, laughing and shaking.

'Daddy'll see them off. You wait, honey, we'll be back in our own beds before you know it.'

'Not tonight we won't,' said Christy, quietly.

The flashing red bulb in the bedroom had failed to waken her and, burrowed deep in bedclothes, she didn't sense the frantic activity in the street.

Unknown to Rosie, Kenny had given Mr McVicar a door key and the warden had no hesitation in using it to let himself into MacGregor's flat. He had already supervised the removal of eighty-six-year-old Mrs Jackson from the top floor and allayed the panic that had taken possession of Mrs Lottman, who had three children under five and a husband at sea. He had personally ferried her tiny, toddling brood out of the close and across to the brick air-raid shelter at the corner of Cowcaddens Arch and St Mungo's Lane. Only then had he gone back into the tenement to fetch out the policeman's wife.

He navigated his way into the bedroom by the light of the warning bulb. Kenny's young wife was so slight that she made hardly a bump under the bedclothes. The room smelled stale, like a sick bay. He wondered what the fastidious Fiona MacGregor would have to say about that when she got home.

He tapped the bump with his torch.

'Rosie, Mrs MacGregor,' he shouted, 'wake up, please.'

She stirred, moaned, dug deeper into the bedclothes.

Mr McVicar peeled back the quilt and blankets. Rosie sat up. The buttons of her pyjamas were undone. The warden caught a glimpse of small, up-tilted breasts and a flat bare stomach, and looked quickly away.

'Whuh . . . ?'

A skirt and sweater, vest and knickers had been tossed across the foot of the bed. He lifted the bundle and handed it to her.

'Uh! Uh! Is it . . . uh . . . ?'

He flapped an arm, stirring an invisible pot, to indicate that haste was essential. There were no sounds of falling bombs yet but he could make out the clang of fire engines and ambulances, and the siren continued to wail.

He glanced round. She was naked, skinny naked, thinner than most of the half-starved children he'd encountered when he'd worked as a porter in the Royal Infirmary. She fumbled, still half asleep, with her clothes.

He went out into the hall and, a minute later, she joined him.

'HOW BUH-BAD?'

'Bad enough,' he shouted, facing her.

'WHUH-WHERE'S KENNETH?'

'I don't know.'

She uttered an angry little *tut* and followed the warden out of the flat and down the dark stairs to the street.

The communal shelter nestled against the wall of a railway cutting. Rosie looked up at the tenements that towered above her and saw a scud of cloud lit by a searchlight. She was awake now, wide awake. She could tell by Mr McVicar's attitude that this was the real thing and that somewhere not far off bombs were falling from the sky.

She felt weak but not unwell. She was, in fact, hungry, which was an odd and inconvenient thing to be right now. She had snatched up her purse but there was nothing to eat in it, not even a toffee or a mint. She had absolutely no idea what time it was. She walked to the door of the shelter and went in. It stank of damp brick, distemper and disinfectant. There were no stoves or heating pipes to warm the dank atmosphere and only three dim blue electric bulbs locked in wire cages against the ceiling gave light.

Rosie peered into the gloom. Benches lined the walls, benches crowded with widows and couples, wives without husbands, a soldier or two, three or four young girls, and a surprising number of young children.

She looked for somewhere to sit and found herself squeezed up against a gaunt, dark-haired woman with two toddlers and a baby clinging to her like monkeys. The children were clad in an assortment of knitted garments, and whined and pawed fractiously at their mother as if they were afraid that she would abandon them in this unwholesome place.

Rosie stared down at her scuffed shoes and wrinkled stockings and endeavoured not to meet the woman's eye.

In the unnatural light everyone seemed inordinately calm.

They dug into pockets and bags, produced buns and apples and tubes of wine gums, lit cigarettes, drank bottled beer or soda pop.

The woman fumbled by her feet, hoisted up a shopping bag and fished from it a feeding bottle and a packet of sandwiches.

Rosie eyed the sandwiches hungrily while the children clawed and clamoured for bread and jam and the baby screeched for milk. How lucky she was, Rosie thought, not to have children.

Then everyone looked up.

A girl screamed.

The dark-haired woman covered the children with her long, ungainly arms. She, like Rosie, wore an old trench coat. She, like Rosie, had wrinkled stockings and scuffed shoes. Unlike Rosie, she was terrified.

The blast shook the shelter and delivered a series of small aftershocks.

Rosie felt them in her stomach and chest and, looking up, watched a trickle of blue-grey dust sift down from the ceiling.

Mute with fear, the dark-haired woman wept helplessly.

Rosie shifted her position.

'Huh-here,' she shouted. 'Give me the damned thuh-thing.' Then detaching the child from the woman's grasp and prising the bottle from her fist, she stuffed the baby into the crook of her arm, squeezed the teat between its lips and, grimly, let it feed.

After the first wave of enemy bombers passed, April lay down and fell asleep.

Babs worried about her daughter sleeping on a damp mattress, especially after Christy told her it was her fault for not being prepared. He read her the riot act about the realities of warfare for ten or fifteen minutes, then he tugged open the wooden door and stuck his head out.

'Is that the all clear?' Babs asked.

'Not yet.'

'Maybe we can go indoors, though? What d' you think?'

'It's a lull, is all.' Christy answered and, to Babs's dismay, pulled himself up the ladder and vanished into the night.

Shaking like a leaf and cold beyond belief, she sat cross-legged on the bunk and peered at the rectangle of not quite darkness.

The carpet of rainwater had turned inky black and she would swear she heard wavelets lapping against the bottom of the bunk. She knew she'd been a fool and deserved a telling-off. She should have paid more attention to the warden's instructions, should have read the civil defence pamphlets that had popped through the door. She had been busy, though, so busy trying to manage the war on her own account that she'd ignored all advice. She'd never forgive herself if April fell sick because of her carelessness.

Five minutes passed, then Christy came skulking back, carrying blankets, pillows and clothing. He waded into the water, passed the bundle to Babs and went off again. Three minutes later he returned toting two bolster cases. He slid ankle-deep into the water, dumped the bolster cases on top of the stove and carefully sealed the door again. He flicked on the torch, opened one of the bolster cases and brought out candles and a couple of her best china saucers. He softened the bottom of two candles with his lighter, stuck them firmly on to the saucers and passed them to Babs.

She took one in each hand and held them out over the muddy water while Christy lit a fire in the stove with kindling he'd brought from the coalhole in the bungalow. Babs began to feel better. Hunkered at the stove, his bum hovering just above the waterline, he looked broad and strong in the crouching shadows, his hair glistening in the candlelight; Babs felt like a goddess of sorts, squatting on the bunk in her nightie with a candle in each hand.

'I doubt if they've given up,' Christy said. 'If they've earmarked targets down river they'll send through a second wave.' The lighter flame bloomed. Babs heard the crackle of sticks and smelled paper burning. 'This is nothing. If you'd been in Warsaw during the siege you'd know what it was like to be scared. There was no place to hide to escape the destruction.'

'You escaped, though,' Babs said.

'I did, yeah.'

'But not Ewa?'

He didn't turn round. Babs could see his hands, small square hands with bitten fingernails, dirty with coal dust, clasp the rim of the Tortoise stove.

He rested his brow on his knuckles.

'I saw the letter,' Babs said. 'Did Ewa survive?'

'I don't know.'

'You left her there, didn't you?'

'I had no choice.'

'Really, no choice?'

'It's none of your friggin' business, Babs.' He scooped a handful of coal nuts from the bolster case and hurled it into the stove. 'You shouldn't have gone nosing through my stuff. If you wanna know more about me, ask.'

'I'm askin' you now,' Babs said.

He swivelled round and glared at her.

Candle flames wavered in the draft from the door. Babs couldn't stop shaking. She put the saucers one on each side of her, and leaned forward.

'Polly's kids,' she said. 'I saw the photograph of Polly's kids too.'

'So friggin' what!'

'Is that your brother? The guy in uniform?'

His shoulder lifted in a massive sigh. 'Yeah. Jamie.'

'You told me you'd never met Dominic.'

'I haven't.'

'Then who took the photograph?'

'God knows. I didn't. Jamie gave me the photograph.'

'Does Polly know all about you? Have you told her all the things you haven't told me?'

'I told her what I had to, no more.'

'You're lyin' again, Christy, aren't you?'

He slammed the little iron door of the stove, lifted himself from the floor, planted his hands on the bunk and looked her straight in the eye.

'I was sent here by the US Government to make a deal with your sister,' he said. 'That's all you need know.'

'It has to do with Dominic, though, hasn't it?'

'Yeah.'

'Is Dominic spying for the Germans?'

'What makes you say that?'

'He always was a shifty bugger. You never knew what he was up to.'

A flickering glow showed in the tiny glass panels of the

stove and a gout of smoke broke from the seam of the metal vent and crawled across the roof.

Christy said, 'We don't know what he's up to either.'

'Oh, I get it now,' Babs said. 'You think we're in it with him. You think we're part of Dominic Manone's mob. Well, we're not. I'm not.'

He put an arm round her and pulled her away from the wall. She let herself go, yielding to him. Her breasts were visible under the damp nightie, her nipples stiff with cold. She could feel his fingers against her spine, strong and hard, and longed for him to kiss her. Instead, he took a bottle from his pocket, uncorked it and swallowed a mouthful of whisky.

'I don't blame you for going through my stuff,' he said. 'I'd have done the same in your position. It's all so goddamned sneaky. I hate being sneaky. I wasn't brought up that way.'

'Were you in love with the girl in Warsaw?'

'No.'

'Did you – were you an' she . . . ?'

'No.'

'I don't believe you,' Babs said, softly.

'Believe what you like.'

'Did you try to get her out of the country?'

'Yes.'

'Why didn't you?'

'She wouldn't leave her family.'

'Will you go back for her when the war's over?'

'No.'

'Why not?'

'Because she won't be there. She'll be gone. Dead, most like. There can be no happy endings to this story. For all any of us know there may be no endings at all.'

'You did love her?'

'Maybe I did.'

'That's sad.'

Babs rested her brow on his shoulder. The tension had gone out of her. She felt sorry for him. She had mothered Jackie and stood up to Dennis but she had never felt sorry for a man before. She leaned on him, saying nothing, listening to the crackle from the stove and, far off, the *pam-pam-pam* of anti-aircraft guns in the hills to the west.

'How long will you stay with us?' Babs asked at length.

'As long as I have to,' Christy answered.

'As long as you can?'

'Yeah,' he said, sighing, 'as long as I possibly can.'

Kenny rode home in an RN gharry with Sir Charles Huserall and two young Wrens who had wangled forty-eight-hour passes and were determined to reach the big city as soon as possible.

The second wave of heavy bombers hadn't materialised. Perhaps British air defences had proved too much for the German pilots or perhaps the Luftwaffe had just been flexing its muscle. The all clear sounded about half-past three a.m. and the gharry left Greenock soon after. Over the river several small fires were visible and on the long stretch past Inchinnan the railway line was up and a fire crew was working to put out a blaze in a clump of scrub alder. There were fires in Paisley too, but not many.

Kenny was almost dead for want of sleep. Sensing his fatigue, Sir Charles said little during the two-hour drive and had Kenny and the Wrens dropped off in George Square.

Bubbling with excitement, the girls said ta-ta and set off, arm in arm, along Cathedral Street while Kenny slogged up hill to Cowcaddens.

Small debris, mainly slates and broken chimney pots, scattered the cobbles, but all the tenement windows were intact and there were no fire engines or ambulances in the vicinity.

Relieved, he climbed the stairs and let himself into the flat.

He peeped into the bedroom.

The bed had been made and clothing put away. A freshly ironed shirt hung from a wire hanger on the wardrobe door. Folded neatly on a chair were clean stockings, a vest and underpants.

Rosie was home, safe and sound.

He went into the kitchen.

She stood at the sink under the blackout, back to him. She wore her best pleated skirt, stockings and heels and a frilly apron. She was washing clothes in the big sink, and singing to herself. She had learned the lyrics of popular songs by plastering her better ear hard against the wireless set but it had been months since Kenny had heard her sing.

Sensing his presence, she swung round.

'Uh, there you are,' she said.

Kenny propped an elbow on the draining board.

'Are you okay?'

'Fine.'

'Did you have an air raid?'

'Uh-huh. Mr McVicar wakened me and tuh-took me down to the shelter.'

'How long did it last?'

'Couple of hours, closer to three, come to think of it.'

'No damage, no injuries?'

'Nuh, none.'

He nodded then, with a little frown, said, 'What are you doing, Rosie?'

'Washing your shirts.'

'Aren't you tired?'

'I had a little nap in the shelter.'

Kenny watched her remove a shirt from the suds, rinse it

in a separate basin, wring it out and hang it on a clotheshorse near the fire.

Drying her hands and forearms on a towel, she faced him. 'When are you due on duty?' she asked.

'Two this afternoon.'

'Greenock?'

'No, I'm finished in Greenock for the time being.'

'Is there much damage down there?'

'Some, not much,' he said. 'Rosie, are you sure you're all right?'

'Fine. Starved, that's all.'

She stepped to the stove and lit a gas ring, slid a knob of lard into a frying pan and shook the pan over the flame. She had placed four rashers of bacon on waxed paper and whipped up a jug of dried-egg mix. She put two slices of bread under the grill and the kettle, already filled, on the big back ring by the bubbling porridge pot. She seemed alert and energetic; too energetic perhaps. Kenny studied her, seeking signs of a frenetic edge to her benign mood, something to account for the sudden change in her.

She glanced over her shoulder, smiling. 'You must be hungry too?'

'Rosie . . .' He checked himself, too eroded by fatigue to pursue the obvious line of enquiry. 'Yes, I am hungry.'

'Porridge to start with?'

'What? Yes, porridge too, please. Thank you.'

'Sit then. Sit.'

Obediently he seated himself at the table.

Spoons, forks and knives were all in place, milk jug, sugar bowl, marmalade and sauce bottle. He felt awkward, almost embarrassed, as if he had stumbled into someone else's kitchen and was about to scoff someone else's breakfast served by someone else's wife.

'Rosie?' She ladled porridge into two large plates. 'Rosie?'

'Uh?'

'Why are you all dressed up?'

'I am going back to work.'

'Are you sure you're up to it?'

'Oh yah,' she said, 'I'm up to it.'

And coming round behind him to deliver the porridge plate, she stooped and kissed him brusquely right on the top of his head.

Heavy taping had protected the glass only in part. One entire pane had fallen into the parlour and lay like a mosaic in the window bay under the torn curtain. An orange vase of some antiquity and one heavy-framed painting of a Dutch sea battle had been shaken from their moorings and lay in pieces in the hearth. The piano lid had been scarred and the back of the big black leather sofa, once Dominic's place of repose, had a gash in it but, all in all, Polly thought, the old homestead had got off pretty lightly.

She surveyed the damage from the parlour door, sniffed the early morning air that filtered in from the park, then with no more than a little sigh, went back to the telephone in the hall and lifted the up-turned receiver.

'No, Bernard,' she said, 'not much damage. Lost a window, that's all.'

'I take it you're not injured?'

'I slept through most of it,' Polly said.

In fact, she had slept through all of it, snug in the cot in the larder. Only the persistent ringing of the telephone had wakened her. She was reluctant to leave her den below stairs but had a feeling that Bernard might call and knew it would be unfair to ignore him. She was clad only in a pair of slacks and a cashmere jumper, her feet bare. She shivered a little in the breeze that weaselled through the broken window.

'Your mother was terribly worried,' Bernard said. 'Have you been round to check on Babs yet?'

'No, actually – what time *is* it?'

'Gone seven.'

'Really!' Polly said. 'Are you in the phone box on Anniesland Road, or are you at work?'

'In the box,' said Bernard. 'I'll have to report to Lizzie before I leave.'

'Well, it's kind of you to call,' said Polly. 'Tell Mammy I'm perfectly all right and I'm sure Babs is too. As far as I can make out there hasn't been much damage in this neck of the woods – or have you heard news to the contrary?'

'The Jerries were after something further down river, I imagine,' Bernard said. 'They may have been attempting to breach the boom defence system to let U-boats into the Firth.'

'Umm,' said Polly, diffidently.

'They dumped some stuff on Paisley; tail-enders probably.'

Polly looked down at her feet. She had amused herself last evening by painting her toenails. It had crossed her mind that someone from New York might be used to girls with painted toenails and might even find them attractive. Her feet were still dainty and the pink-tinted polish made them seem more so. She arched her left foot, put it on the chair by the telephone table and waggled her toes while Bernard droned on about the Luftwaffe. He had probably picked up the BBC's six o'clock bulletin and put Mammy into a panic by exaggerating the importance of the news.

At length, Polly said, 'I gather Knightswood escaped unscathed?'

'Yes, pretty well.'

Consorting with councillors had added an officious note to Bernard's voice. The clumsy old Glaswegian consonants had been pared away and, Polly thought, if the war lasts long enough Bernard would wind up sounding like all the other local government twerps she'd ever known.

'Did you spend the night in the shelter?'

'Three or four hours,' said Bernard, 'quite comfortably.'

'Was Mammy upset?'

'Not greatly, but she's worried about the children. You will pop round to Babs's, won't you, just to make sure she's safe?'

'I have work to do too, Bernard. Besides, Babs has probably left for the office, or will have by the time I get there.'

'Please, Polly.'

Polly admired her painted toenails and wondered again what a certain person from New York would think of them; wondered too if she should call Fin and have him send someone round to help clean up the mess in the parlour and fit boards over the broken window, or if that certain person from New York might turn out to be a handyman as well as a spy.

'Oh, all right, Bernard,' she said. 'All right.'

Babs was never at her glorious best in the morning, and that morning in particular she looked, she thought, a right sorry mess after a sleepless night in a soaking wet, smoke-filled shelter.

When the tramcar dumped her at the Cross she was dismayed to find Archie loitering outside the greengrocer's shop. One arm was folded across his chest and he was puffing on a cigarette as he peered short-sightedly at the tram. As soon as Babs appeared, however, Archie lobbed away the ciggie and darted across the cobbles to greet her.

'You're all right, are you?' he enquired anxiously.

'Do I look all right?' Babs answered.

'Well, I confess I have seen you looking more chipper,' Archie said.

'What're you doin' out here, anyway?' Babs said.

He executed a little pivot on the ball of one foot. 'Nothing,' he said. 'Absolutely nothing. I – erm – I got here early and thought perhaps you wouldn't show up today so before I plunged single-handed into the hectic tide of paper work I decided to—'

'Oh, shut up,' Babs said. 'Point is, do we still have an office?'

'We do,' said Archie. 'Mercifully we still have an office and, by the grace of God, a staff to run it. What happened to you?'

They were walking towards Cyprus Street. The morning was doing its best to be crisp but dampness wouldn't leave the air and the mist over the river seemed more dense than usual.

'What d'you mean – what happened?' said Babs. 'What happened was, I spent the whole bloody night cowerin' in a steel shelter.'

'Me too,' said Archie. 'Mother and I and two cats, one dog and a parrot.'

'A parrot?'

'Skipper.'

'Skipper?'

'My father's final legacy.'

'I didn't know your mother was a widow,' Babs said.

'Has been for years,' said Archie. 'The damned parrot's older than I am. It simply refuses to do the decent thing and die. Are you really as chewed up as you appear to be?'

'Are you kiddin'?'

'Everything's all right, though: I mean, the house, your daughter?'

'Yeah, yeah, yeah,' said Babs.

He put a hand on her arm and, breaking stride, held her back from turning into Cyprus Street. Babs had been too weary, too focused on Archie to notice that a host of strange men in various shades of uniform were scuttling about the junction.

She scowled. 'I thought you said—'

'The office is unharmed, quite intact, I assure you,' Archie said. 'However – look, I don't want you to be unduly alarmed by what you're about to see. It's not as bad as it looks, just another CD fuss, in my opinion, but I suppose they do have the right to be just a mite concerned, really.'

'What the heck are you babblin' about?'

She tugged on his arm, dragged him round the corner – and stopped dead in her tracks. It was, she thought, like a scene from that old Clark Cable picture about the San Francisco earthquake. Even the firemen and the fire engines didn't look real. The great mound of earth that banked the end of Cyprus Street just a hundred yards from the door of the Welfare Centre seemed more like painted cardboard than genuine rubble.

High above the earth embankment jets of water curved into the air and two firemen in oilskins were perched on top of the mound, directing operations with expansive gestures, like semaphore signallers who had lost their flags.

'They missed; the bombers, I mean,' said Archie. 'They left a footprint, but, thank God, they missed the obvious target.'

'If they . . .' Babs's throat was sticky with fear, 'if they missed, how come half the fire crews in the county— Archie, is that an ambulance?'

'It may be, it may very well be.'

'Dear God! Are you tellin' me the fuel dump's on fire?'

'Only a teeny weenie corner.'

'*Archie!*'

'Now, now, dear,' he put an arm about her, 'it's no cause for alarm.'

'They aren't gonna let us in, are they?'

'Well, I admit there was a certain reluctance on the part of the fire chief to acknowledge that we had an important job to do and that any delay would be detrimental to the—'

'*Archie!*' Babs howled.

Both hands on her shoulders, bottle-bottom glasses and greeny-blue eyes in what seemed like four dimensions, pressed close to her nose, Archie explained, 'I talked them into it. I persuaded them, yes, but you can be sure they wouldn't let us anywhere near the building if they thought there was the slightest risk of an explosion.'

'An *explosion!*' Once more, piercing and outraged: '*Archie!*'

'Putting out the fire in the emergency fuel depository is their responsibility,' Archie said. 'Protecting the files in the Recruitment and Welfare Centre is ours. Are you with me on that, Mrs Hallop?'

'Oh God!' Babs thumped her brow against his chest. 'What kind of an idiot do you take me for?'

'One very much like myself, I imagine,' said Archie.

'Oh, God!' said Babs again. 'Oh, God!'

Then, without quite knowing why, she let young Archie Harding steer her over the hoses and round the pumps into the office in Cyprus Street.

Polly was glad that Fin had insisted on giving her driving lessons. She suspected that Fin had it in mind that if the Germans did invade then he and she would motor to one of the distant North Sea fishing ports and sail off to a safe haven in neutral Sweden.

The threat of invasion had receded these past few months, though, the lessons had tailed off, and Polly had only an imperfect knowledge of what to do once she'd hauled off the dustsheet, filled the tank with petrol from a two-gallon can and checked the oil and water levels. She opened the garage doors as wide as they would go, climbed into the driving seat, settled the folds of her coat around her and switched on the engine.

She had watched Fin, and Babs too, do this often enough and wished she'd been as bold and far-sighted as her sister and had taken proper driving lessons while the going was good. She drew a deep breath, tapped the clutch, manipulated the gearshift and released the handbrake.

Rather to her surprise the Wolseley rolled sweetly down the driveway and bumped out into the avenue. She glanced back at the open doors of the garage – an invitation to looters and thieves Fin would have told her – decided to heck with them and, gripping the steering wheel, set off on the circuit of suburban roads that ringed the park.

She could readily understand why Fin was so addicted to motoring, why he loved lean, fast open-top sports cars. If she had any money left after the war ended, she promised herself she'd take proper professional instruction and buy a Morgan or a Riley Sprite – or let Dominic buy it for her.

She didn't know if she'd ever see her husband again, of course, or if by settling in New York Dominic intended to end their marriage. She could hardly blame him for wanting to be rid of her. She had been deceitful and disloyal, had betrayed Dom's trust by embarking on an affair with Tony Lombard. She had thought herself in love with Tony, but it hadn't been love at all, only wilful self-indulgence, made all the more lurid by being conducted under Dominic's nose.

There was no sign of the bomb that had blown out her front-room window, no crater, no smoke and all the trees in the park were still upright as far as she could make out. There were queues at bus stops and children wending off to school and women out with shopping bags, scavenging for off-ration foodstuffs and extra little luxuries to salt away for Christmas; all quite normal for a weekday morning. She drove past the telephone box on the corner of Raines Drive, glanced at it out of the corner of her eye, hastily applied the foot brake and brought the Wolseley to a halt.

She opened the passenger door and, leaning across the seat, looked back.

Christy Cameron emerged from the telephone box and, pausing, lit a cigarette. He looked smaller in daylight, and shabbier. Even as she watched, he hunched his shoulders, stuck his hands in his pockets and, head down, trudged towards her motorcar, quite oblivious to her presence.

If he is a spy, Polly thought, he's a very careless one.

She nudged the horn with her elbow.

He looked up and, to Polly's astonishment, backed away. For a moment she thought he might even take to his heels but then, collecting himself, he came grudgingly up to the car and leaned down to talk to her.

'Hey,' he said. 'Surprise.'

'That much is obvious,' Polly said.

'What do you mean?'

She patted the leather seat. 'Get in.'

He drew the jacket around him and slid into the car. She reached across and closed the door. He glanced down at the handle as if it were still in his mind to make a break for it.

'Phoning home, were you?' Polly said.

'No.' The irony was lost on him, apparently. 'It was just – just business.'

'How's my sister? Did she survive the night?'

He said again, 'What do you mean?'

'Well, I thought the question was clear enough,' said Polly. 'As you seem to be a bit dithery this morning, Mr Cameron, I'll put it another way: was the bungalow damaged in the air raid and did my sister and my niece escape unscathed?'

'Yeah, we – she – we're all okay.'

'Good,' said Polly, flatly.

'She's gone off to the office.'

'And April?'

'School, nursery, whatever.'

'It's business as usual then?' said Polly.

He was sullen and unsettled. She wondered whom he had been phoning and why her appearance had upset him.

'Brockway's,' he said, as if he'd read her mind. 'I was calling Brockway's.'

'Ah yes, you're "served" by Brockway's, aren't you?' Polly said. 'What sort of instructions did you receive? Are you going to come at me with a gun, or just wheedle away until I give in?'

'Jesus, Mrs Manone, you are some piece of work.'

'I've never been called that before. Is it a compliment?'

He settled back in the seat and took the cigarette from his mouth. 'I guess you've every right to be cagey.'

'Cagey is putting it mildly,' said Polly.

He smoked again, peered at the smoke. 'All right, I'll tell you the truth. I've a photographic spread due out, one I think Babs will like.'

'Photographs? Don't tell me you've photographed Babs?'

'Yeah.'

'In – I mean, she's actually *in* the magazine?'

'Yeah.'

'Glamour girl stuff?'

'Hardly.'

'Your reticence is breathtaking,' Polly said.

'Most girls would die for a chance to appear in *Brockway's*.'

'My sister isn't "most girls",' said Polly. 'She has a husband, in case you've forgotten, and Jackie certainly isn't going to be overwhelmed with delight when his wife turns up in a widely circulated magazine famous for its – shall we say? – candour.' She hesitated, then asked, 'When did you photograph Babs?'

'Day we first met.'

'How romantic.'

'That's cheap.'

'Yes,' Polly said. 'Yes, I suppose it is.'

'Don't tell me *you're* gonna make waves about my living with Babs?' Christy said. 'I thought you were a woman of the world.'

'And I thought you were engaged on a mission of national importance,' Polly said. 'Perhaps we're each deceiving the other. Be that as it may, if you've nothing better to do on Thursday I'll take you out to lunch at Blackstone Farm.'

'Why?'

'Do bring your camera,' Polly said. 'There's a very nice pig there.'

Christy was clearly in no frame of mind to be teased. 'You don't just want to show me round some crummy farm, do you?'

'I want to get to know you better,' Polly said. 'After all, if you have been dispatched to Scotland to size me up I don't see why I shouldn't do a bit of sizing up too. I'll pick you up at half-past ten.'

'Can I tell Babs what we're up to?' Christy said.

'Up to? We're not "up to" anything,' Polly said crisply. 'By all means tell Babs where we're going.'

Polly started the car, drove round the long curve of Raines Drive and stopped before the gate of the bungalow.

'What are you going to do now?' she asked.

'Make breakfast,' Christy said. 'Want some?'

'I'd better not,' said Polly. 'I have too much to do today.'

'Like what?'

'Tending my husband's money,' Polly said. 'Thursday: ten thirty?'

'I'll be waiting,' Christy said, and loped off up the steps of the Hallops' bungalow as if, Polly thought, he already owned the place.

⋆   ⋆   ⋆

Polly had never been to Rosie's flat before and had a little trouble locating it, for the tenement looked much the same as all the other tall tenements clustered on the hill. Eventually she found it and parked in the almost empty street outside. An old woman in a canvas apron was sweeping out the communal air-raid shelter and two council workmen with a handcart were clearing debris from the pavement, but the building itself appeared to be undamaged.

Polly climbed the stairs and knocked on the MacGregors' door.

She didn't really expect anyone to be home. Rosie would probably be at work, Kenny on duty. Polly was just on the point of turning away when her brother-in-law, whey-faced, opened the door an inch or two and peered blearily out at her.

'Polly?'

'Oh, I'm sorry. Did I get you out of bed?'

'What time is it?'

'Almost eleven.'

He clutched the collar of the dressing gown to his chest.

'Rosie isn't here,' he said. 'She's gone back to work today.'

'It isn't Rosie I came to see.'

He nodded sleepily, stifled a yawn, admitted her into the hallway and led her directly into the kitchen. He tugged open the blackout curtains, filled a kettle and placed it on the stove.

He looked terrible, Polly thought, a far cry from the dashing young bridegroom of eighteen months ago. He had probably been on night duty and she had wakened him before he'd caught up on his sleep. She didn't feel guilty, though. She regarded policemen, even her brother-in-law, as a breed undeserving of sympathy.

'How large is the flat?' she asked.

'Four rooms. Two bedrooms, kitchen and drawing room.

We seldom use the drawing room. We live in the kitchen pretty much.' He leaned over the sink, ran water from the tap, splashed his face and dried it on a hand towel. 'Haven't you been here before?'

'No.'

'I suppose you dropped in to ask about Rosie?'

'Did I?' said Polly. 'What about Rosie?'

'She's all right again. I didn't realise she would get over it so quickly.'

'Get over what?' said Polly.

'The miscarriage.'

'Miscarriage!' Polly exclaimed. 'Our Rosie had a miscarriage?'

'Didn't Lizzie tell you?'

'No one told me,' said Polly. 'When did this happen?'

'Monday. They whipped her into Redlands, kept her overnight and released her early next morning. The baby wasn't very old. Seven weeks, that's all. It just – I really don't quite know what happened – it just came, I suppose, when she was at work and that – well, that was that.'

'Did you know she was expecting?'

'She hardly knew herself,' said Kenny; an answer, Polly realised, that was both ambiguous and defensive. 'She's all right, though. She was keen to get back to work and I couldn't— I saw no reason to stop her.'

'You couldn't have stopped her even if you'd wanted to,' Polly said with a rueful shake of the head. 'Our Rosie has a mind of her own.'

'It's true,' Kenny agreed. 'I've been in the doghouse because I wasn't here at the time. I was working on a case in Greenock and couldn't be reached. Rosie feels I let her down.'

He shrugged, spooned tea leaves into a teapot and added boiling water. He was unkempt and hollow-eyed and seemed to emanate an air of resignation that was close to defeat. Though she had always loved and protected her little sister, Polly was well aware that Rosie, deaf or not, was a good deal tougher than any of them ever gave her credit for.

Kenny pulled out a chair at the table.

Polly seated herself, took out her cigarettes and lit one.

She watched Kenny produce two cups and saucers from the cupboard and fill each cup with tea. He seated himself at the table and lifted a cup to his lips. 'If you didn't know about Rosie,' he said, 'what brings you here?'

'I believe you went to see Babs?'

'I did.'

'And her lodger?'

'You know fine well I did.'

'What did you make of him?'

Kenny let out breath. 'Don't tell me *you're* going to start— '

'Come off it, Kenny,' Polly said. 'You've used your professional connections to check on him, haven't you?'

'What makes you think I'd do that?'

'Because you're a naturally nosy copper.'

He grunted, amused. 'Cameron's just what he says he is. His folks did come from Clydeside. Parish records are available if you're interested.'

'What else?'

'I can't divulge official information, Polly.'

'Nonsense!'

'He does have a contract with Brockway's. Brockway's will vouch for him right down the line.'

'Of course they will,' said Polly. 'What about the brother, James or Jamie, back in the United States?'

'I didn't pursue things that far,' Kenny said. 'I'm not working up a case against Mr Cameron. As far as I can make out his one and only "crime" is landing himself on your sister.'

'Didn't it cross your mind that he might be one of Dominic's associates?'

'Of course it did.'

'Well,' said Polly, 'that question remains unresolved.'

Kenny put down the cup and rested his chin on his hands. 'I can't have Cameron arrested just on your say-so, Polly.'

She laughed. 'I don't want him arrested, for heaven's sake.'

'What do you want?'

'I'm just making you aware of the situation.'

'*Is* there a situation?' Kenny said.

'There may be,' Polly said. 'I need to be sure I can count on your support if and when required.'

Kenny said nothing for a moment, though he didn't appear perplexed by what she had told him or, indeed, by what she *hadn't* told him. 'Whose support do you need, Polly?' he said at length. 'Uncle Kenny's or Inspector MacGregor's?'

'Inspector MacGregor's.'

'It is Dominic, isn't it? He's up to something. He's trying to involve you and you're not having it?'

'It would be awfully helpful to find out precisely where Christy Cameron's brother is and what he does.'

'Can you give me a clue?' said Kenny.

'He's an officer in the US Navy.'

'Really?'

'That's absolutely all I can tell you.'

'That's probably enough to be going on with,' said Kenny, and, helping himself to more tea, tactfully changed the subject.

Rosie followed the others to the door of the old vestry where the time clock and punch cards were housed. There was no stampede, no pushing to be first to the cast-iron turnstile through which each employee, even foreman Bass, had to pass to gain admittance to the church.

The women went in meekly, like bees into a hive. Some, Aileen Ashford among them, lingered outside to have a last puff on a cigarette or absorb a final mouthful of more-or-less fresh air before their long shift began. In addition to the dentist's wife there were Mrs Findlater, a former school-teacher, Doris Maybury, wife of a general practitioner, and twin sisters, Eleanor and Constance, the spinster daughters of an Episcopalian minister.

Rosie strutted past them with her head high. She punched in, walked down the corridor to the cloakroom, changed into her overall, stuck on her cotton mobcap and headed for her cubicle, which, mercifully, hadn't been reallocated. The unit she'd been working on when she'd collapsed had been removed and the cubicle thoroughly dusted – not only dusted but disinfected, as if miscarriages might be contagious.

She seated herself on the swivel chair and swung around until her thin legs were sticking out into the aisle.

From the steps of the pulpit foreman Bass, whistle in hand, blandly surveyed the scene. He was an elderly gentle-man who had been with Merryweather's for years. He had white hair, white eyebrows and a fluffy moustache, badly tobacco-stained.

Aileen emerged from the cloakroom and trotted down the aisle.

She checked her step when she saw Rosie's legs, checked again when she encountered Rosie's sugary smile.

'Good morning, Aileen,' Rosie said, and got to her feet.

Aileen raised her slender shoulders and pressed her delicate little hands against her chest, like mouse paws. 'Good – good morning, Rose.'

'Rosie. My friends all call me Rosie.'

'Rosie . . . Good morning, Rosie.'

'How are you, Rosie?'

'I beg your pardon.'

'Whuh-what you say next – how are you, Rosie? Rosie, are you well? Rosie, can you still have babies?' Rosie's voice cut through the sudden silence like an intercessory prayer.

Mr Bass stroked his stained moustache and kept the whistle in his fist.

'Rose, I think you should sit down,' Aileen Ashford whispered. 'I don't think you're quite yourself this morning.'

'Course I'm not quite myself,' Rosie said cheerfully. 'I'm not carrying any more. I lost it, if you recall, Aileen. I luh-lost it while you just stood there looking down at the dummy lying on the floor.' Aileen Ashford would have turned on her heel and fled if Rosie hadn't caught her by the sleeve. 'Now, can you hear me clearly, can you make out what the dummy is saying?'

At least Mrs Ashford knew how to maintain grace under pressure. Five years of marriage to a bossy and merciless dentist had taught her how to take her medicine like a man. 'I do believe I can hear you, Rose. Everyone can.'

'Good,' said Rosie. 'I am vuh-very well, thank you, Aileen. I am still perfectly able to bear children and my husband and I will seize every opportunity to ensure that I do.'

'There's no need to . . . You are making such an exhibition of—'

'I'm telling you now so you won't have to go whispering behind my back. I am not going to let you lot chuh-chase me away. If you want to know how I am in future, ask me face to face.'

'I'm sorry you feel you've been victimised, Rose. It has nothing to do with me, of course, but . . .'

Cheeks dappled rosebud red, the dentist's wife ran out of excuses. Tears welled up in the corners of her eyes and she covered her lips with her mouse-paw fingers, not, Rosie knew, because she felt remorse but simply because she'd been singled out and was afraid that she too might become an outcast.

'Thank you for sparing me a moment, Aileen,' Rosie said. 'I do appreciate it.' Then, seating herself, she swung round to face her desk just as foreman Bass, tactfully hiding a grin, blew the whistle to signal the start of the working day.

7

The man and the boy leaned on the gate and peered down into the sty.

'Does the pig have a name?' Christy asked.

'Aye, he's called Ron.'

'Ron? Why do you call him Ron?'

'Dougie says he looks like a Ron,' Angus explained. 'He can be a right bully if he doesn't get his own way.'

'I'll bet he can,' said Christy.

'Dougie says he'd like to get a sow to keep Ron company but Miss Dawlish says if he starts that nonsense she'll pack her bags an' leave.'

'What does Ron eat?' Christy asked tactfully.

'Everythin'. He'd eat you if you went in there. He's fierce, so he is.'

Christy knew little or nothing about pigs. There had been a dozen small grey and white hogs penned behind Ewa's house on the outskirts of Warsaw but they had been slaughtered before the Germans entered the city and the real butchery began. He remembered too the flayed carcasses that hung from hooks in the Washington Market, but they had never looked as if they'd been alive.

He glanced at the boy, who was glowering at the boar, willing him to show his mettle. Ron, however, was not in fighting mood and went on nonchalantly nudging a turnip through the clabber.

The boy resembled his mother, though his hair was tufty

brown, not blond. He had a remarkably deep voice for a kid, Christy thought.

'How come you aren't at school?'

'Gotta rash. Miss Dawlish thinks it might be the chicken-pox. Have you had the chickenpox, Mr Cameron?'

'I guess I have,' Christy said. 'Yeah, I must've had.'

'Don't you remember?'

'Not exactly, no.'

'You'll have to ask your mum,' Angus said. 'Mums always remember when you've been sick.'

'I'll ask her,' Christy said, 'next time I see her.'

'Where does your mum live?'

'New York,' said Christy. 'Know where that is?'

'Aye, it's in America. My uncle lives in New York.'

The pig edged up to the gate and peered at Angus with an optimistic expression as if, like a dog, he expected the boy to toss the turnip for him to retrieve. Angus craned over the gate and rubbed his knuckles against the pig's brow. Ron grunted with pleasure and pressed his snout against the boy's knees.

'You a soldier, Mr Cameron?'

'Not me. I take pictures.'

'With a camera?'

'Yep.'

'Gonna take a picture o' Ron then?'

'Sure, why not?'

'Now?'

'After lunch.'

'Promise.'

'Spit on my hand.'

'Eh?'

'Like – like cross my heart.'

'Spit on your hand.' Angus opened his fist and released a careful droplet of pure white froth on to his palm. 'Like this?'

'You got it,' Christy said and, spitting into his palm in turn, held up his hand. 'Now we shake.'

'Mix the spit?' said Angus.

'Sure.' Christy pressed his palm against the boy's. 'The promise is now binding. Okay?'

'Oh-*kay*!'

Much taken with this new transatlantic ritual, Angus grinned at the stranger his aunt had brought to visit. If 'the Yank' hadn't quite lived up to Angus's high expectations just at first he was living up to them now.

'You gotta six-shooter?'

'Nope, no six-shooter.'

'You gotta a horse?'

'I'm a New Yorker, son, not a cowboy. You have to go west to find the big ranges and wide-open spaces; the prairies.'

'You've been there, but?'

'Once or twice,' Christy admitted.

'You seen Indians?'

The pig, disappointed, slumped down in the mud with a squelching sound and began to gnaw at the turnip. The boy was too full of questions to settle.

Christy recalled an assignment to a Sioux reservation at Waverley Falls. He'd exposed forty-two rolls of film on the trip but the photographs had proved too raw for the editorial board and all but three had been scrapped. That wasn't a story the kid wanted to hear, however. It wasn't the truth that appealed to young Angus Hallop, but the myth, the cheating image.

'Sure,' Christy said. 'I met with Big Chief Running Wolf.'

'Apache?'

'Sioux,' said Christy. 'I pow-wowed with him while the braves danced round the fire. I even got to smoke the peace pipe.'

'What'd it taste like?'

'Pretty nasty.'

'Was that in a wigwam?'

'Tepee,' Christy said. 'They call them tepees out there.'

'What else did you see?' said Angus, agog.

He found it easier to lie to the kid than to lie to the kid's aunt.

The lies he was obliged to tell Polly Manone were on-going half-truths, evasions, prevarications, down-played versions of the way it was, not the way it should have been. They were intended not to inform but to manipulate, which was a basic difference between history and propaganda, Christy supposed.

Polly crossed the yard from the farmhouse where she'd been 'arranging lunch', whatever that meant. She picked her way between the puddles, arms out like a dancer, and looked, Christy thought, gorgeously self-contained.

'Did Running Wolf fight General Custer?' Angus asked.

'Nope, he wasn't old enough to be at Little Bighorn.' Christy gave the boy a loose-knuckled rap on the jaw, man to man and almost as binding as spit on the hand. 'I'll tell you more about the Indians later. Right now I got to go talk to your Aunt Polly.'

'Aunt Polly!' said Angus, grimacing. 'What does she know?'

'For someone with chickenpox, young man,' Polly said, 'you're far too lively. I suggest you go into the house and ask Miss Dawlish to put you to bed.'

'I'm not – I'm not . . .' Angus protested, then realising that he had put himself in a cleft stick, set off at a gallop to hide in the motorcar that Polly had parked by the stable-barn.

'Some kid!' Christy said.

'He can be a handful at times.'

'Is he really sick?'

'No,' Polly said. 'He's taking advantage of the rash to have a day off school.'

'I'm surprised your friend Dougie fell for it.'

'Dougie knows when to slacken the reins. He's very fond of the children. He had two boys of his own, but they died.'

'Jesus!' said Christy. 'I don't know how you survive that.'

'Nor I,' said Polly.

They moved away from Ron's sty.

It was a grey morning, not cold. The sky over the hills was tinted with amber as if the sun might break through before long.

Blackstone wasn't far from Glasgow and you could see all the suburban townships on the far side of the river piled against the hills. Jamie had told him that the counterfeit operation Manone had fronted had been based on a farm; this farm presumably.

Half-finished villas and bungalows peeked over the ridge about a half-mile off. Polly said that the builders had gone into liquidation soon after war began but that when the war ended some smart financier, with more of an eye to the future than the past, would make a killing by reopening the site.

Christy had no plans, no future, nothing beyond acquiring the information Marzipan needed to set up this woman to take a fall. He felt guiltier than he had done when he'd conned Babs Hallop into renting him a room, for Babs was an innocent and Polly was not. She was slim, sleek and sophisticated but the hard, self-protective shell that real painted ladies possessed was missing and behind her clever talk was a melancholy core.

'Do you miss your kids?' he asked.

'Of course I do.'

'Will he bring them back?'

'How do I know what Dominic will do?' she snapped. 'You're the one with all the answers. Is that the price I'll have to pay to get my children back? Will I have to give your government everything I have to ensure that my husband stays out of prison and my children are free to return to Scotland?'

'I can't answer those questions.'

'Can't, or won't.'

'Can't.'

'Tell me the truth; are you being paid to persuade me to hand over all my money to your government?'

'Not paid, no, not in cash.'

'What then? What's in it for you, Mr Cameron?'

'I get my pass to sail with a convoy, take pho—'

'Baloney!' Polly said. 'Is that an appropriate word?'

'It'll do,' said Christy.

'Why are you trying to sell me some ridiculous cock-and-bull story about Italian guerrillas, American double agents and plots to bring down *Il Duce*?'

They had strolled to the gate at the far end of the yard. Beyond was a field, half ploughed. Beyond the field were a cluster of pines and the leafless branches of tall oaks and beeches and little silver birch trees, slender and elegant as Polly herself. Down river, where the hills dipped away, you could see barrage balloons in the sky and thin columns of smoke and a squadron of aeroplanes winging in from the south. In the yard Christy could make out the boy and the motorcar. The old man, Dougie, was standing by the farmhouse door with a cat in his arms, the woman, Miss Dawlish, at an upstairs window, all motionless, like model figures on a model farm.

Polly leaned against the field gate and folded her arms. In the long overcoat and tweed hat she looked, he thought, like an exiled Russian princess. He felt sudden anger at Manone for callously leaving her behind.

He said, 'I've seen the harm they can do.'

'What who can do?'

'The Nazis.'

'Oh!'

'The Paris of the North, they called it. One and a half million people lived in Warsaw before Hitler decided he wanted to own Poland too. They bombarded the city for three weeks. Food supplies were cut off and refugees, three hundred thousand of them, came pouring in from the countryside. Electricity, gas, water, telephones all knocked out. When we thought there was nothing left to bomb the Luftwaffe pilots came in low and machine-gunned the civilian population. Picked them off while they queued for bread or lined up at the water carts or tried to get the wounded to safety, while they buried their dead.'

'You witnessed all of this?'

Christy nodded.

He spoke without emphasis for he had learned not to allow passion to distort conviction.

'Sunday,' he went on, 'Sunday the twenty-fourth of September, they shelled the Church of the Saviour during High Mass and left most of the city in ruins. Next morning they sent in the planes again. From eight in the morning until midnight they bombed the rubble.'

'Where were you while all this was happening?'

'Started out in the Savoy Hotel in Nowy Swiat Street but when the hotel took a hit I followed a family of refugees out into Marshall Pilsudski Square. Even that late in the day the Poles believed they could save the city. Poles, Jews, rich, poor, men, women and kids all running about looking for somewhere to shelter while the Civilian Committee for the Defence tried to organise its last lines of resistance. Resistance! Jesus, who could resist that onslaught; who could resist that brutal, unrelenting *blitzkrieg*, that sort of power?'

He glanced down the valley of the Clyde, at smug suburban villas and tenements, at factories and shipyards protected only by toy aircraft and comical silvery balloons, and then he went on: '*Blitzkrieg* isn't even real power. It's just warfare, just men and machines and organisation. Real power is yellow badges on Jews and trains leaving for Dachau and Buchenwald, trains packed with lawyers, bankers, teachers, priests, all the protectors of that once-beautiful city. What'll happen to them? God only knows.'

'Are you trying to tell me that sort of thing could happen here?'

'Sure it could,' Christy said. 'And it isn't only planes and tanks and guns that'll hold the bastards off, it's the small stuff, the petty stuff too. There are other wars going on, little wars, from two congressmen squabbling about a defence budget on Capitol Hill to – well, me and you and Dominic Manone caught up in a shady deal to underwrite the downfall of the Duce.'

'We had our first real raid two nights ago,' said Polly, almost wistfully.

'I know. I was there,' said Christy. 'That was nothing. You got tickled, is all. Tickled.'

'People died.'

'How many? Forty, fifty?'

'Don't be so callous,' Polly said. 'If one person dies . . .'

'Sure, one is too many,' Christy agreed. 'But one is better than one million and one million's better than having the rats running Europe. You think Fascism is the answer to anything? You think you can sort out the muddles of democracy by rounding up Jews and Catholics, gypsies and Socialists, Communists and Liberals, the schoolteachers and Gospel ministers, actors, artists, writers and—'

'All right,' Polly interrupted, 'I understand.'

'I hope you do,' said Christy. 'I really hope you do.'

'Could it happen here?' said Polly.

'It can happen anywhere,' said Christy. 'Maybe there are those who would prefer to capitulate and not fight against the monster, not to spill more blood, but the monster don't see it that way and when the monster comes stalking you . . .' He shrugged and shook his head. '*Lebensraum*: you British don't know what it means yet.' He shrugged again. 'I guess you could say that's why I'm here.'

'What happened to your photographs?'

'From Warsaw? Confiscated. Every scrap of film, every negative politely but firmly confiscated before I was politely but firmly booted out of Poland. I saved one roll, just one.'

'How?'

'Smuggled it out inside me, wrapped in a rubber contraceptive.'

'And you sold the photographs to Brockway's, I suppose?' said Polly.

'Nope, I ain't *that* mercenary, Mrs Manone. I gave the roll to a guy in the US Government.'

'Because information is also power,' said Polly.

'You didn't really bring me way out here just to eat lunch, did you?'

He remarked her hesitation, her reluctance to admit that his argument was convincing. He hadn't lied about Warsaw; he would never lie about Warsaw. He said, 'I thought Madrid was bad but under the bombing and bloodshed in Spain there was a sense of adventure, of acceptable danger. Not now, though, not now. Franco's no Hitler. He's a megalomaniac pipsqueak, sure, but no barbarian. Mussolini? Italy wouldn't be in this damned war at all if it wasn't for the Duce's overweening ambition to become the noblest Roman of them all.'

'No,' Polly said. 'I didn't bring you out here just to eat lunch.'

'Why did you bring me out here then?'

'To hear what you had to say.'

'Well, I've said it,' Christy told her. 'You've got my side of the story. You know what makes me tick.'

'Do I?' said Polly. 'I'm not at all sure that I do.'

'Okay,' Christy said. 'Don't try to make sense of it, just think about what I've told you and talk it over with your friend.'

'My friend?'

'Hughes.'

'So Babs has been gossiping, has she?'

'If you do decide to liquidate your holdings and turn them into cash then you're going to need Hughes' help, aren't you?'

'Fin won't buy your story. His patriotism is only skin-deep. When it comes to parting with money he'll fight his own little war on his own little terms.'

'Then you'll have to change his mind, won't you?' Christy said.

'Only after you've changed mine,' said Polly.

They had lost the window in Archie's office and some tiles from the roof but otherwise the office in Cyprus Street was undamaged.

Archie set about boarding up the empty window, showing, Babs thought, not only a deal of application but also surprising dexterity for a schoolteacher. He popped out for an hour and returned with four planks of wood balanced on his shoulder and a bag of tools that he'd scrounged from the gateman at Simons' shipyard in Renfrew. To acquire such valuable booty, Archie must have argued his case very eloquently, Babs thought admiringly.

By the time Archie returned, she had swept up all the broken glass and together – he the journeyman, she the apprentice – they had measured and sawn the planks and hammered them into place so tightly that not one breath of air could seep through, let alone one drop of rain. Archie said he'd retile the roof too if he could find a long enough ladder.

Babs was sorry that Archie's ingenuity failed on that point for the beautifully boarded window gave her not only a sense of security but of satisfaction in a job well done.

On Thursday morning Babs arrived late, not terribly late, just late enough to incur Archie's wrath, for now that the fuel repository had been sandbagged and made shipshape and firemen and workmen had gone from Cyprus Street, he would brook no excuse for bad timekeeping.

Twenty minutes to nine o'clock; the office door was unlocked and the business of the day apparently underway.

A handsome middle-aged woman was seated in Archie's office. She was clearly visible through the open doorway, and she was mad, hopping mad.

Archie, it appeared, was in need of moral support and before Babs had time to take off her coat, called out to her in his very best yaw-yaw voice, 'Mrs Hallop. Erm – if I could possibly enlist your assistance for one moment, I would be . . .' Then he projected himself from the chair behind the desk and with a mumbled apology, shot out of the office and closed the door behind him, leaving the client, still fizzing, alone.

'Who is she?' Babs said. 'What's got up her nose?'

'She's Belgian,' said Archie. 'Widow of an Englishman. Very well-to-do, I gather, and exceedingly well heeled. Private means, that sort of thing.'

'What's she doing here?'

'Wants war work.'

'Is she skilled?'

'Used to be a doctor, would you believe?' Archie ran a hand over his hair. 'In general practice in Liège, ages before the war. Married an English consultant and came to live in Paisley. He was a bigwig in hospital medicine until he died of a heart attack in October last year.'

'Children?'

'None.'

'Send her to the Labour Exchange,' said Babs. 'They're crying out for doctors.'

'The Exchange sent her here,' said Archie. 'Well, not exactly, not directly. She tried to enlist in the Red Cross but they turned her down because of her age. Then she canvassed the local hospitals, none of which would accept her qualifications and regarded her with deep suspicion in spite of her late husband's reputation. Paisley General offered her skivvy work, cleaning, which she declined.'

'Can't say I blame her,' said Babs. 'Then what?'

Archie glanced at the office door. There was no sound from behind it but Babs thought she could sense frustration thrumming in the air.

'The Exchange suggested factory work,' Archie went on. 'That's fine. That's okay. The widow's willing. They ship her round for interview by Personnel at Mainbridge Munitions, who keep her hanging around virtually all day while the labour committee hems and haws about her Belgian origins. They're totally boggled by her and eventually decide not to accept her. Now she's really mad, blistering mad, for she knows dashed well it's not her Belgian origins that bother them so much as her posh accent and expensive clothes.

'She hotfoots it back to the Labour Exchange, shouting the odds. There's no placating her. Small wonder: an able-bodied, intelligent woman who wants to contribute because she has family still in Flanders and hates the Jerries and nobody will sign her on. Ridiculous! Absolutely bloody ridiculous! So this morning, not knowing what else to do, they ship her round to us.'

'What can we do for her?'

'I haven't the foggiest,' said Archie. 'She's been dumped on us only because she's too hot to handle. I'm blue-blind if I'll let her go to waste, though, but I do need a little time to evolve a strategy.'

'I'll make tea,' said Babs.

'Big help you are,' said Archie, and went back into his office.

The woman's name was Evelyn Reeder and from the moment Babs clapped eyes on her she realised that the problem was not merely her age, sex or the fact that she hailed from Belgium. Whatever her name had been before marriage or whatever name her husband had been blessed with at birth, it was patently obvious to Babs that Mrs Evelyn Reeder was a Jew.

All the floating prejudices, all the overt slanders that applied to the tribe of Israel came popping into Babs's head and she experienced a little shiver of revulsion and at precisely the same moment a little shiver of revulsion *at* her revulsion, a confusing amalgam of guilt and distaste that almost caused her to drop the tea tray into Mrs Reeder's lap.

Spotting Babs's alarm, and deducing the reason for it, Archie hastened to an introduction: 'Mrs Reeder, my assistant Mrs Hallop.'

The woman turned her head. She had a long neck and a strong chin and – how could Babs ignore it? – a fine, hooked, hawklike nose that set off her heavy-lidded, jet-black eyes to perfection. She looked, Babs thought, like an oil painting, so luxurious, rich and opulent that at first you were daunted, then you were fascinated. She could only imagine the effect that Mrs Reeder might have on men but you didn't need to be Sherlock Holmes to deduce the effect she would have on the little tin gods of industrial middle management.

Babs put down the tray and offered the lady her hand.

'Who are you?' the woman said. 'What can you do for me?'

She had only the faintest trace of an accent and sounded not so much angry as supercilious.

Babs felt herself bristle. She stepped back and busied herself pouring tea. Tea, tea, tea: the answer to every problem. Mrs Reeder didn't want tea. Mrs Reeder wanted work yet she, Babs Hallop, was doing the usual thing, dishing out the brown stuff like a hollow character in a radio play. 'Milk, Mrs Reeder? Sugar, Mrs Reeder?'

'I have no time for your tea,' Mrs Reeder said. 'I have to find a job.'

'It isn't money, is it?' said Archie in a soft wheedling tone.

'No, it is the – the priority.'

'Necessity,' said Archie, even more softly.

Oh God, Babs thought, don't let him start on English lessons, not now, not with this woman. If he starts on English lessons she'll brain him with the tea tray, and if she doesn't, I will.

'Yes,' Mrs Reeder agreed. 'A necessity.'

'How large is your family in Liège?' Archie asked.

'Mother and Father are there. I have a sister and her husband in Amsterdam and two brothers, doctors like me, in Brussels.'

'Have you heard from them since the Germans occupied the country?'

'No.'

Archie nodded. 'So you're entirely on your own, Mrs Reeder?' he said.

'Yes.'

Polly, it was Polly all over, except that Mrs Reeder's husband was dead, not merely absent. Babs had a vision of the woman wandering about some gaunt mansion in one of the high-class villages that hid themselves among the trees of rural Renfrewshire. She saw a shadow of Polly in the Belgian widow: alone, and alienated by her own cleverness. But Polly still had Mammy and Bernard to fall back on and this woman's family was lost to her. She had nothing, nothing but style, money and her skills to protect her from the ravages of petty bureaucracy.

'Your husband's family?' Babs asked.

'A brother in Worthing.'

'Won't he take you in?'

'I do not want to be taken in,' the woman snapped. 'I do not want to be taken care of. I need to find a useful job to do here. I need to find a position of my own. Why will nobody believe me? Is it so hard to understand?'

Archie edged the teacup towards her and made a little gesture of encouragement. The woman lifted the cup and drank. Babs, still standing, offered her a cigarette. Archie lit up for all of them and for a minute or more they smoked in uncompanionable silence.

'There's always voluntary work,' Archie suggested. 'The voluntary organisations are always on the lookout for extra—'

'No, I must be paid.'

'Why?' said Babs.

'Because then I will have worth.'

'Sure,' said Babs. 'Of course. Sorry.'

Archie sat back, pushed his spectacles into place and frowned.

'We need,' he said at length, 'to pull a few strings.'

'What strings?' Mrs Reeder said. 'I have tried to pull strings. You are going to tell me you will do something and send me to another department meanwhile. Then you will do nothing. You will pass me like a buck and be rid of the nuisance.'

'Oh no, ma'am,' said Archie. 'You're barking up the wrong tree if you think we're going to let you go. In this office we take our responsibilities seriously. Are you with me on that, Mrs Hallop?'

'Absolutely, Mr Harding,' Babs agreed.

'Now who do we know who can help us out of a jam?'

'Bernard,' said Babs, surprised at her own acuity.

'Bernard?' said Archie.

'My stepfather,' Babs said. 'He's employed by Breslin Council and they have lots of – of – ladies in that part of the world.'

'Ladies?' Archie tapped his glasses. 'Oh yes, of course, lots of vacancies for – ladies. Did I hear a rumour that they're opening a new military hospital out that way?'

'You did,' Babs said. 'I'll give Bernard a tinkle right now, shall I?'

'Please do,' said Archie.

It struck Polly as odd that Dougie and Christy had so much in common. Dougie had travelled not at all – one or two trips down the Clyde in a paddle steamer was the extent of his journeying – while Christy and his camera had chased all over the globe. But if Christy had experienced at first hand many of the crises of the past half-dozen years the well-read, stay-at-home Glaswegian seemed better able to put those crises in perspective.

Polly helped Miss Dawlish clear away the dishes. The housekeeper had done them proud: rollmop herring, lamb casserole, and mock banana cream pie to finish with. The men drank bottled beer. Angus, on his best behaviour, drank Vimto and, afterwards, 'smoked' the chocolate cigar that Polly had brought him.

Polly listened in desultory fashion to the ebb and flow of conversation. With a big lunch sitting comfortably inside her, she contented herself by watching her energetic little nephew nibble his chocolate cigar. He looked, she thought, more Conway than Hallop, and speculated on the perversity of genes that shaped character and appearance, and wondered how the son of a skinny, unattractive Gorbals guttersnipe could show every sign of turning into a handsome young man.

She hoped that Angus had inherited nothing from her side of the family.

She had met her absent father for the first time only a month or two before he disappeared again, and had been anything but impressed. He was short in stature, huge in ego, and with a nasty streak that bordered on wickedness. Polly wasn't sorry that he had vanished into thin air once more.

Few traces of Conway virtues or, fortunately, Conway vices were evident in her children. With the best will in the world, she had never been able to regard Stuart and Ishbel as other than capricious. What she didn't dare examine, though, was the confluence of genes in her own character for she suspected that she might be more like Frank, her sly and greedy father, than Lizzie, her tender-hearted, hard-working mother.

That calm Thursday afternoon in the farmhouse kitchen at Blackstone, seated on the sofa with her legs tucked under her and her nephew lolling at her feet like a sleepy puppy, Polly didn't feel greedy. If anything, she felt a soothing, almost paralysing sense of being at the mercy of events she could not control, as if something had not so much snapped as loosened within her and she was drifting towards a massive and imperious change.

She knew what the feeling was, of course, what it meant.

She was in process of falling in love.

She turned her head: he was seated at the kitchen table, a glass of whisky in hand, his blunt, boyish features outlined against the light from the window, a cigarette bobbing in his mouth. He had a pretty mouth, almost too feminine for the shape of his face. His hair was untidy and a row of Romanesque curls clung to his brow. She wondered what it would be like to feel those soft springy curls against her skin, if they would be coarser than they appeared to be and if the hair on his wrists and forearms extended to his chest and belly.

Christy was unaware of her scrutiny.

He leaned an elbow on the table and listened to Dougie sound off about the campaign in North Africa.

'Well,' Dougie was saying, 'I know what the newspapers are sayin'. It's the right season o' the year for desert fightin', an' here's General Wavell dug in an' doin' nothin' while the Eyeties consolidate their supply lines an' get on wi' buildin' this wonderful new road they've started. Far as I can make out, though, Wavell's right to hold the line round the Nile an' the Suez Canal. He's got four divisions, sixty thousand men, an' not much more armour than a few dozen heavy tanks. When the race across the Nile starts our heavy tanks will be no bloody use at all. Have you got pals in the desert?'

'Pals?' Christy said.

'Colleagues, photographers?'

'Sure,' Christy said. 'All the news agencies want to put men in the field.'

'Why don't they?'

Polly was listening now.

Angus rolled against the cushions, the chocolate object, steadily melting, clenched in his teeth. He scowled at Dougie. How much the boy understood, how much Dougie had explained to him, Polly couldn't be certain, nor was she convinced that it was entirely healthy for a nine-year-old to be introduced to the details of combat. There was no way to avoid or prevent it, she supposed, boys being what they were.

'It's expensive for one thing,' Christy said. 'The photo mags have generated a demand for high-quality images published with speed. The public wants and expects the stuff to be up to the minute. But this war isn't like the last war. You can't just dispatch a guy to the Western Front with a tripod camera. We're – you're fighting all over the globe so the news agencies have to pool their resources. Anyhow, the military authorities insist on it.'

'Control what you get to see?'

'Try to,' said Christy. 'Official military photographers rule the roost but a few civilian photographers are given a permit, an accredited identification card that allows them to shoot classified subjects.'

'Up on the front line, y' mean?'

'Yeah.'

'An' you haven't got a card yet?'

'Nope, not yet.'

'Is that why you're not in Cairo or Benghazi?'

'I wouldn't be in Africa anyway. I'm on another assignment.'

'To sail with a North Atlantic convoy?'

'Yep.'

'My Uncle Dennis is on a carrier,' Angus chimed in. 'He sends me postcards. He fixes the aeroplanes. Maybe you'll meet him, Mr Cameron.'

Christy glanced at the boy and then, smiling, at Polly. 'Maybe I will, Angus,' he said.

Angus, it seemed, had been patiently awaiting his chance. He got up, pushed the remains of the cigar into his mouth, and said through a mouthful of chocolate. 'You promised to take a photo of Ron.'

'Yeah, I did, didn't I?' Christy said.

'Don't be impertinent, young man,' said Miss Dawlish. 'Douglas and Mr Cameron have better things to do than humour your whims.'

'He promised. He spat on my hand.'

North Africa and the battles of the Atlantic were forgotten. Miss Dawlish advanced from the region of the sink. She moved, Polly thought, with all the grace of a small tank, one hand out to snare Angus by the ear.

Angus darted away and hid behind Christy's chair.

'*He promised, he promised.*'

'Sure did,' said Christy and, finishing off his whisky, gathered the boy to him and got to his feet. 'Let's do it now, while there's still some decent light.'

'Angus!' said Miss Dawlish, hands on hips. 'Behave yourself or you'll be for it when our visitor goes away.'

'Yes, Miss Dawlish.' Angus snapped off a salute that would have done General Wavell proud, then, taking Christy's hand, dragged the man towards the kitchen door.

'Hang on, son,' Christy said. 'Let me get my camera.' He nodded to Polly, who had already begun to unfold herself from the sofa. 'You coming too, Mrs Manone? It's not every day you get a chance to see a pig being shot.'

'I wouldn't miss it for the world,' Polly said, and went out into the hallway to fetch her hat and coat.

Space in the council building was at a premium and Bernard was obliged to share a ground-floor room with three other officers.

Protected by an apron of grass, the broad sandstone edifice stood off the Bearsden-Breslin highway. It had been erected in 1901 with money raised by the sale of common ground to a consortium of businessmen who had hoped to expand the thready transport system and carry the city out into the countryside. The scheme had come to naught in the end but Breslin had acquired a railway branch line and a fine new civic centre by that time, and suffered no financial loss when the speculators' grandiose plans went awry.

Intrigued by local history, Bernard had pored over the archives and was now generally regarded as an authority on who currently owned what. Bungalow, villa or cottage, mansion house or mud hut, Bernard had them all marked down in his little black book, for persuasion was Bernard's game and, not to put too fine a point on it, blackmail where blackmail was necessary to further his selfless ends.

In his day Bernard had been by turns a brave soldier, an efficient rent collector, an effective estate agent in one of Dominic Manone's front companies, but only when war rolled round again and he was appointed billeting officer for Breslin District Council did he finally come into his own. Within the empire of agents, officers, lawyers, surveyors and councillors who inhabited the sandstone building above the highway, Bernard stood out like a colossus.

True, he didn't look much like a colossus, though he no longer had the haggard, hangdog appearance of a rent collector or the nervy twitchiness of an estate agent whose income depended on commissions. He was confident now and fulfilled. It showed in plump jowls and an expanded waistline for, rationing or no rationing, Bernard had developed a bow window that made it increasingly difficult for him to button up his trousers.

He had been surprised but not displeased when Babs had telephoned him. He had done little enough for the girls since Rosie had married Kenny MacGregor and moved into a flat in Cowcaddens, and he had been too busy to pay more than passing attention to what was happening south of the river.

The Hallop kids – his step-grandchildren – were boarded at Blackstone only four or five miles from the council offices, but he'd seen little of them this past year for the billeting arrangement had been none of his doing and he was not officially responsible for checking on their welfare.

Besides, Blackstone was still too closely associated with Dominic Manone for Bernard's liking. It had taken all his strength of character to shake free of Dominic's shady influence. Having done so, he regarded himself as a man of integrity, absolutely incorruptible, and he was convinced that no one would ever again tempt him to stray from the straight and narrow.

'You are Peabody, Bernard Peabody?' Evelyn Reeder enquired.

'Indeed, ma'am. Indeed I am.'

'If you find me work to which I am suited you will also be required to find me lodgings.' No beating about the bush for Mrs Reeder, apparently. 'It is too far to travel from where I live and I am unfamiliar with this part of the country.'

'Where do you live, Mrs Reeder?' Bernard asked.

'Brookfield.'

'Ah yes, deep in the wilds of Renfrewshire; a long way.'

'You see how far I have had to travel to keep this appointment?'

'I do,' said Bernard. 'How well do you know my daughter?'

'Your daughter?'

'Stepdaughter, actually,' Bernard said. 'Babs.'

'Is she the person in the Recruitment Centre?'

'Yes.'

'I met her this morning for the first and only time.'

'Really!' said Bernard.

'Why do you sound surprised?'

'Surprised? Do I? Well, I was rather under the impression that Babs was a friend of yours.'

'We are not friends,' the woman said. 'I do not know her.'

Obviously you don't, Bernard thought, or you wouldn't be asking why I'm surprised. There was nothing altruistic about Lizzie's middle daughter and he wondered why Babs had gone out of her way to do this woman a favour, particularly as Evelyn Reeder was Jewish and Babs had more than her fair share of prejudice against – what was the current phrase? – 'Jews and Catholics and bald-headed men'. The department in which Babs worked was probably under as much pressure as Breslin's own employment services, however, and his stepdaughter had simply been trying to impress her boss by shipping the troublesome Mrs Reeder out of the county.

'I believe you're a doctor?' Bernard said.

'My husband was Gordon Reeder, the surgeon.'

'I take it your husband is – ah, deceased?'

'He is.'

'Didn't he have colleagues who can find you a suitable post?'

'My husband had more enemies than friends in the profession.'

'It's honest of you to admit it,' Bernard said. 'I take it we're up against some sort of prejudice here?'

'Yes.'

'Prejudice against you because you aren't British, because you're female, or because . . .'

'Because I'm a Jew?'

'Precisely,' Bernard said.

One table, two chairs, a coat-rack and a great teetering stack of cardboard boxes filled the little room, which was so cramped that Mrs Reeder almost seemed to be sitting on his lap. He shifted his weight from one buttock to the other and sucked in his stomach to give the woman a little more room. She angled her body to one side and crossed her long legs. She reminded him just a little of Polly, though she was ten or a dozen years older than Polly and much taller. She wore black stockings under a loose black skirt, an expensive black overcoat, and a blouse in pale grey silk: proper widow's weeds, Bernard thought approvingly, and frowned.

'Seven rooms in my house in Brookfield,' Evelyn Reeder went on. 'Seven rooms and a separate apartment for the servants. The *kindergarten* want to board homeless children in my house and it will be taken from me by the law.'

'Requisitioned,' said Bernard. 'Yes, but they can't throw you out in the street. If there's a separate flat in the house they'll insist you move into it while they take over the rest of the place.'

'Then I will have children beneath me, noisy children.'

'Undoubtedly,' said Bernard.

'I thought the *kindergarten* people would find me a post in a hospital but they say that is not their department. I must find my own post. I will put the furniture into store, if I am allowed to do that?'

'Are we not gettin' a wee bit ahead of ourselves?' Bernard said. 'I imagine I can find you somewhere to stay but—'

'With no children?'

'With no children,' Bernard said, 'but I'm not sure I can find you a job.'

'It is not your department?' the woman said, scornfully. 'I have been hearing that from the day I placed myself on the labour market.'

She wore high-heeled shoes in black patent leather. Without straining, Bernard could see one shoe bobbing up and down on the end of a shapely foot.

She was angry and frustrated and he guessed she'd been led a merry dance by officials far and wide. She was a woman alone, at the mercy of authorities who wanted nothing to do with her. She would probably have received more sympathy, more courtesy, if she'd been totally destitute.

He watched the shoe tap up and down.

'All right,' he said. 'What I require from you, Mrs Reeder, are copies of your birth certificate and marriage lines and any documents relating to your qualifications as a medical practitioner. Did you ever work in a hospital, for instance?'

'I trained in medical wards in Bruges and Amsterdam.'

'Are you a surgeon like your husband?'

'There are no females in surgery. I am a physician.'

'Would you be prepared to work in a hospital again?'

'I will not clean floors and lavatories.'

'Good God! Is that what they've been offering you?'

The woman said nothing. She lifted her head, tilted her chin and stared at the little fanlight above Bernard's head.

Bernard had never seen so much pride in anyone before. There was no evidence of conceit, no vanity, no indication that she was posing. He had to think faster than he had been obliged to do in a very long time. With this woman there could be no backtracking, no compromises, no brush-off. He must ensure that the autocratic Jewish lady got everything she was entitled to and perhaps a little bit more to compensate for the raw deal she'd been handed so far.

But he did not dare make promises he couldn't keep.

'Give me three days,' he said.

'To do what?' she said. 'To find another way to be rid of me?'

'To find you a suitable job, Doctor Reeder,' Bernard said.

'And a suitable place to stay?'

'Yes,' Bernard promised her. 'And a place of your own to stay.'

8

It would have been better for all concerned if Jackie hadn't come home on leave. It would certainly have been easier on Babs if her husband's arrival at Euston hadn't coincided with publication of the 9th December issue of *Brockway's Illustrated Weekly*.

By the time he reached London on the overnight train from Devon and fought his way across the city in full webbing and lugging a kitbag, Jackie was not in the best of humours. It didn't matter to him that incendiary bombs had pasted London and that large sections of the city were closed off. He had only one thought in mind – to get home to Glasgow, his family and Babs as soon as possible. Euston was chaotic. Air raids had shot his travel plan to hell and he found himself with three hours to kill before anything vaguely resembling a train would be heading out for Glasgow. To while away the time he bought ten Woodbine, a *Daily Mirror* and the latest issue of *Brockway's*.

Like most servicemen, Jackie enjoyed the illustrated weekly's mixed bag of commentary and news, and photographs in which refugees rubbed shoulders with pretty girls in bathing costumes. He scanned the *Mirror* first, though, for he was somewhat concerned about events in North Africa.

The RAOC mechanics had been working night and day to fit the battalion's armoured vehicles for desert warfare and they'd all had extra jabs, had been issued with tropical kit, had drowsed through boring lectures on unsavoury foreign diseases and in ten days' time would be bundled on to a troop ship, and sent out to service the hardware somewhere in the Western Desert.

Jackie had no curiosity about North Africa, no sense of excitement or fear of the great unknown. One sheep in the khaki flock, he did, more or less, what he was told. He had earned his stripe by being a good mechanic and was more concerned about the effects of excessive heat on the unreliable Nuffield Liberty engines of the new model Crusaders than he was about personal safety.

He scrounged a cup of tea and a bun from a Salvation Army stall and settled down among all the other soldiers, sailors and airmen who were in transit that morning. He was tired, dog-tired, but didn't dare fall asleep in case he missed the announcement about the Glasgow train. He found a spot on the corner of a bench and with his kitbag tucked between his knees, lit a ciggie and flicked open *Brockway's* at an article entitled 'Women of the Clyde', which was made up of thirteen large photographs, some captions and stirring text.

It didn't look like the Clyde he remembered: women in shawls queuing outside a dairy, women in overalls and head-bands huddled round a brazier on a bleak, black-and-white factory floor, a smiling young female riveter with her mask tipped back, four girls in a locker room changing their clothes and showing a lot of bare shoulder and thigh in the process.

Jackie sighed, leaned into the kitbag and turned the page.

And there was Babs, his lovely blonde wife and the mother of his children, posing like a tart in the middle of a cobbled street he didn't even recognise. Her head was tossed back like a film star's and her arms were stretched up as if she were dancing a reel and you could see her breasts pushing through her shirt – *his* shirt, come to think of it – and she was pouting in the same alluring manner she adopted when she wanted him to take her to bed.

Every randy male who bought the paper would be thinking the same thing he'd been thinking when he'd looked at the four girls in the locker room stepping out of their skirts and garter belts. Only this was no anonymous young thing: this was Barbara Conway Hallop, his bloody wife!

He tossed away the Woodbine.

He got to his feet.

He waved the illustrated rag in the air and shouted four or five words so obscene that they would have had him charged if an officer or an MP had been within earshot.

Then he sat down again.

Fingers shaking, he lit another cigarette.

And began, systematically, to read.

Thirteen hours and one pork pie later, Jackie arrived at the bungalow in Raines Drive and started kicking the locked front door.

'What the heck is that?' Christy said, sitting up in the armchair by the fire. 'Are you expecting company?'

'Not me,' said Babs. 'Not at this time of night.'

She put the whisky glass down on the coffee table and got to her feet. Christy was up before her, an arm out to protect her. He tugged at the blackout curtain and found himself staring into the face of a wild-eyed army corporal.

'Bastard!' the corporal shouted. 'You bloody bastard!'

'Dear God! It's Jackie.'

'Jackie?' said Christy.

'My husband.'

'Did you – I mean, did you know he was due home?'

'Course not,' said Babs. 'Would I be sittin' here like this if I had?'

'I reckon,' Christy dropped the curtain, 'he's cottoned on to my piece in *Brockway's*.'

'I told you he wouldn't like it.'

'What the hell are we gonna do now?'

Babs pulled in her stomach, thrust out her chest and tightened the belt of her dressing gown.

'Let him in, of course,' she said.

Three copies of *Brockway's* had arrived in the morning mail and Christy, pleased with the spread, had shown Babs the photograph over breakfast. Because of the excitement, she'd been twenty minutes late for work but the moment she'd slid the paper on to his desk Archie had forgiven her. He'd peered at the picture through his thick lenses, then he'd taken off his glasses and stuck his nose down until it almost touched the page.

'It is you, indeed,' he'd said. 'By Gum, don't you look . . .'

'What?' Babs had said. 'Don't I look okay?'

'Oh yes, okay isn't the word for it.'

'What is the word for it?'

'Scrumptious.'

'Scrumptious?'

'You know what I mean,' Archie had said, and blushed.

Polly and Bernard had both called to offer congratulations and at the lunch break Archie had trotted out to the newsagents on the corner and had bought four copies of the magazine and had had Babs sign them. All day long she had basked in the warm glow of celebrity, with *Brockway's*, open at her photograph, propped on the desk. But she had known in her heart of hearts that sooner or later there would be a price to pay for her fleeting moment of fame.

As she went out of the lounge to open the front door, it crossed her mind that Jackie had deserted his army post and had come all the way to Glasgow just to punish her. When she opened the door she kept her knee behind it but so great was Jackie's ire that he pitched the kitbag from his shoulder and followed it, shouting, into the hall.

Babs staggered back. He had a knife, a long knife, raised

above his head. She covered her face with her forearms, shrieking, '*No, Jackie, no, no!*'

He brought the knife down and stabbed her shoulder with it. She felt the blade stiffen then crumple, then he was swatting her about the head and she realised it wasn't a knife at all but the tattered remnants of *Brockway's Illustrated Weekly* rolled up like a baton.

Jackie clouted her about the ears.

She squealed.

He clouted her again and would have gone on clouting her if Christy hadn't intervened. He caught Jackie's arm, snared the straps of Jackie's webbing, spun him into the kitchen and slammed him against the cooker.

Babs heard pans rattling and the bizarre sounds the men made as they fought, panting and grunting and odd little orgasmic gasps. She kicked the front door shut, switched on the hall and kitchen lights, stormed into the kitchen and shouted, 'STOP IT, THE PAIR OF YOU.'

Rather to her surprise, they did.

'What the heck's wrong with you, man?' Christy gasped.

'*Me?*' Jackie panted. 'You're screwin' ma wife an' you're askin' what's wrong with *me?*' He sank back against the rim of the cooker, the furled copy of *Brockway's* hanging limply from his fist. 'Who the bloody hell are you, anyway? Are you the lodger?'

'Sure, I'm the lodger.'

'I thought you were older. She said you were older.'

'Well, I'm not older,' said Christy, 'though what the hell that has to do with anything—'

'You took these?' Jackie wagged the magazine.

'Yeah, I did.'

'What else did you take?'

'Pardon?'

'What else, what others, the ones they wouldn't print.'

'Oh, for God's sake, man!' said Christy. 'It's one lousy photograph.'

'Lousy?' Babs murmured, frowning.

Her cheeks were the shade of blanched tomatoes and her left ear stung. Her hair was all over the place. Her lipstick was smeared across her chin. She looked a right unholy mess, not at all what a wife was supposed to look like when her brave solider husband returned home.

Tears welled up in her eyes. But she was too angry to cry, too angry at Jackie's assumption that she'd encouraged Christy to expose her in a national magazine, that she was so vain that she would pose nude for the man, let alone go to bed with him.

The fact that she had contemplated going to bed with Christy, that she had – and maybe still did – fancy him was irrelevant. She was angry with Jackie for being angry with her, for being jealous of a man he had never met and, most of all, for cuffing her around the ears as if she was some naughty wee schoolgirl. But rough old tenement habits died hard, she supposed, and under the circumstances this was the only way Jackie could express his feelings.

She experienced a wave of regret at the thought that she had betrayed not her husband but her aspirations by taking a stranger into her home, for Jackie didn't really look like Jackie any more. The scraped-bone flakiness had gone, and with a trim haircut and a weathered tan he looked like just the sort of guy she might have fallen for if she hadn't already been his wife.

She sucked back tears and bit her lip. 'Lousy?' she said again. 'It isn't lousy; it's lovely.'

'You look like a bloody tart.'

'Well, I'm not a tart – or maybe I am. Maybe that's what you always liked about me, Jackie. What are you doing here anyway?'

'Leave.'

'How long?'

'Ten days.'

'Then?'

'Embarkation. The desert, most like,' said Jackie.

'Hey, I'm sorry,' Christy said.

'For what?' said Jackie.

He untangled himself from the taps of the cooker, wrestling with webbing and the weight of his greatcoat. His cap had fallen off and his hair, Babs noticed, had a sprinkling of grey in it. Same old Hallop ears, though, sticking out like handles on a milk jug.

'Listen,' Christy said, 'I took the shot when Babs wasn't expecting it. She didn't realise I intended to have it published. She didn't even know I was a photographer. I guess you've every right to be mad about the photograph but whatever else you're thinking – well, it hasn't happened and it never will.'

'Sod it!' said Jackie, hoarsely. 'Right now I'm too knackered to care. Where are the kids?'

'April's asleep next door. The rest are still out at Blackstone.'

'Aw yeah,' Jackie said. 'Well, tomorrow I'll go get them back.'

Since the night of the air raid Polly had continued to sleep in the larder.

She found the little cubby more comforting than claustrophobic. She had a lamp, a card table and a chair, a flask of hot tea, a wireless and three or four books on the shelf above the cot. The space, still smelling faintly of coffee beans and cheese, was more than adequate for her needs. She preferred it to the gloomy wasteland of the master bedroom and the double bed she had shared with Dominic. Snug in the cot, covered with blankets and a feather quilt, she could read, listen to the wireless or simply drowse and dream in peace and quiet.

Room by room, piece by piece, she had gradually deserted the parts of the house she had once shared with Dominic and the children.

The front parlour, with its broken window and bomb scars, was all but sealed off; the dining room too. Even the airy little breakfast room with its French doors overlooking the garden seemed too open and exposed for Polly these days. She made do with the lavatory under the stairs, washed in the kitchen and climbed up to the bathroom and bedrooms only when it became necessary to bathe, fish out clean clothes or refill her handbag with perfume, lipstick and make-up.

She preferred the basement kitchen and her burrow down in the roots of the mansion, and if she had been less self-centred and hermetical she might even have surrendered to the demands of the local billeting officers and handed the place over to the homeless.

Fin, of course, would have none of it. He needed comfort, space, gloom, the luxury of the big cold master bedroom and a double bed for his Saturday night performance. But as Fin became ever more inventive in giving and taking sexual pleasure, Polly found herself longing not for Dom or Tony but only for peace and privacy and the solitude of her cubbyhole downstairs.

She wasn't asleep when the doorbell rang.

If she had been asleep it's doubtful if she would have heard anything short of a thousand-pounder exploding in the garden.

She no longer needed quantities of gin to push her into unconsciousness. She fell asleep as soon as her head touched the pillow, cradled in the knowledge that now she had fallen in love again she would waken to a nice, shiny-bright new day filled with all sorts of promises and possibilities.

The doorbell continued to ring.

She slid out of the cot, threw an overcoat over her pyjamas, glanced at the clock on the card table and gave a little *tsk* of annoyance at the lateness of the hour. Convinced that it would be some officious Civil Defence officer come to tell her that light was leaking from her window – which it wasn't, of course – she followed the shaded beam of her pocket torch upstairs into the hall.

'Who is it?'

'Me.'

She didn't have to ask who 'me' might be. He had been on her mind all evening long, all day in fact, and it seemed to her then that wishing had conjured him up out of the dank December air. She unbolted the door and opened it.

Christy had a bag with him, a canvas holdall slung over his shoulder. He gave a little shrug of apology and said, 'You wouldn't happen to have a spare bed lying empty, by any chance?'

'Several.' Polly closed and bolted the door behind him. 'Did Babs throw you out or did you just tire of her jolly patter and jump ship?'

'Jackie turned up unexpectedly.'

'What?'

'Embarkation leave. No warning.'

'Did he— I mean, you and Babs weren't . . . ?'

'Nope, but we might as well have been.'

'Presumably Jackie saw the *Brockway's* photograph?'

'Sure did.'

'And threw you out?'

'I threw myself out. I mean, hell, the guy's heading for the Western Desert in ten days' time. It's his house, after all.'

'And his wife,' said Polly. 'Why did you come round here?'

'Babs said you wouldn't mind.'

'What if I do mind?'

'I guess I'll have to sleep in the park.'

Polly laughed. She couldn't help herself. She thought of the double bed upstairs with its fresh white linen sheets and gigantic peacock-patterned eiderdown and also of the cot downstairs, so tight and narrow and warm.

She jerked the torch, tossing a faint beam of light to the head of the stairs.

'Down there,' she said.

His fingers found the flesh of her wrist.

He tapped the bone, two or three quick little taps, like code.

'Is it really okay with you?' he asked.

'Of course it is,' said Polly.

It had been a long time since Babs had looked at her body from that peculiar angle. She saw a stomach ribboned with silvery stretch marks, a tuft of coarse brown hair, plump knees and calves and small feet – though not as small as Polly's – braced against the bed end.

Raising her head, she watched Jackie step out of his army trousers and lay them neatly across a chair. He had never been one for holding back and she was puzzled by his patience. He was ready for her, that much was obvious, but there was something different about him, something reticent, almost modest.

'Hurry, darlin', hurry,' she whispered with more urgency than she felt.

In fact, she felt as if she were speaking his lines for him, trying to erase the months of separation and restore the Jackie of old, brash and bold and ever so impatient to be getting on with it. But he was wary now and deliberate, not the same. Perhaps nothing between them would ever be the same, not until the war was over and the children came home and she had time to make amends.

He had insisted on leaving the ceiling light on. The bulb in its tasselled shade hung over her, swaying slightly in the draft from the hall. He had gone to look in on April but hadn't lifted her up, had let her sleep. He had looked at April with the same indifference as he looked down on her now. Babs wondered what had changed in him, if she had changed him, if one lousy photograph, one trivial misjudgement on her part had made all the difference or if it was something out there, something else.

He folded his shirt, smoothing out the creases, and placed it on top of his trousers on the chair.

Given the state of him up front, his patience seemed ridiculous, almost farcical. It was as if he were preparing himself for a kit inspection, not to make love to her for the first time in months.

She sat up. 'For God's sake, Jackie, what's wrong with you?'

'It's been a long time, Babs, a bloody long time.'

She tried to make light of it. 'Don't tell me you've forgotten how?'

He didn't laugh, didn't even crack a smile.

He said, 'I thought you'd wait for me.'

She punched the mattress furiously with her fist. 'I *did* wait for you. I *did*. Damn it, Jackie, why don't you believe me?'

'I didn't say I didn't.'

'Is it that stupid photo? If it is, I'll—'

'Stand up.'

'Pa'din?'

'Go on, stand up. Lemme look at you.'

She rose from the bed and stood before him, more awkward and self-conscious now than she had been when she'd lain on her back with everything on show. She didn't know what to do with her hands, how to position her legs, whether he expected modesty or contrition.

He said, 'Has he been out on ma bike?'

'What?'

'The lodger; has he been ridin' ma motorbike?'

She had all but forgotten about the Excelsior tucked under a big green tarpaulin in the shed at the side of the bungalow. She hadn't seen the motorcycle since the last time Angus had been home and had insisted she let him sit on it. A tremor of pure rage shot through her. Jackie hadn't been thinking about her at all. He had only been going through the motions.

'No,' she said. 'Christy doesn't even know it's there.'

'That's all right then,' Jackie said, nodding.

He wore an army vest of heavy wool, discoloured by careless washing. He tugged it over his head, folded it and put it too on the chair. His chest was hairless but no longer shrunken. He wasn't fat, would never be fat, but he had acquired muscle, little hard strands and straps of muscle that altered his shape and made him appear strong. He looked, she thought, as smooth and hard as a leather saddle. Her willingness to let him make love to her suddenly flared into need. Impulsively, she flung up an arm, fingers flared, tossed back her head and cocked her hip, mocking the pose in which Christy had caught her that drab November morning on her way to work.

'Is this it?' she said, pouting. 'Is this what you want?'

'Aye,' Jackie said, soberly. 'I think maybe it is.'

She turned away, peeled back the bedclothes, leaped into bed and drew the sheet up to her chin.

'All right,' she said, huskily. 'If you want it, come and get it.'

'Aw hell!' said Jackie. 'Maybe I will at that.'

Kicking off his underpants, he heaved himself into bed beside her and, with all his old impatience, bridged her hips, kissed her on the nose and eagerly set to.

★   ★   ★

They were seated on opposite sides of the kitchen table. He drank whisky. She sipped tea and casually turned the pages of the magazine.

'Where did you take this one?' Polly asked.

'South Street, close to the docks.'

'And the girls in the locker room?'

'Ostler's.'

'Didn't the girls mind taking their clothes off for you?'

'I told them to forget I was there.'

'Easier said than done,' said Polly. 'Why did you photograph Babs?'

'I don't know,' Christy said, shrugging. 'I liked the look of her, I guess.'

'Did you tell her how to pose?'

'Heck, no! I don't make pictures, I find pictures.'

'An artist with a camera,' said Polly.

'I'm no artist. I'm a craftsman, that's all. Camera artists are notoriously slow when it comes to producing the goods. Commercial pressure speeds up your reflexes and you learn not to chew the rug when something gets ruined in processing. Most of the time you work in a vacuum, though, because you can't see what's on the negatives. You shoot the stuff, label the rolls, fill in the caption forms and ship the batch out as fast as you can. All that matters is the feel of the shot and your timing. Sometimes you're lucky, most times you ain't.'

'Were you lucky with Babs?'

'Sure.'

'How would you photograph me?'

'I wouldn't even try,' Christy said.

'Why not? Amn't I pretty enough?'

'I wouldn't photograph you,' Christy said, 'because I'd never be able to catch you off guard long enough to make it seem natural.'

'You just beggared the question.'

'I know I did.'

Polly turned a page, not looking at him.

'When you shoot photographs in a war zone,' Christy went on, 'you learn to stop motion just before the obvious point; that way you capture the unexpected.'

'But this isn't a war zone,' Polly said. 'In spite of what you told me out at the farm, all that doom and gloom and prophetic fantasy, I don't think the Germans will invade Britain now.' She paused. 'Am I not unexpected enough for you?'

'I didn't expect you to be the way you are, if that's what you mean.'

'How did you think I'd be? Like Babs?' She glanced up. 'Am I embarrassing you, Mr Cameron?'

'Yeah, you are.'

She closed the magazine. 'Did you study photography at college?'

'My old man didn't earn enough to send us to college,' Christy said. 'Jamie bummed around for a couple of years after he left high school, then enlisted in the navy. I talked my way into a job as a darkroom assistant at Brockway's. Brockway's was more of a newspaper in those days, running splash stories under big banner headlines. I worked for a guy named Eiber, a German, one of the best photographers in the business. I made the coffee, fetched the doughnuts, lugged equipment, delivered photos, anything and everything. He called me his little *Laufbub*, which is German for "gofer", so pretty soon that's who I became – Bub Cameron.'

He took a mouthful of whisky and held it in his cheek for a moment. 'Poor old Fritzy Eiber drank himself into an early grave. Most of the rest of the guys in the old Brockway's gang from twenty years back are still around, though, still chasing the news, still stalking the unexpected.'

'Bub Cameron,' Polly said. 'The name suits you.'

'Nobody calls me Bub any more,' Christy said. 'I left that name behind years ago.'

'Before you became a spy?'

'For the last time—'

'You're not a spy; all right,' Polly said. 'I believe you.'

'Have you thought about what I asked you to do?'

'A little,' Polly said.

'But you haven't reached a decision yet?'

'No.'

'Or spoken to Hughes?'

'No.'

'You don't want to do it, do you?'

'Of course I don't want to do it,' Polly said.

'I don't see how you can refuse,' Christy said.

'Put it down to traits in my character that wouldn't show on a negative.'

'What do you mean?'

'I mean, why should I give up what I've got to buy my husband—'

'And your children.'

'All right – and my children – American citizenship?'

'If you don't come through,' said Christy, 'my government will probably deport him back to Italy.'

'Dominic's a British citizen.'

'Maybe that's what it says on his passport, but in the eyes of the federal authorities he's the elder son of Carlo Manone and heir apparent to a criminal empire.'

'Surely you're exaggerating.'

'Am I?'

What Christy said was the simple truth. Britain had been ruthless in dealing with immigrants and foreign nationals, and America, she suspected, would be even more so. She was unsure just how much she owed Dominic, how much loyalty. She had a feeling that this was just a beginning and that Dominic was playing another of his deadly little games not just with her but with the Government.

'What's in the bag?' she said.

'My cameras,' Christy said. 'I left most of my stuff with Babs.'

'So you intend to go back there, do you, after Jackie leaves?'

'I hadn't given it much thought.'

'I can put you up,' Polly heard herself say. 'I've lots of room upstairs. You can take the big bed tonight, my bed. It's made up. I'll fill you a bottle.'

'A bottle?'

'A hot-water bottle, to warm the bed.'

'Oh yeah,' Christy said. 'Where will you sleep?'

'Down here,' said Polly. 'I prefer it down here.'

'Because of the air raids?'

'Yes.'

'What if there's a raid tonight?'

'Come down,' she said.

'Down where?'

She got up from the table, crossed around behind him and pushed open the larder door. 'Here,' she said. 'I shelter here.'

He stood behind her, glass in hand, looking at the narrow cot bathed in warm light from the little lamp, sheets and blankets turned back.

'Cosy,' he said.

'And safe,' said Polly, and led him, reluctantly, upstairs.

Jackie opened one bleary eye and peered at his daughter. She looked, he thought, like something off a Christmas card in a heavy red overcoat and a woollen cap.

'Hullo, darlin',' Jackie said. 'Are you glad t' see me?'

'Where's Christy?'

It was pitch-dark outside, the bedroom lit only by a shaft

of light from the hall. It was also cold, colder than it ever got in the barracks where a big barrel stove burned all night. His breath hung in the air and when he moved his legs he found only frosty space beside him. He pulled the clothes up and offered an unshaven cheek to his child.

'Come on, April, give Daddy a kiss.'

She backed away, frowning.

'Where's Christy?'

'What's wrong, honey? Don't you remember me?'

'Yes. Where's Christy?'

From the doorway, Babs said, 'Christy's gone to stay with Aunt Polly.'

'Will he be comin' back?' April said.

'She doesn't remember me,' said Jackie.

'It's Daddy,' said Babs, standing behind April now.

'I know,' said April and, turning on her heel and brushing past her mother, darted out into the hall.

Jackie sighed, sank back and stared at his breath in the air above him.

'Time is it?'

'Half-past seven.'

'She doesn't remember.'

'She's only young,' Babs said. 'Give her time.'

'I don't have time.' He turned his head. 'Where are you goin'?'

'To work,' said Babs.

She got down on her knees beside the bed.

He peered into her face and said. 'I thought you'd be stayin' home today. Can't you phone in, tell them you're sick or somethin'?'

'I can't,' said Babs. 'Anyway, I have to take April to nursery.'

'Stay home, both o' you. We'll go to the farm an' fetch the others.'

'Jackie . . .'

'Christ!' he said, without emphasis.

'I've left out two real eggs an' some bacon. Fry up when you feel like it. There's tinned soup in the cupboard an' a pie as well, if you're hungry.' She kissed him on the cheek and got to her feet. 'You need sleep, m'lad, that's what you need. I'll be home about six.'

'Phone in,' Jackie said in a pathetic whisper. 'Why can't you?'

'I wish I could, darlin',' Babs said, 'but I don't want to let Archie down.'

'Archie? Who's Archie?'

'Mummy,' April called, clear as a bell, from the hall. 'Late.'

'Gotta go.' Babs kissed him once more and tucked the blankets under his chin. 'Great to have you home, honey,' she said, and left him lying there in the darkness, wide awake and all alone.

9

The Anglia had been ordered only weeks before the war. There had been much hemming and hawing in council meetings about whether the order should or should not be cancelled. In the end, delivery of the Ford had been taken on the very forenoon that Chamberlain had made his announcement that Britain was at war with Germany and nobody in the Breslin Council offices had taken much pleasure in the arrival of a motorcar that might in a matter of weeks be blown to smithereens or, worse, be filled with German officers.

Since neither fate had befallen the car so far, however, the scramble among local government officers to use the machine had become intense, a little war within a war, as it were, and Bernard had to pull out all the stops to borrow the car for an hour or so that chill December morning.

He was not the most assured of drivers. He drove, in fact, just as methodically as he did most other things, which included planning his campaign to ensure that the Belgian widow got everything she deserved and perhaps a little more than she bargained for.

Bernard could not explain why he found the woman's plight so affecting. He was neither pro- nor anti-Semitic and, as a rule, suffered none of the emotional confusion about Jewish people that troubled his stepdaughters and most of the district councillors. He drove directly from the council building to Breslin Primary School where Miss Wilma Stewart, the headmistress, and Mr Lachlan Boyd, the janitor, were waiting for him, together with six little evacuees from the lower rungs of the social ladder.

Miss Stewart and Mr Peabody were old friends, for billeting and schooling were two hands in the same glove and, to mix a metaphor, there had been a good deal of mutual back-scratching between the schoolteacher and the council servant since the war began.

A drive in a motorcar was just what the doctor ordered for the sickly six. Their little faces were flushed with excitement as Miss Stewart ushered them into the rear seat of the Anglia and Mr Boyd, fat as a toad and smelling of lavatory fluid, clambered in beside them. They pressed their runny noses to the windows and clutched the seat with cold little hands as the gentleman from the council slid behind the wheel and, with Miss Stewart at his side, drove away from the school and turned uphill into Antonine Way.

Close to the top of the hill, just before the stately mansions of the very rich gave way to rugged moorland, Miss Stewart swung round to face her pupils and began her lesson. 'Now, children,' she said, in a dry Highland voice, 'Breslin is famous for being one of the forts on the Roman wall. The Romans were a bit like the Germans. They wanted to conquer Europe and a man called Julius Caesar led an army over here and conquered the English.'

'But not the Scots, eh?' put in Mr Boyd who, at that opportune moment, had discovered a bag of toffees in his pocket and was quietly handing them out. 'Naw, they Romans never got the better o' the Scots.'

'Thank you for your contribution, Mr Boyd,' Miss Stewart said. 'Now, one hundred and fifty years after Julius Caesar's invasion, the Romans ruled England. They wanted to rule Scotland too but the Scots were not going to have any of it and gave the Romans a lot of trouble by attacking them. So what do you think the Romans did?'

'Runned awa', Miss.'

'Choppit them up, Miss.'

'I'll bet they brung in the tanks.'

'Unfortunately they didn't have tanks in those days, Iain.' Miss Stewart paused and glanced at Bernard, who gave her the nod. 'What the Romans did – ' the Anglia came to a halt exactly on cue – 'was build a wall. That wall.'

Six pairs of eyes swivelled to starboard and gaped out at the misty moor. There was nothing much to see: a ragged birch tree, some gorse and, jutting from the edge of the moor, a jumble of shaped stones.

'That's no' a wa'.'

'Antonine's wall, a piece of it,' said Miss Stewart. 'Antonine was the name of the Roman officer who built it. It stretched all the way from Edinburgh to Glasgow and it had forts on it to keep out the marauding—'

'That's definitely no' a wa',' Iain, the rebel, declared. 'We've got a wa' behind oor hoose an' it never lookit like that in its puff.'

'What's left here,' said Miss Stewart, patiently, 'is only a fragment, a small part of Antonine's wall. It's nearly two thousand years old, after all, so we're very lucky to have it.'

'Aye, well, Miss, y' can keep it.'

'Enough lip out o' you, son,' said Mr Boyd in a voice that would have made the bravest Roman quail. 'Listen t' Miss Stewart an' see if you canny learn somethin' useful for a change.'

But the educational portion of the trip, such as it was, had ended.

'Well,' the headmistress said, 'now you've seen it, you can tell all your friends there's a piece of Antonine's wall still here in Breslin.' She paused then said, 'I believe you have some business to attend to in the vicinity, Mr Peabody.'

'As it happens, I do,' said Bernard.

Angus was feeling rotten. The fact that his sisters were feeling even more rotten gave him no satisfaction.

The doctor, a lady, had called first thing. She had embarrassed him by stretching him out on top of the blankets without his pyjamas and lifting up his winkle with her big cold hands so that she could look at the spots on his thighs.

He had developed a rash, a serious one this time, on his back and arms, and almost overnight bigger spots had sprung out in his hair, on his face and the front of his chest, and the itch had got worse. He found cold air soothing and lay very still while the doctor examined him. His throat was sore too and when he spoke his voice sounded queer, like Ron grunting. He knew what the lady doctor was going to say, for Miss Dawlish had told Dougie last night what it was and Dougie had told him: 'You've got the pox, son, the chickenpox.'

Angus had said, 'Have they got it too?'

'What, the chickens?' Dougie had said.

'My sisters?'

'They have.'

'Worse than me?'

'Just as bad.'

'Worse?'

'Aye, worse.'

Angus had taken Dougie's word for it for he could hear May whimpering through the wall that separated their bedrooms and, at an early hour of the morning, before daylight, he'd wakened to hear Miss Dawlish talking soothingly to the girls and May, or maybe it was June, retching.

Dougie had told him not to scratch with his fingernails and had shown him how to rub the rash lightly with the back of his wrists and he had lain awake in the darkness feeling rotten, rubbing away at his hair and chest with the back of his wrists until, with Miss Dawlish still talking to his sisters and a chink of light showing under the door, the itch had eased and he had fallen asleep.

Next thing he knew the lady doctor was coming upstairs.

After the doctor had gone next door to examine the girls Dougie came in to help him back into his pyjamas and tuck him into bed again.

'Is it the pox?'

'Aye, just chickenpox, not scarlet fever,' Dougie said.

'Can you die of chickenpox?'

'Nah.'

'Can you go to school wi' chickenpox?'

'Nup, no school for you this side o' the New Year.'

'Hurrah!' said Angus, croaking.

'No nowhere for any o' you for a fortnight at least. You're contagious.'

'Am I?'

'You are,' said Dougie and stroked his forehead, soothingly.

Later Dougie brought up a paraffin stove and fiddled away until he got it going for the doctor had said Angus must keep warm.

Later still Miss Dawlish brought up porridge, two pieces of soft toast and a mug of milky tea. He was glad of the tea but couldn't face the porridge, never mind the toast. Miss Dawlish took it all away without complaining about waste, which made him realise that he really was ill.

Then Miss Dawlish came back with a baking bowl half full of milky liquid, and a sponge. She bathed him with the stuff and told him it was boric acid and that it would take the itch away for a while.

While he was being bathed he could hear Dougie talking to his sisters next door, and May still whimpering.

Then after Miss Dawlish had gone away again he had to get up to pee but when he put his feet on the floor he felt as if his head was a barrage balloon floating on a cable and he shouted and Dougie came in quickly and brought him the pot, which was very embarrassing and made him feel worse.

He got back into bed as fast as he could and lay there, smelling the stink of the paraffin stove and the stuff Miss Dawlish had bathed him with and listening to the mouse sounds of his sisters fretting in the room next door.

Then Dougie opened the curtains and grey daylight filtered into the room and he said, 'What time is it now, Dougie?'

And Dougie said, 'Half-past nine.'

'Is that all?'

'Aye, son,' said Dougie. 'That's all.'

Arthur Hunter Gowan was having breakfast in the big front room of his house on Antonine Way when the Anglia appeared out of the evergreens.

As a rule Arthur Hunter Gowan wasn't given to breakfasting late but he had endured an overnight journey from London and even his wealth and influence had not been able to protect him from the vicissitudes of wartime railway travel. In addition, he had struggled to find a cab driver willing to take him as far out of the city as Breslin and even his equitable temperament had been challenged by the excess fare charged and the sauce the cabbie had given him when he had politely disputed it. When he'd finally reached home he'd found his wife, Miranda, in tears at something the day-maid had said and it had cost him the best part of a half-hour to smooth her ruffled feathers.

For these reasons Arthur Hunter Gowan was breakfasting at a quarter to ten o'clock instead of his usual hour of seven thirty when the Anglia crept up the long driveway and parked in front of the window.

Arthur called to Miranda to fetch the maid from the kitchen to answer the door but, receiving no response, hoisted himself from his chair at the dining table and went to answer it himself.

The man on the second step down was well enough dressed, though not, Arthur knew, a gentleman. He touched his hat but didn't remove it, nor did he back down when invited to state his business.

'Billeting,' the man said.

'Billeting?' said Arthur Hunter Gowan. 'Here?'

'Four public rooms, seven bedrooms, two toilets,' the man said, 'and just three permanent residents, not counting serving personnel.'

'Billeting what?' said Arthur. 'Whom?'

His eagle eye had already sighted the faded old woman in the front seat of the motorcar and the man, obviously her husband, crammed into the back fighting with what appeared to be a gang of unruly children.

When he scrutinised the faces pressed against the window he felt a curious pang of pity for the children who had been uprooted from their burrows in the warm dark heart of Glasgow and whisked without warning to this strange, no doubt alien environment. He had tended their like in hospitals all over the city and tended them still from time to time, for his scalpel neither knew nor cared whose flesh it cut into. Having a carload of the little blighters on his gravel driveway, however, lay close to the limit of his sympathy.

'Do you know who I am?' he asked.

'I do indeed, sir,' said the man. 'You're Mister – have I got that right? – Mister, not Doctor, Hunter Gowan. I have you listed as a surgeon.'

'You, I presume, are a council officer.'

'Bernard Peabody, sir. I have identification if it's required.'

One of the advantages of a privileged education is that it

develops not only character but also perspicacity, and Arthur Hunter Gowan sensed immediately that there was something 'off' about this little charade but in spite of his weariness and the great load of more pressing concerns that weighed upon him, he was sufficiently intrigued to step out of the house and close the front door behind him.

'How many children are in the vehicle?'

'Six,' Bernard Peabody answered.

'Are they homeless?'

'Uprooted.'

'Evacuees?'

'Yes.'

'Do you propose that they move into my house this very minute?'

The billeting officer frowned. 'Not necessarily this very minute.'

Arthur Hunter Gowan stepped down on to the gravel and peered into the Anglia. 'Tell me, Mr Peabody', he said, 'do you propose that I should also provide a billet for Miss Stewart, given that she has a perfectly good home of her own only a quarter of a mile from here?'

'Ah!' said Bernard.

'My three sons,' Arthur said, 'are serving King and country at this present juncture but the first four years of their school lives were spent under the tutelage of that lady there who is, if memory serves, still headmistress of Breslin Primary. What do you really want from me, Mr Peabody?'

'Your influence, sir.'

'Influence? What sort of influence do you think I have when it comes to finding homes for your evacuees?'

'It isn't the evacuees,' said Bernard. 'I need to place a doctor and I thought that as you're on the governing board of the new hospital at Ottershaw it might be possible—'

'Good God, man!' said Arthur Hunter Gowan. 'I'm chief

of surgery, not a damned personnel officer. What sort of doctor is he?'

'It's a she, in fact, a Belgian lady, a widow.'

'Not Reeder's widow?' said Arthur Hunter Gowan.

'Yes, sir. Do you know her?'

'I know of her,' the surgeon said. 'I knew him – slightly. What's she doing in this neck of the woods? I thought she lived in Renfrewshire?'

'She does,' said Bernard, 'but apparently there are no openings for qualified female medical personnel in Renfrewshire, or in Glasgow, for that matter. She's having to move to find work.'

'I take it you didn't know the husband?'

'No, sir,' said Bernard. 'I never had that pleasure.'

'An awkward customer, believe me, and frightfully ambitious.'

'Isn't that what they say about all of them?' said Bernard.

'Now how do I answer that,' said Arthur Hunter Gowan, 'without displaying prejudice? Yes, Mr Peabody, I'm well aware that the late Mr Reeder was a Jew. Does that answer your question?'

'Not exactly,' said Bernard.

'What connection do you have with this woman?'

'She turned up at the council offices and asked for assistance,' said Bernard. 'And just in case you're wondering, no, Mr Hunter Gowan, I'm not one of the tribe of Israel.'

'You're not above a little bit of blackmail, though, are you?' the surgeon said. 'Did you really suppose I'd raise my hands in horror at the sight of a car full of snotty-nosed evacuees? For your information, Mr Peabody, I've just returned from a series of meetings at the War Office, arguing the toss with Treasury officials who seem to imagine that one can build, equip and staff a brand-new military hospital for half a crown. When it comes to blackmail, I'm a better hand at it than you will ever be. Is this woman available for interview?'

'She's ready and waiting.'

'Bring her to Ottershaw at ten a.m. on Thursday.'

'Will you be in attendance, sir?'

'Of course I'll be in attendance.'

'And you will interview her personally?'

'Yes,' the surgeon said. 'Personally. Now get those blessed ragamuffins out of my driveway, if you please.'

And Bernard, mission accomplished, left to drive his little band of accomplices back downhill to school.

Swimming in barley water and dozy with the fumes of paraffin and boric acid, Angus lay on his back with the blankets up to his nose and tried not to scratch. He was bored, tired and restless, and had no idea how much of the morning had passed since Miss Dawlish had last popped in to see him.

Dougie had brought him two comics but he hadn't the strength to read them and left them on the blanket where he could look at the colourful covers. In the window he could see clouds passing and a fleeting smear of sunlight and was briefly diverted from his misery by a robin that hopped about on the sill and peeped in on him with its cheery little eye. He wondered if Dougie had remembered to feed Ron and who would help Miss Dawlish scatter grain for the chicks since May, June and he wouldn't be allowed out of doors for a fortnight.

A fortnight! He couldn't imagine a fortnight shut up indoors. He tried fixing his mind on Christmas by subtracting fourteen from twenty-five and adding on the number of days in the month that had already passed, but couldn't remember what date it was today. He'd never really had to think about dates before. He was more at home with Mother Nature's broad scale of things than clocks, watches and calendars.

His sisters were whining for Mum but Dougie had told him that his mother couldn't visit in case April caught chickenpox too. He loved his youngest sister quite a bit more than he loved his middle sisters, though he didn't recognise it as love, of course, and thought he was just looking after them while Dad was away fighting the war.

He turned his head and stared out of the window.

Two rooks flew past in strict formation, black against a pale blue sky.

He wished he could fly. He wished he was old enough to drive a tank. He wished they would let him join the navy and sail on the *Illustrious* and dive-bomb German battleships like his Uncle Dennis. He wished . . .

He scowled.

He sat up.

His head went whirly for an instant, then steadied. He scratched his ears frantically with his fingernails, listening to the sound in the distance.

'Excelsior,' he muttered. 'That's our Excelsior.'

Then with a wild leap that scattered comic books and blankets across the floorboards, he was out of bed and heading for the window.

'Daddy,' he shouted. 'It's Daddy.'

And it was.

Jackie had never been to Blackstone before. Dom had cut him out of the counterfeiting caper. Maybe Dom had thought he was too dumb to take part in a big money scheme. And maybe Dom had been right.

One thing Jackie had learned in fourteen months in khaki was the limit of his own intelligence. He wasn't dumb, of course, but he wasn't as near smart as he'd always supposed himself to be.

The blistering nervous energy that had driven him when he was a kid, plus all that false pride, would have landed him in real trouble sooner or later. The coming of war had been the best thing – next to marrying Babs – that had ever happened to him – to Dennis and Billy too he reckoned, for it had released them from the culture of moral laxity, of trying to get something for nothing.

Army ranks were sprinkled with spivs and fly men, sharp-witted Londoners who always had some black-market scheme or other on the boil, plus hard tickets from Liverpool, Cardiff or Newcastle who would nut you as soon as look at you. None of them had ever heard of Dominic Manone and didn't give a toss about Jackie's Italian connections or his motoring salon or his cutthroat life in Glasgow during the Depression. He was nothing to them but a bragging little twerp who couldn't hold his liquor.

He had learned quickly to keep his mouth shut and his head down, and even before he'd emerged from basic training had begun to realise that he was better than they were, better at what he did under the bonnet of a staff car or the hull plate of a Crusader, and to appreciate that a wife and four lovely kids were worth a lot more than pie-in-the-sky dreams of easy money. He longed to see Babs and the kids again, if just to remind himself what he was fighting for and to make sure that Babs understood that when he returned to civvy street he would be content to earn an honest dollar doing what he did best.

That bloody photograph in *Brockway's* had shaken his faith in the future, however. It had reminded him that he wasn't the only one who'd been changed by the war. Dennis's wife had left him for another guy. Billy's sweetheart had had a kid to a married man twice her age. And now Babs, Babs and her Yankee reporter, this cuckoo whom she'd welcomed into her nest; Jackie didn't know whether to believe her story or whether her hugs and kisses might turn out to be as dud as one of Dominic's fivers. He couldn't forget April's face, though, when she'd found him in bed that morning, couldn't put out of his mind her shrill little cry, 'Where's Christy? Where's Christy?'

Now he needed to see the kids, was desperate to see the kids, just to make sure that they hadn't forgotten him too.

He pulled the covers off the Excelsior with a sigh.

The bike was untouched, just as he'd left her.

He'd left her with a full tank of petrol and, even allowing for evaporation, she would have the best part of three gallons still inside her.

He took his scarred old leather coat from the hook on the back of the shed door and put it on. It smelled musty but that smell would soon go once he was out on the open road. He buttoned up the coat and belted it, hung a pair of goggles around his neck, tucked his trousers into his stocking tops, rammed his forage cap down over his ears, and flung a leg over the saddle.

She felt good, just right, just the way she'd always felt.

He switched on, turned her over, gently warmed her up.

Sweet as a nut she was, smelling of oil, his beloved Excelsior Manxman, 297 pounds of polished, well-preserved machinery waiting for him, unchanged.

He got off, kicked open the shed door, kicked up the stand, rolled her forward on to the paving, mounted her once more and roared off around the curve of Holloway Road and down the long straight to Paisley Road, down by the back ways and byways that he knew so well, down to the ferry that carried him over the river. Then out along the broad streets of Yoker, heading north-west to Breslin in search of his missing kids.

'You can't come in,' Miss Dawlish said.

'Who says I can't?' said Jackie.

'I do,' the woman said. 'We're in strict quarantine.'

'Quarantine?'

'We've got chickenpox.'

'Bugger that,' said Jackie. 'I wanna see my kids.'

'Have you had the chickenpox, Mr Hallop?'

'Corporal Hallop.'

'Very well, Corporal Hallop, have you had—'

'Aye,' Jackie said. 'Naw: I dunno know, do I, but?'

'Chickenpox can kill a grown man.'

'Are you tellin' me my kids're dyin'?'

'Of course not. They're young. They'll soon recover.'

'Then I'll risk it. Let me in.'

'Are you on embarkation leave, by any chance?'

'What if I am?' said Jackie.

'Just think, you're halfway to wherever you're going and you fall sick with a lethal dose of a childhood ailment,' Miss Dawlish said. 'Even if you survive the disease, think what a laughing stock you'll be thereafter.'

Jackie glanced up at the window under the eaves. He could see all three of his children there, little faces pressed against the glass, hands waving frantically as if this bitch of a woman had them locked up in a tower. Maybe she had too; he wouldn't put it past her. Miss Dawlish had never liked him. All the days she'd worked for him in the motor salon, she'd despised him. She'd been a good worker, though, a terrific accountant, he'd grant her that, but the woman who stood, arms folded, in the doorway was so altered that he could hardly believe it was the same Miss Dawlish. She looked like a bloody scarecrow now, a male scarecrow, with her pudding-basin haircut, baggy corduroys and clumsy big boots.

Exhilarated by the cycle ride and still seated on the Excelsior he glanced up at the window and waved.

The girls had vanished, however. Only Angus remained: his Gus, his boy, banging his forehead against the glass like a bumblebee trapped in a jam jar.

'Is he locked in?' Jackie said. 'If so, why?'

'He isn't at all well.'

'Has the doctor been?'

'First thing this morning.'

'Can he not come down, just for a minute?'

'Dougie's with him.'

The bitch had his boy under lock and key. He was tempted to gun the bike and run her over, storm the farmhouse door and might have done so too if Giffard hadn't appeared in the doorway.

Giffard was one of the old school, one of Carlo Manone's original gang from before his, Jackie's, time. He had always believed that all the old timers were hard men but Giffard was just a shabby wee brown-skinned guy in a cloth cap and a tattered jacket whom you could blow away with a fart.

'Bad timin', Jackie,' Giffard said.

'I want to see the boy.'

'Are they sendin' you overseas?'

'Aye.'

'How long's your leave?'

'Ten days.'

'It'll be North Africa I expect, with the tanks.'

'Who told you that?' said Jackie.

'Angus,' said Giffard.

'What does Angus know about North Africa?'

'It's the tanks Angus knows about,' Giffard said. 'It's me reads the newspapers. You'll be part o' the build-up for Wavell's strike against the Eyetie forts on the Libyan coast: Sidi Barrani, Bardia then Tobruk. Anyway, I'll bring the boy down if you promise not t' touch him. It's not you I'm worried about; it's April. You wouldn't want t' give the pox to poor wee April now, would you?'

'I suppose not,' Jackie agreed.

He hated being sensible but something told him that Giffard and the woman had only the kids' best interests at heart. He propped the bike and swung himself from the saddle. He stripped off his cap and let the cold wind ruffle what was left of his hair. He looked at the long line of the Old Kilpatrick Hills sliding down into the valley of the Clyde, at barrage balloons, and white, cold clouds gathering away to the west, then he heard Angus shouting, the familiar gravel voice even deeper than he remembered it.

'Dad! Daddy! We've got the chickenpox.'

Angus was too big to be carried but Dougie Giffard managed it somehow, the boy's legs, pyjama-clad, trailing down the front of the man's body; socks and sand shoes, a dressing gown, a blanket thrown around his shoulders. It felt strange to see his son in another man's arms, held up like a big, sad doll.

Miss Dawlish appeared in the doorway with May and June. The girls too had changed, had grown taller. Even all wrapped up Jackie could see the sort of women his daughters would become, the sort of wives they would make if any poor bloke ever managed to separate them long enough to get them to the altar. They blinked impassively, cheeks flushed and tear-stained. But the tears they shed weren't tears of joy at seeing him again. They were crying only because they were ailing.

Jackie yielded to helplessness once more, all the fight, all the vigour draining out of him for a moment. He put a hand to his face, covering his eyes in case he would cry too, then with the wind blowing the stink of pig and chickens across the yard, he braced himself, rammed the cap back on his head, kicked away the prop, and leaped on to the saddle of the Excelsior.

'Watch this,' he shouted, and gave the machine the gun.

Crouched low over the handlebars like a Manx TT racer, he roared away, inches from the farmhouse wall. He aimed at the narrow gate that led out to the vegetable plot at the back of the house then, with less than inches to spare, swerved, stabbing down with his left foot and swinging the bike round into the big yard again. He added throttle, punched forward, racing along the side of the outbuildings, bike and body bouncing high over the rough cobbles. He targeted an open gate that led to a field and drove through it on to rough pasture slippery with recent rain. He snaked the Manxman up on to the crest of the hill and braked. Looking back, he could see them huddled in the doorway, the woman, the old guy, his daughters and his son all watching him.

He lifted his arm, closed his fist and punched the air, jerked the bike round and drove back through the field gate as fast as he dared. He hit the cobbles at the end of the track, soared high off the saddle and thumped down, jarring every bone in his body. He focused on the doorway, on his children, saw his girls scream, half afraid, half excited, saw them retreat into the tiny hall, saw Angus drop from Giffard's arms and stand up, arms flung out as if he expected Dad to reach down, pluck him up and ride off with him.

Jackie swerved, spraying grit and muck, brought the bike round broadside and slithered to a halt just three or four feet from his son.

'It's the best I can do, Angus, since you're sick,' he said. 'Next time, we'll go out together. Okay?'

'Okay, Dad, okay.'

'You get well now, y'hear me.'

'Aye, Dad.'

'Girls, do what Miss Dawlish tells you.'

He didn't need an answer, didn't need acknowledgement, didn't need to hear them say they loved him. He loved them, and that was enough.

He touched his knuckles to his lips, threw them a kiss and crouching low now to hide his tears, rode off towards the Breslin Road, leaving nothing of himself behind but the fragrant odour of exhaust.

* * *

Polly had no idea what time it was. She seldom did these days. She opened one eye and then the other and sat up.

The aroma of coffee was strong in the air. She fumbled for the lamp switch and flooded the larder with light. Blinking, she consulted the clock on the shelf above the cot. Ten minutes past ten. She needed to pee but was too tired to get up just yet; no, not tired – happy.

'Knock, knock.'

She smiled. 'Who's there?'

'The big bad wolf.'

'Oh, good,' she said. 'Come in.'

He opened the door with his elbow and peeped in on her.

She sprawled against the pillows, looking, she supposed, like something the cat had dragged in. She didn't much care about her appearance, though, and neither, apparently, did Christy for, carrying a coffee mug in each hand, he looked decidedly rumpled too.

'May I?' he said.

'You may.'

He squeezed to the side of the cot and sat down. Polly could see daylight in the kitchen and a faint, hot haze of smoke from the region of the stove. He said, 'I took the liberty of making some breakfast. I hope you don't mind.'

'Coffee in bed,' Polly said. 'Of course I don't mind.'

'There's a bacon sandwich too, if you want it.'

'In a moment.' Polly took the mug, touching his wrist to steady his hand. 'Let me enjoy this first.' She sipped the strong black coffee. 'Did you sleep well?'

'Yeah.'

'Were you cold?'

'Maybe a little.'

'It is cold up there,' she said. 'It's impossible to heat this house properly.'

'Is that why you sleep down here?'

'Hm, probably,' Polly said. 'Are you cold now?'

'Nope. Okay now.'

She reached out and touched his wrist again. 'Are you sure?'

She had never been a 'touchy' sort of person, unlike Babs, who was full of nudges and dabs and playful slaps. She wondered why she wanted to touch this man, not only to touch him but to have him touch her, to put his hands on her breasts, to reach down under the blankets and feel how warm she was, how appallingly warm.

She felt his weight press against her thigh. She wished she didn't have to pee. If she didn't have to pee she could linger here all morning, talking, just talking and sipping the strong black coffee that he had brewed in her kitchen.

'Sure,' he said, 'I'm sure.'

'What,' she cleared her throat, 'what do you intend to do?'

'How do you mean?'

'Today? What's your programme?'

'I guess I'll go find some place to stay.'

'No,' she said, too quickly, too eagerly. 'You don't have to do that.'

'I can't go back to Barbara's.'

'Stay here.'

'Really?'

'Yes,' Polly said. 'It's silly not to.'

'I wonder what your sister will have to say about that.'

'My sister?' Polly said, thinking of Babs.

'Rose.'

'Rosie. Yes. Well, Rosie will just have to wonder, won't she?'

'Wonder?'

'If you've – if you're being friendly with both Babs and me.'

'What's wrong with being friends with both of you?'

'My little sister may be deaf . . .' It was a step too far, too quickly. Polly pushed her mouth down into the coffee mug.

'But she ain't dumb, is that what you mean?' Christy said. 'I think you'd better finish your coffee and get up now, Mrs Manone.'

'Why?'

'Because, appearances to the contrary, I still like to kid myself I'm a gentleman.'

'Aren't you?'

'Not all the time.' He pushed himself from the cot. 'Look,' he said, 'you know why I'm here and what I'm supposed to do and if you think having me stay is gonna make it easier on both of us . . .'

'Easier?' Polly laughed. 'Easier to do what?'

'Collaborate.'

'Is that what this is, a collaboration?'

The larder was too small; retreat was impossible. He had her pinned in the cot and she couldn't get up even if she wanted to. She was, in a sense, at his mercy, would, in a sense, have to await his pleasure. She squeezed her knees together and raised them under the blankets. If Christy chose to touch her now she would yield to him, would give herself up without a qualm of conscience or thought of consequence. In all the months she had spent with Fin Hughes she had never felt like this, not remotely like this.

She clung to the coffee mug as if it were a rock.

Christy nodded. Then he said, 'Listen, you've a telephone upstairs. Do you mind if I make a couple of calls?'

'What?' said Polly.

'The telephone, in the hall, do you—'

'No, no, of course not.'

'Anyhow, I guess you'll want to get dressed.'

'I think I'd better,' said Polly.

'Then I'll just . . .' He gestured with his thumb, 'upstairs.'

'Yes,' she said. 'Yes, by all means,' and with a mixture of relief and disappointment watched him go out into the kitchen and, like a perfect gentleman, discreetly close the larder door.

IO

'Is this the best that you can do?' Evelyn Reeder said.

'Oh, come now,' Bernard said, 'it isn't that bad.'

'Do you know what I am leaving to come here?'

No, Bernard thought, but I can guess.

He watched her move about the small square room, brushing the surface of the sideboard with the back of her hand, patting cushions on the two-seater sofa, stroking the length of blackout curtain that screened the view of the monuments and the hills.

Mid-afternoon: he had squandered the best part of a working day on Dr Reeder. He had driven her to Ottershaw, then, in spite of grumbles from other council officers, had hung on to the car to pick her up after her interview and stand her lunch while she made up her mind about Hunter Gowan's offer. Her credentials had obviously impressed Hunter Gowan for he had personally given her the grand tour of the new operating theatres. To Bernard's way of thinking it was a pretty generous offer and exactly what the woman claimed she wanted.

'What will you do there?' he'd asked her. 'What post will you hold?'

'I will be clinical assistant to the Chief Medical Officer.'

'Do you know who that is?'

'George Gillespie.'

'Do you know him or, more to the point, does he know you?'

'He knows who I am. He worked with my husband once.'

'I assume,' Bernard had said, as tactfully as possible, 'that confirmation of your appointment will depend on Doctor Gillespie's approval.'

'Gillespie will not go against Hunter Gowan's wishes.'

'Are you sure of that, Dr Reeder?'

'I am sure.'

'Sure enough to accept the appointment?'

She'd hesitated, then said, 'Do you have a place in which I might live?'

'I do.'

'I will not share.'

'I wouldn't expect you to.'

'And there are no children?'

'None that will give you bother.'

Directly after lunch he had driven her out to Breslin Old Parish Church. He wished that the weather had been more cheerful for Breslin Old Parish was nothing if not picturesque. The church gate was not the main entrance to the cemetery or the shortest way into the lodge, but it was, Bernard thought, the one that would cause Dr Reeder least alarm. As a doctor she surely wouldn't be disturbed by the presence of dead folk who, Bernard thought, never seemed quite dead at all but merely reposing under their handsome markers in a reticent middle-class manner.

Personally he preferred the old part of the graveyard, that swell of ground to the north-east where farmers and their wives and children had been laid to rest over the past century and a half. He had never been a country boy, had never yearned to be a country boy, yet he felt a curious affinity with the sons of the soil who lay under the sod beneath the willows and gnarled oaks.

'Is this where you are bringing me, to a graveyard? Is this where you expect me to stay?'

'Not in the graveyard, no.'

'Where then?'

'In the lodge house.'

He had always fancied the lodge house for himself, though he knew that Lizzie would never condone a move from Knightswood.

The lodge tower was in fact a late Victorian replica of a baronial keep, three storeys high. Until September 1939 it had been white but in a fit of invasion panic council workers had painted it a mottled shade of green. Bernard had tried several times to billet families there but nobody was willing to live in the middle of a cemetery. What a fuss the townies made, what a furore they created, with wild claims of howling in the night, of apparitions and spectral entities, of furniture being moved and taps turned on and at least one report of a midnight convention of witches up in the north-east corner.

Bernard had opened the creaky door with a long key and had led Dr Reeder up the spiral staircase to the apartment on the third floor.

Parish clerks had resided here until the early thirties but then attitudes had changed and the clerks chose to occupy a council house nearer to the centre of town. Since then the apartment had lain empty, still decently furnished, cleaned from time to time, and regularly fired in winter. It was, Bernard thought, the perfect place for a lady who hankered after a quiet retreat.

'How will I get to Ottershaw from here?'

'Buses pass the main gate. The service isn't great,' Bernard said, 'but they do run pretty much to time. They'll drop you right at the hospital.'

'What time is the last bus at night?'

'I really don't know.'

She gave a little sigh and seated herself on the wing chair beside the empty fireplace, her hands folded in her lap. She looked, Bernard thought, almost regal but her great sad eyes were filled not with hauteur but with a strange vulnerable despair that stirred all his protective instincts.

She said, 'You have been very understanding.'

'It's part of my job to be understanding, Dr Reeder.'

'No, you have done more than your job demands.'

She smiled for the first time in his presence and when she did so he glimpsed the beauty in her, a dark, self-reliant sort of beauty that knew its own worth. He felt his throat close and his knees turn to jelly.

It was all he could do, at that moment, to speak.

'May I take it,' he said, 'that the accommodation is satisfactory?'

'It will do,' Evelyn Reeder said. 'Yes, Mr Peabody, it is satisfactory.'

'When will you—' He cleared his throat. 'When will you move in?'

'At the weekend.'

'I'll be here,' Bernard said.

'Will you?' she said. 'Why?'

'To hand over the keys,' said Bernard.

'Marzipan?'

'Yes,' guardedly.

'I've been trying to reach you all goddamned day.'

'Well, now you have me. What's the problem?'

'It isn't a problem. I'd say it's more of an advance. I'm in.'

'In?' said Marzipan. 'What do you mean by "in"?'

'In the house, with the— with her.'

'Is she there with you now?'

'Nope, she's gone out.'

'Are you calling from a box?'

'I just told you, I'm calling from the house, her house.'

'Haven't you ever heard of telephone bills?' said Marzipan, testily.

'She isn't gonna check her telephone bill,' Christy said. 'Jesus, I thought you'd be pleased.'

'I am,' Marzipan said. 'I just wish you'd be a little more cautious.'

'That's one of the things I wanna ask you: just how cautious do I have to be?'

'I don't understand the question.'

'How much can I tell her?'

'As little as possible but as much as you have to.'

'That's some help, that is,' said Christy.

'What more do you require?'

'Clear guidelines,' said Christy. 'For one thing, pretty soon she's gonna want to know how you intend to ship the money out of the country.'

'That's up to her.'

'I think you've lost the thread, Marzie, old boy,' said Christy. 'It *isn't* up to her. You can't have it both ways. If you intend to skin her of all her money the least you can do is *pretend* to co-operate while you're doing it.'

'Ah, yes,' Marzipan said. 'Technically it's called creating dependency.'

'Call it what the hell you like,' said Christy. 'Soon, real soon, you'll have to tell me what's going on and trust me to take it from there.'

There were several seconds of silence on the line. Christy, leaning against the wall in Polly's hallway, could almost hear Marzipan's brain ticking.

At length, Marzipan said, 'You do have a point.'

'I know I do,' said Christy.

'I'll give the matter my consideration.'

'What you mean,' said Christy, 'is you'll have to consult your superiors. Who are your superiors, Marzie? How far up the heap does this thing go?'

'I'll get back to you.'

'How?' said Christy.

'By letter.'

'I guess you have her address.'

'And I,' said Marzipan, 'I *guess* you have more parts of your anatomy than your feet under her table.'

'Oh nasty!' said Christy. 'Look, don't send letters to this address. For someone as addicted to caution as you are, letters are a giveaway. *I'll* call *you*, all right?'

'All right,' said Marzipan, and rather huffily, Christy thought, hung up.

The quarrel had nothing much to do with Christy Cameron or the *Brockway's* photograph or even Babs's frustration at being unable to visit her sick children.

She spent much time in the office writing letters and wrapping up little parcels of sweets and comics to send them. Archie uttered not a word of reprimand and even donated several bars of chocolate to add to the packets. Archie, it seemed, had changed his tune about the offspring of working mothers, though he pretended he was only being nice because he valued Babs's contribution to the production war and didn't want to have to break in another assistant.

In Raines Drive, however, things were less serene and Jackie a good deal less than co-operative. His unexpected arrival had completely disrupted Babs's routine and his insistence that she spend all her time with him seemed unreasonable. She couldn't make him understand that she had a life of her own now and that, in eight or nine days, he would be gone and all she would be left with was the life she had created for herself. It was only when she refused to trail across town to the Gorbals to visit his mother, however, that Jackie lost his temper and accused her of being a snob and a selfish cow.

She might have agreed with him save for the fact that she knew she couldn't give Jackie what he really wanted.

He wanted everything back the way it had been before the war, before Dominic had flown the coop, before he'd lost the motoring salon. He wanted her to be the way she'd been when they'd been living in squalor off the Calcutta Road. He wanted her to pretend that he was cock of the walk again, a big fish in a small pond, a flash Harry with cash in his pocket, not just a good competent mechanic with a wife and kids to support.

'Have you seen her lately?'

'Who?'

'My mother.'

'No, Jackie, I haven't.'

'Why not?'

'I haven't had time.'

'Half an hour away on the tram an' you haven't had time.'

How could she explain that she feared the Hallop influence on her children and wouldn't risk letting old Ma Hallop into her life again. When she did take the children to visit Gran and Grandpa Hallop she was greeted with sly and greasy indifference. The children hated the tenement in Lavender Court. Even Angus was intimidated by the bony old woman with her stale smell and wheedling ways, and the girls were frightened of the old man, reeking of beer, who sprawled like a hog on the chair by the fire with his trousers unbuttoned.

'Your mother never comes to visit us,' said Babs.

'She's an old woman.'

'Not that old,' said Babs.

'She's got nobody t' look after her.'

'She's got your father an' the girls, your sisters.'

'They don't care.'

'Well, heck, Jackie, if they don't care why should I?'

'God, but you're a cold-hearted bitch.'

'I'm not going to Lavender Court, an' that's flat.'

'Then I'll take April on the bike an'—'

'Damned if you will.'

'Who's gonna stop me?'

'Not the bike, Jackie, please.'

'Aw right then, on the tram.'

'I – I don't think April will want to go.'

'She's a kid. She'll do what she's told.'

'She won't want to miss a day at nursery.'

'She'll come for a ride on the tram wi' her dad?'

'No, Jackie, she won't.'

'Are you tellin' me I can't take ma daughter to see her gran?' Jackie cried. 'Jesus Christ! What kind of a homecomin' is this? What kind of a wife have you turned into? Nothin's the way I thought it'd be.'

'It's the chickenpox . . .'

'Chickenpox, bloody chickenpox,' Jackie shouted at the top of his voice. 'It's got nothin' to do with chickenpox. It's you, you an' – an' everyone else.'

Then he began to call her names, all sorts of filthy names and though it was late in the evening and raining, he rushed through the kitchen into the garden and, a minute or so later, roared away into the darkness on his motorbike and didn't come back that night.

'Is this your office?' Polly asked. 'If it is, I don't think much of it.'

'It isn't my office,' Kenny told her. 'It's an interview room.'

'Where you beat the truth out of suspects?'

'What do you want, Polly?'

'I shouldn't really have come here, should I?'

'No,' Kenny said. 'You shouldn't.'

'I didn't want to bother you at the flat.'

'I'm seldom there,' said Kenny.

'How is Rosie, by the way?'

'She's still not well,' Kenny said. 'She works too hard.'

'Has she been to see a doctor?'

'Won't go. Refuses point-blank.'

Polly nodded. 'Rosie's always been stubborn.'

'Polly, I don't have much time at my disposal.'

'Nor do I,' said Polly. 'I just thought I'd pop in to inform you that I am now living with the enemy or, rather, that the enemy is living with me.'

'Plain English, please.'

'I've taken in the American. Rosie *will* be scandalised.'

'Has she reason to be?'

'God, not you too, Kenneth. I thought you had more sense.'

The room was very small and very dirty. Polly was surprised at the lack of hygiene. Scraps of food and cigarette ends lay on the floor under the scarred table and an abandoned bottle of milk sprouted green mould on the window ledge. She could see nothing from the window, not even sky.

'I've taken him in,' Polly said, 'as an emergency measure and on a temporary basis only because Jackie turned up out of the blue. No,' she held up her hand, 'it's not what you think, Kenneth. Our Jackie hasn't deserted. He's being shipped out in a week's time and this is official leave.'

Kenny lay back in one of the two hard wooden chairs with which the room was furnished. He wore a bulky wool overcoat buttoned up to the throat, and looked, Polly thought, not only cold but exhausted. He surveyed her with what appeared to be a complete lack of interest and she wondered for a moment if he was actually in the process of falling asleep.

She had always felt herself superior to the young policeman but here in the heart of his territory she was much less sure of herself.

'Does Jackie know where he's being sent?' Kenny said.

'North Africa, probably.'

'Poor bastard!'

'You don't envy him then?'

'I do not.' Kenny drew in his legs and propped an elbow on the table. 'Did Cameron send you here?'

Surprised by the question, Polly said, 'No. Why?'

'Because Cameron is just the point man on something big.'

'Point man?'

'The tip of an iceberg,' said Kenny MacGregor. 'Everyone's treading cautiously at the moment. US Military Intelligence is pretty much a closed shop. They're disinclined to trust us after the débâcle in France, though some sort of uneasy alliance has been forged between the chaps in Whitehall. I'm not cleared to receive field intelligence unless it relates to Irish Republican activity or illegal arms dealing, so I can't tell you much more than that.'

'And even if you could, you probably wouldn't?'

'I certainly wouldn't,' Kenny said.

'Because I'm married to Dominic Manone?'

'That's it.'

'And you aren't really nice Uncle Kenny, are you?'

'No.'

'Do I have to be careful of you too?'

'Yes, Polly, you do.'

'All right,' Polly said. 'I appreciate your candour. One last question and then I'll go. Who do I have to watch out for, who can do me most harm – Dominic or Christy Cameron?'

'It's too early to say.'

'Are you telling me I'm out on a limb?'

Kenny hoisted himself from the chair, walked around the table and opened the door. 'You'll have to go now, Polly.'

'Wait,' she said. 'Are you trying to tell me that I have to make the running on my own?'

'I'm not telling you anything.'

Polly rose, straightened her skirt, adjusted her hat and followed him out into the corridor. He walked a half-step ahead of her and she noticed that the long, steady stride of the beat constable had been replaced by a shambling gait that made her brother-in-law seem furtive.

He stopped at the head of the stairs and looked down the spiral of the banister rail, down at clerks and uniformed officers visible on the landings below, then he turned, put a hand on her arm and drew her close.

'Hughes,' he said softly. 'I'd watch out for Hughes, if I were you.'

'Fin, but—'

'Goodbye, Polly. I'm sure you can find your own way out.'

'Yes, I'm sure I can,' said Polly, and with more bewilderment than gratitude, kissed him quickly on the cheek and hurried downstairs to the street.

He felt like a heel, a real piece of low-life, but that didn't stop him prowling through the house. He started on the top floor and worked his way down, room by room, consoled by the thought that Polly would expect nothing less of a spy. He hadn't been trained in the so-called art of spying, of course. He had been shoved into the field with only his wits and a contact number to guide him and wasn't even sure that Marzipan and Jamie were working towards the same end.

Funding the Italian Resistance? Yeah, right! He'd watched the Polish Resistance in action and had been less impressed by their organisational skills than by their courage. Italian soldiers, sailors and airmen weren't shedding their blood because they despised Mussolini, however, or because the Nazis were prodding their asses with bayonets. He'd seen for himself the situation in Spain. He knew why Franco had so far refused to declare for Hitler. Spain was flat broke and gripped by famine, and needed to maintain trading relations with Britain, Canada and the USA. When it came to Italy, though, he was forced to rely on what Jamie had told him and for that reason felt that he was no better than a spear-carrier standing at the back of a very big, very crowded stage.

Goddamn it, he was a seasoned photojournalist who'd been in some pretty rough spots so what the hell was he doing in an empty house in Scotland rifling through a lady's drawers? What secrets did he hope to uncover in Polly's closets that would help the Allies win the war?

The lady's drawers, though, did contain a few surprises.

First off there was the matter of the passports.

Mrs Manone had two of the precious things.

They were hidden where you'd least expect to find them, not tucked under her frillies in the master bedroom or in a shoebox on the top shelf of a closet. They were up in the nursery suite, or what had once been the nursery suite. Christy was surprised to find the rooms untouched since that morning sixteen months ago when Manone had lifted his kids from their beds and carried them off to New York.

The beds had been made in both the little bedrooms and in the nanny's room – Patricia's room – too.

Clean sheets, pillows plumped, windows unmarred by blackout material; pretty curtains printed with goldfish and mermaids, let in a flood of daylight. Toy boxes, books, a doll's house, teddy bears, a rank of lead soldiers, a miniature fire truck, the low, square table in the centre of the playroom still set with cups and plates. All that seemed to be missing was buttered bread and strawberry jam – and the kids themselves, of course.

In the smaller of the toy boxes were jigsaws, comic papers, colouring books, a paint box all dried out, and, right at the bottom, a pale blue stationery box fastened with a cute blue ribbon.

Kneeling, Christy fished out the stationery box and untied the ribbon.

At that precise moment, he reckoned he knew how Babs must have felt when she found the photographs of Polly's kids in his bag: a feeling of guilt justified, of minor misdemeanours excused. He wondered if Babs had sat back on her heels and let out a grunt of satisfaction too.

The passports had never been used. One was date-stamped June 1937 and might, Christy reckoned, be obsolete. The other was new issue, a wartime special with the blind stamp of a government department impressed on the cover. He held it to the light and read the blood-red letters stamped across the top of the page: 'Travel Approved'.

Travel where? Approved by whom?

He had no idea, just a vague suspicion that the lawyer Hughes might have supplied Polly with the valuable document in case he and she ever had to make a break for it.

He looked at the photograph.

Poor lighting had leeched the shadows from her face and her mouth was prominent, lip rouge pure black as if it had been inked in afterwards. She had longer hair and a startled, wide-eyed expression that made her appear almost childishly naïve. He studied the photograph for several seconds then put the passports back in the stationery box and examined the rest of the papers.

Letters, letters from her children, from Stuart and Ishbel, postcards of New York landmarks with polite pencilled greetings on the back. No suggestion of codes or secret messages and nary a mention of Patricia or of Jamie, which indicated either unusual juvenile discretion or censorship on Manone's part.

There was no correspondence from Manone hidden in the

stationery box or the nursery or, so far as Christy could discover, anywhere in the house. And only when he'd finished his search did it dawn on him that what he'd really been seeking in the lady's drawers was evidence of duplicity, some shred of proof that Manone was playing the US State Department for a sucker, and that Polly was part of it. If she was, she was playing it clever, too clever for a dim-witted, half-baked amateur to stumble on at his first fumbling attempt.

No, if he wanted to catch Polly out he would have to make her trust him enough to be careless or – and the thought made him wince – convince her that he loved her and that come hell or high water, he wouldn't let her down.

'Oh, for God's sweet sake, Polly,' Fin Hughes said, 'don't tell me you're falling for this chap?'

'I'm not that much of a fool.'

'Oh, you are, you are,' Fin said. 'You may not care to admit it but you're just like all the rest.'

'The rest of what?'

'Women, snuggling up to any chap who gives you a bit of attention.'

'Is that why I "snuggled up" to you?'

'Of course it is,' Fin said, 'in addition to the fact that I represent a degree of stability in troubled times. I also know where the bodies are buried.'

Polly glanced up sharply. 'Bodies?'

'Purely a figure of speech. Are you really giving me the heave-ho?'

'You have the audacity to criticise women and yet you can stand there and ask me a daft question like that. Dear God, Fin, all I said was that it might not be a good idea to pop over on Saturday night because Christy Cameron is staying at my house temporarily. Do you hear me – *tem-por-arily.*'

'I'm not deaf.'

'Sometimes I wonder,' Polly said.

'Where's he sleeping?'

'In my bed.'

The defence of civil liberties had earned Fin a small fortune in the months since emergency legislation had been introduced. He had been quick to realise that trade union officials would read threat in the small print of the acts, would vigorously resist any government censorship on union meetings and would regard the new anti-strike laws merely as weapons in the eternal struggle of Labour against Capital. In rational argument Polly couldn't hope to get the better of him but she possessed persuasive powers of another kind and did not hesitate to use them.

'He sleeps in my bed and I sleep downstairs.'

'Tell you what,' Fin said, 'I'll lob him a fiver and he can take himself off to a top-class hotel for the weekend.'

'Now you're just being silly.'

'How long will he stay with you?'

'I'm not sure, probably until Jackie goes back to his unit.'

'And then you expect him just to pack his little bag and trot meekly back to your sister's house?'

'I don't see why not.'

'Because by that time you and he . . . Oh, never mind,' Fin said.

He had come stalking into her office at half-past three still clad in formal morning dress. Polly had to admit that he looked mighty impressive. She had seen him naked just once too often, however, and no man, even one at the peak of his profession, could maintain an air of authority when you'd watched him crouch in a few inches of tepid water in a bathtub or wrestle for his share of the quilt in a bedroom as cold as a tomb.

She had been writing when he'd entered, compiling a first rough draft of holdings she might be able to liquidate without excessive interference. Folders lay on her desk, box-files stacked by her chair.

Fin had spotted them immediately.

'What are you doing, Polly? What *are* you doing?'

'A little basic arithmetic, that's all.' She strove not to appear nervous. 'I'm just curious as to what I'm currently worth.'

'To me,' Fin said without warmth, 'a very great deal.'

'Thank you,' Polly said. 'Now what's that in pounds, shillings and pence?'

He came over to the desk and perched on it, blotting out light from the window. He looked so intimidatingly severe that she was surprised when he leaned over the folders, snared her chin with one hand and kissed her.

'Immeasurable,' he said. 'Quite immeasurable.' He drew back, eyeing her all the while. 'Give me a couple of hours and I'll take you to dinner.'

'I can't,' Polly said.

She expected him to wax sarcastic or at least ask her to explain why but he was too shrewd to fall into that trap. He stood up, stretched his arms above his head and performed a little knee-bending exercise, then said, 'Cameron's not blackmailing you, by any chance, is he?'

'Blackmailing me?' Polly laughed shakily. 'Of course he's not blackmailing me. Whatever put that idea into your head?'

Fin shrugged. 'He's a photographer. I thought perhaps . . .'

'That because he photographed Babs, he also has designs on me?' She laughed again, even less convincingly. 'You've been reading that Raymond Chandler novel again, haven't you, the one you said was depraved?'

'If you need cash,' Fin said, 'ask me.'

'I am asking you.'

'How much do you need, Polly?'

'A very great deal.'

'For him, isn't it? For Christy Cameron?'

'No, for Dominic.'

Fin nodded, unsurprised. 'Why does Dominic want his money now? Does he think Britain is going under?'

'I've no idea what Dom wants it for,' Polly lied. 'I'm not even sure he wants it all. He has merely requested a tally.'

'Through this Cameron chap?'

'Yes.'

'A letter, a cable—'

'Might be intercepted.'

'That's true.'

'If you recall,' Polly said, 'you're the one who suggested I wait for Christy to come to me. Well, he did, and now we know what he wants, or at least we *think* we know what he wants. It isn't me, darling. He has no interest in me whatsoever. He's after money, money that Dominic feels he has claim to – which, I suppose, he has.'

She hadn't forgotten Kenny's parting words, his warning.

She would give Fin only a few pieces of the puzzle and only because she couldn't advance without him. She wished that Dom's accountant, Victor Shadwell, had still been hale and hearty for she had always trusted Victor. But he was an old man now, very frail and rather inclined to wander mentally. She really was out on a limb with no one to support her or catch her if she tumbled, not Fin, not Dom, not Kenny MacGregor and most certainly not Christy, the man she was falling in love with, who, for all his charm, might turn out to be more of a rotter than any of them.

'Selling stock at this time,' Fin said, 'is highly unwise.'

'I'm well aware of that and so, I suspect, is Dominic.'

'You know, of course,' Fin said, 'that all your holdings are registered and that your American dollar securities cannot be transferred? Have you seen the list of securities that the Treasury can call up at any time?'

'I don't believe I have,' said Polly.

'Massive,' said Fin, 'massive and all-inclusive.'

'Do you mean we can't sell anything at all?'

Fin hesitated before answering. 'Not quite. Regulations state that the prices paid for securities taken over shall be not less than their market value.'

'Who sets the rating?'

'The Treasury.'

'Based on what?'

'The sterling equivalent of dollar quotations on the New York or Montreal stock exchange on the day of call-up.'

'What if we choose to sell securities before they are taken over?'

'We, as holders, are free to seek permission so to do.'

Polly put a hand to her brow. 'It's all very complicated.'

'Of course it is,' Fin said. 'That's why you have me.'

'Our assets—'

'What assets?'

'The lease on the warehouse,' Polly said. 'We could sell the lease on the warehouse. Lincoln Stephens are desperate to buy the place, are they not, and the original agreement will expire in – what – six months' time?'

'Eight,' said Fin. 'I thought you said you'd never sell the warehouse?'

'No, I said I would hold on to it until Dominic came back.'

'I see. Now you're not so sure that Dominic will come back.'

Hand to brow once more, Polly said, 'I don't know what to think.'

Fin fashioned a courtly little bow. 'Madam, I am your servant,' he said. 'I am paid to do your thinking for you. So, if Dominic is in a bind regarding cash flow, allow me to see what can be done to raise the wind without selling off your assets or securities.'

'By borrowing, do you mean?'

'That is a possibility.'

'Really?'

'Really,' said Fin.

'At what rate of interest?'

'Obviously that remains to be seen,' said Fin. 'Now are you sure I can't treat you to an early dinner? There's a rumour going about that the Caledonia Club has meat on the menu; beef, I believe, not horse. What do you say, old Polly, shall we sally forth and dine in solemn state?'

And in spite of her desire to hurry home to Christy, Polly forced a feeble smile and said, 'Why not?'

No matter how Babs tried to kid herself that Jackie would come back in his own good time, when she got in from work she was dismayed to discover that he still hadn't returned. Before she removed April's coat and hat, she hurried outside to check that the motorbike was still missing, for she had a sudden dreadful feeling that poor Jackie might be lying mangled on a slab in the Southern General or, even worse, jiving the night away with some tart he'd picked up at the Palais.

'Where's Christy?' April asked for the umpteenth time.

'I told you, he's staying with Auntie Polly.'

'Is Daddy staying with Auntie Polly too?'

'No, honey, he's – he's gone to see Grandma.'

'Grandma Lizzie?'

'Grandma Hallop.'

'Oh!' said April. 'Poor Daddy.'

Babs strove to reassure herself that Jackie had probably gone drinking with his old man or one of his sisters' husbands and was having the time of his life; but Jackie had never been much of a drinking man and had no more time for his sisters, or their husbands, than she did.

She fried Spam, made chips, warmed up a tin of beans, fed herself and her daughter, washed up, lit the fire in the living room, bathed April and got her ready for bed. While April played on the rug in front of the fire, she rushed through a washing and hung clothes – Jackie's as well as April's – on the kitchen pulley, after which she went into the living room, sat April on her knee and read her a story from an old *Girl's Crystal Annual*, for April was fascinated by the mischief that passed for adventure before schoolgirls wore tin hats and siren suits and captured German spies in the classroom.

By half-past eight April was almost asleep. She made no protest when Babs carried her through to bed. She settled her head on the pillow, fluttered her eyelashes, murmured something that may have been 'Good night' and sank instantly down into that unaffected place where little children go in search of dreams. Babs returned to the living room, poured herself a drink, lay back in the big armchair and closed her eyes.

She was too tense to fall asleep, too worried to dream. She thought of Christy seated with Polly in the spacious basement kitchen in Manor Park, of how much fun he would have with Polly and how Polly would flirt with him in the ladylike manner that she, Babs, had never been able to emulate. She thought of Jackie in his khaki greatcoat and stiff, constricting webbing and how stricken he'd been when he'd caught her with Christy. Drifting off now, she thought of Archie Harding peering at the parrot, Skipper, though the bars of a gilded cage while he lectured it on the value of industry in time of war.

Then she opened her eyes and sat up.

At first she thought the bombers had come again, then she realised it was only the sound of Jackie's motorcycle and a minute or two later he clumped into the living room without a word of greeting or apology.

He wore army-issue trousers, stockings and boots and

the big ragged sweater he sported only when he rode the Excelsior. His hair, stiff with moist night air, stuck up like a halo around his head. His nose and ears were red and she could see the imprint of the goggles on his cheeks. There was no rage in him now, however, no trace of anger. He tugged off his gloves with his teeth and spread his fingers out to the flickering flames of the fire.

'Well,' he said, 'that was a bloody waste o' time.'

'Didn't you see your mother?'

'Aw yeah, I saw her all right.' Jackie seated himself on the matching armchair and began to unlace his boots. 'She's got herself a job.'

'A job?'

'Aye, up at the steelworks.'

'Your mother's a steelworker?'

'Naw, naw, in the canteen. She loves it there. She does the bloody nightshift every time she's asked. Never been chirpier, never had more money comin' in. Jeeze, I hardly recognised her, all dolled up. Thinks she's a soddin' glamour puss just because the guys chat her up.'

Babs tried not to laugh at the notion of pint-sized Mrs Hallop being chatted up by anyone.

Head down, his fingers making hard work of his muddy bootlaces, Jackie went on, 'She never even gave me ma dinner.'

'Where's the old man these days? Still on the railway?'

'Transport officer, that's what he calls himself. Sixty-one years old, pickled in draught heavy, an' some idiot upstairs makes him responsible for supervisin' the shipment o' danger-ous freight.' Jackie seemed stunned by the rise in his family's fortunes. 'I never knew none o' this. Not one o' the buggers thought t' drop me a line tellin' me what was goin' on. Did you not know, Babs, what was happenin' over there?'

'Nope, it's all news to me,' Babs said.

She was relieved that he had come back to her, that disappointment had replaced anger and that her indiscretions had been swallowed up by the Hallops' indifference to their soldier son.

'Went round to the sister's. She's out at the bloody fire station, mannin' the telephones. Her hubby's at home, pressin' his ARP uniform an' actin' like he was winnin' the war single-handed. The tosser couldn't even spare five minutes for to come out for a pint.'

'So where have you been all night?'

Jackie abandoned the bootlaces. He flopped back in the armchair and arched his arms over his head the way Angus did when he was about to sulk. 'I drove down to Govan to see if I could get into the Rowin' Club. Remember the Rowin' Club, Dominic's hideout? By God, the times we had there.'

'Jackie . . .'

'I know, I know. It's not the Rowin' Club any more.'

'It's for servicemen, for sweethearts,' Babs said, frowning. 'Is that where you were all night, Jackie?'

'Fat bloody chance!' He paused, sighed loudly, then confessed. 'They wouldn't let me in. Two big bruisers wi' dog collars on – Christians, some Christians! – said I wasn't bony fleddy.'

'Bony fleddy?'

'Aye, like in Latin, like bloody RCs.'

'*Bona fide.*' Babs had acquired an accurate pronunciation from Archie. 'Didn't you tell them you were a soldier?'

'Never had my paybook nor ID on me.'

'Oh, Jackie.' She put the whisky glass down on the carpet and kneeled before him. 'Oh, Jackie, what a slap in the face that was.'

'Wasn't it, but? I told them I'd be fightin' the Eyeties eyeball to eyeball when they were singin' carols round the manger, but they never took no heed. I bought a fish supper an' went back home – I mean to Ma's house. He was out an' she never came in until half-past one, then all she wanted to talk about was what this guy had said to her an' what that guy had done – that, an' our Dennis. Now he's a real hero, our bloody Dennis, even though he's in the Fleet Air Arm. Know why? Because he's been blown up twice.'

'I didn't know that,' said Babs, alarmed. 'Is he all right?'

'Don't you start.'

'No, Jackie, is he all right, really?'

'His wife runs off wi' another man, does that matter? Aw naw, all that matters is, he's been twice in the drink.' Jackie craned forward and blinked as if he were seeing her for the first time. 'Aye, aye, Dennis's okay. Got fished out without a scratch on him. But he's the hero, not me, an' not our Billy neither. Billy's up in Lossiemouth guardin' a big gun or somethin'. Safe as bloody houses in the Highlands. Maybe I'll have to get blown sky high before anybody round here'll take me seriously.'

'Jackie, oh, Jackie.'

Babs leaned against his knees, pressing her breast on his shins and when that seemed to have no effect on his despondent mood, bent down and began to unpick his laces. She tugged off one boot then another and placed them neatly on the hearthstone. She took his right foot in both hands and kneaded the coarse damp woollen stocking as if she were trying to wring it dry.

'Slept in my old bed,' Jackie said. 'First time I ever had the bloody thing to myself. Felt funny wi' no bugger kickin' me or fartin' in ma face.' He gave a wry chuckle. 'Slept for hours, though, bloody hours an' hours, just the way I used to when I was a kid.'

'Why didn't you come home?'

'I didn't think I was welcome here.'

'This is me, this is your house. You belong here.'

'I shouldn't have said all those bad things.'

'Forgotten, all forgotten.'

He nodded gravely. 'Drove over to Blackstone again this afternoon. Saw the kids through the window. Old Dawlish wouldn't let them come near me, though.'

'They're still infectious.'

'Aye, aye, I know.'

'Did you do tricks for Angus on the bike?'

'I did, near jiggered ma backside doin' them, an' all.'

'I take it you saw the pig?'

'Aye, I saw the pig.' Another wry chuckle. 'Angus fair dotes on yon pig, doesn't he? I'm thinkin' we'll need to build a sty in the back green for Ron when the war's over an' the kids come home for good.'

'When you come home for good.'

'Aye,' Jackie sighed, softly this time, 'when I come home.'

'Well, it wasn't a wasted day after all, not really,' said Babs. 'At least you got to see the kids again an' they got to see you.'

'It's not the same, but, is it?'

She sagged against him, head on his knee.

'No, darlin',' she said. 'It's not the same.'

Then she got up and went out into the bedroom.

She lifted April gently, wrapped her in the softest blanket, carried her through to the living room and put her down into Jackie's arms.

He looked up, surprised.

April, her eyes barely open, looked up too. 'Daddy,' she murmured, then snuggled in against him and went straight back to sleep.

And that was how Babs would remember him, not dancing, not ranting, not idling away his days, not even roaring up Raines Drive on the big Excelsior Manxman, but seated in the armchair by the fireside with his little daughter sleeping soundly in his arms.

'Okay?' Babs said.

'Okay,' said Jackie, and watched her go off to unearth the pale peach housecoat that he had given her one Christmas, long ago.

11

'The Wife is Always the Last to Know': there it was in black and white, staring up, slightly bloodied, from under the lamb chops that Mr Maitland, the Co-op butcher, had doled out that morning. Lizzie lifted away the chops, smoothed the wrinkled newspaper on the draining board and read the not-very-sensational report on marital infidelity from first word to last.

She found it difficult to identify with any of the case histories and certainly couldn't imagine Bernard consorting with the sort of women who were depicted in the blurry photographs, sleek, blonde girls with big chests and long legs who, in spite of the little strips of Elastoplast that masked their eyes, looked more like film stars than prostitutes. Polly had had more than her fair share of men friends and Babs had had her photograph in *Brockway's Illustrated Weekly*; Lizzie wondered if allowing your photograph to be printed in a newspaper automatically meant you were sliding downhill into – what did the article call it? – 'a morass of moral depravity'. Somehow she doubted it.

She placed the lamb chops on a saucer and clapped a bowl over them, made herself a cup of tea and, still in her overcoat and hat, read through the blood-stained article once more.

She had no idea what sort of temptations Bernard might be encountering out at Breslin. He was very popular with women. He had reached an age when men are at their best and women have already begun to slide downhill. Unlike the

wives in the newspaper article Lizzie yearned not for what she
had lost but for what was hers by right and which, without her
knowing how or why, seemed to be slipping away from her.

'Rubbish!' Bernard would have told her if she'd ever
expressed her fears outright. 'Absolute rubbish!'

Until recently she would have believed him and been
soothed but now that doubt had entered her thinking there
was no keeping it at bay.

Whenever he arrived home late or popped out to attend
yet another neighbourhood meeting, Lizzie wondered if some
adoring young thing like Irene Milligan was plotting to lure
him away from her, someone fresher, someone not lack-
ing in energy and confidence, someone without wrinkles,
fat and falling hair, who would drag her poor unprotesting Bernard down into the morass of depravity and steal
him away.

Bernard slipped on his overcoat and kissed her cheek.

Lizzie said, 'Are you goin' out again?'

'It's business, Lizzie, council business.'

'On Sunday afternoon. Is it a meetin'?'

'No, I'm helping a – a family move house.'

'Can nobody else do it?'

'It's my placement, my responsibility. I have to be there.'

'Where?'

'Breslin. Well – near Breslin.'

He looked just the same as he'd done when he'd come in
from church shortly after noon, shaved and smooth, his hair
slicked down. He looked the same, he smelled the same and
yet there was something different about him.

'Will you be home for your dinner?'

'I'll try my best, but,' Bernard said, 'no guarantees.'

'I'll keep something hot.'

'Yes,' he said, 'you do that.' Then he went out by the front door, whistling a jaunty little hymn tune more suited to Easter than Christmas.

On Saturday evening instead of trotting round to Raines Drive to pay her respects to her brother-in-law, Polly had gone to the pictures with Christy. They had queued for the best part of an hour to see Gary Cooper and Ray Milland behaving nobly in *Beau Geste*, and afterwards had strolled along Paisley Road eating fish suppers and laughing.

Home again, Polly had drunk one gin and tonic to Christy's three whiskies and had kissed him before she'd gone to bed. During all the time they had spent together Christy hadn't once mentioned Fin Hughes and by Sunday morning Polly had given up waiting for the axe to fall.

The thin grey rain had eased not at all and the garden was drowned in fine grey mist; a winter Sunday, still and timeless, church bells silenced by the war. The kitchen below stairs was warmed by the odours of fried bacon, coffee and cigarette smoke. The Sunday newspapers that Christy had fetched from a corner shop on the far side of the park were scattered on the table and Polly, revelling in idleness, lolled about in her dressing gown and pom-pom slippers as if she had no intention of dressing at all that day.

Christy knew nothing of her past beyond the few scant facts his masters had provided and the half-baked gossip he had picked up from Babs.

She wanted him to ask about Dominic, if she had ever loved him, if Dominic had treated her well. For years she had scorned the mundane values by which others lived and had taken a lover, a dangerous lover, Tony Lombard. When Tony had deserted her she had taken up with Fin Hughes only because she preferred to trust an enemy rather than a friend. But now, suddenly, she was free of constraint, free to give everything away – the empty house, the ill-wrought fortune, the motorcar, her fine clothes, her body, even her heart.

'Christy,' she said, 'whatever you want, whatever you need, whatever you've been told to do, I'll help you if I can.'

He stared at her solemnly, almost sorrowfully, then reached across the table, pinched the collar of her dressing gown between forefinger and thumb and tugged it down. He took the folds in both fists and pulled them apart.

He was rough like Tony and gentle like Dominic, less practised and calculating than Fin, but when he slid his hands inside her pyjama top and placed them on her breasts she felt the dominating force of his self-assurance.

Balanced awkwardly on the kitchen chair, she leaned forward so that he could peel down the garment and kiss her but when, out of habit, she tried to push her tongue into his mouth, he resisted, pressing his lips together. And Polly thought: he knows, he knows what it means and how it will change things and what I'm offering him and he will take it because that's the sort of man he is.

She was wet now and waited not patiently but passively for him to kiss her again. When he did, she knew why he wouldn't let her work her tongue into his mouth and pretend that this unromantic intimacy wasn't love and that what would happen next wasn't as natural and mundane as love itself.

'Do you want to go upstairs,' he asked in a thick little whisper, 'or is this not a proper time?'

'No,' she heard herself say, 'this is a proper time. Yes, this is the time.'

The doorbell rang.

They stared at each other.

Christy blew out his cheeks and said, 'Seems not.'

'Ignore it,' Polly told him. 'Whoever it is, they'll go away.'

'Do you want them to go away?'

'Yes, I do.'

'What if it's Babs?'

'What if it is?'

'She'll jump to the wrong conclusions.'

Polly laughed wryly. 'The *wrong* conclusions?'

The doorbell continued to ring, its persistence jarring in the calm half-light of the winter forenoon.

'All right,' said Polly. 'Stay right here. Don't move.'

She hurried upstairs to the hall and opened the door.

Fin stood on the top step, a glove in his mouth, his big bare forefinger thrust into the bell push. When he saw her he removed the glove from his mouth and said, 'Ah, you're in. Did I waken you?'

'Fin,' Polly said, 'what do you want at this hour?'

'I come on a mission of mercy.' Fin waved an arm towards the drive. 'Sorry if it isn't convenient but it isn't easy to find glass, let alone glaziers, these days and you have to take it when you can get it.'

Clutching her dressing gown about her, Polly peeped outside.

Fin's Vauxhall was parked close to the house. Behind it was a small blue-painted van with pine-wood framing bolted to its side. In the frame, padded with straw and canvas, were several large sheets of glass. Leaning against the bonnet of the van were two men, one old, one very young, both dressed in brown overalls and cloth caps.

'The window?' Fin said, raising an eyebrow. 'In the lounge?'

'Yes,' said Polly. 'The window, of course.'

'Shouldn't take long,' said Fin. 'Half an hour or so then you can go back to what you were doing when I so rudely interrupted you.'

'You'd best come in,' Polly said.

Fin signalled to the workmen, who immediately began to tease a pane of glass from the padded frame. Then, leaning close to Polly, he said, 'Is he here?'

'Yes.'

'Is he up?'

'Of course,' Polly said. 'We're having breakfast.'

'Breakfast? Why, it's almost lunch time.'

'Not in this household, it's not,' said Polly and, stepping back, allowed Fin and his little team of workmen to enter the hall.

On Sunday mornings Margaret Dawlish bathed, trimmed her nails and hair and put on a tailored suit, a black swagger coat and the sort of high-crowned hat that never went out of fashion.

If it hadn't been for the floppy rubber boots Dougie might have been tempted to go down on one knee and request her hand in marriage there and then, but she carried her shoes in an oilskin bag to change at the end of the track and hid the Wellingtons in a clump of gorse to collect on her return from church.

Dougie's only connection with church was to deliver Babs's children to afternoon Sunday School. He didn't know if the simple preaching of God's eternal love made any impression on his young charges and pointedly refrained from engaging in theological discussion with June who, unlike her sister and brother, seemed to take the whole thing seriously.

Now and then Dougie was tempted to remind June that the God who made the sun to shine, who shaped the little lambs and clad the lilies of the field was precisely the same God who created the germs that gave you chickenpox and influenza but, of course, he did nothing of the sort, for however much tragedy and booze had destroyed his personal belief in the divine, he envied the young their innocence and would do nothing to undermine it.

He tapped a finger gently on Angus's breastbone. 'I'll be gone for a quarter of an hour, so stay right where you are, an' make sure your sisters stay right where they are too. Got me?'

'What if the house catches fire?'

'The house won't catch fire.'

'What if it does, though?'

'Then you'll have t' carry your sisters out into the yard,' said Dougie, 'but make sure you get the cat out first.'

Angus laughed. He was feeling better. Boric acid had cooled the itch to the point where it bothered him hardly at all. The bed was covered in comics, books and toffee papers, and the wireless set that Dougie had lugged upstairs droned out some dreary English church service in the girls' room next door.

'Are we not going to Sunday School?'

'Not today,' said Dougie.

'What about the Christmas party?'

'We'll have t' see about the Christmas party,' said Dougie.

'I want to see Santa.'

'Santa!'

'I know it's only Miss White wearin' a beard, but it's good for a laugh.'

Dougie sighed.

Angus said, 'Do you think Mum'll come today?'

'I doubt it, son. Maybe next weekend.'

'What about Dad?'

'Possibly,' Dougie said.

'If Dad hasn't any petrol left for the bike maybe Auntie Polly'll bring him over in the motorcar with Mr Cameron.'

'Maybe she will,' said Dougie. 'Look, I'm walkin' Miss Dawlish—'

'Down to the road,' said Angus. 'Stay put. Message received loud an' clear, Admiral.'

'Admiral!' Dougie muttered and, shaking his head, went downstairs.

Margaret and he had barely left the shelter of the yard

before she took his arm, something she had never done before.

'What's wrong,' Dougie said. 'Are the knees bad today?'

'My knees are my own business,' Margaret said. 'Anyway, it's not my knees that are bothering me. It's that American chap.'

'Why should he bother you?'

'What's he up to?'

'I don't think he's up to anything, nothin' that concerns us.'

'What concerns those children concerns me.'

Dougie said, 'Any business Christy Cameron might have wi' this family would hardly be likely to affect the children.'

'Polly's keen on him, is she not?'

'Is she? Can't say I noticed.'

'Take it from me, she's very keen on him,' said Margaret. 'Why hasn't she been to visit us lately?'

'Babs'll have warned her off.'

'I wonder what Jackie has to say about it.'

'Jackie's a man o' the world.'

'Hah!' said Margaret, scornfully.

For a woman she had a fair length of stride; it was all Dougie could do to match his step to hers. He glanced at her out of the side of his eyes. She had dusted her fiery cheeks with powder and defined her lips with lipstick. She didn't look at all mannish in her Sunday morning garb and he experienced an odd little tug of desire, an emotion so unfamiliar that he almost failed to recognise it for what it was.

'Don't you like the American?' Dougie said.

'I like him fine,' Margaret said.

'But,' said Dougie, 'you're wonderin' why Polly brought him here.'

'Rivalry between sisters,' Margaret said, by way of an answer, 'can be terribly destructive.'

'Rivalry?' said Dougie. 'You think they both fancy him?'

'I'm sure they do.'

'If you were younger . . .' Dougie paused, tactfully. 'I mean, if you were one of the Conway girls, would *you* fancy him?'

'Wouldn't I just?' said Margaret.

'Funny, I never thought you'd fancy anyone.'

'What do you mean by that?'

'I always had the impression you weren't much interested in men.'

'There are,' Margaret Dawlish said, 'men and men.'

Dougie was tempted to ask if she'd ever had a boyfriend or a lover, how she defined maleness, what made one man attractive and another repulsive and what category he fell into, if he fell into any category at all.

'They might be Barbara's children,' Margaret went on, 'but Polly pays the bills. If Polly were to do anything rash, or if Babs and she were to fall out . . .'

'Uh-huh!' Dougie said. 'You think we'd be left high an' dry.'

'Well, wouldn't we?'

'We'd struggle through somehow.'

'If she took away the farm . . .'

'She can't,' said Dougie.

'Why can't she?' said Margaret Dawlish.

'Polly doesn't own the farm,' Dougie said.

'Really? Who does then? Dominic?'

'I do.'

'You?'

'I thought you knew that, Margaret?'

'No, I most certainly did not know that.'

'So, there you are,' Dougie said smugly. 'You're not walkin' arm in arm with a mere caretaker; you're walkin' arm in arm with a landowner.'

'Well!' Margaret said. 'Well, well, well! How much land?'

'I sold the land.' Dougie immediately regretted his candour. 'Not all of it, though,' he added. 'I still have a few acres put by for a rainy day.'

'How many acres?' Margaret said.

Dougie smiled. 'Put it this way: more than enough for the two of us.'

'The two of us?'

'Us plus the kiddies, if Polly does decide to fly the coop.'

'Douglas, what are you suggesting?'

'I'm not suggestin' anythin',' Dougie said. 'I'm just puttin' your mind at rest, Margaret, that's all.'

'Hold me,' she said.

'Pardon?'

'Give me something to hold on to while I change into my shoes.'

'By all means,' said Dougie, and gallantly stuck out his hand.

'Polly,' Fin Hughes said, 'why don't you trot upstairs and make yourself decent while Mr Cameron and I exchange pleasantries?

'I wasn't aware that I wasn't decent,' Polly said.

'Well, you aren't,' Fin said. 'If not indecent, distracting, lounging about in that revealing bathrobe. What do you say, Mr Cameron? Don't you find the presence of this lovely lady *en déshabillé* just a tad distracting?'

Christy laughed and shook his head. 'Now that's what I'd call a loaded question, Mr Hughes.'

'Loaded? I don't understand.'

'Of course you do, Fin,' Polly said. 'You're not going to catch Christy out with such an obvious variation on the old "Have you stopped beating your wife?" trick. However, if the sight of me in a dressing gown offends your Presbyterian sensibilities, I will take myself upstairs. Christy will make you fresh coffee, or tea if you prefer it.'

'Coffee will do very nicely, thank you.'

Christy made no move to refill the pot, however, and watched Polly go out of the kitchen into the corridor without a word.

'Isn't she a treat?' Fin said after a pause.

'Yeah, she is.'

'You're a very fortunate fellow, you know.'

'Am I?' Christy said.

'Polly's the sort of person who keeps herself to herself as a rule,' Fin said. 'By which I mean that she doesn't distribute her favours lightly.' He lifted the coffee pot, shook it and dribbled a small quantity of black liquid into a cup. 'What are you doing here, really? Why are you hanging about Glasgow when you should be out in Libya with your little camera?'

'I'm waiting for clearance to sail with an armed convoy,' Christy said.

Fin drank the black coffee, pulled a face and reached for the sugar bowl.

'A credible excuse, I suppose, but it is only an excuse, isn't it, Mr Cameron? I know why you're here. Polly told me. You want Polly to dismantle her financial holdings, accumulate as much cash as possible and give you this money to transport back to Dominic Manone in New York.'

'No,' Christy said.

He didn't like Fin Hughes, didn't trust him. He had met guys like Hughes before and he had never figured out a way to deal with them.

'No?' said Fin. 'I've obviously been misinformed.'

'First off, I won't be toting a sackful of dollar bills back to Manone. The money will be handed over to the Government.'

'Is Dominic buying American citizenship?'

'I don't know what he's doing,' Christy said.

'Haven't your masters told you?'

'Nope.'

He could hear the workmen in the big front parlour smashing glass and listened for the sound of Polly upstairs, longing for her to come back and give him support. Ten minutes ago he had been on the point of making love to this man's lover and still had no qualms about it. He would steal Polly from Fin Hughes without giving it a second thought.

Fin said, 'Of course, it's much in my interests to co-operate, to do what Polly wants and see you, as it were, speedily off the premises.'

Christy said nothing.

Fin said, 'Aren't you going to ask me why?'

'Nope.'

'It isn't quite as easy as you seem to imagine,' Fin went on. 'For instance, selling stock in the current climate and under the current weight of financial restriction requires a great deal of negotiation. I cannot guarantee to have you out of here much before February or March.'

'Can't you sell now?'

'You may be a wizard with a camera, Mr Cameron, but you clearly know nothing of the stock market.'

'That's true.'

'Are you, by any chance, a man divided?'

'I don't know what you mean,' Christy said.

'Have you somewhere you'd rather be?'

'I told you, I'm waiting for clearance to sail with—'

'Balderdash!' Fin put down the coffee cup and leaned an elbow on the table as if he were about to challenge Christy to a bout of arm wrestling. 'You're either committed to obtaining Manone's funds for your government, or you're not. I don't believe you're acting altruistically.'

'I have a job to do here. When it's done, I'll be gone.'

'And Polly?'

'Polly?'

'What will become of Polly?'

The question was baffling. He hadn't given any thought to Polly's future, had assumed he would leave her behind, not because he was forced to but because, like Ewa, Polly would want it that way.

'If you think,' Fin Hughes said quietly, 'that I'll pick up the pieces, that I'll accept second-hand goods and consider it a bargain then you are wrong. I'm not taking leftovers, Mr Cameron. If you fleece Polly Manone of all she possesses she will become your responsibility.'

'You're making a mountain out of a molehill.'

'Am I? I think you know what I'm talking about, and it isn't just money.'

'Polly – I guess she knows what she wants.'

'Ah yes!' Fin Hughes said. 'But what if what she wants is you?'

'Me?'

'I'm not blind. I know what's going on and why this mysterious agency your President has sanctioned has recruited you for its silly little mission. You're no matinée idol, Cameron, but I imagine you've had a certain success with the ladies, have you not?'

'Yeah, yeah,' said Christy, sarcastically. 'Okay, so I'm Mata Hari in baggy underpants; make your point.'

'If Polly decides to do what her husband asks then it will be because of you, not out of any obligation to Manone or any cause which he may wish to support,' Fin said. 'If Polly makes that decision then I will do whatever she asks of me. But afterwards – no, afterwards, she becomes your responsibility and I will wash my hands of her.'

'Does Polly know how you feel?'

'Polly isn't in love with me,' Fin said. 'I am under no illusions on that score, Mr Cameron.'

'Are you . . . ?'

'No – I don't know. No.'

'In other words, Polly's free to do as she chooses.'

'Precisely,' Fin Hughes said. 'As long as she stays in Scotland she has no husband, no children, no ties and if we proceed with this far-fetched scheme that your government has cooked up she'll have no income either. She'll have nothing, nothing except you.'

'She has family.'

'Family won't be enough.'

The sounds of smashing glass from the big room upstairs had ceased. Christy imagined the glaziers applying themselves to the windowpane, thumbing in putty, adjusting the fit, trimming off the edges with that little diamond-hard tool they used. Another raid, another bomb dropped in the vicinity of the park, however, and the window would shatter again.

At that moment it struck Christy how pointless everything was right now, how random. He wondered what it would be like to return to Scotland when the war was over, to marry Polly, to earn a living by going out on Saturdays to shoot the action in soccer games for some provincial rag or by taking photographs of wedding couples in a gloomy little studio in town: wondered if Polly would be worth it, if he could really make her happy, or if the responsibility that Hughes talked about would quickly become a burden.

He was irked at Hughes for making him consider a future that might be no future at all and the consequences of an affair that hadn't even begun.

'You're making too much of it,' Christy said.

'Am I? When Polly gets round to calling the tune,' Fin said, 'will you be prepared to dance to it?'

'Knock, knock.' Polly put her head round the kitchen door.

She wore a cross-check skirt and a cashmere sweater that showed off her figure. She had combed her hair and applied a little make-up and looked fresh and young and vital.

Christy stared at her for a moment then, without turning, said, 'You know, Mr Hughes, I might. I might at that.'

'Might what?' said Polly, frowning.

'Nothing,' said Fin and Christy in unison and, breaking away from the table, headed shoulder to shoulder for the sink to refill the empty coffee pot.

With a fire lighted in the grate and a lamp lit, the lodge had become friendly and free of ghosts.

Bernard's main concern now was that he might become too comfortable and outstay his welcome. He was also conscious of the lateness of the hour and the fact that Lizzie was stuck at home with a shepherd's pie or an Irish stew congealing in the oven. He tried not to think of Lizzie or his wasted dinner but to relax, sip brandy and enjoy the company of a mature and intelligent woman with whom he could discuss politics and persecution on equal terms.

Dr Reeder seemed to be quite at home already and lay back against the cushions of the sofa as if she had lived in the cemetery flat all her life.

Bernard envied her ability to remain unfazed by new experiences.

She crossed her long legs.

He tried to look elsewhere but her legs seemed to dominate the hearth so that to look at her at all, to be polite, he had to lift his gaze and stare into her sad, dark eyes.

'Did you pay the removal men?' she asked.

'Yes.'

'Out of your own pocket?'

'I'll recoup it from the billeting account.'

'Are you entitled to do that?'

'Oh, yes, of course.'

'Will questions not be asked?'

Bernard wondered where politics had gone to.

Five minutes ago he had been expounding his theory that the rise of the National Socialist Party owed as much to Gallic indifference as Teutonic lust for power and Dr Reeder – Evelyn – had been instructing him on certain aspects of recent European history that hadn't received mention in the *Glasgow Herald*. Then, between one little sip of cognac and the next, she was talking about personal matters and the fate of Europe had been put to one side.

He said, 'The accounts department won't quibble if I have a receipt.'

'What was the cost?'

'Thirty-eight shillings.'

'Extortion!'

'Van hire is always more expensive on a Sunday.'

'Did you give the carriers a gratuity?'

'Couple of bob – I mean, two shillings – each.'

'Were they grateful?'

'Grateful?' Bernard frowned. 'Yes, they seemed to be.'

'One cannot always count on gratitude these days.'

'I suppose not,' Bernard said.

Dr Reeder swirled the brandy in the globe in her hand and recrossed her legs. He could see her knees peeping out from beneath the hem of her skirt and that darkness, that hypnotic darkness folding away under her thighs.

He stared intently into her eyes.

'The blonde girl who sent me to you, is she really your daughter?'

'Stepdaughter, actually.'

'How many children do you have?'

'Three, all girls – women now, married women.'

'You have never fathered a child of your own?' Evelyn Reeder asked.

'They're Lizzie's girls but I've always thought of them as my own.'

'Your wife, your Lizzie, she is older than you?'

'Well, aye – yes, she is, as a matter of fact.'

'I,' said Evelyn Reeder, 'am fifty-two.'

'I'd never have believed it,' said Bernard courteously.

'And you?'

'Me?'

'You are not so old, are you?'

'I'm not so young as all that,' said Bernard, embarrassed by all this talk of age. 'I fought in the Great War, you know.'

'For the British?'

Bernard laughed, rather too loudly.

He assumed that she was making a joke but her expression remained unchanged and he saw that she was serious and wanted an answer. What sort of men had Dr Reeder been acquainted with, he wondered, that she required him to declare his allegiance?

'Hm,' he said. 'For the British.'

'It was not a good war.'

'No, it certainly was not.'

He let out his breath; they were moving back on to safer ground now, back towards politics and history.

'You are able to father children?'

'What?'

'I have seen men who could not have children because of that war,' said Dr Reeder, without a blush. 'Damage to their testicles, to the system necessary for reproduction, made them incapable.'

Bernard swallowed, glanced at his wristwatch, said, 'I really must be on my way, Dr Reeder, very soon now.'

'I will cook for you.'

'No, no, really.'

She made no move to get up. 'After all that you have done for me, I will cook for you. You will stay and have supper with me.'

'Another time,' said Bernard.

And then it dawned on him that now that Dr Reeder had got herself a job and a flat the only thing that was missing from her life was a man.

'We will have more brandy and then I will cook something for you.'

'My wife—'

'She will understand that if you are late it is business.'

'No, I have to go,' he said.

'And leave me alone?'

How could anyone so sophisticated and matter-of-fact be so devious as to put him in her debt with just a word? Her assumption that he wanted something from her, that he was 'interested' in her was too accurate for comfort.

He rose and buttoned his jacket, juggled the brandy globe and put it on the shelf above the fireplace.

'Right,' he said. 'Right, I think everything's tickety-boo here, Dr Reeder, so I really must be on my way.'

'Tickety-boo?'

'Squared away, shipshape, apple-pie order.'

'Tickety-boo,' she said again, and laughed.

She laughed in such a way that it caused Bernard pain. For an instant he was tempted to show her what sort of a man he really was and pluck the brandy glass from her hand, pull her to her feet and kiss her; not just kiss her but slip his hand up under that tempting black skirt, up into the dark and mysterious region at the top of those long, taunting legs.

She lay back, watching him, smiling.

He tugged his overcoat and hat from a hook behind the

door but so great was his fear of her now that he didn't pause to put them on.

Coat folded over his arm and hat in hand, he pulled open the door that led out to the top of the stairs.

'Bernard, I am grateful to you,' she said from the depths of the sofa. 'I hope that you will visit me again.'

'Yes, of course.'

'Soon?'

He didn't answer.

He only managed to deliver something midway between a nod and a shake of the head then, closing the door behind him, tiptoed away to hunt down a bus to carry him safely home.

12

Christy was a considerate lover, persistent rather than demanding. He lacked Fin's selfish refinements and the aggression
that had made her affair with Tony so exciting. Afterward
they lay in each other's arms in the big bed upstairs and
listened to the empty rattle of tramcars trolling the length
of the Paisley Road.

'I have to ask you,' Christy said, 'about Hughes.'

'What about him?'

'Are you finished with him?'

'Yes.'

'Do you think he knows you're finished with him?'

'I think he's known for some time.'

'Don't you love him, even a little?'

'It was, I suppose, a sort of marriage of convenience,' Polly
said. 'Does that make me sound like a slut?'

'Not in my book,' Christy said.

His hair was slicked with sweat, his eyelids heavy with sleep.
She felt sleepy too, not leaden but light, almost feathery, but
she had no desire to leave the upstairs room and scuttle down
to her foxhole in the basement.

She said, 'I think Fin realised I was falling for you even
before I knew it myself. It all happened so quickly. Do you
ever feel that everything is speeding away from you and you
have to catch it before it disappears?'

'Polly, I won't be here for ever,' Christy told her. 'As soon
as Christmas is past, next month or the month after—'

'Let's not talk about it, not right now.'

The curtains sighed in window frames loosened by blast. The whole house had been shaken, in fact. One more bomb in the neighbourhood and Polly had a feeling that Dominic's handsome little mansion would simply fall apart.

'Someone will have to tell Babs,' Christy said.

'Oh, God!' Polly said. 'Why does it have to be so complicated? I thought falling in love was supposed to solve everything.'

'Only in books,' said Christy.

The motorcar had no insignia and no official flag in the bonnet. Even so, Kenny spotted it for a wrong 'un as soon as he stepped out of the close.

It was a quarter past eight on a Monday morning, the sky lidded with heavy cloud and a sniff of snow in the air. Cloud had kept the bombers away and there was a faint, unrealistic supposition even among case-hardened coppers that Goering might keep his dogs leashed until Christmas was past.

Kenny lit a cigarette and studied the long, low-slung motorcar out of the corner of his eye; a Lancia – he hadn't seen one of those in ages and certainly didn't expect to find one parked in Cowcaddens. He was wary, almost jumpy, for he'd been responsible for rounding up the Glasgow end of a Liverpool-based gang who had been selling illicit explosives and the Irish had threatened reprisals. He preferred to keep Rosie in the dark about the cases in which he was involved and was relieved that she had left the flat before him.

There was only one man in the Lancia, the driver.

Kenny tossed away his cigarette and crossed the street.

He advanced on the motorcar from the rear. If the driver had a shooter he would have to open the car door to fire and Kenny had already worked out an advantageous angle of attack. He mightn't spend hours in the gymnasium or running round the sports ground but he was still nimble enough to tackle one man with a gun. Officially he wasn't supposed to carry a weapon but he kept a six-inch metal ruler, honed to a cutting edge, in his pocket. He slipped the ruler from his pocket, wrapped it in a handkerchief and held it down against his trouser leg as he came abreast of the car.

'May I be of some assistance?'

'I certainly hope so,' the driver said. 'Inspector MacGregor, is it not?'

The window had been rolled down six or eight inches but the driver was sensible enough not to stick out a hand.

'I don't know what you're talking about,' said Kenny.

He heard the man laugh. All he could see of him was a shabby tweed sports jacket with leather-patched elbows, and some tight, fair curls.

'I was under the impression,' the man said, 'that you SPU Johnnies were supposed to be awfully phlegmatic. Is that a knife you have there?'

'Who are you and what are you doing here?'

'Spot of unofficial business,' the driver said, 'concerning our mutual friend from across the Atlantic.'

'Show me your identification.'

''Fraid I can't. It wouldn't serve much purpose in any case,' the driver said. 'I've more identity cards than you can shake a stick at. If you must have a name to conjure with, call me Marzipan.'

'Marzipan?' said Kenny. 'Oh yes, that sounds about right.'

Keeping the metal ruler snug against his leg, he walked around the Lancia and opened the passenger door. The silly code name had already given him a clue, and the toothbrush moustache and military-style knot in the chap's necktie confirmed his suspicion that he was dealing with a commissioned officer.

He slid into the passenger seat and closed the door.

'Headquarters?' The driver reached for the ignition switch. 'Save you the tram fare, if nothing else.'

Kenny nodded, heard the roar of the big engine and felt the thrust of acceleration against his back as the Lancia surged forward and headed downhill towards the centre of the city.

In spite of the cold, Marzipan wore no overcoat, but a long, striped scarf was tied about his chest like a bandolier. He drove casually, almost recklessly.

'I'll come directly to the point,' he said. 'You've been making enquiries about one of our running-mates, Commander James McAfee Cameron of the United States Navy. I've been given the task of discovering why you're interested in this fellow.'

'No you haven't,' said Kenny. 'Some clerk in the Admiralty may have tipped you the wink about my enquiry but you already know the answer. You're here to tell me to lay off Christy Cameron.'

'Actually, I hadn't realised you were laying into Christy Cameron.'

'He's lodging with my wife's sister, that's all.'

'Come now, that's far from all.'

'All right,' Kenny said. 'I know he's some kind of a spy.'

'The Americans are frightfully prickly about their intelligence sources,' Marzipan said. 'They're new at the spying game and therefore need our co-operation to set up networks and consolidate sources. Cameron's one of several hundred brand-new, inexperienced agents. Hard-line West Pointers detest them, of course, because they blur the line between civil and military authority.'

'Which side are you on?' said Kenny. 'Civil or military?'

Sandwiched between a double-decker tram and a truck laden with rough timber, the Lancia came to a halt.

'It's a combined operation,' Marzipan said. 'It may seem eccentric to you, Inspector, but believe me this plan is much more practical than many of the harebrained schemes the secret services have dreamed up so far.'

'Like incendiary bats and phosphorescent foxes, you mean?'

'Ah, you've heard those preposterous tales, have you?'

'Hardly more preposterous than encouraging a criminal to fund an uprising in Italy. That's what this meeting's about, isn't it? Manone, his wife, and some Communist guerrilla group in Italy that needs cash to buy arms?'

'Organised resistance in Italy doesn't exist yet.'

'So it's a pie-in-the-sky project, is it?'

The car started forward again, weaving between traffic in the general direction of St Andrew's Street.

'The Americans are hot on the idea,' Marzipan admitted. 'Christy Cameron was recruited by his brother, who has, I believe, a passing acquaintance with Dominic Manone. Manone made his initial approach through US Naval Intelligence. In return for his generous contribution to the fighting fund in Italy he'll receive immunity from deportation, a clean bill of health and all the rights and privileges of full American citizenship.'

'And his family?'

'Here, or over there?'

'Over there,' said Kenny. 'The old man, Carlo, and the brother are big-time racketeers. I don't imagine that the FBI will just pat *them* on the head and tell them to run off and play.'

'No, I don't imagine they will,' said Marzipan. 'However, that isn't my concern. My concern is making sure that you don't upset the applecart by asking too many awkward questions.'

'And?' said Kenny.

'To keep an eye on our boy.'

'Cameron, you mean?'

'Of course.'

'What about Hughes?'

'Hughes?' said Marzipan. 'Who the devil's Hughes?'

'He's my concern,' said Kenny. 'Hughes is Polly Manone's partner.'

'Looks after the investments and controls the money, does he?'

'Yes,' Kenny said, 'and I have good reason to believe that Dominic Manone controls him.'

'Curiouser and curiouser!' said Marzipan.

'By the by, Hughes is sleeping with my sister-in-law.'

'What, Manone's wife?'

'Yep, Polly,' said Kenny. 'Polly's the key to this mess. Polly's the puzzle because, sister-in-law or not, I have no idea whose side she's on or what particular game she's playing.'

'Are you sure that she's playing any sort of game?'

'Polly?' said Kenny. 'You bet.'

The Lancia bumped over broken cobbles and nosed down a lane adjacent to St Andrew's Street. Marzipan hadn't finished with Kenny, however. He halted the motorcar facing the gable of the old Saltmarket bath house, which had been sandbagged out of all recognition and now housed the fire service's equivalent of a flying squad.

'Do you have a dossier on her?' he asked.

'On Hughes and Manone, not on Polly,' Kenny said. 'How do I know that Polly's playing a game? For the simple reason that she's her father's daughter. She'd murder me for saying so but she has the same devious streak in her as the late, unlamented Frank Conway. She lacks the old man's viciousness but she's just as self-seeking. Once she sets her mind on something there's no stopping her.'

'You don't have a very high opinion of the lady, do you?'

'On the contrary,' said Kenny. 'If you get her on your side she could be your most valuable asset. She'd make a wonderful spy.'

'But we don't know whose side she's on, do we?'

'Isn't that why you've imported the American?'

Marzipan grinned and rubbed his moustache. 'Damn and blast it! And I thought we were being awfully clever.'

'Do you want to see the file on Hughes?'

Marzipan shook his head. 'Not necessarily. Now that we understand each other, Inspector, I think I'll leave Mr Hughes to you.'

'And Polly?'

'Hm,' said Marzipan, still stroking his moustache. 'No, I think we might safely trust our American friend to bring Polly round. You will, however, tread cautiously in future, will you not?'

'Very cautiously,' Kenny promised. 'Will you contact me again?'

'Absolutely.' Marzipan leaned over and opened the passenger door. 'Just as soon as your dear sister-in-law decides which way to jump.'

Christy hadn't touched a camera in weeks. Although he was still being paid by Brockway's, personally and professionally he was in limbo.

Polly had gone shopping. He was alone in the house when the packet of photographs arrived from Brockway's. He opened the packet and spread the prints on a clean sheet of newspaper on the kitchen table.

Somebody had already weeded out the duds. Christy wondered if some idiot in editorial thought that shots of pigs and chickens, small children and pretty ladies constituted treason and that Blackstone Farm was really a school for spies.

Ron looked up at him from the table top, wet-snouted, long-lashed, ears cocked, more quizzical than belligerent.

The print had been roughly trimmed but he would tidy it up with scissors to improve the composition and make the pig look even more cute. There was nothing he could do to make Angus look cute. Leaning against the fence, elbows hooked around the rail, Angus looked as tough and sour as a Texas ranch-hand.

Christy gave a little nod of self-approval. He had done the kid proud and the kid had done him proud. The photo would never make the cover of the *Saturday Evening Post* but it caught Babs's son to perfection.

Polly too: Polly in her long black velvety overcoat and Russian-style hat stood behind Angus against the grainy-grey wall of the cottage, a hand on the boy's shoulder. She seemed to be looking straight into the lens but Christy knew she was looking at him, watching him with a degree of admiration that nothing he'd been doing at the time had justified.

Somewhere up in Glasgow he would find a photographic shop that stocked mounts. He gathered up the prints, slipped them into the big cardboard-backed envelope, went upstairs to collect his jacket and scarf, and a full hour before Polly arrived home, set out on the bus for the city.

'Where have you been?' Polly snapped. 'Why didn't you tell me you intended going out?'

'Something came up unexpectedly.' Christy said. 'It's a surprise.'

'Oh, is it?' said Polly. 'Have you been to see Babs?'

'Babs?' Christy said. 'Why would I go see Babs?'

'To keep your options open.'

'Polly, what's gotten into you?' he said. 'I went up town, that's all.'

'You didn't take your cameras.'

'Nope, I didn't take my cameras.'

'If you're tired of me, just say so.'

'Polly!'

She was seated at the kitchen table, groceries spread about

her in little paper packets. She had flung her overcoat across a chair and her hat and scarf lay on the floor. When he tried to kiss her she drew away, haughty and irritable, like his ma on those rare occasions when his old man had staggered home drunk. Christy propped the big parcel by the chair, placed a hand on her shoulder and, refusing to accept her rejection, kissed her ear.

'Jackie goes back tonight,' Polly said.

'Are you sure it's tonight?' said Christy.

'I met him at the shops. He was mooching around like a lost soul. He misses the children. Babs had to go to work and April's at nursery and he seemed so – I don't know . . .'

'Are you angry because I wasn't here,' Christy said, 'or because Jackie's leaving and you think I'm gonna run back to Babs?'

'He seemed so pathetic. As if he didn't belong here.'

'He's a soldier,' Christy said. 'He doesn't belong here.'

'Callous, that is so callous.'

'I don't belong here either.'

'Yes, yes, you do. We have things to do together.' She turned her face up and allowed him to kiss her, then said, 'Babs needs you more than I do.'

'Not true,' said Christy.

'No,' Polly admitted. 'Not true.'

He wondered if this little performance was calculated to tighten her hold over him or if she was really afraid of losing him to her sister.

She sniffed. 'Did you call in on Fin?'

'Uh?'

'To carve it up between you?'

'Carve what up?' Christy said.

'Me,' said Polly. 'My future.'

'Hey,' he said, 'I'm not in cahoots with Hughes.'

'Tolerance, communication, thoughtfulness,' said Polly, 'but not trust – is that what you're offering me, Christy?'

'Jeeze,' Christy said, 'you sure know how to spoil a surprise.' He brought up the big square parcel and unwrapped it. 'If you must know, I went up town to buy mounts for these. They cost me an arm and a leg, too.'

'Oh!' said Polly, chastened.

He placed the heavy, velvet-soft grey card mounts before her and exhibited the photographs with which he had intended to surprise her.

'Gifts,' he said, 'for Christmas.'

He watched her expression soften. She glanced up at him.

'Is one for me?' she said.

'Sure,' Christy said. 'The pig's for the boy, but any other you fancy . . .'

'There isn't one of you. I want one of you.'

He was pleased and flattered. 'What the hell for?'

'To remember you by,' said Polly.

Everyone knew Danny Brown's, the big posh restaurant on St Vincent Street. Rosie had often passed it when she'd worked in Shelby's bookshop and had peeked through the plate-glass windows and wondered what it would be like to be one of the elegant ladies who dined amid the potted palms.

When 'the girls' at Merryweather's began planning their Christmas dinner Rosie wasn't at all surprised when Danny Brown's came top of the list.

By choosing Brown's, of course, the ruling élite excluded those poor souls who simply couldn't afford to stump up seventeen shillings and sixpence for a night on the town. Rosie no longer felt much affinity with those who struggled to make ends meet, however. Ever since her confrontation with Aileen Ashford she had been accepted as one of the ladies of the line and in a remarkably short space of time had adopted all the airs and graces that she had once despised.

What really turned things in Rosie's favour was the revelation that her husband was acquainted with Sir Charles Huserall. Rosie knew little of the connection between Kenny and Sir Charles, and when the ladies of the line became too inquisitive she simply invented three or four dark little cases that were vague and plausible enough to leave the ladies agog for more.

'Brown's?' Kenny said, when Rosie informed him that she was dining out with the girls. 'Well, well, you are going up in the world, aren't you?'

'It's my money,' Rosie responded. 'I can spend it how I please.'

'It isn't the money,' Kenny said, mildly. 'It isn't anything. I'll grab a bite at the canteen. You go off and enjoy yourself.'

'I will,' said Rosie. 'Believe me, I will.'

Instructed by the ladies of the line, she had learned to assert herself in a dozen little ways that her mother had never dreamed of to keep her husband on the hop, and as soon as the girls were seated around the long table in Brown's, Aileen asked, 'What did your husband say when you told him you were going out without him? Made a great song and dance, I'll be bound.'

'He said he'd eat in the canteen,' Rosie replied.

There were fourteen at table. Rosie had been placed in the middle so that she could lip-read the conversations without bobbing up and down.

'Oh, the poor chap,' said Eleanor Brough, sarcastically.

'He's trying to make you feel bad,' said Aileen.

'Playing the martyr,' said Constance. 'Men are all the same.'

'Did you leave him something in the oven?' Mrs Findlater asked.

Rosie glanced down at the napkin in her lap. 'I think he may be going to a meeting later this evening.'

'A meeting?'

'Oh, we all know what that means, don't we?' said Doris Maybury.

'A meeting with Sir Charles,' said Rosie.

She had learned to fib without a blush but she was a cautious liar and had scanned the *Glasgow Herald* to make sure that Sir Charles Huserall hadn't popped off that morning. She certainly wasn't going to admit to the ladies of the line that whatever business had brought her husband and the political dreamboat together had been concluded and that Kenny had gone back to dealing with criminals and crusty-faced lawyers.

'Did he say as much?' Aileen asked.

'Oh, nuh-no,' said Rosie. 'He can't say much.'

'Official Secrets Act.' Doris Maybury nodded as knowingly as if she had drafted the document herself.

Fortunately at that moment a grey-haired waitress appeared at the table and began distributing menus.

The good old days of slim-hipped young men in green waistcoats and tight black trousers were gone. The wine waiter was a man but he was about a hundred and ten years old and remained unimpressed by a bunch of snotty women out on the tiles. He recommended something cheap and sweet which, after much discussion, the ladies ordered, one bottle at a time.

Brown Windsor, split-pea and cauliflower, beef consommé, pigeon pie, beef steak and mushroom, mock goose patties, potato croquettes, onions in butter – 'If that's butter I'll eat my hat' – prune roly-poly, American creams, royal fruit mould and a dozen bottles of wine later it seemed that the ladies had buried their differences and shed their inhibitions.

Eleanor and Constance, who 'rarely touched a drop', were listing in their chairs, Doris Maybury was in danger of descending into sentimental tears and Aileen was humming carols under her breath. Two ladies, whose names Rosie had forgotten, were kissing each other under a sprig of mistletoe.

Three or four or five glasses of wine had made Rosie's ears buzz but she was just sober enough to realise that the ladies of the line were making fools of themselves. She thought of Kenny, picking over pie and beans in police headquarters, of her nephew and nieces exiled in a lonely farmhouse in the country, of Mammy growing old and wrinkled with worry about the war, and Bernard, dear, darling Bernard, who had always looked out for her before she'd married Kenny and embraced independence. Thought of Babs, and Jackie going off to war, and Polly and Dominic and how her big sister had wrung so much out of life and how she had wrung nothing worth talking about. Then, still dwelling on Dominic, so smooth and handsome and urbane, she opened her mouth and said, 'We should have gone to Goodman's instead.'

'Goodman's?' said Aileen, blinking her blue eyes. 'Why Goodman's?'

'My sister has a stake in Goodman's.'

'I've been in Goodman's,' said Mrs Findlater. 'The steaks are excellent.'

'Nuh-no,' said Rosie. 'A stake, a holding. She owns it.'

'No, she doesn't,' said Eleanor Brough, scornfully. 'The Italians own it.'

'Or did,' said Constance, 'before the war.'

'My sister is married to an Italian,' Rosie said.

Silence swept the length of the table like an icy draft and Rosie, realising that she had made a dreadful mistake, fashioned a helpless little gesture with her hands as if to erase her last remark.

'Where is the fellow now, this Eyetie?' said Mrs Findlater.

'Prison,' said one of the kissing ladies. 'Where he should be.'

'Too good for him,' said Doris Maybury. 'He should have been shot.'

'He's in America,' said Rosie. 'He – uh – he . . .'

'Wait one moment, young lady,' said Mrs Findlater. 'If I'm not mistaken Goodman's was once owned by one of the Manones.'

Rosie fluttered her hands again. The singing in her ears had become strident. She watched Aileen lay a cigarette carefully on the rim of a crystal ashtray and saw Aileen's lips open and close like the petals of a dahlia.

She sensed that Aileen was shouting.

'Are you related to the Manones?'

'What if I am?'

'Are you? Are you?'

'Dominic Manone's my brother-in-law,' Rosie said and, broken by her stupid confession, covered her face with her hands.

'There, there now,' Kenny said. 'It wasn't your fault. You had a drop too much to drink, that's all.'

'I'm nuh-not drunk.'

'No, no, of course you're not.'

He put his arms about her and drew her to him.

She had been lying on the bed when he'd arrived home, face down, fully clothed and sobbing her heart out. When he'd touched her she'd swung round with such force that she'd almost knocked him to the floor, then she'd thrown herself, sobbing, into his arms. She was more than a little drunk and when he learned that the gang from Merryweather's had abandoned her on the pavement outside Brown's, he felt an anger that was hard to disguise as compassion.

Rosie was so limp and exhausted that it took him all his time to undress her. Whatever brittle truce she had managed to forge with her colleagues at Merryweather's was well and truly broken. He would have to get her out of there, persuade her that given her handicap and his recent promotion, she had no need to work at all.

He kneeled by the bed and peeled down her stockings.

She shivered violently.

He tugged down her underskirt and knickers and reached behind him to find her nightdress. When he turned back she was lying naked across the bed with an arm over her face. He could see everything he had ever loved in her, not just her delicate hips and the long curve of her belly but her helplessness, her vulnerability. He wanted her as he had never wanted her before. It was all he could do not to unbutton his trousers and thrust into her, take her just as she was. Biting his lip, he sat beside her, slipped the nightdress over her head, pulled back the bedclothes and helped her into bed.

She lay flat under the blankets, head on the pillow, staring up at him.

'I tuh-told them about Dominic,' she said. 'Why did I have to tell them about Dominic?'

'I don't know,' Kenny said.

'I wanted to impress them. I wanted them to like me.'

'But you don't like them, Rosie, do you?'

'Nuh-no.'

'Well,' Kenny said, 'for what it's worth, dearest, I like you.'

'Do you?' She frowned. 'I thought you hated me?'

'Of course I don't hate you. I love you.'

'How can you love somebody like me?' she said. 'After what I've done to you. After the – the buh-baby. I – I wanted the baby, Kenny. I didn't want to lose the baby.' She began to cry again. 'Oh, Kenny, I did want the baby.'

'I know,' he said. 'I know you did.'

His desire for her melted into an odd mixture of compassion, tenderness and anxiety that could only be interpreted as love. He sat with her, shivering in the cold bedroom, until she talked herself out and, with a final little sob, a little sigh, turned on her side to sleep.

Archie insisted that she leave the office at half-past two and spend the rest of the afternoon with her husband.

On her arrival at Raines Drive, however, Babs found that Jackie and the motorbike were both missing and assumed that he had ridden over to Blackstone to say goodbye to the children. She prepared dinner and then went round to the Millses' house to pick up April.

It was Jackie's last evening at home and she didn't know how to cope.

Jackie had told her that once the Italians surrendered he would be sent back to Devon or, at worst, to somewhere in France or Holland which, when she looked at a map, seemed a whole lot closer to home than the backside of Africa.

She collected April and carried her home through a grey-etched wintry darkness. Plenty of cloud overhead, Babs noticed, which might stave off the threat of bombing. Please, no raid, tonight, she prayed, as she piggybacked April up Raines Drive, not tonight when, raid or no raid, Jackie would have to catch a bus to the railway station. She'd hate to have to say goodbye from the depth of an Anderson shelter with bombs falling, uncertain if he would reach Glasgow in one piece, let alone Southampton, let alone North Africa.

April tugged at Babs's earlobe and said, 'Daddy.'

He was pushing the Excelsior, stooped into it, shaped to the motorcycle. He wore the scuffed leather coat and a Balaclava, goggles pushed up on to his brow like an extra pair of eyes. She could hear him grunting as he struggled to keep the bike moving on the slope of the hill.

'Run out of petrol?' she called.

He looked up. 'Aye, squeezed out the last bloody drop to reach Govan.'

'Have you pushed it all that way?'

'Aye.'

Babs swung April from her back and placed her in the saddle. 'Hold on tight, honey,' she said. 'Daddy an' I are going to push you home.'

One hand on her daughter's back, Babs applied herself to the offside handlebar and threw her weight into the machine. April nodded stoically and gripped her father's forearm with both hands as he pressed forward. The bike picked up a little speed, trundling along the edge of the pavement.

'How are Angus an' the girls?' said Babs.

'On the mend. She had Gus up an' dressed. She thought I'd show up today,' Jackie said. 'She let me take him out on the bike. If I'd had more bloody petrol I'd have taken him for a proper spin but he was happy enough with goin' round the farmyard a few times.'

'Do they know you're leavin' tonight?'

'I'm pretty sure they do.'

'Didn't you tell them?'

'I told the boy.'

'Did he cry?'

'Nah.'

'I don't know what to do about Christmas,' Babs said.

'Uh?'

'Go over to Blackstone or bring them back here. What do you think?'

'Go over to Blackstone,' said Jackie.

'Will they be well enough?'

'Aye, I'm sure they will.'

It was a small thing, petty and personal, yet Babs would always feel grateful that she had asked her husband's opinion about Christmas. It was the last conversation she could remember with any clarity, though they talked over dinner, talked quietly in the living room with April drowsing on Jackie's knee, talked again while he shaved and dressed himself in his uniform.

He said nothing about Dennis or Billy, nothing about Polly, nothing about Christy Cameron. It was as if at last he had learned to trust her or as if, she thought, he knew he wasn't coming back.

She accompanied him down the steps on to the pavement.

He was strapped into his webbing, the kitbag on his shoulder and looked strong now, not like her weedy Jackie at all, not like the flash Harry from the backstreets of the Gorbals whom she'd married only because he was a heck of a good dancer and had money in his pocket.

When he kissed her she burst into tears.

'Aw, Jesus, Babs,' he said. 'Aw, Jesus!' and, turning, marched off into the darkness, swaying under the weight of the kitbag.

That was the last Babs ever saw of him.

At dawn on 21 January, backing an Australian attack on Tobruk, the tank that he was repairing was blown sky high and Corporal Jackie Hallop was killed outright.

March

13

After the snows of January and February the weather in March was glorious. The rooks built early in the tall trees, crocuses gave way to daffodils, and drifting from the hill pastures you could hear the crying of the first lambs.

Double summer time meant longer light in the evenings but monkeying with the clock upset the hens' laying pattern and Dougie was at his wits' end trying to persuade the bloody birds to roost at a reasonable hour. Margaret Dawlish's suggestion that Ron – well over thirty weeks old and weighing in at a remarkable twenty-one stones – was ready to meet the slaughter man had filled him with trepidation. The tragic news from North Africa and the fact that the children needed pampering had saved old Ron from being reduced to faggots and chitterlings. You might even say that the shell that took poor Jackie Hallop's life saved Ron's bacon, but that was an irony too grim to contemplate and not one Dougie was inclined to share with Angus.

Seeking relief, he fished out his spade and set about a programme of digging that left him so exhausted that he fell asleep by the fire as soon as he'd eaten supper, thus avoiding bedtime tears and questions he could not answer.

'I know he's dead, our daddy, but where's he *gone*?'

'He's gone to heaven, dear.'

'Where *is* heaven? Is heaven up *there*?'

'Yes, my love, heaven's up there, above the sky.'

'How can you be *above* the sky?'

'I don't know. You just can.'

'Did God take him there?'

'Yes, God and Jesus took him to their bosom.'

'What does bosom *mean*?'

'Didn't they teach you that at Sunday School?'

'No, but Miss White says we'll meet Daddy in heaven when we die. Will we have to die soon to meet Daddy?'

'No, dear, you won't have to die soon.'

'What if Daddy forgets who we are?'

'Daddy won't forget.'

'Doesn't he want us to die soon?'

'No, he wants you to live until you're very old ladies.'

'Older'n you, Miss Dawlish?'

'Much, much older than me.'

Angus seemed less curious than his sisters. The boy's silence troubled Dougie. He recalled the pain that the deaths of his wife and children had caused him but he'd been a grown man, an adult, and couldn't for the life of him imagine how a child coped with loss. Tactfully, he allowed Margaret, Babs and Polly to deal with May and June but, for better or worse, he was the man in Angus's life now and regretted that the poor wee guy had no better example to follow than a middle-aged ex-counterfeiter who had drunk himself out of a job.

He wielded the spade mainly to impress the boy, to pretend that he was still vigorous. He repaired fences, mortared walls, dug long evenly spaced trenches, spread the quantities of manure that Ron thoughtfully provided, and on the walk to and from school answered the questions that popped up out of nowhere, like thistles in the grass.

'Was it a bullet?' Angus asked.

'Naw,' Dougie answered. 'We're told it was a shell.'

'Blew Dad up?'

'Aye.'

'Was he really fightin' the Eyeties at Tobruk?'

'Repairin' a tank, I think.'

'The Australians took Tobruk.'

'They did.'

'Captured thousands of Eyetie prisoners.'

'Thousands.'

'Dad's not a prisoner of war, Dougie, is he?'

'No, son, he's not a prisoner of war.'

'I didn't think so, really,' Angus said.

And they walked on, not touching, behind the little girls.

So Dougie dug, his trousers tucked into his stockings, his shirt, soaked with sweat, sticking out at the tail, and when he simply had to rest he trudged over to the farm at Drumry and spoke to the land girls about seeding and planting. Until the children arrived, he had only been playing at gardening. What was required of him now was effort, concentration and a certain mysterious affinity with the seeds and shoots and leafy green things that struggled out of the earth. While he dug and planted, a peculiar feeling stole over him, a feeling too vague to be defined, that if he made himself a better gardener he might become a better father too.

The moment he'd seen Polly's motorcar slithering up the track through the January snow he'd known that something terrible had happened.

Miss Dawlish had been making pancakes. The yard had been filled with the smell of the griddle. He had been out in the barn with Angus and the girls checking stocks of pig feed and chicken meal.

He would never forget the look on Angus's face when his mother had emerged from Aunt Polly's motorcar, how all the energy, all the spirit had drained out of the boy. Polly had shepherded Angus and the girls indoors while he, like the coward he was, had stayed helplessly in the shelter of the barn, smoking a cigarette and listening to the little wails that floated out from the house. Then he had gone upstairs in the barn, up to the floor where the printing press had been, and had found Frobe asleep on the straw and had held Frobe in his arms, petting and patting the fat old cat, until Polly had come looking for him to tell him that which he already knew.

He had followed Polly across the yard, the cat still in his arms, and had entered the farmhouse and had looked at Babs with the girls on her lap, all three of them crying, then at the boy squatting alone in a corner, knees drawn up, white as a sheet. He had slipped the cat to the floor and hunkered down in the corner facing the boy, expecting Angus to crack, for truth to dawn, but there was no truth, no experience of loss to move the wee lad, only the blameless selfishness that is the prerogative and protection of the young.

'Will we have to go back to Glasgow now?' Angus had asked.

'I don't know,' Dougie had said. 'Do you want to go back to Glasgow?'

'Somebody'll have to look after April.'

'That's true.'

'We couldn't take Ron with us, though, could we?'

'Ron wouldn't be happy in Glasgow.'

'I wouldn't want anythin' to happen to Ron.'

Dougie had rolled forward on the balls of his feet and whispered. 'I don't think anybody knows what's goin' to happen, son. It's too early to make plans. Why don't we just wait an' see what your mama wants to do.'

'Uh-huh,' Angus had agreed. 'Too early to make plans.'

Saturday had been filled with tears, muttered conversations between the sisters, vague attempts to plot the future and do the right thing for the children's sake. Eventually Babs had gone off with Polly to locate Bernard at the council offices, then they had driven across town to Lavender Court to inform the Hallops. Lizzie had already been told and was looking after April. Bernard was familiar with 'the drill' for war widows.

Bernard, bless him, would tell Rosie and tomorrow, Sunday, they would all meet up at Mammy's house to decide what to do for the best.

In the end Angus and the girls had stayed on at Blackstone and went on doing what they'd been doing as if nothing had changed.

In a sense, nothing had changed, for as far as the children were concerned their circumstances had been altered not one jot by Jackie's demise.

What had been taken from them was the promise of a settled future and a return to normalcy when the war ended but that sort of future, with its roots so firmly embedded in the past, was not something that children could possibly understand, which, Dougie reckoned, was probably just as well.

Archie had enough sense not to try to comfort her. He really wanted to take her in his arms and offer her a shoulder to cry on but Babs was bristling with all sorts of conflicting emotions and he contented himself with polite enquiries as to how things were faring at home.

By March enquiry and response had been reduced to code.

'All right, Babs?'

'Yeah, all right.'

So far Babs hadn't sought his advice, though now and then she had let off steam. He'd gathered that matters on the domestic front had been fraught with difficulties and frustrations. Her stepfather had been a tower of strength, of course, and had steered her through the depressing business of registering for widow's benefit and child support, and her mother had stayed with her for a week, a kindness that according to Babs had almost driven her nuts.

February had been difficult. The husband's family had tried to siphon off a portion of Babs's entitlement by claiming that they had been financially dependent on Jackie. A lawyer friend of her sister Polly's had put paid to that sleazy little scheme and the Hallops had taken the huff.

There was a will, a decent insurance policy and no outstanding mortgage on the bungalow. All in all, Babs was not hard up. If she had been Archie would have found a means of helping her out. He worried about her, though, for she'd lost weight and he suspected that she wasn't eating enough.

Only once did Archie's tact desert him and he received an earful of abuse, and a good deal of interesting information, by way of reprimand.

'What about your lodger, the American chap? Is he still with you?'

'That bastard, that conniving bastard! Not that that's any of your business, Archie, but he's living with my sister now.'

'Oh!' softly.

'Take that look off your face, Archie Harding. I know what you're thinkin'. What can I offer him that Polly can't? Four kids an' a bungalow in Raines Drive? It's not as if she needs the money, though I doubt if he's paying her a penny.'

'Perhaps you're mistaken.'

'I am not mistaken. That terrible Saturday, just after I got the telegram, I went round to Manor Park and more or less found them in bed together. Christy Cameron lyin' there like butter wouldn't melt in his mouth. The minute he moved in with Polly, I said to myself, "That's that. I've lost him," and by God I was right.'

Archie arranged his features into an expression of non-judgemental blandness as Babs went on, 'He's supposed to be helpin' my sister liquidate her husband's assets so he can take the money back to America. All very hush-hush. I was right in the first place, Archie. He is a spy.'

'I assume,' said Archie, cautiously, 'that he hasn't asked you for money?'

'We're not talkin' pennies here, Archie. We're talkin' thousands and thousands of pounds. He's using her and I'm amazed that Polly doesn't see it.'

Archie had only a dim perception of what the American really wanted with the sisters and why a photographer had been sent to Scotland on official government business.

Stranger things were happening in this war, however, and according to all the books the secret service was a law unto itself. If he met the sister, if he met the American perhaps everything would become clear. As it was he simply couldn't imagine Barbara Hallop being involved in the fate of nations.

Heartache, he thought, or resentment? What's really troubling my Girl Friday?

He had no way of knowing and no means of finding out.

Bernard was on his way down the hall, heading for the door, when the town clerk's assistant came scuttling after him and informed him that there was a telephone call on the line in the surveyor's office. Bernard strode back to the office in question and picked the receiver off the counter.

'Peabody here.'

'Why is it you have been ignoring me?'

Bernard glanced surreptitiously over his shoulder and closed the office door with the toe of his shoe. 'Evelyn?'

'Did you not promise to come on Saturday?'

'Evelyn—'

'I cooked for you.'

'Evelyn—'

'Are you afraid to see me? Is it over?'

'Is what over?' said Bernard. 'Look, I told you, I've lots of problems at home right now. My daughter lost her husband and—'

'If you make promises, you must keep them.'

Bernard glanced at his watch. 'Look, I have to go now but what time do you knock off?'

'Knock off?'

'Finish your shift.'

'I am on until seven o'clock tonight.'

'That's too la—'

'I will be at the gate at ten minutes past the hour.'

'All right. We'll go for a drink or something.'

'You will have the motorcar?'

'No,' said Bernard. 'I will not have the motorcar.'

'Ten past,' Evelyn said, 'at the gate.'

Selling inscribed securities in non-sterling areas was an infinitely complicated procedure, apparently, and Polly had no alternative but to grant Fin further powers of attorney and put up with the delays.

She signed all the documents that Fin placed before her and in due course, towards the end of February, Fin presented her with a cheque for eight thousand, eight hundred and forty-four pounds that Polly deposited in a registered account in Croft & Sutter's Mercantile Bank.

She was surprised at the ease with which the bank handled the transaction and suspected that Fin or Christy, or someone higher up the monkey-puzzle tree, had smoothed the way. She was also surprised to discover that Dominic held large blocks of shares in Argentine Tin, Straits Oil and Nigerian Copper, holdings that had until recently provided substantial dividends.

Jackie's death distracted her, however, and for the best part of a month she was too involved with family matters to confront Fin and demand an explanation why he had neglected to tell her about the foreign stock.

It was odd to be so embroiled with the family again, to have to listen to Bernard's pompous platitudes and Mammy keening over the loss of her son-in-law, to Babs's insistence that she wanted nothing from any of them.

At night in the bed in Manor Park Avenue, however, Christy and she continued to make love as if there were no grieving widows and fatherless children and the war was something that was only happening to other people. The war, however, had not gone away. The Italians were routed in North Africa, Cyrenaica conquered, Egypt and the Suez Canal made safe. Churchill spoke on the wireless and praised the generals who had made victory in North Africa possible and to Polly, lying against Christy, spooned into his back, it seemed as if poor Jackie Hallop had already become as faded as yesterday's newspaper.

Fin had been in Stirling arranging a compromise between the Miners' Union and the Ministry of Labour's regional commissioners. He had been at his best in the tribunal hearings and when he returned to Glasgow late on Friday afternoon he was still buoyed up by conceit. Gratified to find Polly waiting in his chambers, he threw off his overcoat, tossed his briefcase into a corner, leaned over and kissed her.

'What now?' he said. 'Another threatening letter from the Hallops?'

'No, I think we've heard the last of them.'

'What then, my Polly? Have you come to invite me to dinner?'

'I've come to invite you to get a move on, Fin.'

'A move on? A move on? Now what sort of a move on would that be?'

'Stop playing the fool,' Polly said. 'Why are you dragging your feet on this, Fin?' She held up a hand. 'Now don't tell me it's the Treasury or the stock market in Montreal. You've had this on your desk for almost four months.'

'I can muster your money in a week, Polly.' Fin seated himself in his chair and put his feet on the desk, something she had never seen him do before. 'Oh yes, I'll contact an authorised broker who'll sell the remaining foreign securities "forward". I'll settle the taxes, deduct commissions and ensure that the transactions are protected against adverse changes in the rate of exchange. Selling off the Scottish holdings, such as they are, may take a little longer but the bulk of the money lies in those foreign holdings which, as you may have guessed, were built up not by Dominic but by his father in the years before and just after the Great War. Surely you didn't imagine that illegal street bookmaking and a little local racketeering was enough for the Manones.'

'Stop lecturing me, Fin, please,' said Polly. 'Eight thousand is far short of what's required. What's still to come? How much?'

'Thirty,' said Fin. 'Thirty-five at most.'

'That's not enough.'

Enough for what?' said Fin. 'Forty thousand pounds will buy you a great deal of goodwill even in the United States of America.'

'There was talk of sixty or seventy thousand.'

'Piffle!'

'You wouldn't cheat me, Fin, would you?'

'Ah, my dearest Polly, of course I'd cheat you. I'd cheat you without batting an eyelid. But what I will not do is cheat your husband.' He swung his long legs from the desk and planted his feet so firmly on the carpet that the floorboards creaked. 'You and your damned American!' He shook his head. 'It had been my intention to sit out the war with my boots under your table, in a manner of speaking, and see what Dominic made of things. However, your dear husband is far too clever to allow me to play a waiting game. Besides, this damned war might last for ever and I'm bored. Yes, I admit it: I'm bored with you, my Polly, and will be even more bored with you when you're penniless. I'm also more than somewhat leery of what Dominic might do to me if I stick my snout in his trough.'

'Your admission has been duly recorded,' said Polly stiffly. 'I want to put an end to this stupid game as soon as I possibly can. Fin, where's my money?'

'Tell me, Polly,' Fin Hughes said, 'have you or your American friend given any consideration as to what will happen once your fund is salted away in Croft & Sutter's? All financial operations that do not serve the collective needs of the community are ruled out by law. All financial operations in the nature of transfers of capital abroad are banned.'

'I know that,' said Polly.

'So too,' Fin went on, 'is the export or transfer of realisable capital assets, by which is meant art works, postage stamps, diamonds, precious metals, et cetera, et cetera. Therefore, my dear Polly, may I ask how you intend to convey this considerable sum to Dominic so that he may hand it over to the Government of the United States? Perhaps that's where your lovable American boyfriend will enter the picture and prove his mettle.'

'Yes, I expect it is.'

'Does he know what he's doing?'

'I believe he does.'

'Proof of the pudding,' Fin said, 'proof of the pudding, my Polly. The chap may be proficient in the bedroom but is he going to be proficient when it comes to smuggling cash out of the country?'

'How much and how soon?'

'My, my! Aren't we impatient? Is this patriotism or panic, I ask myself.'

'Prudence,' said Polly. 'A bomb could fall through the roof tonight, Fin, and then where would we be?'

'We? Meaning you and Christy Cameron, I assume, not thee and me?'

'Meaning Dominic and my children.'

'Ah! Evidence of conscience at last,' said Fin. 'Still, you do have a valid point there. It won't have escaped your notice that the Luftwaffe have been creeping up the west coast in their search for industrial targets. Sceptics and gainsayers will tell you otherwise but the little raids we experienced before Christmas may develop into a full-scale blitz at any time. You're right to be alarmed.'

Polly slapped her hand down on the desk. 'For God's sake, Fin, will you please shut up and answer my question?'

'I can't,' said Fin. 'Not off hand. I can, however, promise you an answer very soon. Monday, in this office, at eleven.'

'Word of honour?' Polly asked.

'For what it's worth, yes,' Fin answered. 'Oh, by the by, perhaps you should bring along the boyfriend.'

'Christy? Why?'

'Because,' said Fin, 'he's the fellow who'll be in the firing line.'

In the wards of Ottershaw hospital the curtains had already been drawn but the sky to the west was lilac- and lavender-ribbed with pink-tinted cloud, and you could still see the bare bones of the oak trees outlined against the twilight and one rackety tractor trailing a plough across the crest of the hill.

The last of the afternoon visitors had come and gone, and apart from a few nurses and porters the long avenue that split the site was deserted and Bernard, loitering at the gate, felt decidedly conspicuous.

Stepping out from behind a stone pillar, he peered in the direction of the old manor house, which was silently melting into the gloom. Even the gatehouse had grown dark enough to show the firelight within, but when he glanced at his wristwatch he was surprised to discover that Evelyn was not late but that he had been early. Then he saw her striding down the avenue towards him and, feeling foolish, waved.

Evelyn waved back.

Expectation, guilt, the fulfilment of the moment rendered Bernard awkward, for Dr Reeder looked as he'd always imagined a lover would look, tall and confident and stylish, a gas-mask holder hitched over one shoulder, a large black leather bag over the other.

She reached him and took his arm.

'I did not think you would come,' she said.

'Why not?' Bernard said.

'You have been avoiding me.'

'Not intentionally,' Bernard said. 'My daughter's husband—'

'Yes, a victim of the Italians.' She steered him on to the roadway. 'Do you know where it is we are going?'

'Anywhere you fancy?'

Bernard tried to calculate how long it would take to reach Breslin on foot, to walk through the town and up the long hill to the lodge in the graveyard. An hour, he thought, an hour and a half.

The last bus to Anniesland left at half-past nine.

He couldn't very well pour a drink or two down Evelyn's throat, tip his hat and leave. With any luck there would be an air-raid warning and Mr Grainger would see Lizzie safely out to the shelter and he, Bernard, would have a valid excuse for rolling home late.

Dear God, he thought, what am I coming to, depending on the Luftwaffe to get me out of a jam?

Evelyn said, 'I have heard of a bar called the Greyhound?'

'Yes, at the crossroad,' said Bernard. 'The Greyhound will do nicely.'

He quickened his pace and allowed her to grip his arm

more tightly, his gas-mask holder and her gas-mask holder bumping together, hip to hip.

'Is the work going well?' he asked.

'It is going better,' Evelyn admitted.

'Are you still on the wards?'

'I am learning to assist.'

'What?' said Bernard, impressed. 'Surgery?'

'In the unit for burns.'

'Nasty.'

'It is interesting work. The sailors are brought up from the landings at Greenock. The elementary treatment they receive on board the rescue ships is often inadequate. Many die.'

'How many?'

'One in every three,' said Evelyn. 'The younger nurses blame themselves when a sailor dies. I tell them, it is not we who fail the sailors but the convoy commanders. It is the oil that does the damage.'

'The oil?' said Bernard.

'Burning oil. When a ship is sunk and the sailors thrown into the sea they must choose between drowning or burning. There is no escape.'

Mention of suffering brought back memories of trench warfare. Trench warfare was nothing to write home about these days, a horror all but forgotten. Though he was proud to be walking out with a woman who saved lives, Bernard resented the fact that he couldn't separate Evelyn from what she did, for she, more than anyone or anything, even poor dead Jackie Hallop, had carried home to him the barbaric realities of modern warfare.

Twenty minutes' fast walking brought them to the quaint old public house.

Bernard had visited the Greyhound once before when a councillor with whom he'd been sharing the Anglia had insisted that drink was necessary to survival and had dragged

Bernard in for a pint. He was not at all sure that the pub had accommodation for ladies or that the inhabitants of the bar would welcome someone like Evelyn Reeder. But when he ushered Evelyn through the door he found to his relief that times had changed in rural Ottershaw just as they had changed everywhere else.

The pub's long low-ceilinged room buzzed with activity.

Bernard glanced towards the fireplace where several land girls were gathered round an old shepherd who was entertaining them by playing a melodeon and singing a traditional risqué ballad that had just reached its climax with a naughty word. There were no dainty sherry schooners on the table, only tankards and pint pots, and the girls were clad in boots, trousers and bulging woollen sweaters.

By the bar three nurses were hanging over a wireless set, laughing uproariously. Corner tables, the snug, the nook were also occupied, and it took Bernard all his time to find a bench close to the door that led out to the lavatory. Evelyn was not dismayed by the lack of privacy and while Bernard went to the bar she shucked off her gas-mask container and leather bag and shed her overcoat, then, lighting a cigarette, stood up to survey the room.

Bernard purchased two pints of beer and was in process of steering the pots back to the bench when he noticed that Evelyn was waving to someone, waving more enthusiastically than she had waved to him, waving in a manner that made her seem girlish. Bernard looked behind him and saw Arthur Hunter Gowan, also on his feet, beckoning to Evelyn and pointing at a table that he had managed to commandeer.

Evelyn had gathered her stuff and was on the move before Bernard could change direction. He followed her round the group by the fire, beer slopping and trickling down the sides of the mugs, wetting his fingers and wrists.

Arthur Hunter Gowan wore a grey two-piece suit and a

stiff-collared shirt in the vee of which nestled a college tie. He looked fresh, his hands pink and muscular and assured as he clasped Evelyn's shoulder and brought her lips down to brush his cheek.

'Well,' Bernard said, 'I didn't expect to find you in a place like this, sir.'

'Whyever not, Peabody?'

'I thought you'd have your own place to go for a drink.'

'My own place? Do you take me for a snob?'

'No, I didn't mean—'

'Nothing wrong with the Greyhound,' Hunter Gowan said, 'even if it does get rather crowded on occasions.'

Evelyn snuggled in beside the surgeon, leaving Bernard to perch precariously on a small stool. Prejudice put aside, the surgeon and the Belgian widow leaned shoulder against shoulder in an intimacy that may, or may not, have been forced.

Bernard knew then that his 'affair' with Dr Evelyn Reeder was over before it had begun. He had imagined the unimaginable and tricked himself into believing that because he had a bit of power in the council offices he was as good as she was; nothing could have been further from the truth.

He licked the sticky taste of beer from his fingertips and listened to Hunter Gowan describe some elaborate piece of surgery he had performed that morning. There was nothing in the conversation to latch on to. The doctors had no time to waste on a mere billeting officer. They were the life-savers and unless he missed his guess, were, or soon would be, lovers. They would be discreet, of course, for they were more devious and duplicitous than he could ever be and, oddly, he admired them for it.

Bernard spread his knees to keep balance on the stool and felt within his chest a sudden, sad deflation as if his heart, or his hopes, had shrunk.

Half an hour later they left the pub together, Evelyn hanging on to Hunter Gowan's arm.

The motorcar, a lovely old Humber Super Six, was hidden beneath the trees behind the pub. Hunter Gowan was considerate enough to drop Bernard off at Breslin railway station before he drove Evelyn away to the lodge in the cemetery which was, after all, a perfect little love-nest for a lonely widow and a respectable married man.

Angus wakened screaming in the night. Dougie was out of bed and had dashed upstairs before Miss Dawlish could find her dressing gown and stumble out of her room. Roused by their brother's shrieks, May and June sat up in bed, hugging each other. Dougie left the girls to Margaret and, blackout or no blackout, switched on the light. Angus was standing on the bed, eyes wide open, arms stretched out like aeroplane wings.

'*Daddy, Daddy, Daddy, Daddy, Daddy!*' he shrieked.

'All right, son, all right,' Dougie said. 'I'm here now. I'm here.'

He clasped the boy about the waist and eased him on to his back.

Angus's arms and neck were rigid and there was spittle all down his chin.

Whatever he had seen, whatever dream or nightmare had speared his brain would not go away.

Dougie lay by him, cradling him in his arms.

'Now, now, now, Angus. Waken up, waken up, please.'

It was cold in the bedroom; you could feel the clear cold night air pressing upon the slope of the roof. You could feel moonlight on the hill and the loneliness of the hill and the silver ribbon of the river running down to the sea far away.

The boy's eyes clicked like a doll's. He blinked and returned from wherever the dream had taken him.

Dougie stroked his brow.

'There, son, there now. You had a bad dream, that's all. You're safe now, Gus. It's all gone now.'

'Daddy?'

'It's me, Angus,' Dougie said, 'just me.'

Margaret stood behind them in the doorway. She was draped in the monkish overcoat that served as a dressing gown, barefoot and thick-legged, looming and solid in the dim light from the bulb above the landing. The girls clung to her, skinny and angelic in their cotton pyjamas. They were scared too, and Margaret, without looking round, gathered them to her.

Dougie's pyjamas had slipped down. He was bare-bummed and halfway to being indecent but he gave dignity not a passing thought. He leaned close to Angus and whispered, 'Was it Daddy, son? Did you see your daddy?'

'There in the corner. He came for me.'

'Angus, Angus,' Dougie crooned. 'It was just a dream.'

'I wanted to go with him.'

'No, no, no,' softly, so softly.

'Then you came in.' Angus punched a fist into Dougie's ribs, punching and punching. 'You came in an' he went without me. He went away without me.'

'Brandy, do you think?' said Margaret Dawlish from the doorway.

'A drop in warm milk, an' a hot-water bottle,' Dougie said.

'It's all your fault.' Angus punched him again but feebly, without conviction. 'He'd have taken me away with him if you hadn't put on the light.'

'You were dreamin', Angus. It was just a bad dream.'

The boy's face was wet with tears. He looked, Dougie thought, less like a young man than a tiny child lost in the empty reaches of a world that had no meaning. He cried naturally, though, his face – and his tears – pressed against Dougie's chest.

'It *wasn't* a dream. It *wasn't*, it *wasn't*. He was *there*, right *there*.'

Dougie peered into the corner where the roof sloped down to meet the wall. He almost expected, almost hoped, that he would see the shade that Angus had seen, that for the boy's sake the shadow of the father would still be there. Then, disappointed but not surprised, he slid his gaze from the empty corner to the doorway, empty too now that Margaret had taken the girls downstairs.

'Why did he go away?' Angus said through his tears.

'He had to, son. I expect he had to.'

'Was it just me dreamin', really?'

'Aye.'

'He's dead, Dougie, isn't he? He's really, really dead?'

'Aye, son, he is,' said Dougie, and held the sobbing child to his heart.

14

Fin booked the call through a transatlantic operator before he went out to dine. By the time he got back to Baltic Chambers the building was almost deserted, apart from a covey of fire-watchers on the roof.

The elevator was still functioning, though, and the caretaker switched on the night bulb on the landing and Fin didn't need the little torch that was clipped into his pocket with his fountain pens.

At exactly three minutes to eleven o'clock, he let himself into his office.

He checked the blackout curtains, switched on the desk lamp and seated himself behind the desk.

He had drunk very little with dinner and wished now that he had drunk more. He was far too sober for his own good.

There was something unnatural about making a telephone call to a foreign country, something that made him nervous. He couldn't imagine an undersea cable stretching all the way across the Atlantic, deeper than the keels of the U-boats, deeper than a depth charge or a torpedo could reach, and he didn't like the idea of his voice running along a wire at the bottom of the ocean. He was also agitated because he was about to talk to Dominic Manone, for in spite of occasional letters he had no idea how much Dominic knew of the true state of affairs in Manor Park Avenue or precisely how much he, Fin, should tell him.

At exactly eleven Fin reached for the telephone and summoned the number of the transatlantic operator who, after
several minutes' delay, opened a line to the number he had
given her.

There was a crackle on the wire, like static on a wireless
set, then abruptly a clear, familiar voice said, 'Manone.'

'Dominic?'

'Yes.'

'It's Fin.'

'What time is it over there – about ten?'

'Eleven.'

Dominic's soft Scottish accent was unmarred by an American
twang. He sounded, Fin thought, just as he always did,
perfectly calm and controlled.

'Have you had air raids?'

'A few,' said Fin. 'None serious.'

'Tell me why you're calling,' Dominic said.

'This scheme you have in hand isn't working out as
smoothly as you supposed it would.'

'What's the problem?'

'Restrictions on dealing in foreign stock.'

'How much have you raised?'

Fin swallowed. 'Only about eight thousand.'

'Who's your broker?'

'Donald MacDonald.'

'MacDonald is honest enough.'

'It's the South American stuff,' said Fin. 'Every blasted
transaction has to be cleared with the Treasury.'

'Haven't you got shot of the South American stock yet?'

'Not all of it, no.'

'What about the warehouse?'

'The lease doesn't expire until the autumn.'

'Get rid of it now.'

'Dominic—'

'What about the house?'

'The house?' Fin said.

'In Manor Park, my house.'

'I thought the house belonged to Polly.'

'It hasn't suffered any damage, has it?'

'No, but—'

'Tell her to put it on the market.'

'This is no time to shift property, Dominic.'

'Shift it nonetheless,' Dominic said.

'What about Polly?'

'What about her?'

'Is it your intention to leave her homeless?'

'She understands my situation.'

Fin swallowed again. 'I'm not so sure she does. I'm not sure any of us do. That chap you sent over – Cameron, the photographer – he appears to be no better informed than the rest of us.'

'Is he still with you?'

'Yes, he is,' said Fin. 'Look, it's been somewhat rough over here lately. I take it you've been informed that your brother-in-law was killed.'

'MacGregor?'

'No, the other one – Hallop. Killed in action in Libya.'

A pause: 'How's Babs making out?'

'From what I gather,' Fin said, 'as well as can be expected. Look, Dominic, you'll have to talk to Polly.'

'No.'

'Give her a call, talk to her, make her see sense.'

'No.'

'What's wrong with you, man? Why won't you talk to her?'

'Doesn't she trust you?' Dominic said.

'I'm afraid not, no, not entirely.'

'What about Cameron, doesn't she trust him?'

'She's confused,' Fin said. 'It's a very confusing time for all of us.'

Dominic said, 'I'll tell you what I want done, Fin. Given the profit you're making on fees I expect you to do it immediately.'

'Go on.'

'Sooner or later America will enter the war,' Dominic said. 'When it happens I'll be deported or interned. The FBI are breathing down my father's neck. My father's a sick man. He probably won't last much longer. My brother can look out for himself. My concern is with the children.'

'Send them back here.'

'Don't be ridiculous,' Dominic said. 'I've no intention of being separated from my children. And I've no intention of being deported or interned. I've a deal on the table with the secret services, but they won't wait for ever. The Americans have already coerced certain undesirable elements – all right, gangsters – into helping them contact the forces in Italy who'd like to see Mussolini deposed. I've few family connections left in Italy but I do have money and the operation is in desperate need of finance. If I help fund the Italian partisans I can get myself and my children out from under the net of a federal investigation. In other words, I have to prove I'm not my father's son before the Government will allow me to apply for citizenship.'

'Call Polly. Talk to her. Tell her what you've just told me.'

'At the end of this month,' Dominic went on, 'I'll be flying to Lisbon.'

'Lisbon.'

'Lisbon is crawling with spies and double agents. I won't be out of their sight for one moment. My job is to hand over fifty thousand pounds to an Italian financier. Once that's done—'

'Fifty thousand pounds!' Fin exploded. 'You can't ferry hard currency out of Britain, Dominic, not without risking arrest.'

'It won't be hard currency,' Dominic said.

'What then?'

'Diamonds.'

'Diamonds!' Fin manufactured a laugh. 'Oh, yes, of course. Bless me, I'd forgotten about diamonds. What? Do you expect me to stroll into a jeweller's shop on Argyll Street and say, "Give me fifty thousand pounds worth of assorted gemstones," and walk out with them in a nice little brown paper bag?'

'Once Polly has the money,' Dominic went on, 'the purchase of the diamonds will be arranged by someone else and you can go back to robbing the unions or whatever racket you're into these days.'

'I trust I won't be expected to transport the diamonds to Lisbon?'

'Polly will do it.'

'Polly! Oh, my God!'

'She'll be given instructions on how to set up the trip. And she won't be travelling alone.'

'Why must you involve Polly at all?'

'She's the only one I can trust.'

'Are you sure about that?' Fin said. 'She – Polly isn't . . .'

'Fin, what are you trying to tell me?'

'Nothing,' Fin said. 'Nothing.'

'Polly is, after all, my wife.'

'True, that's true.'

'Our time's running out,' Dominic said. 'We'll have to break the connection in a moment. Do you understand what I want from you, Carfin?'

'Yes, dispose of everything you own.'

'And leave the rest of it to Polly.'

'Dominic . . .'

'What?'

'The American, Christy Cameron . . .'

'What about him?'

'Is he really a US Government agent?'

'What makes you think he isn't?' Dominic said.

'It's just that . . . No, no, of course he is. Of course.'

'Any other questions, Fin? Any other doubts?'

'What if I can't raise all of the fifty thousand in time?'

'You'd better,' Dominic said, and hung up.

The mist over the potato fields had burned off early and the light was incredibly pure. There were land girls on the long patches of tilled ground and a tractor – two tractors, in fact – ploughing the flat horizon, a great skein of seagulls swirling in their wake. Sunlight lay on the roofs of the old aerodrome, and there was just enough of a breeze to make the barrage balloons tethered across the river shimmer against the pale blue sky.

The tram driver responded to the fine spring weather by bursting into song now and then and the conductor, his sinuses dry at last, dangled from the platform rail and bawled threats to startled rabbits and one large hare that only just avoided being turned into mincemeat by the speeding tram.

'Look, look,' the conductor shouted. 'Look at that wee beggar go.'

Babs hoisted herself from the seat just as she'd done in the dreary days at the beginning of winter when she'd scouted out for Christy Cameron. She twisted against the motion of the tram and watched the hare dart across the field.

The conductor shouted down the length of the car, 'You ever eat one o' them, dear?'

'Not me,' said Babs.

'Beautiful, they are. Beautiful. My old ma, she does 'em a treat.'

'I wouldn't even know how to pluck one,' Babs said.

'Pluck?' The conductor roared with laughter. 'Hear that, Wendell, lady here thinks you *pluck* a hare for the pot.'

The driver shouted over his shoulder, 'Well, don't you?'

'Daft beggar. Those aren't feathers. Those're fur.'

Babs said, 'Wendell? Did you call him Wendell?'

'Certainly,' said the conductor. He shouted, 'Hoy, Wendell, lady here thinks you got a funny name.'

'Hah bloomin' hah,' Wendell called back.

'Call the beggar Wendy, lady. He loves bein' called Wendy.'

'I think I'd better not,' Babs said.

For the first time in many weeks she laughed.

A ripple of guilt passed through her at the realisation that she had forgotten about Jackie long enough to laugh.

How odd it seemed to have no one to betray but herself.

Back in November she had yearned for excitement; now all she could think of was security. She knew that Jackie wasn't coming home again and that if the war went on long enough she might lose Dennis too. Dennis was the only guy, apart from Jackie, whom she'd ever contemplated going to bed with, until Christy came along. Dennis was Jackie's brother, though, and even if his wife had left him, Dennis would never be the man for her. God, the man for her! What sort of phrase was that to pop into her head when poor Jackie had been dead for not much more than a month.

It would have been easier if there had been a body, a funeral. Jackie was buried in a war grave outside Tobruk and she didn't think he would be all that happy lying in the sand in a place so far from home. And here she was, still riding the tramcar every damned morning, still going dutifully to work, still shopping, cooking, cleaning, mending clothes, still trailing April round to the Millses every morning and visiting Angus and the girls every Sunday.

She had always considered herself tough but she wasn't as tough as all that. She still needed a man to cherish and spoil her as Jackie had done, but in the unpredictable spring sunshine, ripping down the old aerodrome road, she suddenly experienced a lift in spirits that indicated that at least some of her resilience remained intact.

'Hey, Wendy,' she called out. 'Wen-deee, it's my stop.'

'Don't you start,' the driver shouted.

'I'll stop when you stop,' Babs yelled.

'Bloody women!' the driver muttered, and obediently applied the brake.

'Boy!' said Archie. 'Am I glad to see you.'

'That's nice,' Babs said. 'What's up?'

'We have a problem.'

'We usually do,' Babs said. 'Who's in the toilet?'

'The problem's in the toilet.'

'Not another Belgian widow?' Babs said.

'Worse,' said Archie.

'Two Belgian widows?' said Babs.

'Do not be facetious.'

'How long is the problem gonna be in the toilet?'

'Lord only knows,' said Archie. 'How long does it take to feed a kid?'

'A kid?'

'Mother attached,' said Archie.

'How old is the kid?'

'Still on the— you know.'

'Is breast the word you're searching for?'

'Oh my, aren't we in a jolly mood this morning,' said Archie. 'Flippancy is the last thing I need right now. A lactating Irish girl and a banshee child are quite enough to be going on with, thank you.'

Babs took off her coat and hat and seated herself at her desk. She was used to Archie's states of harassment and was more amused than dismayed by his sarcasm. Nothing, it seemed, could dent her buoyant mood this morning, not even the prospect of having to deal with another displaced person.

'Does the fair Colleen have a name?' Babs said.

'She's down in the documents as Doreen Quinlan.'

'What the kid's name?'

'I didn't dare ask.'

'Pretty?'

'Who? The kid?'

'The girl.'

'I don't know, do I?' said Archie. 'How long is she liable to be in there? How long *does* it take to feed an infant?'

'Patience, lad,' said Babs. 'What are we expected to do with her, anyway?'

'The usual,' said Archie. 'Find her work and a place to stay.'

He tipped up his glasses, rubbed his eyes then, to Babs's surprise, rested an elbow on her knee and peered up at her. His eyes weren't really like those of a mole or a vole; they were grey-green and slightly bloodshot.

He said, 'Last night, just after you'd left, Labour Exchange officer phoned to offer us a woman worker, untrained. Thanks, say I. She has a baby, eighteen months old. Thanks again, say I. She's from Belfast. Super, say I. He sticks her up in a hostel last night and when I arrive here this morning she's sitting on the doorstep clutching the kid, her papers and a pathetic little bag of worldly goods.'

'Archie, do you have to lean on my knee?'

'Sorry,' he said, shifting position. 'I'm just giving you the background. I thought you'd be interested.'

'I am interested, but I can hear you perfectly well without your elbow diggin' a hole in my leg.'

'The hostel in Paisley fed her breakfast, gave her three shillings out of the kitty and booted her out. She trails down here because here is where she's been told to come. Know something, Babs, I'm becoming thoroughly disheartened at being made the dumping ground for every waif and stray nobody else knows what to do with.'

'You'll feel better when you've had your tea.'

'Probably. Anyhow, our fair Doreen trots into the toilet to feed the child while I examine her papers. It seems she worked in a clothing factory in Belfast before she joined the ATS, from whose ranks she was discharged on "Medical Grounds"; only "Medical Grounds" has been scored through and replaced with the euphemism "Compassionate Release". Checking the dates it would appear that the little stranger began its journey into this vale of tears about the same time as Mumsy joined the ATS. In other words . . .'

'She was pregnant when she joined up,' said Babs.

'Indeed,' said Archie. 'Pregnant – and no wedding ring.'

'So there's no husband?'

'When I put that very question to her she informed me, quite cheerfully, that she doesn't know where hubby is. She has an aunt in Belfast – the address is on the form – but my guess is that she smuggled the kid out without the Belfast Labour Office even realising that she had it.'

'What's she doing in Scotland?'

'I have no idea,' said Archie.

'Perhaps we should ask her?'

'I already did,' said Archie. 'She doesn't know herself.'

'Could the husband – the daddy, I mean – could he be lurking somewhere in the vicinity?'

'It's possible, of course,' said Archie, 'but somehow I doubt it.'

'What are we expected to do with her?'

'Find her a billet and a job to keep her going.'

'Untrained?' said Babs. 'With a baby?'

'I've been racking my brains to think where we could put her and I've come up dry. Perhaps,' Archie hesitated, 'perhaps your stepfather might be able to help out again, do you think?'

'I don't think,' said Babs. 'From what Bernard's told me the last one we dumped on him gave him enough trouble. Anyway, the girl's our problem.'

'What a big heart you have, Barbara,' Archie said. 'Who'll take in an Irish girl with a kid, even if we guarantee the rent?'

At that moment the door of the toilet swung open and Doreen Quinlan emerged with the baby, a very robust and buxom baby, slung over her shoulder.

The baby, a boy, was warmly dressed in a romper suit with a pointed hood. The suit had been knitted from blue wool that had faded with washing, and looked, Babs thought, like a tiny suit of chain mail.

The girl wasn't much older than eighteen. She had broad, open features, blue eyes and a dimple – my God, Babs thought, a dimple – on each cheek. She was as blonde as a cornstalk and almost as slender. She wore a short red flannel jacket and a long, trailing skirt of a sort that had gone out of fashion thirty years ago. Her blouse was baby-stained but otherwise she was clean and tidy and very pretty in a naïve kind of way.

'I was havin' to change him,' the girl said. 'I was havin' to use the sink for to wash his bott. I cleaned up, like, afterwards.' Her voice had the casual attitude to vowels that Glaswegians were used to. 'He's a right greedy guts, his majesty, so he is now. I'll be needin' to find milk an' an egg for him soon.'

'You're weaning him, I take it?' Babs said.

'I am, I am.'

'How old is he?'

'Eighteen months, close to.'

'He's a big chap for eighteen months.' Archie walked around the girl to peer through his spectacles at the child. 'Has he got a name?'

'David. I call him Davy.'

'After his dad?' Babs said.

The girl gave her a little smile, more mysterious than patronising. 'Nah, nah,' she said. 'Now you won't be catchin' me out that way.'

Archie extended a forefinger and wiggled it, a gesture that young Master Quinlan ignored. He was sleepy and sluggish, at least for the moment.

'I'll – erm – put on the kettle, shall I?' said Archie.

'Aye, I could be doin' with a cup o' tea, so I could,' said Doreen Quinlan and, hoisting the baby down from her shoulder to her lap, seated herself on Babs's chair and gave a weary sigh. 'It wasn't much o' a breakfast they were showin' me at that hostel place.'

'It was probably the best they could do,' said Babs and then, on impulse, detached Davy from his mother's arms and lifted him up.

He reared back and glared at her as she tugged down the chain-mail hood and stroked the fringe of dark hair that hung over his brow. He gave Babs a thorough scrutiny then used, perhaps, to taking succour where he could find it, settled against her shoulder and closed a fist over her breast.

'Not me, pal,' Babs said.

Gently detaching Davy's fingers from that tempting part of her anatomy, she strolled up and down the length of the office with him in her arms while an idea, a fine malicious little notion, tumbled softly into her head.

'I take it,' Polly said, 'that this is some kind of a joke.'

'Homelessness is no joke, Poll,' Babs informed her.

'You,' said Polly, 'what's your name?'

'Walter George,' said the area council officer whom Archie had summoned with one telephone call. 'I think we've met before, Mrs Manone. Would you care to inspect my credentials?'

'I don't give a damn about your credentials,' Polly said. 'I don't give a damn if you're acting on orders from Winston bloody Churchill, I am not – let me repeat myself – I am *not* taking that woman and that child into my house.'

Mr George was much older than Archie. He had been an ambulance driver on the Somme during the last conflict and a dedicated worker in the Church ever since. He was, so Archie said, an inspirational lay preacher and as honest as the day was long. Though well over sixty, he was handsome, tall and broad-shouldered, with a mop of fine white hair and a trim moustache. If Polly's profanity offended him, he gave no sign of it. No doubt, thought Babs, he had heard a lot worse in his day. He reminded her a little of Bernard, though Mr George wasn't as pompous as her stepfather, wasn't pompous at all, in fact.

It had been a stroke of genius on her part to think of dumping the Belfast girl and her baby on Polly, but an even greater stroke of genius on Archie's part to insist that she take Mr George along for support.

Without Mr George's gentlemanly presence, Polly would probably have kicked her out by now. As it was, the Belfast girl and her baby were downstairs in the kitchen, tucking into a second breakfast that Christy had rustled up.

Christy hadn't been in the least put out by the arrival of a stranger with a baby or a council officer brandishing a hastily drafted requisition order. He had been sloping about in pyjama bottoms, thick stockings and a reefer jacket at ten thirty in the morning. Polly hadn't been in much better shape, all tousled and baggy-eyed and without a scrap of make-up to emphasise her superiority.

Babs wondered, rather maliciously, if they had actually been 'at it' in Polly's foxhole in the basement when Walter George had rung the doorbell.

'I'm terribly sorry, Mrs Manone,' said Mr George, 'but I'm afraid you have no choice in the matter.'

Polly pulled her dressing gown about her with an angry flick of the wrists. 'Do I not? Well, we'll just see what my lawyer has to say.'

'If you mean Mr Hughes,' said Walter George, 'I question if Mr Hughes will be able to do much about it.' He glanced at the paper in his hand. 'What I have here is a draft requisition to utilise a portion of your house. It is, I stress, only a draft, and draft documents are notoriously tricky to revoke, as Mr Hughes will, I'm sure, be first to acknowledge.'

'Draft documents,' said Polly, 'aren't worth the paper they're written on.'

'True, they're not binding,' said Mr George, 'but in my experience they represent an important first step to legal enforcement.'

Sunlight streamed through the windows and made the big front parlour look like a museum. The furniture was scarred and the wallpaper showed white where two framed paintings had been removed. The carpet was gritty underfoot and little splinters of wood and plaster littered the ledge of the mantelpiece. Even the huge leather sofa upon which Mr George and Babs were seated felt greasy and unwholesome.

Polly paced up and down, her agitation palpable. If she hadn't stolen Christy Cameron away, Babs might even have felt sorry for her sister.

'I will not take in lodgers,' Polly said.

'What about the guy downstairs then?' Babs said. 'Isn't he a lodger?'

'Oh, so that's it,' Polly snapped. 'It's revenge, is it? Do you think you can land me with some snotty-nosed brat just to pay me back for taking in . . .' She caught herself in time and reverted to a flat, dead tone of voice. 'Mr Cameron is not a lodger. He is a guest. His stay here is only temporary.'

'I see.' Mr George took a small notebook from his pocket, extracted a pencil no thicker than a darning needle, licked the lead and made a note before hiding the notebook in his pocket again. 'I assume that your guest occupies a separate bedroom from your good self?'

A dusky red flush spread from Polly's throat to her cheeks. 'Of course.'

'Two rooms out of ten,' said Mr George with a little cock of the head, 'one in temporary occupancy.'

'Babs, you're a complete and utter bitch,' said Polly. 'I will not let you do this to me. I'll – I'll sell the place first.'

Babs glanced at Mr George, who cocked his head again, in the other direction this time.

'That,' he said, 'is your prerogative, Mrs Manone. However, I should warn you that the asking price will be controlled by the council housing committee and that council will have first refusal to purchase.'

'What?' Polly cried. 'First refusal on a price they set?'

'I know it seems unfair—'

'Unfair!' Polly shouted. 'It's criminal, bloody criminal.'

'On the other hand,' said Mr George, almost casually, 'if you were to take in a temporary guest or two then I expect the requisition order would not be enforced. Thus, when the situation eases and restrictions are lifted you would be at liberty to put the property on the market and get what you can for it by private barter.'

'Are you telling me I can't even sell my own house?'

'Mrs Manone, the war—'

'Damn the war!' Polly threw herself down in an armchair

and stretched out her legs. She stared at the plaster chips on the mantelpiece and then, chin tucked to her chest, said, 'This girl you've brought me, she isn't sick or anything?'

'No,' said Mr George. 'She isn't sick.'

'What about the kiddie?'

'Master Davy appears to be in bounding good health,' said Mr George.

'Where did you find her?' Polly asked Babs.

'I didn't find her; she found us.'

'Oh, wasn't that convenient!' said Polly.

'You'll be paid for housing her,' Babs said. 'There's a scale of payment to cover billeting costs. Am I not right, Mr George?'

'Quite right, Mrs Hallop,' Walter George said. 'The girl will be given a ration card and work papers but billeting fees will be paid directly to you.'

'What does she do, this girl?'

'She's a housckeeper,' Babs said.

'Oh, is she now?' said Polly.

Mr George slapped his hand on his knee and got to his feet. He glanced at his watch, buttoned his overcoat and, looking a lot less impartial than he had done a moment ago, put the papers down on the sofa table.

'I see you're not amenable to negotiation, Mrs Manone, so I'll leave these documents for your solicitor to examine. I'm sure he'll confirm everything I've told you. Meanwhile, Mrs Hallop and I will take the girl and the child back to the hostel in Paisley until we can find—'

'Wait,' Polly said, chin still stuck to her chest. 'Is there a husband?'

'Nope,' said Babs. 'No husband.'

'How much will you pay me to take her in?'

'For the child,' said Mr George, 'ten shillings and sixpence. For the mother, billet without board, eight and sixpence.'

Polly gave a little snort of disgust. 'You certainly have a nerve, Babs, given that I'm shelling out more than that every week to keep your kids at Blackstone.' She glared up at Walter George. 'Take your papers away. I haven't time to be bothered with that nonsense right now.'

'And the girl?' Mr George said.

'Leave her. I'll find a place for her.'

'I'm afraid I'll have to inspect the accommodations, Mrs Manone.'

'Oh, for God's sake, inspect them and get out of here.'

'With your permission?'

'Go on. Do it. Get it over with.'

The sisters watched the council officer leave the room and head downstairs. Polly didn't move until a lusty wail floated up from the kitchen, then she thrust herself out of the armchair and stalked to the window.

Babs watched her warily. She had been so enraptured with the idea of taking revenge that she had forgotten all about Polly's generosity in allowing May, June and Angus to stay at Blackstone. She had also forgotten that Miss Dawlish was officially Polly's housekeeper and that Polly would be quite within her rights to summon the woman back to Manor Park.

She felt mean now, mean and rather despicable at what she had done, yet a little niggling part of her was glad that she had put one over on Polly and forced her sister to face up to harsh reality.

Staring out at the ragged hedge and shabby evergreens, Polly said, 'You don't have to worry, Babs. I won't throw your children out of Blackstone. I'm surprised at you, though. I didn't think you were so spiteful.'

'It isn't spite,' Babs said.

'What is it then?' Polly glanced over her shoulder. 'Is it because you lost Jackie? Do you think I don't know what it's like to lose a husband?'

'It hasn't seemed to bother you much.'

'Oh, it has. It has bothered me.'

'I see: you can't stand to be without a man. Is that why you took up with the lawyer chap?' Babs said. 'Is that why you won't let Christy come back to stay with me?'

'Christy and I are doing business together. It's just business, Babs.'

Babs said. 'Well, Polly, console yourself with the thought that what I've done today is just business too – my business, my job.'

'I hope you realise that you're ruining my life,' Polly said.

'What life?' said Babs, and, rising, followed Mr George downstairs.

'I'm sorry, Polly.' Christy flopped on to his back. 'I guess I'm too tired.'

'Would you be less tired if we went downstairs?'

'I don't think it would make much difference.'

'It's them, isn't it?' Polly said. 'It's having strangers in the house?'

'Yeah, I suppose it might be.'

In fact she had no more desire in her tonight than he had and when she'd wrapped her arms and legs around him it had been out of a sense of obligation, almost defiance, rather than sexual need.

She sat up and switched on the little bedside lamp.

'Look at me, Christy, look at me.'

He lifted his head, nose barely visible above the blankets.

'Okay,' he said. 'I'm looking at you.'

'Have I changed since this morning? Have I become old and ugly?'

'Of course not.'

'Then why are you so reluctant to share a bed with me?'

'I am sharing a bed with you.'

'But you're not listening to me.'

'Yeah I am.'

'You haven't paid me a blind bit of attention since that girl arrived.'

'I can't help it.'

'Can't help what?' Polly demanded.

She didn't really require an answer. She knew that Christy Cameron was no boor, no callous philanderer. American or not, he was burdened by scruples. He had spent most of the day amusing the baby, trying to make the baby and the girl like him. That was his flaw: he wanted everyone to like him. He'd cooked for her, had found toys for the kid to play with, had even taken the kid out into the park for a half-hour and let him toddle about on the grass. But when the girl had bared her breast to feed her greedy little monster, he had hurriedly left the kitchen and had vanished upstairs.

'Look,' Polly said, 'that girl doesn't care whether we're married or not. She's not going to be shocked by anything we do. In any case, for all I know she thinks we're married. I mean, I do have a wedding ring on my finger – which is more than she has.' She nudged him with her foot under the bedclothes. 'You didn't tell her we weren't married, did you?'

'I figure she knows,' Christy said.

'You told her, didn't you?'

'Nope.'

'It doesn't mean a thing to you, does it?' Polly said. 'It isn't your house. It isn't your children's nursery that's been possessed by some half-witted tart from Belfast. It isn't your daughter's cot that—'

'You *told* me to dig out that cot and fix it up.'

'What else could I do? Let the baby sleep on the floor?'

'The kid's all right,' said Christy. 'He doesn't know what's going on.'

'And the girl? I suppose you feel sorry for the girl too?'

'Pretty much,' Christy admitted.

'It's those damned dimples, isn't it? I'll bet you wouldn't feel half so sorry for her if she was a warty old hag.'

Christy laughed and, in spite of herself, Polly gave a rueful little snort.

'Oh, very well,' she said, 'I admit that the dimples are—'

'Cute?' said Christy. 'Yeah, they're cute all right.'

'Would you prefer to share a bed with her and her dimples?'

'Right now,' Christy said, 'I just wanna get some sleep.'

'Well, I don't. I'm not in the least sleepy.'

Christy sighed and sat up.

Polly glanced at him critically. 'Are you wearing a vest?'

'Yeah.'

'That's disgusting.'

'What's disgusting about it?'

'It's unhygienic.'

'It's also goddamned freezing,' Christy said.

'How can it be freezing?' said Polly. 'It's March.'

'That's practically high summer here in the Highlands, right?'

'This is not the Highlands.' Polly paused then asked, 'Does she remind you of your Polish girl, the girl you left behind in Warsaw?'

'Nope.'

'Are you sure?'

'Sure I'm sure.'

'She isn't a refugee, you know. She's just – feckless.'

'Feckless?'

'Flighty,' Polly said. 'Irresponsible.'

'She looks after the kid well enough.'

'Meaning that I don't, that I haven't?'

'Jesus!' Christy said. 'What's wrong with you, Polly?'

Polly let out a loud sigh and threw her hands over her head.

She lay back against the pillows. 'I don't know. I honestly do not know. It's the uncertainty of it all. I mean, what's going to happen when you go – and you will go, won't you, you will leave me too?'

'I have to.'

'I'll be left alone here with very little money and a houseful of unwed mothers and screaming children.'

'One, one of each,' Christy said.

'Not if Babs has her way.'

'At least you still have a husband, even if he is six thousand miles away.'

'A husband who'd like to be shot of me once and for all.'

'How can you be sure of that?' said Christy.

'It's entirely my own fault,' Polly said. 'I should never have married him. I should never have fallen in love with him in the first place.'

'Maybe you're still in love with him.'

'No,' Polly said. 'I'm in love with you.'

She wanted him to kiss her, take her in his arms, give her a tangible sign that she was as needy and pathetic as the girl from Belfast.

'Listen,' Christy said. 'What's that noise?'

His head was turned away, one hand cupped to his ear in a gesture so artificial, so off-puttingly synthetic that Polly was tempted to slap him.

'Don't tell me she's singing to that damned baby at this hour?'

'No,' Christy said. 'It's the phone in the hall. Can't you hear it? I guess you've a call coming through.'

'At half-past midnight?' Polly was too irritated to be alarmed. 'Dear God! What is it now?' she exclaimed and, throwing back the bedclothes and snatching her dressing gown from the chair, hurried downstairs to find out.

★   ★   ★

It had been eighteen months since last she'd heard his voice. He sounded not one whit different. She felt a thud in the region between her stomach and her heart, a palpable blow, like a punch. She gasped and pressed a hand against her ribcage.

'Dom – Dominic, where are you?'

'New York: Staten Island. Did I wake you?'

'I wasn't asleep.' Her heart was racing so fast that she could hardly catch breath. 'Are the children with you? Let me talk to them.'

'The children are at school.'

'Oh!'

'Have you spoken to Cameron lately?'

She lied without hesitation. 'Not for several days.'

'What about Hughes?'

'Yesterday.'

'Polly, are you clear about what I want you to do?'

'I'm not clear about anything right now.'

'Sell everything.'

'Fin's attending to it – but there are problems.'

'When I say everything, I mean everything. The car, the house—'

'The house?' Polly said. 'I can't sell the house.'

'Why not?'

'Aren't you coming back when the war ends?'

'Didn't Cameron tell you anything at all?'

'For God's sake, darling, what's going on? Is he one of yours?'

'He is what he says he is,' Dominic told her. 'Sell the house.'

'I can't.'

Had Dominic found out about Tony? Had he always known about Tony, about Fin, perhaps even about Christy? Was he stripping her of everything, even the roof over her head, to

take revenge for her infidelities? It was as if Dominic were
here in the house, watching her every move. Polly peered up
the darkened staircase and saw Christy, a grey shape, glide
across the landing, listening like a good little spy, listening to
every word she said.

'Why can't you?' Dominic asked.

'The house has been requisitioned.'

'Since when?'

'I couldn't do anything to stop them.'

'Stop who?'

'The billeting authorities. It's the law, Dominic. Emergency
powers act.'

There was no trace of frustration in his tone. 'All right,'
he said crisply. 'Forget the house. Hughes will have to come
through with enough cash to do what we have to do.'

Polly had never much liked the mansion in Manor Park
Avenue. It had always remained the Manone family home,
no matter how much she had done to make it less masculine,
less formidably Italian. Now that Dominic was trying to take
it from her, however, to kick away the last shaky prop in their
marriage, she resisted. The arrival of the Belfast girl and her
obstreperous toddler had, it seemed, been no calamity but a
gigantic stroke of luck.

'Stuart and Ishbel, are they—' Polly began.

Dominic cut her off. 'Polly, listen to me. Hughes knows
what he's got to do but after he's done it, you walk away from
him. Understand?'

'Yes.'

'After you have the money Cameron and his crew will take
over. Do what they tell you to do and don't ask questions.'

'Can I – can I trust him, Dominic?'

'You don't have much choice,' Dominic told her. 'Listen,
you'll be bringing the money to me in Lisbon.'

'Me?'

'Yes, you.'

'I can't – I can't leave Scotland right now. Babs needs me.'

'You and nobody else, Polly. It's part of the deal, my deal.'

'Dominic, are you in trouble?'

'Yes.'

'The children—'

'The children are safe. It's me they're after, not the children.'

'Is Patricia with you?'

'She's still here, still looking after us.'

'Oh, I see.'

'No, you don't see,' Dominic said. 'You don't see at all.'

'You can't deny that you ran off with her?'

'I needed someone to look after Stuart and Ishbel. Patricia was eager to leave Scotland. I didn't have to force her. Whatever you may think, she came for the sake of the children, not to be with me, not to sleep with me.' He paused then said, 'Anyhow, she's engaged to be married. Didn't Cameron tell you?'

'Christy, why would he tell me that?'

'She's marrying his brother.'

'Ah!' said Polly. 'Ah, yes, of course.'

'In September, I think.'

'Yes,' Polly said. 'Yes, I see. I do see.'

'Let it go, Polly, just let it go. I don't have time to explain right now. Go along with the arrangements that Cameron makes on your behalf. He'll tell you how to package the money and he'll accompany you when you bring it over to Lisbon. But remember that he's their guy, not mine.'

'Their guy,' said Polly. 'Yes.'

There was a little pause, a breath. She could imagine Dominic drawing in smoke from one of the small cigars that he liked so much, blowing out smoke, thinking out his next line, how much, or how little, he should tell her.

He said, 'I was sorry to hear about Jackie. Is Babs okay?'

'She's coping,' Polly said.

'He didn't deserve to die like that,' Dominic said, 'not Jackie Hallop.'

'Nobody deserves to die like that,' said Polly.

'Is Babs okay for cash?'

'Why, do you want her to sell her house too?'

'Polly, Polly!'

'When do I have to meet you in Lisbon?'

'End of the month,' Dominic said.

'That's impossible.'

'It better not be,' Dominic said. 'If I don't close the deal with the federal authorities by then, then they'll close the deal on me.'

'Is it that bad?'

'Yes, that bad,' Dominic said. 'Now listen, Polly, when Hughes comes through with the cash, as much as he can or will rake together, go to Dougie Giffard and tell him it's done. You, nobody else.'

'Dougie? What does he have to do with all this?'

'Nothing,' Dominic told her. 'Nothing much, at any rate.'

'Then why—'

'Withdraw all the money from the private bank account, every penny, deposit it into your account with the Bank of Scotland, then go to Dougie and tell him what you've done.'

'Dominic, I don't understand what's going on.'

'You will, Polly, you will soon enough.'

'All right,' Polly said. 'I'll – I'll see you in Lisbon, darling, won't I?'

But the line, rather curiously, had gone dead.

15

Bernard came home at half-past six. He ate his supper and promptly fell asleep in the armchair by the fire, still wearing his outdoor shoes. Lizzie had a suspicion that he should be somewhere else but hadn't the heart to wake him.

She cleared the table as quietly as possible, washed the dishes, and put a ham bone to boil in a pot of water on the gas stove. She had been lucky to get the ham bone. Leaning her plump elbows on the sides of the stove, she peered admiringly into the pot as the small red-flecked object began to release its store of flavoursome fats.

The kitchenette was clean and cosy. For once there were no clothes dripping from the pulley overhead. It had been a wonderful spell of drying weather, sheets, blankets, shirts, vests, stockings and knickers all flapping in the back green like bunting in a victory parade. Bernard and Mr Grainger fretted about clear skies and moonlight. Lizzie understood their concern but didn't share it. Even in the darkest days of her time in the tenements, when you could hardly see the sky for soot, she had always been cheered by the coming of spring.

Out in the back green the wee birds were already thinking about nesting, the daffodils that had escaped the spade were showing yellow, and tender green shoots had nosed up through the clay, much to the satisfaction of the menfolk who now vied to produce a great crop of vegetables just as they had once competed to train sweet peas or coax blood-red roses into bloom. Even in the middle of a war Knightswood in spring was a pleasant place to be and now that Bernard was spending more time at home and Babs appeared to be settling down after Jackie's death, Lizzie experienced a strange surge of euphoria.

At a few minutes to nine o'clock, she made tea and carried a cup through to the living room.

Bernard was awake.

He yawned loudly, then reared up and said, 'What time is it?'

'Nearly nine.'

'Dear God, I should've been at ambulance practice an hour ago.'

'You needed the sleep.'

'I suppose I did. Old Grainger can potter on without me for once.' He took the cup and saucer and settled back.

'You're not going out now, are you?' Lizzie asked.

'No, not now. It's too late.'

'You'll be missed.'

'I doubt it,' Bernard said, sipping tea.

'Irene will miss you.'

'Irene?' He frowned. 'Oh, Irene Milligan, you mean. She's gone.'

'Gone? Gone where?'

'Sidcup, in Kent.'

'What's she doing there?'

'Services training.'

'Has she joined up?' Lizzie asked.

'She's thinking about it.'

'What does her mother have to say about that?'

Bernard shrugged. 'Not much she can say, really.'

'Why didn't you tell me?'

'I thought Mrs Milligan would've told you.'

'Well, she didn't. What else have you been keeping from me?'

Bernard laughed uncomfortably. 'What do you mean?'

She hadn't set out to harass him, for Bernard always seemed to have right on his side and to know so much more about everything than she did but something in his manner made her press on.

'What else haven't you told me?'

'Heavens, Lizzie,' he said, 'the girl only left yesterday.'

'Did she kiss you goodbye?'

'Lizzie!' He was flustered, plainly flustered. 'Don't be so daft!'

Lizzie moved to her chair on the opposite side of the fireplace. The battleground for domestic conflicts wasn't a thousand miles of desert but three square feet of hearthrug. She had been a fighter once, back in the old days. She had fought to protect her daughters and give them a better life than she'd ever had, but marriage to Bernard had robbed her of her fighting spirit. He had become her battleship, her Spitfire, her tank, and all she had to do was keep him in working order.

'Daft, am I?' Lizzie said.

'Oh, look,' Bernard said, 'it's nine o'clock: time for the news.'

'I'm not that daft,' said Lizzie. 'What's going on?'

He laughed, a nervous whinny, and shifted in the armchair, slopping tea into the saucer.

'Now see what you've made me do,' he said.

'It's another woman, isn't it?'

He paused then, leaning over, placed the teacup and saucer on the carpet by the side of the chair. Lizzie watched, her heart pounding, and wished that she had never asked the question.

'Yes,' Bernard said, 'it's another woman.'

'Are – are you leavin' me?'

'Don't be ridiculous, Lizzie. Of course I'm not leaving you.'

'Aren't you in love with her?'

'I thought I might be – but it turned out I wasn't.'

'Why are you tellin' me this, Bernard.'

'Because you asked.'

'You don't have to tell me. You *shouldn't* be tellin' me.'

'Who the heck else can I tell?' Bernard said with a trace of exasperation, 'if I can't tell you.'

'Is it Mrs Milligan?'

'Now that *is* daft, that *is* crazy,' Bernard said. 'She's a doctor at Ottershaw, if you must know. Babs sent her over to Breslin and I found her a post at the hospital and a place to stay.'

'Are you still seein' her?'

'No, I'm done with her,' Bernard said. 'She's fixed up now, not just with a job and accommodation but also with a man. That's what she wanted, I think, a man to look after her, a shoulder to lean on.'

'And it wasn't your shoulder?' said Lizzie.

'No, it wasn't my shoulder.'

'Did she turn you down?'

'I turned her down,' Bernard said. 'Oh aye, I admit I thought about it, but then I walked away. I did, Lizzie, I walked away.'

'A doctor,' Lizzie said. 'Oh my!'

'She's not young,' Bernard said. 'I mean, no spring chicken. A widow. From Belgium. Lost her family. Doesn't know where they are.'

'Is she a Jew?'

'Yes, but it wasn't her religion that put me off.'

'What was it then?'

'She wanted me to help her but she wouldn't let me feel sorry for her.' He was taken aback by his own admission. 'Dear God, Lizzie, I never realised it until now. That's it! I wanted her gratitude and she wouldn't give it.'

'Didn't you sleep with her?' Lizzie said.

Bernard shook his head.

She knew instinctively that he was telling the truth. She was so relieved that his fancy piece wasn't Mrs Milligan or Ella Grainger, say, that she felt almost sorry for him.

'It's been botherin' me, though,' he said, 'the thought that I might have.'

'But you didn't.'

'No, I didn't.'

'That's all right then,' Lizzie said.

'It isn't all right, Lizzie,' said Bernard. 'I shouldn't have put myself in that position in the first place. I did no more than my job and did it well but I did it for all the wrong reasons. I felt sorry for Evelyn Reeder – that's her name, by the way – because there's so much dislike of foreigners floatin' in the air these days. I did the right things but for all the wrong reasons.'

'She'll find another man soon enough, I expect.'

'She has already,' Bernard said. 'Another doctor.'

'Is he married?'

'He is.'

'I wonder what his wife'll have to say about it?'

'She'll probably never know,' said Bernard.

'Then good luck to them,' said Lizzie.

He blinked, startled by her statement.

'It isn't doing wrong that's wrong then?' he asked.

'No, it's being found out,' Lizzie answered.

'If it had been me, would that be a different story?'

'It would,' Lizzie told him. 'It most definitely would.'

'Well, dearest,' he sat back in the armchair, 'you do surprise me.'

'Do you feel better now, Bernard, now you've got it off your chest?'

'Oddly enough, I do.'

'What time is it?' said Lizzie.

'Just after nine.'

'If you want to listen to the news . . .'

'You sure you don't mind?'

Lizzie shook her head. 'No, I don't mind.'

And just as Bernard reached out to switch on the wireless set and Lizzie kneeled to pick up his cup and saucer the first wave of German bombers swept down the Vale of Leven and the Clydeside blitz began.

The house shook and shook again. Dougie tumbled out of his armchair. He heard the aeroplanes roaring overhead. He thought: north-east, they're in coming from the north-east. A flare lit up the yard, a brilliant yellow flash so bright that it penetrated the fabric of the curtains. He heard the thump and chuckle of an incendiary container striking the roof. Frobe leaped screeching from the window-ledge and hid under the table. Dougie flung himself belly down on the floor, groped under the table, grabbed the cat by the tail and dragged her out. He clutched her in his arms, claws digging into his chest, kicked open the pantry door and tossed her inside. He slammed the door and latched it, trying to blot out her screams. He hoisted up the bucket of sand from behind the kitchen door and dumped the contents on to the coal fire for there was more risk of losing the farmhouse to carelessness than to German bombs.

He had been listening to the BBC nine o'clock news bulletin when the planes arrived. The night was clear as crystal with a near-enough full moon. He had been out at the field gate only fifteen minutes before, sniffing the sweet spring air and had come back indoors only to catch the news.

The kids had just gone upstairs to bed. Margaret was with the girls. Angus would probably be pottering about his bedroom, playing with his toy soldiers or reading a comic by the wan light of the ceiling bulb. The paraffin stove was still lighted, though: the bloody paraffin stove! Dougie took the stairs two at a time, crowding into Margaret and the girls as they stumbled out of the bedroom.

'Gus,' Dougie shouted, 'turn off the stove.'

Another blast shook the farmhouse, not so violent this time. He heard the whistling *pop* of something coming down near the house, a parachute mine, perhaps, or another bloody incendiary.

Cursing the ineptitude of German pilots who couldn't tell a sheep field from a shipyard, Dougie grabbed May, lifted her over his head and put her down on the stairs behind him. She was as slippery as an eel inside a bath towel and squealed more in modesty than fright. June, in pyjamas, came next. He swung her over and past him on the narrow stairs then plunged up into Angus's room.

The paraffin stove glowed with soft blue light. He dived at it, screwed frantically at the tap and killed the flame.

He looked up and round.

The ceiling light had been extinguished.

Angus had flung open the blackout curtain and was leaning out of the open window. Little dabs of red and yellow tinted the silvery-blue air. Balanced on his belly, Angus shook his fists at the sky.

Dougie grabbed the boy by the leg.

'What're you doin' son?' he shouted. 'What the hell are you doin'?'

'Look at them,' Angus shouted back. 'Heinkels. Hundreds of them. The bastuds, the bastuds. What're they bombin' us for?'

'They're after the shipyards,' Dougie said. 'If they don't get the shipyards, they'll make damned sure they get the shipwrights. They're tryin' to scare us into submission.'

'They won't scare us, Dougie,' said Angus. 'Will they?'

'No, they won't scare us,' said Dougie. 'Come on, son, it's high time we got out o' here, don't you think?'

'Yeah, you're prob'ly right,' said Angus.

Kenny had Rosie halfway downstairs when a bomb fell on the tenement in St Aidan's Street. You could feel the blast rivering through you and the rumble of falling masonry was deafening. At first it was only noise and vibration, then like a fist punching into the back of the building, the stair window exploded inwards. Rosie buckled at the knees and clasped a hand to her face. Kenny hoisted her into his arms, tucked her head into the folds of his overcoat and headed for the patch of moonlight that marked the street below.

Smoke billowed in from the backs, not smoke but dust, a great gritty cloud of dust. Kenny pressed his tongue to the roof of his mouth, trying not to breathe. Behind him something came crashing down, a chimney-head or guttering. Two small girls huddled against the wall at the close mouth while their mother, a soldier's wife, tried to resurrect her baby.

The baby, caught by flying glass, looked as if it had been flayed.

It made no noise at all as the woman tried to breathe life into it.

'*Rosie*,' Kenny shouted. She couldn't hear him, of course. '*Rosie?*'

He lowered Rosie to the step and propped her up.

There was blood on her cheek and one eyebrow hung on a little tatter of skin but she was fully conscious and quite aware of what was going on.

She cupped a hand to her eyebrow and squeezed.

'*Yes*,' she said, very loudly. '*Yes*.'

His face an inch from her face, he said, 'Can you walk?'

'*Yes*.'

'Take the girls to the shelter.'

'*Yes.*'

'Do you know what you have to do?'

'*Yes.*'

'I'll stay here.'

'*Oh-kuh-kay.*' She took her hand from her face and let blood flow into her eye, winking at him. '*I've got them. Don't worry.*'

She lifted the younger child as easily as she might have lifted a kitten, pulled the other child against her skirt and hurried down the steps to the street and the shelter.

Kenny kneeled by the silent woman and the silent little bundle on the steps and very quietly said, 'Let me.'

'Sure an' I don't mind if you watch,' Doreen Quinlan said. 'It's a natural thing an' nothing to be ashamed of.'

The child looked big, almost gargantuan, nestled on the girl's lap. He seemed to be eating his mother's breast rather than sucking on it. He was clad in a short-sleeved vest and flannel bodice, the lower half of his body bare.

The electric lamp flickered.

Christy had brought in a packet of wax candles, two boxes of matches and a bundle of other necessities, including bottles of gin, whisky and tonic water. He had put them on the little folding table by the cot.

The girl was seated on the cot, her head resting against the wall.

She was totally unfazed by the air raid and had moved swiftly downstairs to the larder shelter while Christy had gathered pillows and blankets from the nursery and, thoughtfully, one large chamber pot.

If it hadn't been for Master Davy and his mother, Polly might have found it exciting to be locked up with Christy in the middle of an air raid. As it was, she was crushed into a corner with a blanket round her knees, drinking gin and tonic and smoking a cigarette. She couldn't even bring herself to sit on the bed with the girl from Belfast and her baby.

'You're taking it very calmly, Doreen,' Christy said.

'Been through it all before,' the girl said.

Polly sipped gin and tonic water and watched the lamp flicker.

'Where?' said Christy. 'In Belfast?'

'Down the Smoke.'

'London? When were you in London?'

'Before the war,' the girl said.

Christy laughed. 'They weren't bombing London before the war.'

'Went back there after it started too.'

'What were you doing in London?' Christy said. 'Looking for work?'

'Looking for his daddy,' said Doreen Quinlan, unabashed.

'Whom you didn't find, of course?' said Polly.

Crockery rattled on the dresser shelves and something smashed on the stone-flagged floor. The adults, and Master Davy too, watched the larder door shake.

'Umm!' Doreen said. 'Bit close for comfort.' She pressed a forefinger against Master Davy's fat cheek and guided his mouth to her nipple again. 'Nothing for you to worry about, boy, just get on wi' what you're doing.'

Polly was more afraid of the girl and the baby than she was of the bombs. She had encountered Doreen's type before and knew that girls like Doreen Quinlan invariably prospered. There would always be some man eager to take care of a girl with fair skin, dimples and a wide-eyed expression.

Polly said, 'Just how old is Davy?'

'Eighteen months, thereabouts.'

'Thereabouts? Don't you know?'

Doreen gave Polly a sweet smile and a shrug by way of an answer.

Christy said, 'Does that mean he was born before the war began?'

'Must have been, I suppose,' Doreen answered, 'just about.'

'In which case,' said Polly, 'you were never in the ATS at all.'

'He's a year,' said Doreen. 'Birthday last month.'

'He's a heck of a size for a one-year-old,' said Christy.

'We're all big in our family.'

'His father,' said Polly, 'was he a big man?'

'Was he not now?' said Doreen. 'He was big all right.'

'What was his name?'

'Garry.'

'Was he your sweetheart?' said Christy.

'Yea.'

'What happened to him?'

'Done the bunk.' Doreen shrugged again. 'His old man wanted to murder him for puttin' one in me.'

'Why?' said Christy.

'Good Catholic boy like Garry, set to be a priest, and me a Proddy.'

'What about your family?'

'No family. Just Auntie. She tossed me out on my ear.'

'Is all this true, Doreen?' said Christy, frowning.

'True as I'm standin' here,' the girl said.

'I don't think it's true at all,' said Polly. 'I think you're making it up. I think it's some story you read in a book.'

'Don't read books,' said Doreen. She transferred Master Davy from one breast to the other and dabbed perspiration from his brow with her sleeve.

'Have you no idea where Garry is now?' Christy asked.

'Told me he was going to the Smoke but I didn't find him where he said he'd be, staying with his mates in Fulham.'

'What sort of mates?' Polly asked.

'Workin' chaps,' Doreen said. 'They've joined up now, most o' them.'

'Were you really in London during the raids?' said Christy.

Doreen nodded. 'In Fulham. Daylight raids as well as night-time. Never got no sleep for near a week. Wore out, I was.'

'How long did you remain in Fulham?' said Polly.

'Six months, thereabouts.'

'Waiting for Garry to show up again?'

'Yea.'

'But he never did?'

'Never did,' said Doreen.

'How did you support yourself?' Polly said.

'Not the way you think.'

'And what way is that?' said Polly.

'I never done nothin' bad.'

'What did you do for money?' said Christy.

'Worked for the woman who ran the boardin' house. Mrs Duggan looked after me an' Davy. I cleaned an' cooked. Mrs Duggan was still taking in Irish but more girls than men was comin' over an' she never liked doin' for girls.'

'Why did you leave Fulham?'

'The house got blowed up.'

'What happened to Mrs Duggan?'

'Went back to Belfast. I went with her. But it was no good.'

'Why was it no good?' said Christy.

'Labour Exchange couldn't do nothing for me, not wi' a kid.'

'Is that why you came to Scotland?'

'Yea, I heard a rumour Garry was on the boats. Heard he'd signed wi' the Clan Line an' was sailing out o' Glasgow. The Clan Line never heard o' him, though, and the Merchant Seaman's Union never had him registered. So there I was, stuck for work in the Port o' Glasgow, until your sister brought me here for to work for you.'

'Work?' said Polly. 'I don't have any work for you to do.'

'I can cook,' the girl said. 'I'm reliable.'

'Hah!' said Polly.

'What about Garry?' Christy said. 'You won't find him here, you know.'

'I'm coming round to thinking he doesn't want to be found,' the girl said.

'Oh, really!' said Polly. 'I wonder what gave you that idea?'

'Polly!' Christy said, not quite chidingly.

To Polly's dismay the girl suddenly detached her son from her breast and held him out like an offering.

'I'm not thinking about Garry now,' she said. 'I got him here to think about and that's enough. It's all right for you, missus, you got a fine big house and a car and a man in your bed, but what about them empty beds upstairs. Where are they then, where are *your* kiddies?'

'Do not be impertinent,' said Polly.

'They've gone, ain't they? They ain't here no more.'

'It's none of your damned business.'

'Got rid o' them, did you, missus? Well, I ain't getting rid o' Davy, not now and not ever.'

Polly flung the gin glass to the floor and got to her feet.

'For your information,' she said angrily, 'my children are in America.'

'Yea,' said Doreen, undaunted, 'but they ain't with you, Missus Manone, are they? They ain't with their ma where they should be.'

'Easy, Doreen,' Christy warned. 'Take it easy.'

'You don't – don't know what . . .' Polly stammered, '. . . what you're talking about, you stupid woman. My children – my children are . . .'

'Yea?'

'Polly,' Christy said, 'sit down, please sit down.'

'Don't you tell me what to do.'

'Sit down, goddamn it,' Christy said. 'We're in the middle of an air raid.'

'Look, look at him now,' said Polly, close to tears, as Master Davy released a stream of pee on to the blanket. 'This place will smell for days.'

'For God's sake, stop fussing,' Christy told her. 'He's only a kid.' He pulled the little boy from Doreen's arms and held him over the chamber pot to complete what he had started. 'Don't you have any diapers?'

'Towels,' said Polly. 'There are towels upstairs.'

'Where?' Christy said.

'In the big cupboard on the first-floor landing.'

'I'll fetch them,' said Doreen. 'You know what he's liable to do next, so keep holdin' him over the pot, Mr Cameron.'

'Wait,' Christy said.

But the girl had already gone.

The lamp flickered and went out. Davy began to cry. Polly fumbled for matches, struck one, found the pocket torch and switched it on.

Christy was kneeling on the floor, holding the struggling toddler over the pot. Polly held the match flame to the candle wick. She hated what was happening, not just the raid but the intrusion. Most of all she hated an open door that revealed not the familiar outlines of her kitchen but only darkness. She longed for the girl to return so that she could close the door again.

Matchstick and candle wick fused into one long slender flame. She saw flame reflected in the child's dark eyes, the wet, red cavity of his mouth. At that moment he seemed to be yelling not at but for her, like a little succubus. Then she heard whistling. Christy snatched the baby from the pot. He turned away, sinking into the pillows on the cot. Then there was light, a brilliant flash, like sheet lightning. Then there was darkness. Then noise filled Polly's ears like water and she was flung back into the corner. Then the candle flame snuffed out and she was left with a wisp of pale grey smoke to stare at before the table fell on her and bottles, biscuits and the lamp tumbled on top of her. Then there was a long moment of silence before the house began to fall around her, creaking and groaning, and something thudded just above her head.

Polly covered her head with her arms.

There was nothing to see except a dart of light from the torch on the floor and four or five little rivulets of dust cascading down the wall of the larder.

Christy said, 'You okay?'

'Yes – I think so.'

'Not hurt?'

'No.'

'You sure?'

'No.'

Christy pulled back from the cot with the baby.

To Polly's vast relief Master Davy let out a piercing yell and glimpses of chubby legs and curled toes appeared in the torchlight.

'He's messed himself,' said Christy.

'I'm not surprised,' said Polly.

She found the torch and propped it upright.

The overhead beams were intact. The cracks from which plaster ran were confined to the angle of the wall.

Polly pulled her legs out from under the table and untangled herself from the cord of the lamp. Her skirt was torn, her stockings ruined. There was a graze on her knee that seeped a little blood but she was otherwise undamaged.

She struggled to her feet, lifted the torch and directed it at Christy.

All she could see was the baby, all legs and belly, like a cherub in an Italian painting.

'Was that a direct hit?' Polly asked.

'If it had been, we'd be dead by now.'

'Can't you shut him up?'

'I doubt it.'

Christy rose stiffly and seated himself on the edge of the cot. He held the squirming child tightly.

The racket from the avenue was louder now. Polly was reminded of afternoon visits to the theatre and how intrusive sunlight and fresh air seemed when the exit doors were opened, how unreal the world outside became. She heard fire bells and a soft, fluctuating roar like ocean waves and smelled the garden, moist and earthy in the cold night air.

'Listen,' Christy said. 'I'd better go look for her. Take the kid.'

'No.'

'Polly!'

'Look at him; he's filthy.'

'It's only poop. Take him.'

'I'll find her,' Polly said.

'All right, but be careful. We don't know what sort of damage has been done to the house. Don't go lighting any cigarettes in case there's a gas leak.'

Polly eased out of the larder.

The kitchen window had been blown in. It lay over the sink, glass and debris everywhere. The dresser, tipped forward, had shed its cups and plates, and broken crockery littered the table and the floor.

She picked her way upstairs into the hall.

The hall seemed to be intact. The clock was still ticking and, curiously, the telephone was ringing in short intermittent bursts. Polly ignored it. If the kitchen had caught it, the breakfast room, with its big French windows, would be devastated too. She moved to the foot of the staircase and looked up the length of the torch beam.

'Doreen?'

Torrents of small debris cascaded down the staircase. The light fitting, a great brass pendant, had become detached from its moorings and swayed on a frayed cord. Even by the scant light of the torch Polly could see that the blast had struck the rear wall of the house, smashing through windows, scouring passageways and corridors and battering open cupboard doors.

'Doreen, are you all right?'

No answer.

Cautiously Polly picked her way upstairs.

The light pendant, like a Damoclean sword, dangled just above her head. She ducked under it and pulled herself into the first-floor passageway.

Through a gaping hole in the wall at the far end of the passage she could make out moonlight, and flames. Flames soared from one of the houses that backed the Avenue, sparks shooting high into the night sky. The gap framed the scene like a parlour painting and for an instant Polly was entranced. Then she moved forward, stepping over glass, smashed frames, lumps of masonry and pale hummocks of linen that had been sucked from the cupboard and blown down the length of the corridor.

The girl was lying on her back, skirt over her face.

Her legs were bent backward and there was a gigantic hole in her stomach. Her blood looked like treacle in the torchlight.

Polly got down on one knee and lifted away the skirt.

Doreen's face was unmarked except for a frond of blood clinging to her parted lips. She was still dimpled, still pretty. Her eyes were wide open.

'Doreen?' Polly whispered.

She expected no answer for even to Polly it was obvious that Doreen Quinlan was dead.

The German pathfinders had done their work well. Marker fires raged all through Clydebank and across the slopes of the Old Kilpatrick Hills. The oil tanks at Dalnottar released great shawls of black smoke and the pungent odour of whisky stung the throat; the distillery at Yoker was burning too. Across the river in Renfrew incendiaries had taken a heavy toll and the entire horizon, from east to west, was ablaze.

The view from Blackstone Farm was breathtaking.

Dougie leaned in the open doorway of the barn, a cigarette in his mouth, an arm about the boy.

Angus had refused to go indoors and curl up between the straw bales like his sisters. Dougie couldn't blame him. If he had been Angus's age he would have been gripped by an experience that was no longer an air raid but more a force of nature, awful and awe-inspiring at one and the same time.

'Do you really think Ron'll be all right?' Angus asked.

'Well, if he's wise,' said Dougie, 'he'll be hidin' in his shed.'

'Maybe we should go back there, see if he needs anything.'

'We're staying right where we are,' said Dougie.

'They're not dropping anything on us now,' said Angus.

'It's half-past four in the mornin', son,' said Dougie. 'This is the longest air attack we've had yet. No sayin' how many more planes are to come.'

'Look,' Angus shouted, excitedly. 'Look, look at that, Dougie.'

'I see it,' said Dougie.

'What is it?'

'Probably the timber yard at Singer's.'

'*Whoosh!*' Angus shouted. '*Whoosh!*'

'There're people down there,' Dougie said, 'remember.'

'They'll be okay, though, won't they, in the shelters?'

'Not them all,' said Dougie.

He had extinguished the two incendiary canisters that had fallen into the yard, one with a dustbin lid and the other with a shovelful of slurry from the pit by Ron's sty. The pig had been nervous and skittery but Dougie had hurled a handful of rotten apples into the sty to give Ron something to chew on before he'd scuttled back to the stables where, tucked among the straw bales under the gallery floor, Margaret had bedded down the girls.

May and June were asleep now, their fears calmed and put aside. There was the smack of adventure about sleeping in blankets in the stable-barn, Dougie supposed, but it would become a whole lot less adventurous if the Luftwaffe made a habit of raiding Glasgow, and the sight of the sky on fire would pall quickly enough when the kids saw the damage that bombing caused. Dougie promised himself that he would keep them away from Clydebank for God knew what horrible sights might greet them there.

'There!' Angus pointed again. 'See the steeple. Is that St John's?'

'I dunno. It's kinda far away. It might be St Jerome's?'

'Where's that?'

'Over the river, where your mama works?'

Angus swung round. 'Mum's not there, is she?'

At last it had dawned on the boy that people were dying.

'She won't be at work in the middle o' the night,' Dougie said. 'She'll be safe at home in the Anderson shelter, with April.'

'What if she's not?'

'She'll be fine, Angus.'

'What if she dies? What'll we do if she dies?'

'Angus, they're not bombing Raines Drive.'

'I don't want her to die.'

'Your mama will be fine.'

'How do *you* know? Look at it,' Angus shouted. 'It's terrible.'

'It's all that,' Dougie agreed.

'Why are they doing it? Why are they bombing us?'

'Because they want to win the war.'

'But why – why is this the way to win the war?'

'There are all sorts o' ways to win a war, son,' Dougie said.
'I wish I had a gun,' said Angus, grimly. 'A great big gun.'
'And just what would you do with a gun?' Miss Dawlish
asked.

She appeared behind them with a blanket to drape over
the boy's shoulders and two beakers of tea poured from a
Thermos flask.

'Shoot them,' Angus shouted. 'Shoot them all,' then with a
blood-curdling cry, crouched and fired an imaginary weapon
up into the burning sky.

Ten minutes after Babs tucked her into the cot in the Anderson
shelter, April gave a little sigh and fell fast asleep. She wakened
only once when something big and heavy thundered along
Raines Drive.

'Daddy's not fighting now,' she murmured, sleepily.

Babs, seated by the cot, said, 'No, dearest, Daddy's not
fightin' now.'

'Where's Christy?'

'He's takin' care of Auntie Polly.'

'That's good,' said April, and closed her eyes again.

Christy had drained water from the shelter with a stirrup
pump, put candles into holders and a torch with spare batteries
in an old biscuit tin. He had even laid out kindling and coal for
the stove but Babs didn't have the sense to light it for a kind of
paralysis came over her as soon as April fell asleep.

She wished that Christy was with her now for as the night
wore on she became scared and lonely, fretting about Mammy
in Knightswood, Rosie in town, even about Polly over in
Manor Park. She was less worried about Angus and the girls,
whom she assumed were safe in the countryside.

About half-past four, she opened the door and peeped out.

Noises in the Drive: the imperious shouting of wardens and
the shrilling of whistles relaying tuneless messages across the

moonlit gardens. She crawled up the steps on her knees, glanced up at the sky, navy blue and deep, and at the moon and the flushed cloud that formed a canopy above the rooftops.

She stood up. She could make out the glint of moonlight in the glass of the villas and bungalows round about and, heartened, clambered up the slope of the shelter on to the roof.

'*Get down, woman! Get down from there!*'

Babs peered into the shadows by the side of the bungalow and saw a tin helmet, a gas cape, the flicker of a torch.

The warden advanced to the edge of the lawn.

'Are you tryin' to get yourself killed?'

Because she was at work all day, she had no contact with Civil Defence groups and didn't know the warden's name. She slid down the slope of the shelter and flounced across the lawn. Through gaps between the bungalows she was aware of flames but she saw them out of the corner of her eye, not focusing.

Hands on hips, she said, 'What's up? What's happening?'

'There's been no all clear. Get back into your shelter an' stay there.'

The fiery red sheet behind the man expanded and at that moment Babs realised its significance. She made to move past the warden, heading for the path at the front of the bungalow, but he checked her progress, snatching at her arm.

'No,' he said, growling. 'No, lady, don't look.'

Babs broke free, ran down the narrow path, and stopped in her tracks.

Everything was on fire, everything. The river, the hills, the townships were all illuminated by great ghastly sheets of flame.

She clapped her hands to her cheeks.

'Oh God!' she cried out. '*Oh God!*'

'I told you not to look, didn't I?' the warden said and snaring her by the waist, led her, shocked and unprotesting, back to the safety of the shelter.

*　　*　　*

Army mattresses had been laid on the dirt floor at the end of the communal shelter and all the little ones settled down, some of the older women too.

The two children whom Rosie had picked up at the close mouth had been calmed by the arrival of the dark-haired woman, Mrs Lottman, and her children. They were friends of Mrs Mavor, the woman whose baby had been injured. Mrs Lottman was very concerned about Mrs Mavor's baby and asked for news from the wardens and welfare workers who drifted in and out of the shelter but they could provide no information. The fact that Kenny hadn't returned yet didn't worry Rosie. She assumed that he was helping with rescue work or had been summoned back to St Andrew's Street.

She sat very still by Mrs Lottman's side and watched the children sleep.

The air in the shelter was clammy and condensation glistened on the walls but at least the floor was dry.

Rosie pressed the pad of lint that a warden had given her against her torn eyebrow. If she took her hand away she felt sure that the lint would remain in place, pasted to her flesh by blood. Her eyebrow hurt hardly at all but the cut cheekbone throbbed. She had a bit of a headache and her vision was blurry but Mrs Lottman peered into her eyes and told her she'd be all right.

Mrs Lottman showed no sign of the panic that had affected her last time. Perhaps, Rosie thought, we're adapting and will soon become blasé about spending nights out of bed. Perhaps we will become refugees, drifting from place to place and there will be nothing solid left to hang on to except air-raid shelters and community canteens.

She had assumed that working in Merryweather's would help her make sense of the war. She'd been wrong and if she hadn't been cursed with a stubborn streak she would have packed in the job months ago. Only Mr Bass and two or three of the younger girls ever tried to converse with her now that Doris Maybury had put it about that Rosie MacGregor wasn't really the wife of a policeman but the mistress of an Italian collaborator.

If the fiction hadn't been so vicious Rosie would have laughed it off, but malice and prejudice were home-grown evils that corrupted everyone in time and Rosie was thankful for her deafness and the numbing concentration that assembling small parts hour upon hour demanded.

As the night wore on and the threat of bombing receded, Rosie slipped into a light, not unpleasant sleep. She had no idea what time it was when Mrs Lottman dug her in the ribs. Rosie opened her eyes and read the woman's lips.

'That's the all clear and unless I'm mistaken, that's your hubby.'

Rosie, stiff and sore now, got up from the bench.

Nobody seemed to be in a hurry to leave the shelter. Mothers were lifting children from the mattresses – sleepy little faces, cross at being wakened – and men were helping the older women to their feet. One old woman was gathering up blankets, shaking and folding them as if the shelter had already become her home. Smoke curled away into the faint pre-dawn daylight through the open door at the far end of the shelter and, looking in that direction, Rosie saw Kenny standing against the light.

He was covered in dust, his hair, normally so neat, standing up about his head as if he'd been electrocuted.

He was grinning, though, and holding up his thumb.

She eased her way along the wall of the shelter to greet him.

He put his hands on her shoulders and kissed her.

'You look terrible,' he said.

'You don't look so good yourself. What about the Mavor baby?'

'She's in the children's ward at Yorkhill. They've patched her up pretty well. She lost the little finger on her left hand, poor wee lass, and she'll have some scars on her face when she grows up but her eyes weren't damaged and there were no major injuries.'

'Where is Mrs Mavor?'

'She'll be back soon.'

Mrs Lottman, her baby in her arms, joined them.

'How badly are our houses damaged?' she asked.

'Most of the windows are out and the gas has been cut off but otherwise they're just about habitable,' Kenny told her. 'Watch out for the glass, though. There's tons of broken glass everywhere. I'd sweep out the kitchen first, if I were you, and put the kids in there until you can clear the rest of the rooms. The council will send workmen round to board up the windows.'

'If that's the case, I'll take care of Mrs Mavor's girls,' Mrs Lottman said.

Rosie said, 'I'd take them but I have to go to work.'

Kenny put out a forefinger and dabbed the blood-caked pad of lint that clung like a barnacle to her eyebrow.

'Not with that wound, Rosie,' he said, 'not until you've seen a doctor.'

'Listen to your man, Mrs MacGregor,' Mrs Lottman told her and, gathering the sleepy brood about her, herded them towards the door. 'Tell Mrs Mavor where they are, will you please?'

'Will do,' said Kenny, then with an arm about her shoulder, steered Rosie out into the blackened street.

16

By rights Babs should have been on her knees by breakfast time for she hadn't slept a wink all night. Instead she was filled with defiant energy and pursued her usual routine as if there had been no air raid at all.

The houses in Raines Drive and Holloway Road had escaped unscathed, and when Babs reached the Millses' house she found the usual little band of children waiting to be led to the nursery. Mr Mills told her that Clydebank had been severely damaged, though, and many people had been killed. He warned her that she would be lucky to make it as far as Paisley, let alone St Jerome's. He also asked her to be back before nightfall for predictions were that the Germans would come again to pound what was left of the city and Mrs Mills and he just weren't capable of looking after children in the event of another raid.

Babs pursed her lips, kissed her daughter and set off for Paisley Road.

She was much more anxious now, fearful for her children, her sisters and her mother. For two pins she would have abandoned her trek to Cyprus Street and headed for Manor Park instead. She passed a telephone box with a queue outside it, hesitated, then walked on. All she had to hang on to was her need to reach Cyprus Street. Archie would be there. Archie wouldn't let a little thing like an air raid keep him from doing his duty. My duty, she thought, that's what I'm doing, my duty to King, country and Archie Harding. Hang on to that, honey, and just keep walking.

Babs wasn't the only worker on the hoof that morning, not by a long chalk. Power lines were down at Govan Cross and no trams were running. The thoroughfare hummed with ambulances, fire engines and military vehicles, and, now and then, a police car hurtled past at high speed.

Babs walked for the best part of a mile and was just beginning to think of giving up when a single-decker bus appeared out of a side street and halted at the kerb to let passengers off.

Babs ran up to the cab and shouted, 'Where are you going?'

'Paisley depot – if I can get there.'

'Room for one more?'

'Hop in.'

Forty minutes later, having skirted floods from burst water mains, rubble-strewn streets and cul-de-sacs ringed by fire engines, the bus reached Paisley, nosed into the depot and stopped.

Babs and the dozen or so passengers who were left on board got off.

She had seen enough damage to be sure that the news Mr Mills had picked up on his wireless set was accurate. Clydeside had taken a hammering and she felt selfish, almost cruel, about neglecting her family.

She had made it this far, though, and would press on. With luck the office phone would still be functioning and she would be able to contact Polly at home, Bernard at his office in Breslin and maybe even Kenny in Glasgow to make sure that everyone was all right.

She set off down lanes and side streets between passive old tenements and corner shops and at length found herself on Aerodrome Road with an unimpeded view of the shipyards and the river.

Her heart sank.

Dense black smoke coiled over the townships on the far

side of the Clyde, and in strengthening sunlight she could
make out a mass of ruined buildings.

She headed along the straight with tears running down her
cheeks and her legs shaking. It was the worst time, there would
never be another quite so bad, for it seemed to Babs then that
she had lost everything, her children, her mother, her sister too
probably, that everything had gone up in smoke and that all
she would have left would be files and telephones and a legion
of slackers and shirkers, without pride or shame, demanding
their rights.

The Aerodrome Road was remarkably quiet, though.

Tramway tracks shimmered in the sunlight. Gulls were
strung out in a long white line across the furrows. In the
distance, near the old aerodrome buildings, a barrage balloon,
dimpled like a pillow, floated only feet above the ground and,
even as Babs watched, collapsed in a flapping heap. A Co-op
delivery van passed, heading towards Paisley. It was followed
by two Red Cross vehicles, not ambulances but motorcars
and, of all things, an open-topped double-decker bus packed
with children who cheered and waved as they passed.

Babs wiped her eyes with a soggy handkerchief and tried
to pull herself together. She was nowhere, though, going
nowhere, running from nowhere to nowhere. She began to
cry again, to keen softly for Jackie and all the folk she loved
whom she might never see again.

Then far down the road she noticed an ungainly little figure
pulling towards her from beneath the smoke cloud's shadow.
Steering an erratic course between the tram rails, head down
and tail in the air, Archie Harding pedalled into view and
gradually approached.

Sniffing back tears, Babs watched the bike swerve towards
the verge and brake. Archie threw one long leg across the
handlebars and dismounted, catching the bicycle neatly by
the saddle.

'Well, well,' he said, panting just a little, 'what a surprise.'

'What's surprisin' about it?'

'I didn't expect to see you today.'

'If you didn't expect to see me today what are you doin' this far out on the Aerodrome Road?'

'Taking a spot of exercise, that's all.'

'Really? Did you pedal all the way from Scotstoun on that thing?'

'That thing, I'll have you know, is a priceless antique, just one step up from a penny farthing. Been in our family for years. How are you, Mrs H.?'

'Not so bad really,' Babs said. 'Are we in business?'

'Hanging on by our fingernails,' said Archie.

'That smoke,' Babs said, 'isn't from our fuel dump then?'

'Fortunately not,' said Archie. 'Our fuel dump received a handful of incendiaries but the firemen were on to it at once. They've been spraying down the containers more or less constantly ever since. The black smoke is from the Admiralty oil tanks at Dalnottar. Only one of the seventy-odd tanks is actually on fire, though three tanks were hit. The rest of the smoke is from schools and churches and tenements. I skirted Clydebank to get to the ferry and it doesn't look good. You?'

'All right. No sleep. Not much damage.'

'Family all right?'

'I don't know yet.'

'Well, not surprisingly our phone's out of order. I've reported it through a line at the warden's post and the Exchange has promised to have it repaired as soon as possible. We've lost all the windows, of course, and some of the plaster but given what it's like over the river . . .' He shrugged. 'Anyway, we've lots to do, lots and lots to do.'

'Archie, why did you come lookin' for me?'

'I'm responsible for the welfare of all personnel.'

'Archie?'

'I knew you'd come, Babs. I knew you wouldn't let me down.'

'Is that the only reason?'

'We're two peas in one pod,' said Archie, evasively. 'And we are now about to be two peas on one bicycle. Shape your haunch to the crossbar, Mrs Hallop, and I will provide the locomotive power.'

'I perch, you pedal.'

'Precisely,' said Archie.

She felt better now, relieved of fear and pessimism by Archie's cheerful presence. She hoisted herself on to the crossbar, skirt hitched up and legs dangling and Archie, with considerable care, cocked a leg over the saddle, twined an arm about her middle and, steering with one hand, sent them bowling off along the road to St Jerome's.

'For God's sake, Polly,' Christy said, 'don't be unreasonable. I'm only asking if I can borrow your motorcar.'

'I'm out of petrol.'

'You're not. You've half a goddamned tankful.'

'And I'll need every drop.'

'For what?'

'To get rid of him for a start.'

'Rid of him?'

'Take him back.'

The parlour was the only room in the house that had not been damaged. The windowpanes bulged against their strips of tape but otherwise the room was just as it had been before the bombing. Christy had spread out his cameras, lenses and packets of film on the carpet and was in process of packing them into a canvas bag. He wore his reefer jacket and ankle-length boots, and Polly realised that whether or not she gave him permission to borrow the motorcar he intended to leave her here alone with Doreen Quinlan's child.

She looked down her nose at Master Davy, who had developed an affinity with the huge black leather sofa and was pulling himself around it hand over hand, his little bare feet curling into the carpet, his fat little legs bowed.

Now and then he would glance up at Polly as if he expected praise for his achievements; none was forthcoming.

'Take him back where?' said Christy.

'To Babs, or to that man – George whatsisname – let them deal with it.'

'You can't return him, Polly. He's not damaged goods.'

'He isn't ours, Christy. He doesn't belong to us.'

'Who does he belong to then?'

'He isn't our responsibility.'

Doreen's body had already been removed, a simple procedure, quickly executed. Within an hour of Christy reporting the girl's death to a warden, two mortuary attendants and a doctor from the Procurator Fiscal's office had turned up in an ambulance. Polly had given the Fiscal's representative a brief, not quite accurate statement of what had happened and Doreen's body had been stretchered down from the first-floor corridor, hoisted into the back of the ambulance and driven away.

'If he's not our responsibility,' Christy said, 'how come you lied to the guy from the Coroner's office?'

'Fiscal,' said Polly. 'We don't have coroners in Scotland.'

'Whatever,' said Christy. 'Why did you tell him that Doreen was your cousin on a visit from Belfast? Why didn't you just tell him the truth?'

Polly shook her head. 'Too complicated.'

'You could have handed the kid over right there and then.'

'No,' Polly said.

Christy strapped up the canvas bag and got to his feet. He pulled a Spanish-style beret from his pocket and stuck it on his head. 'We'll talk about it later, okay? Right now I gotta get down to the docks and start earning my keep. I'm a photographer, in case you've forgotten. This is what I do, Polly.'

'I'm sure your bosses at Brockway's will be delighted to have yet more photographs of smoking ruins and weeping children.'

'Polly, this is the news,' he said. 'Now do I get to borrow the car, or not?'

'The ignition keys are on the table in the hall.'

'Does that mean yes?'

'Yes.'

He kissed her perfunctorily on the cheek while Master Davy tried to clamber up on to the sofa and, failing, fell back on to the carpet with a yelp of annoyance.

Polly said, 'What am I supposed to do with him?'

'You've raised kids, haven't you? You should know what to do.'

'Nanny Patricia raised my two,' Polly said. 'I only watched from a safe distance. I wonder if he's almost fully weaned.'

'Well,' Christy said, 'if he isn't, he soon will be.'

He kissed her again, then went out into the hallway, picked up the keys from the table and left the house.

Master Davy wailed.

Polly picked the toddler up, carried him to the window and together they watched the Wolseley nose down the drive and turn into the Avenue.

Master Davy peered up at her.

'Ma,' he said, quite distinctly. 'Ma. Ma. Ma.'

And Polly, all too swiftly, lugged him out into the hallway in the hope that the telephone was working and that she could somehow get through to Babs.

*   *   *

Archie's belief that they would have lots to do turned out to be false. Without a telephone connection the Welfare Centre in Cyprus Street seemed to have slipped right off the production map. Babs spent the remainder of the morning sweeping up piles of broken glass while Archie, ever inventive, glued umpteen cardboard folders together and nailed them, layer by layer, over the shattered windows.

They worked undisturbed for there were no scroungers looking for hand-outs, no homeless waifs in search of accommodations and, to Archie's consternation, no outriders from the Labour Exchange to check on their welfare and deliver the Friday pay packets.

Shortly after noon, a tram car rattled down to the Cross.

Shortly after that the fire engines left the vicinity of the fuel store.

Around one o'clock two army privates parked a lorry outside, sauntered into the office and claimed they were looking for Renfrew, but they were really in search of a hot cup of tea, which Babs was only too pleased to provide. Garrulous souls, the soldiers imparted much information about the state of the roads and the havoc that the air-raid had caused. They stayed for half an hour, ate biscuits, drank tea, smoked two of Archie's cigarettes and left again, heading heaven knew where.

It was just on two o'clock when the telephone in Archie's office chirped.

Babs snatched it up immediately.

'Thank God, I've reached you,' Bernard said. 'I thought we might be cut off for days. Are you all right?'

Babs told him that she was.

Archie was standing on his desk trying to repair a damaged light fitting with window tape and string.

Babs looked up. Archie looked down. She mouthed, 'My stepfather.' Archie nodded and went back to what he was doing.

Tense now, Babs leaned her shoulder against Archie's trousers leg and said to the mouthpiece, 'Have you seen the kids?'

'Popped out to Blackstone as soon as I possibly could,' Bernard told her. 'Everything's fine there. The school's still open. There hasn't been much damage in Breslin, thank heaven. I wish I could say the same about Knightswood.'

'Mammy, is she—'

'Bombed out,' Bernard said. 'The cottages copped a lot of blast from a parachute bomb. I've moved her to Blackstone until the windows are replaced and gas and electricity restored. We could've muddled through, I suppose, but moving out temporarily seemed by far the most sensible thing to do under the circumstances, especially as there may be another raid tonight.'

'Blackstone's handy for you too.'

'Very,' Bernard admitted. 'Has Polly contacted you yet?'

'Not yet. The office is only just back on line.'

'She will,' Bernard said. 'She's all right but the mansion took a fair walloping, I gather – and she has a problem.'

'What sort of problem?'

'Look, dearest,' Bernard said, 'it's a complete madhouse over here. We've inherited an enormous number of bombed-out persons scrambling for safe billets, so I'll have to go.'

'What's Polly's problem?'

'I leave her to tell you that herself.'

'Everyone over there is all right, aren't they?'

'Right as rain,' Bernard assured her, and hung up.

Babs returned the telephone to the cradle and rested her head as well as her shoulder against Archie's shin.

She blew out her cheeks and sighed.

'Not bad news, I trust?' said Archie from on high.

'Nope, not bad news at all,' Babs said as he climbed down and seated himself on the desk beside her. 'My mother's gone to stay at Blackstone farm with my kids and my sister Polly has a problem, but I don't know what it is.'

'Call her,' Archie said. 'Go on, do it now before the powers that be discover we still exist and all hell breaks loose.'

'I'll pay for the call, of course.'

'No, no, Mrs H.,' said Archie. 'Have this one on me.'

Soon after Christy left, Master Davy's wails became too loud to ignore and Polly ventured downstairs into the wreckage of her kitchen. She carried the toddler with her for she was afraid to leave him alone. He was a curious wee beggar and would take off on all fours the instant her back was turned, and with the house full of steep stairs and broken glass, Polly had a horror of some harm coming to him, some injury for which she would be blamed.

So far Davy seemed not to have noticed that his mother was missing and his wailing was occasioned by hunger and discomfort rather than emotional distress, so Polly told herself.

When she carried him into the kitchen he stopped crying at once, though teardrops still clung to his eyelashes and he sobbed deeply from time to time.

'My goodness me,' said Polly, 'will you look at all this mess.'

Master Davy peered down at broken dishes, at the dresser toppled across the stove, at the hole in the wall where the window frame had been. He uttered a sound, a variation on 'Ma-ma-ma', and pointed at the lawn that sloped down towards the wall like a smooth yellow blanket, a chimneypot, absolutely whole, propped in the middle like a garden ornament.

Polly stepped cautiously through the wreckage.

Shattered Italian plates, china jars, pots, saucepans, cutlery and jugs were scattered everywhere. The table was covered in shards and splinters and the chairs were overturned. To her left she could see the larder, her shelter, dark as a cave.

The baby bounced in her arms. He wanted down, wanted to explore. She held him as tightly as she dared.

'Patience, m' lad, patience,' she told him. 'First we're going to have to find something for you to eat, then we're going to have to find a means of cooking it and something to serve it in.'

Davy studied her with the same sort of concentration that Rosie displayed when lip-reading.

One-handed, Polly righted a chair, cleared space at the table and sat down. For a brief moment she felt overwhelmed by all the things she would have to do just to perform the simplest of tasks, like boiling an egg or making oatmeal. She looked around, detected a pan, a milk pan, and shifting the chair like a hobbyhorse, stooped and slid the object from beneath the dresser. She spotted a jar almost full of sugar, hobbled to it and picked it up.

She placed the items on the table and, rising, moved further into the room, scavenging like a magpie for anything that might prove useful. She retrieved a tin of dried egg powder and, miraculously, a pint bottle of milk still with the cap on, some spoons, a knife and, squashed under a drawer of the dresser, a packet of lard and a box of oatmeal.

Soon she would have to go upstairs. She hadn't been upstairs since the Quinlan girl's body had been taken away. She was afraid of what she would find there, not just blood on the floor but all the detritus of her comfortable life with Dominic scattered or destroyed.

Davy had stopped sobbing. He shifted about in her arms, wriggling not to escape but to see what little piece of treasure would next emerge from the debris.

Five minutes of foraging gave Polly most of what she needed. She wrapped the items in a sheet from the cot in the larder and carried the bundle, and Davy, back upstairs to the parlour.

She put the bundle on the top of the piano where Davy couldn't get at it, then, lifting him again, lugged him into the ground-floor toilet to see if the water had been turned on again, which, to her relief, it had.

The sight of clear cold water trickling thinly from the tap pleased her enormously. She poured a glass of water, gave the baby a sip and drank the rest herself, then, refreshed if not exactly rejuvenated, took a great deep breath and headed upstairs to rummage through the bedrooms in search of towels, clothes, documents and ready cash and, if she could find it, the pushchair that had last been used when Ishbel was a toddler.

Some time later, close on one o'clock, with a fire of broken sticks crackling in the grate and the baby fed, washed, changed and fast asleep in a nest of pillows on Dominic's big black sofa, Polly went out to the hall to telephone Babs once more.

'Where the devil have you been?' were Polly's first words. 'I've been trying to reach you all morning. Didn't Bernard tell you?'

'Nope,' Babs answered. 'He just told me you had a problem.'

'A problem.' Polly's voice crackled on the wire. 'That's putting it mildly. I'm stuck here on my own with that Irish child. He won't leave me alone. You didn't tell me he was mobile. He can row himself about on his bottom like a turtle. I can't turn my back on him for a moment. And the floors are covered in broken glass. And I've no hot water, gas or electricity. I had to cook on a wood fire in the grate in the parlour just to give him something to eat.'

'Whoa,' said Babs. 'Calm down. Let me talk to Christy.'

'Christy,' Polly snapped, 'has gone out to take photographs.'

'I see. Did the Belfast girl go with him? Is that the problem?'

'The Belfast girl's dead . . .'

'Dear God! Bernard didn't tell me that.'

'. . . and I'm saddled with the kid.'

'Bomb, was it?'

'Flying glass. She was caught in the upstairs corridor when
the windows were blown in. Killed instantly. The mortuary
attendants took her away this morning. Very efficient they
were too, I'll give them that.' Polly checked herself and
strove to sound more rational and controlled. 'I take it you're
all right.'

'We're fine,' said Babs. 'I even made it to work.'

'Oh good,' said Polly. 'Good for you. Now how long will
it take you to send a man over here to collect the child?'

'You're joking!'

'I'm not.'

Archie had strolled into the outer office but was still within
earshot and when Babs covered the receiver and called out to
him he returned at once. He leaned on the desk and peered
enquiringly at her through his bottle-bottom glasses. Babs
kept her hand over the mouthpiece and hissed, 'The Belfast
girl, Quinlan, was killed last night. My sister wants us to take
the baby back. What shall I tell her?'

'Tell her to hang on to him meanwhile.'

'I doubt if she'll want to do that.'

'Try her,' Archie said.

Babs spoke into the telephone. 'Polly, I don't know if you
realise that things are pretty bad everywhere at the moment.
I mean, there are hundreds dead an' thousands injured,
thousands more without a roof over their heads. Could we
possibly ask you to look after—'

'Oh, for God's sake! I have things to do, Babs. I'm *busy*.'

'Well, we're all kinda busy, Poll,' Babs said, evenly. 'It's not as if we know who the kid belongs to now. Far as we can make out the father's unknown, certainly untraceable. We do have an address for an aunt in Belfast but I doubt if we'll be able to get in touch with her immediately an' I doubt if she's gonna come rushing over to take the child away. Fact, I doubt if she'll take him at all.'

'This isn't good enough,' Polly said.

Archie's eyebrows formed an arch under his hairline. He signalled for the phone and Babs, with some reluctance, yielded it to him.

He straightened, brushed his dusty lapels with his knuckles, then said, 'Mrs Manone? Archibald Harding here. Now, what's the problem?' He listened, nodding, while Polly went off into another rant. Then, drily, he said, 'Very well, Mrs Manone, I do believe I have grasped the situation. I sympathise with the inconvenience it has caused you. Most inconsiderate of the mother to get herself killed, I agree. Now, here's what you must do: collect all the personal belongings of the child and deceased mother, including all and any documentation that pertains to identity. Take them and the child along to a police station. The officers on duty will attend to his welfare and you will be absolved of all further responsibility.'

'Archie?' Babs hissed. 'What the heck are you doing?'

She heard Polly say, 'What will happen to the child then?'

'That will not be your concern.' Diplomatically Archie hesitated for just a fraction of a second before he continued. 'As a matter of information, the child will be transported to an orphanage or council home and kept there until such time as the next of kin can be traced. That, alas, may take some weeks given the pressure that . . . No, Mrs Manone, I'm afraid there is no other alternative.'

Archie's brows rose once more and even through the thick lenses Babs could make out the angry glint in his eyes.

He thrust the receiver towards Babs. 'She wants to talk to you.'

'What?' Babs said. 'Didn't Mr Harding make it plain enough, Polly?'

'I – I can't do it,' Polly said, 'not like that, not in cold blood. Won't you – won't you come over and take him from me?'

'Me?' said Babs. 'What could I do with the kid that you can't?'

'You could take him in and look after him.'

'Oh, I would,' said Babs, 'believe me I would. But it's impossible. Surely even you can see that, Polly. I can't care for a toddler, not when I have to go out to work every day. It's difficult enough with April, God knows, but a baby, no.'

'You did this deliberately, didn't you?' Polly said.

'I didn't know there'd be a bloody air raid.'

'All right,' said Polly. 'All right.'

'What does *that* mean?' said Babs.

'I'll do it myself.'

'You mean, look after him?'

'No,' Polly said. 'I'll take him to the police.'

'An' just dump him?'

'Of course,' said Polly curtly, and rang off.

The taxi couldn't make it to the top of the hill. Lorries blocked the street below the cul-de-sac in which Rosie lived and an odd-looking vehicle with a jib-crane on a flat-bed had been backed into the tenements and was unloading four or five huge wooden beams that, Polly supposed, would be fixed in place to support the building's sagging gables.

She paid the taxi driver, drew Ishbel's pushchair from the luggage nook and strapped the bundle of Davy's belongings on to it. She pushed the chair with one hand and held Davy against her body with the other. He'd had a good sound sleep and had eaten most of the dried-egg omelette that she'd made for him. He had even allowed her to dress him in a clean nappy and the knitted romper suit without too much fuss. It struck Polly that young Master Quinlan was well used to being looked after by strangers and handed round from pillar to post.

She ploughed on uphill, by-passing coppers and work-men.

Davy goggled at the sight of a huge beam swinging on the end of a chain and chattered incomprehensibly in Polly's ear. He was an active child, very alert for his age, though Polly had no idea what age he really was for Doreen had been evasive on that point and there had been no birth certificate among the young woman's documents.

The cul-de-sac was strewn with debris. Three men in gas board uniforms were peering into an open manhole. There were no warning signs, however, and the buildings were occupied so Polly assumed that it was safe to proceed.

In Rosie's close three women of about her age were shov-elling up glass and an older woman was already scrubbing the stairs.

'I'm looking for my sister, Mrs MacGregor,' Polly said. 'Do you happen to know if she's at home?'

'She is,' a dark-haired woman told her. 'She took a knock on the head an' her hubby had her round at the doctor's for stitches. She's up upstairs now, I'm sure. You sure, Mrs Mavor?'

'Aye, I'm sure she's at home.'

Polly thanked the women, navigated a route between the heaps of broken glass and, hoisting the pushchair into the crook of her arm, man-handled it, and Davy, up to Rosie's landing.

She pressed the big ivory-white button, waited, pressed it again, then turned the little brass knob of the door lock and gave the door a push.

It swung open.

Still carrying Davy, Polly stepped into the hall just as Rosie, blinking and rubbing her eyes, emerged from the bedroom.

'Oh!' Rosie said in a hoarse whisper. 'It's you, is it? I thought it might be Kuh-Kenny, or another air raid. What time is it?'

'Just gone four,' said Polly.

Rosie looked alarmingly skinny, Polly thought, dressed in nothing but an old skirt and blouse. A pure white, unsullied bandage covered half her head and dipped across her left eye, flattening her hair. A small crisscross of pink sticking plaster adhered to her cheekbone. All in all, she gave the appearance of a doll got up to instruct an ambulance class in the basic principles of first aid.

Rosie wiped her good eye with the ball of her thumb.

'And who's this?' she said.

'His name's Davy.'

'Hullo, Davy,' Rosie said, and grinned.

Polly had drawn the blackout curtains early, pinching the ragged ends together with safety pins and tacking them snugly to the window frame.

She was ravenously hungry now and watched a tin of macaroni-and-cheese knock and bobble in warming water in a blackened pot. In a second saucepan a tin of rhubarb pudding drummed an accompaniment.

On the lid of the piano were plates and spoons, bottles of Chianti, gin and whisky and a large jug filled to the brim with water from the tap in the ground-floor lavatory.

Polly kneeled on the carpet before the blaze, smoking a cigarette and feeling uncommonly pleased with herself. Dominic's house might be wrecked but with a fire roaring in the grate and candles lighted, she had made a cosy refuge for herself. She was tired but it was a satisfied tiredness and she was certain that when the siren sounded and she was obliged to seek refuge in the larder she would sleep like a babe in arms.

She didn't know when Christy would bring her motorcar back. She didn't care. She didn't need it now. She had everything she needed right here.

She sat on her heels and watched varnish blister on the chair leg she'd chopped up with one of Fin's hammers. A supply of wood was stacked against the sofa, pieces of the dresser, broken chairs, even fragments of window frame that she had lugged upstairs. She had, however, filled a bucket with earth from the flowerbed in the garden for she was not so far gone into Never-Never land that she would ignore the basic rules of safety and leave a blazing fire alight if and when the bombers came again.

She didn't hear the motorcar pull into the drive.

The first indication she had that Christy had returned was when he flung open the door of the parlour and called out, 'Polly, what's burning? What the hell is burning now?'

'Supper,' she said. 'You're just in time for supper.'

She knew how attractive she looked, kneeling in the glow of the firelight in a tweed skirt and cashmere two-piece, all groomed and made up.

'Are you nuts?' he said. 'You can't stay here.'

'Why ever not?'

'The building isn't safe.'

'Nonsense. It's as safe as it ever was, or ever will be.'

He looked even more dishevelled than usual. Smears of soot, like tribal marks, highlighted his cheekbones. He eased the canvas bag from his shoulder and placed it on the carpet.

Polly said, 'Did you take lots of lovely pictures, darling?'

'I wouldn't call them lovely,' Christy said.

'A document,' said Polly. 'You made a document of destruction.'

'What the hell is wrong with you?'

'Absolutely not a thing.' Polly peered into the pot and watched the label separate itself from the can. 'Heinz' best,' she said. 'A feast fit for a king. It's amazing what you can find when you really try. Aren't I clever?'

'Yeah,' Christy said. 'Very clever.'

He went to the piano, found a teacup and poured himself whisky. He held the cup in both hands and drank. Whatever he had been up to that day, where ever he had been, whatever sights he had seen had shaken him badly.

'You look quite done in, darling,' Polly said. 'Come, rest your weary old bones while I fish for our supper with a can opener.'

He drifted to the sofa, which was still padded with pillows.

'Where's the kid?'

'Oh, the kid,' Polly said. 'I got rid of him.'

'Rid of him? How?'

'Babs told me to ask a policeman, so that's what I did.'

'Have you been drinking?'

'Not a drop, I swear, not one single drop.'

'Where is he? What have you done with him?'

'I went one better than asking a policeman,' Polly said. 'I took him to a policeman or, to be precise, to a policeman's wife. Fortunately my sister was at home today, nursing six stitches in her forehead and, I might add, feeling terribly sorry for herself.'

'You took him to Rosie's?'

'Of course.'

'Why?'

'Because if I'm going to Lisbon with you I can't keep him here.'

'Poor little bastard.'

'On the contrary,' Polly said. 'It might be the best thing

that ever happened to Master Davy Quinlan. Rosie will take very good care of him.'

'Sure she will,' Christy said.

'And I, in turn, will take very good care of you.' She tugged at his sleeve and drew him down on to the sofa, kissing him on the brow. 'How much petrol did you use?'

'What?'

'Petrol, in the car.'

'Some, not much. I drove down to Renfrew and crossed to Clydebank.' He shrugged, and drank from the cup. 'It's bad, Polly, very bad.'

'Did it remind you of Warsaw?'

'Pretty much,' Christy said, then shook his head. 'No, it's not as bad as Warsaw because you don't have the Germans crouched on your doorstep. What will your sister do with the kid?'

'Keep him,' Polly said.

'And what will Inspector Kenny have to say about that?'

'Inspector Kenny,' Polly said, 'will do exactly as he's told.'

Word had come through the Air Defence unit that the Third German bomber fleet had left its base in Western France and appeared to be heading for Clydeside.

Every officer in St Andrew's Street had been mustered for rescue service, including CID detectives and SPU interrogators most of whom, like Kenny, had been on their feet for thirty-six hours. The raiders were expected to arrive just after nine o'clock and at half-past six Kenny left headquarters on a strict one-hour stand-down.

It was still broad daylight and traffic was heavy in those parts of the city that hadn't been sealed off. Down by the docks the riverside warehouses were still burning and a tarnished haze masked the sky to the west. Kenny hit the pavement at a dead run and sprinted to the station at St

Enoch in the hope that underground trains would be operating which, fortunately, they were. Twenty minutes later he arrived at the door of his flat and let himself in with his key.

He peeped into the kitchen which, to his surprise, had been swept and scrubbed and made almost habitable.

On the table were milk bottles, saucepans and a bowl containing the remnants of a gooey substance that he couldn't identify. Hanging from the rope of the pulley, high against the cracked ceiling, were eight or ten small towels, an under vest that would have fitted a doll and – Kenny frowned – what looked like a miniature suit of armour knitted out of blue wool.

Kenny took off his hat, fanned his sweaty brow and stared, mystified, at the objects on the pulley rope.

'Rosie?' he said, pointlessly.

He crossed the hall and went into the bedroom.

She was lying on top of the bed, covered by a light blanket. Her eyes were open and she was turned on her side, looking not at the door but at a baby nestled in the crook of her arm.

Kenny tiptoed to the bed.

Rosie swivelled her head a little and glanced up at him.

The baby was dark-haired, broad-browed and sturdy-looking, not really a baby at all, Kenny realised, but a toddler of fourteen or fifteen months. He was fast asleep and snoring.

'Rosie,' Kenny said, stooping close and speaking softly, 'what's that?'

'What duh-does it look like? It's a baby.'

'Yes, but whose baby is it?'

And Rosie answered fiercely, '*Mine.*'

17

The centre of the city was more bruised than battered that Monday morning. Much of the bomb damage had been cleared from the streets, riverside fires extinguished, bridges reopened and trams and buses were running almost normally. Two nights of heavy bombing had dented the Clydeside's defences but not the pride of its people. What had been strengthened by the severity of the mid-March raids was communal unity; what had been lost was the illusion of invulnerability, the vague, swaggering Glaswegian belief that pugnaciousness and hard-nosed stoicism would keep old Adolf at bay.

Polly and Christy travelled into town by tram.

Polly was down to her last four gallons of black market petrol and couldn't count on Fin to supply more now that she had given him the heave-ho. Kenny's warning had come in the nick of time; not only had she allowed herself to become dependent on Fin Hughes she had also become complaisant. She had always known that the relationship had been skewed, a cold-hearted affair entered into without love, and that she had betrayed not only her husband but her own vestigial integrity by sleeping with a man who was even more self-centred than she was.

Fin was waiting in the office, not a hair out of place, not a crumb of brick dust or a fleck of mud on his polished shoes, as if he had travelled to the Baltic Chambers in a bubble, immune to all damage and disruption.

'I wasn't sure you would come, Polly,' he began. 'Why didn't you telephone me?'

'Because,' Polly answered, 'I knew you'd be here.'

'Really? I could have been dead under a pile of rubble, you know.'

'It'll take more than German bombs to kill you, Fin,' Polly said. 'I assume you were safely out of town?'

'I was, as a matter of fact. I obtained a place for my ageds in a nice quiet hotel in Perthshire, drove them up there and stayed over. My flat suffered some damage but nothing major, nothing irreparable.' He paused and studied her. 'I take it that you both escaped without a scratch?'

'Sure did,' Christy said. 'I guess we were lucky.'

'And the house, Dominic's house?' Fin said.

'Not in the best of states,' said Polly.

Four months ago, before Christy had stepped into her life, Polly would have told Fin all about Doreen Quinlan's death and what she had done with the child, would have fished for Fin's approval and pretended that callousness not concern had motivated her to hand the orphan over to her sister. Now, however, she decided to say nothing about the girl, the child, or her transatlantic telephone call from Dominic.

'Habitable?' Fin said. 'The house, I mean.'

'Barely,' Polly said.

'But you're still there, still living there?'

'Yes.'

'Both of you?'

'Yes.'

She waited for him to offer to set in motion a little chain of events that would wind up with her installed, like his parents, in a private hotel in the country but Fin too had apparently reached the end of his tether. She could hardly blame him; in a sense, she had cheated Fin out of what he regarded as his just rewards and, with Christy seated by her side, could not pretend otherwise.

'Fin,' she said, 'do you have the money?'

'Strange as it may seem,' Fin said, 'I do.'

She had expected him to stall, to offer the blitz as an excuse for holding back, for holding on to her a little longer. He was still studying her – he had hardly so much as glanced at Christy – and what she saw in his eyes now wasn't resentment or anxiety but a peculiar sadness.

She said, 'You managed to sell the foreign holdings, did you?'

'Yes,' Fin said. 'I sold them "forward" for much less than their worth.'

'How much less?' said Polly.

'I have a cheque for forty thousand, four hundred and ninety pounds.'

Christy let out a low whistle, hardly much more than a breath.

'After or before taxes and the extraction of your fee?' said Polly.

She tried not to let Fin see that no matter how much she distrusted him she had never despised him, that all the games they had played together, in the bedroom and out of it, had added up to something that had come close to being a satisfactory relationship. In fact if she had been just a little more selfish they might even have forged a marriage and made it work.

'After.' Fin opened a desk drawer and took out a single sheet of paper to which a cheque was clipped. 'The summary,' he said. 'Brokerage fees, taxes and my percentage are all accounted for. The cheque represents the balance.'

Polly glanced at the paper, neatly typed, dated and signed.

Forty thousand pounds was all that Fin had mustered all told.

The Scottish holdings, such as they were, the house, the car and a few other bits and pieces wouldn't add much to the total. She wondered if forty thousand pounds would be enough to buy Dom respectability. It seemed a trivial amount compared to the vast sums nations were spending on arms, and a mere drop in the ocean to the Government of the United States.

'Are you disappointed?' Fin said.

'Yes.'

'It's the best I could do in the time allotted.'

'I'm not blaming you, Fin.'

'Good,' he said. 'Good. What will you do now, my Polly?'

'Deposit the cheque and await further instructions.'

'From Dominic,' said Fin, nodding at Christy, 'or from this gentleman?'

'We'll be told what to do next,' said Christy.

'Are you going with Polly to Lisbon?'

'Yeah, I guess so.'

'How romantic!' Fin said, with just the ghost of a smile. 'And how unfortunate that Polly's husband will be waiting to greet you at the other end. I wonder if Dominic knows what's really going on? What do you think, Mr Cameron?' Christy didn't answer, didn't even shrug. Fin got to his feet. 'Well, my Polly,' he said brusquely, 'I do believe our business together is concluded. I've done all that's been asked of me.'

'And been well paid for it,' Polly reminded him.

Fin gave a little bow. 'Very true. When do you leave for Lisbon?'

'Next week, or the week after.'

'All that remains then,' Fin said, 'is to wish you *bon voyage.*'

He shook Christy's hand and then, stepping from behind the desk, took Polly into his arms and kissed her with a tenderness that she had never encountered in him before. She held the kiss a moment longer than she'd intended and then, with the cheque in her purse, followed Christy out into the hallway and along to the elevator.

'He isn't in love with you, Polly, is he?' Christy asked while the old machinery cranked them down to the ground floor.

'No,' Polly said. 'No, of course not.'

'Forty grand,' Christy said. 'It's not much, is it?'

'I'm sure Fin's been feathering his nest at Dominic's expense,' Polly said, 'and he thinks I'm going to let him off with it.'

'No,' Christy said, 'he thinks you aren't coming back.'

'Not coming back? Of course I'm coming back,' said Polly with a lot more conviction than she, at that moment, felt.

Blackstone was hardly another country and Knightswood wasn't much more than fifteen miles away but Lizzie had always been a townie and Bernard had expected her to pine for her kitchen in the cottage row and badger him to take her back there as soon as possible. To his surprise Lizzie settled quickly to life in exile and seemed content to stay right where she was.

The children had a great deal to do with it. She'd missed the children more than he'd realised. Angus, June and May were pleased to have Granny Lizzie around and soon co-opted her as an ally in their little wars with Margaret Dawlish. Lizzie was careful not to tread on Miss Dawlish's toes or rub the housekeeper the wrong way, though, for however out of her depth she might be when it came to coping with a world gone mad, she was, Bernard realised, much more in tune with family feelings than he would ever be.

Poor old Dougie had been ousted from his room. Lizzie slept there in the narrow single bed while Dougie and Bernard dossed down each night in sleeping bags on the gallery floor in the stable-barn.

Fortunately there was no sting in winter's tail and Bernard

knew that there were worse places to lay your head than a stable-barn. Legions of folk were camped out in schools and church halls or crammed into spare rooms in other people's houses, suffering not only the stress of being homeless but the even greater stress of being dubbed scroungers and layabouts by their landlords. So great was the pressure on him to find lodgings for the displaced that he had even been forced to board two families with Arthur Hunter Gowan. Naturally the surgeon's wife had kicked up Hades but Hunter Gowan had been oddly acquiescent, even, in his way, welcoming, for Bernard and he shared a secret now and were bonded by it.

Lizzie wasn't alone in enjoying the novelty of staying at Blackstone. Bernard also found the experience salutary.

After a chaotic day at the council offices, he would trudge up the farm track in the gloaming with a real sense of release, for family life, or a fair approximation thereof, appeased his guilt and pushed the affair-that-never-was further into the background. His lingering regrets about not being man enough to embark on a sexual adventure vanished when he gathered at the table with Babs's children, his wife and new-found friends. This, he thought as he looked around the supper table, was what he had risked losing for the sake of a furtive fling with a woman who was more admirable than admiring and whose sorrows he could never hope to understand, let alone relieve.

If he had been sharing a bed with Lizzie on those mild mid-March nights he might have whispered to her that he had been a fool to contemplate straying from the fold, might have told her that he loved her and that anything else had been but a silly aberration. Then to show that he not only loved but wanted her, he would have pushed up her night-gown and stroked her stomach, soothing and easing the way for lovemaking, for the satisfaction of that ineluctable and inexplicable desire that made a good marriage what it was.

Alas, he wasn't sleeping with Lizzie. He was dossed out in the stable-barn with Dougie Giffard wheezing and grunting in the straw at his side and the faint musty odour of the lumpy ex-army sleeping bag teasing his nostrils the way memory teases the mind.

'What's wrong wi' you, Bernard?' Dougie rasped. 'Can you not lie still?'

'I was thinking of things,' said Bernard.

'Things? What things?'

'Just . . . things.'

'Aw aye,' said Dougie. 'I know all about those "things" too.'

'I don't mean women,' said Bernard, hastily.

'Women?' said Dougie. 'I never thought you meant women. What've women got to do with anythin' at our age?'

'Speak for yourself, Giffard.' Bernard tried to make light of it. 'I'm a long way short of a trip to the boneyard.'

'Aye, but you're married.'

'Happily married,' Bernard added.

'It's the kids I worry about,' said Dougie. 'Angus without a proper father; the girls too, poor wee things.'

'Babs will take care of them,' said Bernard.

'Aye, I'm sure she will, but who'll take care o' her?'

'Oh, someone will come along,' said Bernard. 'Never mind the children, Dougie; what will become of us?'

'Nothin',' Dougie told him. 'Once this war is over we'll have had our day an' the rest will be up to the kids.'

'God, that's a cheerful thought,' said Bernard.

'Isn't it the truth, but?'

Bernard lay motionless on the bed of straw, arms by his sides, the sleeping bag drawn up to his chin. The ending of the war had become like a gigantic punctuation mark preceding a blank page and until that moment he had never considered what would become of him when the war ended.

He would continue to live in Knightswood, he supposed, in the house in the cottage row. He would hang on to a council job and support Lizzie until one or other of them died. He would watch Babs's children grow up and take as much pride in them as if they were his own. He would suffer when they made mistakes and would try not to impose on them all the old verities, all the outmoded values that he had learned before he went to fight in Kitchener's war, the sterling, imperishable truths that Fritz had tarnished beyond redemption in the trenches of the Somme.

Dougie was right: once the war was over the Giffards of this world, and the Peabodys too, would sink down into a haze of nostalgia, a soft, slow, coiling fog of remembrance and regret, and all that would be left to them would be the pride they'd once had and the shadow of the hopes they'd lost along the way.

'Yes,' Bernard admitted. 'It's the truth,' then turned on his side to sleep.

'What can you tell me about Mr Giffard?' Margaret Dawlish said. 'Does he really own land round about here or is he just spinning me a tale?'

'I don't know,' Lizzie said. 'I mean, I've only just met the man.'

'But surely,' Margaret said, 'you've heard your girls talk. They must have let something slip.'

'Slip?' said Lizzie, frowning. 'Is it a secret what Mr Giffard does?'

'Not what he does – I know what he does – but what he owns.'

The women were alone in the farmhouse kitchen, sipping cocoa and nibbling ginger biscuits. The fire had burned low but Margaret was reluctant to put on more coal in case the bombers came again.

'He used to be a printer, didn't he?' Lizzie said.

'A long time ago. He drank himself out of job after job, so I've heard.'

'His wife and children died,' said Lizzie.

'Well, that's his excuse.'

'It's a good excuse in my book,' Lizzie said. 'Why are you askin' me all these questions?'

'He fancies me.'

'What?'

'He fancies me, so there's very little likelihood he'd tell me the truth.'

'Don't you fancy him?'

'Phooh!' Margaret blew out her cheeks in scorn. 'Look at him!'

Well, Lizzie thought, you're not exactly an oil painting yourself.

She sipped cocoa, said nothing.

Margaret Dawlish went on, 'On the other hand, if he has a bit of money tucked away I wouldn't be averse to settling down here on the strict understanding that it would be a marriage in name only. I'll cook for him, wash his socks and clean his house but I won't – well, you know what I mean.'

'I don't call that a marriage,' said Lizzie.

'Anyway, I expect Dougie's well past it.'

'Past what?'

'All that lovey-dovey nonsense,' said Margaret.

Lizzie had her doubts that Douglas Giffard was anything like past it. He seemed to be as vigorous as any man of his age, which, she'd learned, was almost exactly her age. She was more embarrassed by Margaret Dawlish's callous attitude than by her oblique references to sex. Even now, after years of marriage, she loved having Bernard's arms about her, to feel the warmth of his body, his manliness, against her and to take him, welcomingly, inside her.

'Would you . . . ?' Lizzie hesitated. 'Would you marry Mr Giffard just for his money?'

'I like it here at Blackstone.'

'Aye, it's a nice enough spot,' Lizzie agreed.

Reluctantly, almost sheepishly, Margaret Dawlish admitted, 'Besides, I've nowhere else to go.'

'I'm sure Polly will take you back.'

'Polly!' Margaret said, with a hefty sigh. 'Yes, I expect she might – if she's still in Glasgow.'

'Of course she'll be in Glasgow,' said Lizzie. 'Where else would she be?'

'She might go chasing after him.'

'After who?'

'Her husband,' Margaret Dawlish said. 'Or she might go tramping off with that American instead.'

Confusion clouded Lizzie's thinking. She was rattled by the fact that this woman, this stranger, seemed to know more about her daughters than she did. Margaret Dawlish had been associated with Jackie and Babs for many years, of course. She'd managed the business side of Jackie's motoring salon and, according to Babs, had done a very good job of keeping Jackie in check. But Lizzie had never even seen the motoring salon and had rarely visited Babs and Jackie in their lovely bungalow in Raines Drive.

The river, the broad brown band of the Clyde, had separated her from her daughters and their affairs. She was vaguely aware that their lives had a density and texture that her life lacked but when she thought back to the time of her youth she realised that her life had been no less rich and her history no less colourful then than theirs was now.

Quite deliberately she had chosen a quiet life with Bernard in Knightswood and all the striving and stramash that had marked her days in the Gorbals seemed far behind her. She watched now from a distance and suffered only obliquely when events caught up with her children, when Rosie miscarried and Babs lost her husband, for instance, and Polly found herself abandoned by that smooth, crooked devil, Dominic Manone.

It wasn't that she loved her daughters less or was indifferent to what happened to them but rather an awareness that she was so far removed from how they lived their lives that she could no longer solve their problems for them or protect them from the inevitable consequences of folly and misjudgement.

She had heard of the American, Christy Cameron, of course, had learned from Rosie that he was Babs's fancy man, but he remained vague and faceless, like a person in one of those thick books without illustrations that Rosie had devoured; how he had suddenly become attached to Polly was more than she could fathom.

'Polly's got nothing to hold her here,' Margaret Dawlish said, 'not now her husband's left her. She's a poor soul, your eldest, in spite of her money, her cars and her clothes. If she went off with the American I wouldn't blame her. He's a lot nicer than the lawyer.'

Lizzie lost the thread, found herself unable to make the ellipses that linked Babs's American to Polly's lawyer, though she remembered the unpleasant Sunday afternoon before Christmas when all three of her girls had staged a quarrel in her living room and she had retreated with April to see Mrs Grainger's cats. Perhaps she should have stayed. Perhaps she would have learned something that might help her understand what was going on now.

'Aye,' Lizzie said, defensively. 'Aye, he's all that.'

'As for Jackie Hallop—'

'Jackie's dead,' Lizzie put in. 'I'll not hear a word against Jackie.'

'All I'm saying,' said Margaret Dawlish, 'is that Babs could have done better for herself.'

'He gave her four lovely children.'

'Any man who's any sort of man could do that.'

Suddenly weary of feeling weak and inadequate in the face of this mannish woman's tittle-tattle, Lizzie blurted out, 'Have you ever been married, Miss Dawlish?'

'Not me, oh no.'

'Have you ever had a man?'

'I'm not interested in men.'

'You seem interested enough in Mr Giffard.'

'He's different.'

'Is he?' Somewhere deep within her Lizzie discovered a spark of her old self. 'So you'd take Dougie for a husband but you wouldn't let him be a husband. What makes you think a man should be treated any different from a woman when it comes to respect? My daughters might have made mistakes but they've never wanted for love, not when they were young and not now. What they do is their business but I'd advise you not to turn up your nose at Mr Giffard if and when he does make an offer of marriage. You'll be lucky to have him, I think, for he strikes me as a good catch – and if you think I don't know what a good catch is then you've only to look at my Bernard.'

'I'm sorry.' Contrition did not sit well with Margaret Dawlish. 'I really am sorry. I didn't intend to insult you or your daughters.'

'I should hope not,' said Lizzie haughtily, 'considerin' they've provided you with a livin' for the past ten years.'

Then putting down the cocoa cup, she took herself off to bed.

Kenny had been at the docks since before dawn. The SPU had been drawn into an investigation involving a shipment of black market meat that Customs inspectors felt might prove to be the tip of an iceberg of unregistered importation. There was nothing much to go on yet but the case had all the hallmarks of becoming a long, dreary haul, and Kenny had already opened a logbook and would soon set about gathering information from Port authorities and other less official sources.

He arrived home just before noon.

He knew that Rosie would be at home for she had said she would go out early to join the food queues with the baby, well wrapped up, strapped into the old pushchair that Polly had provided.

As far as Kenny was concerned the only good thing to come out of this latest turn of events was that Rosie had quit her job at Merryweather's. He had telephoned the personnel officer and informed him that Rosie had suffered a minor nervous breakdown and would not be returning to the line. The officer seemed neither surprised nor dismayed and, to Kenny's relief, hadn't asked for a medical certificate.

The reason for Rosie's resignation – the minor nervous breakdown – was seated on the kitchen table, legs akimbo, gnawing on a Farley's rusk and smearing goo on Rosie's hair while she, with an arm about his waist, read aloud from a big green volume entitled *Every Woman's Home Doctor*.

'Uh-uh,' she said, 'listen to this, Davy. This is a guh-good bit. "Mother may pick him up at five o'clock for a little play-time, which will help to develop the baby's senses and strengthen the link between parent and child." Five o'clock, see. I thuh-think you're supposed to sleep until five o'clock or maybe that's when Mummy gets in from her round of golf.'

'Mmmmmaw!' Davy exclaimed.

'Quite right!' Rosie glanced up from the book. 'By the way, I think you're supposed to eat that rusk and not shuh-shampoo Mummy's hair with it.'

Davy laughed as if he'd understood the joke. He looked different when he laughed, all petulance dispersed by a deep, gurgling chuckle and a glimpse of teeth showing through pink gums.

He attacked the rusk again, fisting it into his cheek.

Rosie read on: '"On no account should baby be over-stuh-stimulated by too many caresses, however; such over-stuh-stimulation is bad for the child's suh-suh-psychological development." There you are, my lad, hugs and kuh-kisses are on the ration from now on. What do you have to say to that?'

'Mmmaw, mmmaw,' Davy answered, then, like an alert little watchdog, heard Kenny enter the kitchen and swung round to face the door. 'Ma, Ma, Ma, Ma,' he chanted and wriggled so energetically that Rosie had to grab him before he tumbled off the table.

'He's got teeth,' she said. 'Eight teeth.'

'Has he?' Kenny took off his overcoat and hat.

'Feel them.'

'I'll take your word for it, sweetheart.'

'According to the buh-book, the appearance of back molars means he's at least fifteen months old.'

'By the way he's tackling that biscuit,' said Kenny, 'I'd put him down as fast approaching school age.'

'Incidentally, where is the nearest primary school?'

'Rosie!'

'Whuh-what?'

'It won't be up to us where he goes to school.'

'Yes it will.'

'Rosie, he has relatives somewhere in Ireland, in Belfast, we believe. He'll have to go back to them. He's not ours to keep.'

'Of course he is,' said Rosie. 'You're mine, honey, aren't you?'

She removed Davy from the table top and held him firmly on her lap.

'Rosie,' Kenny spoke in a soft, well-articulated voice, 'I'm a policeman. I can't ignore the law. I just can't. It's incumbent—'

'Pah-pardon?'

'I'm legally obliged to trace the child's next-of-kin.'

'Polly told you: there is no next-of-kin.'

'I can't allow you to keep a child who belongs to someone else.'

'He belongs to me,' Rosie said. 'Polly brought him to me. It was fuh-fate, Kenny, that's what it was.'

'What if someone comes looking for him?'

'You've heard the stuh-story. You know nobody cared about the girl. And nobody cares about him. Nobody except me.'

'Rosie, I'm going to have to find out where he came from.'

'If you tuh-take him away from me, Kenny MacGregor, I'll nuh-never forgive you, nuh-never.' And so saying, she hoisted Master Davy high into her arms and carried him off to the bedroom across the hall.

In bright spring sunshine Greenock looked almost festive. Those elements of the fleet that had dispersed into the open sea as soon as warning of an air attack was received had returned, and repair yards and victualling quays were bustling with activity. Out in the Firth, licked by a light March breeze, were cruisers and destroyers and a host of patrol boats, and sitting proud in deep water off the Cloch lighthouse, HMS *Titania*, a Clyde-built warship, rode at anchor.

Christy paused on his way up from the railway station. He wished that he had brought along his cameras, though photographing naval vessels was strictly forbidden and might land him in jail. In any case he had sent Brockway's fourteen rolls of film documenting the devastation that the German raiders had wrought on parts of Clydeside and regarded his contract as fulfilled, at least for the time being.

The Alba Hotel had changed somewhat since his last visit.

Sandbags had been stacked against the façade and the windows were so latticed with tape and plywood that the place resembled a medieval keep. The shy little serving girl, her hair tied up in a blue bandana, her narrow hips shrouded by a canvas apron, was scrubbing the front steps.

Christy stepped over her and went up into the long dark hallway.

Marzipan was leaning against an ornate piece of furniture in the hall, sipping coffee from a china cup.

'You're late,' Marzipan said.

'Don't blame me, blame the railways,' Christy said. 'Where are we? In the lounge?'

'Yes.'

The front room was crisscrossed by bars of shadow, dust thicker than ever in the air. Christy lit a cigarette and seated himself on the ancient sofa. There was something different about Marzipan today, something definite, almost forceful.

'Does she have the money?'

'She does,' Christy answered. 'Forty grand, sterling.'

'Are you sure?'

'Sure I'm sure. I was there when Hughes gave her the cheque. She's taking it to the bank this morning.'

Marzipan wandered about the lounge with the stupid little coffee cup stuck to his middle finger. 'Has she said anything to you about diamonds?'

'Diamonds? What the hell are you talking about?'

'Money is useful,' Marzipan said, 'but diamonds are the real inducement. You need permission to ferry diamonds out of Britain and permission is seldom granted.'

'Why not?'

'Oh, come now, Cameron, don't be naïve. Diamonds are

essential to most industrial processes, particularly weapons manufacture. Venezuela is the main source of supply but South America is currently stiff with German and Italian sympathisers.'

'In other words, diamonds are in short supply.'

'Indeed, they are. Consequently we're taking a leaf from the Germans' book by releasing funds to purchase diamonds.'

'Is that the racket that Manone's mixed up in?'

'If only it were,' said the control officer.

He put the coffee cup down and seated himself on the sofa so close to Christy that their knees were touching. It was almost as if he were being courted, Christy thought, or seduced.

Marzipan said, 'Four and a half million Italians reside in the United States and Mussolini's half-cocked theories of racial superiority and national advancement appeal to those who are poor and politically immature. Refugees from Fascism and a resident minority are bitterly opposed to Mussolini, however, and among them are the bosses of the Amalgamated Clothing Workers of America and the Garment Workers unions.'

'You've lost me now, Marzie,' Christy said.

'From those sources our American cousins hope to recruit agents for dispatch into Italy. One or two agents are already feeding information back to the Intelligence services via a revolutionary who has contacts all over Italy.'

'Presumably the revolutionary's the guy who needs financing?'

'Yes.'

'And you're not going to tell me his name.'

'He has more names than I have,' Marzipan said. 'Let's just call him Emilio, shall we? British Security Co-ordination—'

'That's you, is it?'

'British Security Co-ordination,' Marzipan went on as if he hadn't heard the question, 'have landed the task of handling this touchy and suspicious character for the simple reason that we have very good relations with the Portuguese. In fact, I visited Lisbon last summer with the Duke of Kent's party to attend Portugal's Tercentenary celebrations.'

'In the middle of a war?'

'Diplomacy must go on,' said Marzipan. 'Besides, Great Britain's history has been linked with that of Portugal since the Crusades and there exists between our nations the oldest alliance not just in Europe but in the world. While I was there I was approached by the Americans and, not by coincidence, by one of Emilio's chums. He – Emilio – wants money to establish networks inside Italy. He had already been in negotiations with US Naval Intelligence. Problem: Emilio doesn't trust anyone, not the British, not the Americans, certainly not the Spanish or the French. He's an outlaw and he puts his trust, if you can call it that, only in other outlaws.'

'Gangsters, you mean?'

'Quite.'

'Which is where Dominic Manone steps in.'

'Old Carlo Manone still has considerable "influence", shall we say, over some of the lesser Italian unions and he's known to, if not exactly a friend of, the big labour bosses. Dominic used his father's connections to offer himself to Emilio as a trading agent and broker.'

'Through my brother, Jamie?'

'So I believe.'

'So it wasn't Jamie's idea?'

'Manone made the offer; Jamie relayed it; Emilio accepted.'

'Are you telling me,' Christy said, 'that the only guys Emilio regards as trustworthy are crooks?'

'A beautiful irony, don't you think?'

'Yeah,' Christy said drily, 'beautiful.'

'Manone suggested that he represent himself as a diamond

trader – Lisbon is full of them, by the way – to control the
flow of funds to Emilio's organisation. However, none of
the intelligence services was willing to hand over a hundred
thousand dollars worth of diamonds to a known criminal.
Manone upped the offer. He said he would supply his own
stock and trade with his own money – on two conditions.'

'American citizenship?'

'Yes.'

'What's the other?' Christy said.

'He wants his wife back,' said Marzipan.

Archie was in the back office and didn't hear the motorcar
draw up. He had been rushed off his feet since the moment
he'd arrived that morning and had almost reached the screaming stage when the policeman made his appearance. Clad in
a belted raincoat and slouch hat, his identity card held out
before him like a talisman, the chap fitted Archie's image of
a detective to a tee.

Inspector MacGregor's first words were, 'Is that what I
think it is down at the end of the street?'

'An emergency fuel dump,' said Archie, 'yes.'

'My God! How do you put up with it?'

'Well,' said Archie, 'I confess it does provide one with
a certain *frisson* when the siren sounds, but so far we've
been lucky.'

The Inspector was looking around without appearing to
look around.

He said, 'Why did the Labour Exchange people stick
you out here in the middle of nowhere where nobody can
find you?'

'Precisely because it is the middle of nowhere and nobody
can find us,' said Archie. 'You're Barbara's brother-in-law,
aren't you?'

'I am,' said Kenny. 'Where is she?'

'Powdering her nose,' said Archie. 'I trust you're not the bearer of more bad tidings?'

'Official business,' said Kenny.

'What could the Glasgow CID possibly want with us?' Archie raised an eyebrow and adjusted his glasses. 'Unless, of course, it pertains to the poor young woman from Belfast, who is lately deceased?'

Kenny smiled. 'I can see why Babs likes you.'

'Does she?' said Archie, gruffly. 'I – erm – I wasn't aware of that.'

Kenny glanced at the door of the lavatory with, Archie thought, a certain apprehension. 'The Belfast girl, Doreen Quinlan, left an orphan child, Davy, who is now in our care.'

'I know,' said Archie. 'Babs told me. Your wife took the child in.'

'Temporarily.'

'Ah!' said Archie. 'She wants to keep him, does she?'

'Strictly speaking,' Kenny MacGregor said, 'it's a matter for the district authority but, given the unusual circumstances . . .'

Behind the painted door of the toilet the cistern flushed.

Kenny dug his hands deeper into his overcoat pockets and looked, Archie thought, not so much nervous as depressed.

'Kenny!' Babs emerged from the toilet. 'What brings you here?'

She kissed her brother-in-law on the cheek and stepped back, frowning.

'He's in search of documentation relating to Doreen Quinlan,' Archie said, 'to enable him to trace the little boy's next-of-kin.'

'Oh! Doesn't Rosie want to keep him?'

'Unfortunately,' said Kenny, 'Rosie does want to keep him.'

Archie cleared his throat. 'Would you like me to leave you two alone?'

'No,' said Babs. 'Stay. We might need your expertise.'

'I have to do what's right,' Kenny said.

'What's right for Rosie or what's right for you?' said Babs.

'I can't just snatch a child from the street and pretend he's ours.'

'Of course you can't, Inspector,' Archie put in. 'Every effort must be made to trace the father and ensure that he takes responsibility for his offspring's welfare.' Babs shot him a look that would have made a lesser man quail. Archie ignored her and pressed on. 'Of course, the probability exists that the chap in question will deny that he is the father or that he ever had intimate relations with Doreen Quinlan.'

'Even if we do track him down,' said Babs.

'Which,' Archie said, 'will make it necessary to uncover marriage and birth certificates and, given what I believe to be Miss Quinlan's reckless disregard for the truth, let alone her reckless disregard of legal obligations and formalities, will almost certainly take – pardon my French – for bloody ever.'

'Have you spoken to Polly?' Babs asked.

'On the telephone this morning,' Kenny answered.

'She told you the whole story, I assume?'

'Some garbled tale about the girl living in London, yes.'

'Polly has a lot to answer for.' Babs shrugged. 'I suppose I do too, since it was my idea to stick the poor girl and the kid with Polly in the first place.'

'Why did you?' said Kenny.

'Spite,' said Babs.

'Expediency,' said Archie. 'There's a lot of it about right now.'

Kenny took off his hat and stroked his hand over his hair. 'If – and I'm only saying if – Rosie and I wanted to adopt the little boy I assume we'd have to go through the whole procedure.'

'A paper chase,' Archie chipped in. 'Oh yes, an intermi-
nable paper chase. Dealing with the Irish authorities at this
time will not be easy.'

'What would happen to the boy while all this is going
on?'

'He'll be made a ward of court, I think,' said Archie.

'And kept where?'

'In an orphanage,' said Archie. 'In actual fact I have the
impression that he'd be shipped back to Northern Ireland,
given that's where his mother hailed from originally.'

'What about the aunt?'

'The aunt threw Miss Quinlan out.'

Kenny seated himself on the edge of Babs's desk and
fingered his hat brim. 'This trail of paper, where does it
begin and where does it end?'

'Lord knows where it begins.' Archie paused, glanced at
Babs, then said, 'But it ends right here in that big green filing
cabinet.'

'May I see the documentation?'

'By all means,' said Archie. 'Babs?'

The drawer grated open, the brown card folder emerged;
Babs handed it to Inspector Kenny, who laid it on his lap
and opened it. He bent forward, frowned, and looked up. 'Is
that it?'

'That's it,' said Babs.

'One sheet of paper?'

'Form number eight-o-nine-nine-one to be exact,' said
Archie. 'Where and when will the girl be buried?'

'Tomorrow,' said Kenny, absently, 'in the old Manor Park
cemetery. Polly made the arrangements.'

'Who holds the death certificate?' said Archie.

'Polly, I expect.'

'There's no marriage line, no birth certificate?'

'None.'

'Well then,' said Archie, 'what we have in our possession are two small pieces of paper that represent the full available record of Miss Quinlan's life and death. We'd better preserve them carefully, had we not, Inspector? If, say, one were to go missing – destroyed in the bombing or lost in the files – there would be no feasible means of tracing next-of-kin and the child would belong to anyone willing to care for him, at least until the war's over, by which time he might be grown up, married and have children of his own.'

'You don't want him, Kenny, do you?' Babs said.

'Rosie does.'

'I didn't ask about Rosie,' Babs said. 'I asked about you.'

'I just want Rosie to be happy.'

'So?'

'God knows what my sister, Fiona, will have to say about it.' He picked the form from the folder and scanned it again. 'I can't do it,' he said. 'I can't ignore my legal responsibilities and destroy evidence.'

'Evidence of what?' said Babs. 'Evidence of neglect, of indifference, of prejudice? What sort of life is the wee guy gonna have if you hand him over? Better than the life Rosie and you can offer him? I doubt it.'

'I don't even know who he is or who she was.'

'She had dimples,' said Archie, 'that much I can tell you.'

'Dimples,' said Kenny. 'Dear God!'

'However,' said Archie, 'I'm afraid I can't condone the destruction of government property either. Unless you come up with a warrant, Inspector MacGregor, I do not intend to relinquish Miss Quinlan's form of registration.'

'Archie!' Babs shrieked. 'What are you saying?'

'So, Inspector, if you'd be kind enough to step into my office,' said Archie with a flourish, 'I will provide you with a fair copy of the next-of-kin's address while retaining the original form for our records.'

'*Archie!*'

'My office, Inspector, if you please.'

Hesitantly Kenny followed Archie into the back room. Babs stood in the open doorway, hands on her hips, her plump cheeks flushed with anger. She watched Archie lay down the form, place it casually across the big glass ashtray on his desk then, fishing in his pocket, produce a packet of cigarettes. He offered a cigarette to Kenny who shook his head.

'Mind if I do?' said Archie. 'Soothes the nerves, and all that.'

'Please smoke if you wish,' said Kenny.

Archie struck a match, lit his cigarette and dropped the match, still burning, into the big glass ashtray.

Together Kenny and he watched the paper ignite.

'Oh dear!' said Archie. 'Oh dear me! I do believe there's been an accident.' He stooped and blew – gently – on the sheet of paper, watched the flame spread and Form 80991 char and blacken. 'Goodness, wasn't that careless of me?' He looked up. 'I'm afraid the form is no more, Inspector, unless you want to gather and preserve the ashes?'

'I don't think that would serve much purpose, do you?'

'Actually, no,' said Archie. 'Dreadfully sorry.'

'Accidents,' Kenny said, 'do happen.'

Babs covered her mouth with her hand, her eyes round with astonishment as her brother-in-law poked at the burned sheet with his forefinger and Doreen Quinlan's last known home address melted away like snow.

'I thought you'd be pleased,' said Marzipan, 'to be sailing with an armed convoy. Isn't that what you want?'

'Why don't you fly us over?'

'Too risky,' said Marzipan.

'Riskier than U-boats in the English Channel and the Bay of Biscay?' Christy said. 'How long will we be at sea?'

'All in, about a week,' said Marzipan. 'Emilio's meeting with Manone is scheduled for the last day of the month.'

'That won't give Polly much time,' said Christy.

'I question if she needs much time,' said Marzipan. 'I have the distinct impression that your Mrs Manone is one step ahead of us.'

'You mean she already has the diamonds?'

'Or knows where to find them,' said Marzipan. 'You'll be sailing in convoy from Greenock on Friday night and will link up with another section from Liverpool to join the main convoy at Milford Haven. Thirty-eight merchant ships, plus five escorts and a rescue ship.'

'All bound for Lisbon?'

'Lord, no. Your vessel will peel off and the others will carry on to Montevideo.'

'Cargo?'

'None. You'll be sailing under ballast,' Marzipan said. 'I won't deceive you, Cameron, it won't be a luxury cruise.'

'What about papers?'

'I'll be on the quay to furnish you with everything you'll need.'

'Except the diamonds,' Christy said.

'Yes,' Marzipan agreed, 'except the diamonds.'

Rosie was swaddled in a blanket in the chair in the kitchen. She had stoked up the fire in the grate and opened the vent as wide as it would go. There was a breeze that night, the first sign that the settled spell of fine spring weather was about to change, and the draft of air in the chimney had drawn the fire into a soft red glow.

Rosie was drowsy but not asleep. The baby was cradled in her arms and she was crooning an old Scottish lullaby in a quaint, quacking, tuneless voice. Davy was dressed in a nightshirt and dressing gown, both new, that Rosie had purchased with the last of her clothing coupons. Even in the gloom of the kitchen, with the window boarded up and blackout curtains drawn, there was a certain homely charm to the sight that greeted Kenny when he returned from St Andrew's Street at a little after nine o'clock.

He stood quietly in the doorway until the child, sensing his presence, lifted himself up and peeped sleepily around the wing of the armchair then, curiosity satisfied, flopped down into the folds of the blanket, stuck his thumb in his mouth and rested his head on Rosie's breast once more.

'Are you on fuh-fire-watch?' Rosie asked.

Kenny placed himself before her. 'No, not tonight.'

'Good,' Rosie said, smiling. 'Once I put him down, we'll have supper.'

'Where's he sleeping?'

'With me. You can have Fiona's room.'

Kenny nodded stoically then reached out. 'Give him here.'

Rosie shrank back, pressing herself into the blanket. 'Yuh-you're not taking him away?'

'No,' Kenny said. 'I'm not taking him away.'

He touched her arm, drew it back and lifted the toddler.

For an instant he was awkward and unsure, but when Davy sagged against his shoulder Kenny suddenly discovered how easy it was to support him.

'Well, Master Davy Quinlan MacGregor,' Kenny said, 'I think you're here to stay. What do you have to say to that now?'

But Master Davy Quinlan MacGregor had nothing to say, for in spite of Rosie's yelp of delight, he had quietly fallen asleep.

The day was grey and windy with a spit of rain. Eleven funerals were taking place that afternoon and several retired council workers had been drafted in to help keep traffic flowing.

Mourners were crowded between the monuments and hearses were lined up on the gravel driveway like tanks on a production line. Babs found it hard to believe that death had undone so many for there were mounds everywhere and, even as Doreen's coffin was carried along the pathway, workmen were digging more graves.

Polly wore fur, black fur, and the Russian hat. Christy Cameron looked disreputable by comparison, his reefer jacket buttoned up to the throat. Rosie and Kenny were models of respectability, however, in their Sunday-best clothes, the baby, in a faded romper suit, clinging like a limpet to Kenny's chest. He seemed to be aware of the sober nature of the occasion and was unusually quiet. Babs and Archie came last, Archie looking dignified and mature in a navy-blue three-piece, pinstripe suit, topped by a bowler hat. Babs had sponged her best black skirt and had dyed a pair of stockings to a shade that approximated black, but her one black coat was thin and threadbare and she had settled for a charcoal grey swagger instead.

Archie had closed the office at one. They had come up by tram to Paisley Cross and had eaten lunch in Hubbard's tearooms. It was odd to see Archie detached from the office, to watch him use a fork and eat his pudding with a spoon, to ride up to Manor Park in the back of a taxicab with him.

The droning voices of priests and preachers rose and fell in the air. The cemetery was situated above the suburbs and provided a panoramic view of shipyards and factories and a multitude of tenements, villas, bungalows and mansions, the pattern pierced by steeples and cranes all wreathed, all shrouded in the silent advance of the rain.

Polly had arranged everything, had paid for everything. Possession of money and a telephone certainly made life a lot simpler, Babs thought. The only thing Polly had been unable to do was find a minister to commit poor Doreen Quinlan's body to the ground. Archie had taken care of that and Walter George's brother was already positioned at the graveside, his robes flapping in the wind. He clasped a Bible in one hand and looked, Babs thought, not bored or indifferent but weary, for, so Archie had told her, he had been burying the dead in his parish across the river all week long and his faith in the Resurrection and the Life had been shaken because of it.

There were flowers on the coffin, flowers from Kenny and Rosie, flowers from Polly and Christy. The cards looked white and mournful, the ink beginning to run in the lightly falling rain.

Babs felt guilty at not having taken flowers to the funeral home. She wondered how it was done, how the body was picked up from the morgue, what formalities were called for, what signatures. She trusted Polly – Polly and Kenny – to keep everything within the letter of the law, or almost so, for the orphan who wasn't really an orphan added a certain shiftiness to the proceedings and strengthened her need to have it over and done with.

Halfway through the committal, just as two hard-pressed grave-diggers in overalls and flat caps came loping up to lower the coffin into the ground, Babs began to weep. She hadn't expected to shed tears and didn't know whether she was crying for the Belfast girl, for herself, or for Jackie. She watched the toddler swing and kick in Kenny's arms, restless now and beginning to grizzle, watched her brother-in-law divert him, tickling him with his forefinger. She heard Davy laugh. She watched the coffin going down and saw the wind riffle the pages of the Bible and the minister, his muddy black shoes close to the edge of the grave, mouth words of farewell – and she wept for Jackie, just Jackie.

Rosie scowled and shook her head. Polly leaned into Christy, touching his shoulder, taller than he was in her Russian hat and leather boots: Lizzie Conway's girls gathered together at the grave of a stranger who had been caught in a web of her own naïve desires, who had searched for the man who had loved her in the forlorn hope that he would love her still.

Babs wept until the first spadeful of earth struck the coffin lid and Kenny put Master Davy down to toddle along the path and Polly went to thank the minister and, presumably, pay him for his trouble; then she blew her nose on a handkerchief Archie had whipped from his breast pocket and, leaning close, whispered in his ear, 'God, but I'm dyin' for a cigarette.'

'Don't pretend you're not upset,' Archie told her. 'I know you're thinking about your husband.'

'Yeah,' Babs admitted. 'Be odd if I wasn't.'

'Well,' Archie said, 'take comfort, Mrs Hallop; wherever they lay our mortal remains it's the same short road to heaven for all of us.'

'Heaven?' said Babs, surprised. 'Don't tell me you believe in heaven?'

Very tentatively, Archie took her hand and gave it a reassuring squeeze.

'Of course,' he said. 'Don't you?'

18

Angus was sure that his sisters were up to something. He was too straightforward a chap to spy on them but during the past few days he had detected a change in their behaviour that he'd found puzzling.

As a rule he didn't have much to do with May and June and they were so self-contained that they more or less ignored him, apart from a bit of bickering about who got the last pancake on the plate or the last wine gum in the packet. Angus was too gallant to argue over trivialities and invariably let them have their way, not out of a sense of inferiority or because his sisters intimidated him but simply because they were girls.

He was surprised when May and June took to the woods, though, and rather resented the fact that his sisters had invaded his kingdom without asking his permission or suggesting – as if they would! – that he provide an escort.

There were no dangers in the woods, no leopards waiting to pounce or head-hunters skulking in the ferns. Primroses and daffodils grew wild in the clearings and if May or June had been astute enough to gather a posy or two to bring back to the farmhouse then Angus wouldn't have thought twice about it, particularly after he overheard Miss Dawlish tell Grandma Lizzie that the girls were growing up and spreading their wings, though he wasn't quite sure precisely what that meant.

He kept a wary eye on the pair from the top of the wall by Ron's sty as they headed, hand-in-hand, along the dirt

path that led to the fence that bounded the trees. If Grandpa
Bernard had been there or Aunt Polly's American friend he
might have persuaded them to accompany him on a little
sortie just to see what the girls were up to. But Grandpa
Bernard was at work and Mr Cameron hadn't been back
since Christmas, and he had a feeling that if he told Dougie
then Dougie would accuse him of being a tattle-tale.

On Thursday afternoon, with light rain falling, the girls
trotted in from school, ate the scones and jam that Miss
Dawlish had laid out for them, changed shoes for Wellingtons,
overcoats for oilskins and, with a casualness that didn't fool
Angus for one minute, announced that they were going out
for a walk.

Outside in the yard, Angus shouted after them, 'Hang on,
I'll come with you,' but May glanced at June, June at May,
and the pair, giggling, took to their heels and left him standing
there with a bucket of pigswill clasped to his chest, and egg
all over his face.

Frowning, he poured swill into Ron's trough and rubbed
Ron's head with his knuckles while Ron grunted and snorted
and lapped up the slop. Then, deciding that his little sisters
were definitely up to something, Angus dumped the bucket
and set out for the woods.

He slipped along the back of the stable-byre where Dougie
and Grandpa Peabody slept, darted across open ground to the
hawthorn hedge and, using the hedge as cover, ran down to
the fence, climbed over it and headed for the big beech tree
that had been blown down by a gale the year before he'd
been born.

The branches had been sawn off and carted away long
since but the trunk, grey and smooth as elephant-hide, still
lay where it had fallen, and he had 'camped' under it many a
time to observe the rooks feeding their chicks in the tall elms
and squirrels rooting about in the birch and willow trash. He

pulled himself up on to the slippery surface of the beech and, braced like the Jungle Boy, like Mowgli, cupped a hand to his ear and listened to the faint, ever-present mutter of industrial activity from the valley far below and, much closer, the flighty alarm call of a blackbird.

The woods were uncannily quiet this afternoon. The rooks had abandoned their spiky half-built nests and there wasn't a squirrel or a rabbit to be seen.

Then he heard it, a tiny, tinny, unnatural *Tink*.

Angus rotated his head.

Tink. Tink.

He slid from the beech and crept stealthily towards the sound.

He could make out his sisters' frail voices now. He was used to hearing them complain, whisper, cajole and giggle, but excited chattering was so unusual that it made the hair on the back of his neck rise as if a cold wind had blown over him from behind.

Tink, tink, clink.

May saying, 'Oh, you silly. That isn't going to do. If you're going to do it you have to do it properly.'

June saying, 'I'm telling you, we'll never manage it. We need a rope or a ladder and where are we going to get a rope or a ladder?'

'There's a rope in the barn, I think, but what good would a rope do?'

'I don't know. We could lasso it, I suppose.'

And May saying, 'Try another stone.'

Clink, clang – then a skittering sound, like rats running over grain.

'See, see,' May cried out. 'It moved. I saw it move.'

The girls had their backs to him and were so intent on what they were doing that a German tank could have come crashing through the undergrowth and they wouldn't have noticed.

Angus watched May fish another stone from her oilskin pocket, a pebble that she'd brought down from the field or had collected on the road home from school. He felt a strange surge of annoyance when she stood under the broken branches of the pine tree and tossed the stone up, a typical girl's throw, so feeble as to be laughable. The pebble failed to reach its target.

May jumped back as the stone fell to the earth.

Angus said, 'I wouldn't do that if I were you.'

May and June spun round.

'Go away,' June snapped. 'Go away. It's got nothing to do with you.'

'It's ours,' May snapped. 'And we're not sharing.'

'What do you want it for anyway?' Angus enquired.

'It's a nice piece of material and it's just going to waste,' said June.

'Grandma Lizzie can sew it up for us,' said May.

'Make dresses,' said June and, stooping, picked up the pebble and weighed it in her hand.

'Don't *do* that,' said Angus.

'Will if we like,' said May.

'Don't you know what that is?' said Angus.

'It don't belong to anybody,' June said. 'It's ours. We found it.'

'It's a parachute mine,' said Angus. 'It's dangerous.'

'Nonsense!' June told him.

'It could go off at any time,' Angus said. 'We'll have to report it.'

'It's ours, it's ours,' June cried and, fired by anger, turned and pitched the pebble high into the branches of the pine.

The mine was enormous, much bigger than Angus had ever thought a mine would be. It had an odd shape, not spherical, more like the hull of a sail boat. It was made out of a light grey metal so clean and pale that you could see the little screws in their sockets and the two curving welds that held the plates together. It dangled on eight or ten cords, all twisted, from a ragged balloon of material that had hooked itself on one of the pine branches.

Angus watched the pebble tumble through the branches like the ball in a machine in an amusement arcade. It took a little hop, struck the edge of the mine casing and dropped to earth.

The mine swayed and the tree branch creaked.

'Bloody hell!' said Angus.

'You swore. I'm telling Miss Dawlish you swore.'

The mine reversed direction, spun slowly and ponderously clockwise as the twisted cords unravelled. Then it sagged, jerked down eight or ten inches and the parachute above it ripped a little more.

'See what you're doing,' June shouted. 'You're ruining it.'

She dipped and snatched up the stone and raised her arm.

Angus cuffed her open-handed across the mouth. He saw her mouth open and her tongue flick spit on to the fuzzy lapel of her oilskin coat and heard May scream and felt her little fists pounding ineptly on his shoulder.

He didn't move, didn't apologise, didn't fend her off. He stared up at the object in the pine tree and watched it sway again and sink a little further towards the ground. Then he swung round, grabbed May by the belt of her oilskin and dragged her back, tripping and lurching, dragged her away from the menace in the tree while June, her face scarlet and tears jumping from her eyes, scooted for the fence and the farmhouse, shrieking at the pitch of her voice:

'He *hit* me. Angus *hit* me. Angus hit me and – and – he *swore*.'

When Christy told her that they would be sailing from Greenock on Friday night Polly indulged herself with a moment of absolute panic. She threw up her hands and let out a cry that seemed to come from the pit of her stomach, and when Christy sought to console her by taking her in his arms she pushed him off so violently that he stumbled and almost fell.

Polly's fit wasn't brought on by fear but, rather, by the weight of the duties and obligations that lay upon her and the realisation that one hitch could ruin Dominic's elaborate plans and possibly send him to jail.

History, her history, had been a long series of ill-timed miscalculations, and she was so furious at Dom, and Christy too, for giving her so much to do and no time to do it in that she drank more gin than she had done in months and wakened on Thursday morning bleary-eyed and alone in the cot in the larder.

Electricity had been restored but not gas. The rooms at the back of the house were boarded up, the breakfast room beyond repair. She locked the door on it and promised herself that when she returned from Lisbon, with or without Christy, she would find someone to render the house habitable again.

She brewed coffee on an electrical plate, drank three cups, black, and tottered upstairs to wash and change.

Christy was not in the master bedroom. He had hit the whisky almost as heavily as she had hit the gin and had fallen asleep, fully clothed, on the couch in the parlour, which from Polly's point of view was all to the good. Much of what she had to do that day was her secret or, rather, Dominic's secret, the beginning of the last act of their marriage that she would play out as instructed before she handed herself over to Christy Cameron and the men who cut his orders.

Four gallons of petrol in the tank of the Wolseley; a hundred and twenty miles of travel or perhaps a little more. Greenock and back would notch up sixty. Babs would drive them to the dock and keep the motorcar in the garage at Raines Drive until she returned from Portugal.

Leaving Christy asleep in the parlour, she eased the car down the driveway and headed for Glasgow, blissfully unaware that everything that could possibly go wrong, would.

It had been her intention to transact banking business in the morning, snatch a spot of lunch in town and drive out to Blackstone before the children returned from school. Fat chance!

The teller was reluctant to part with forty thousand pounds in hard cash and even the deputy manager went into a tailspin. He was full of apologies, of course, but contrition didn't make up for inefficiency and it was after midday before funds were accumulated, forms filled in and the money, in ten- and twenty-pound notes, packed into the briefcase that Polly had brought with her. When the briefcase proved too small to accommodate all the money the deputy manager took twenty minutes to find a canvas carrier large enough to contain the surplus.

Lunch time by now, doors locked, staff vanished; another delay while the keys were found and Polly, staggering under the weight of case and carrier, was left to make her own way around the corner to the Wolseley. Toting forty thousand pounds through the streets of Glasgow in broad daylight made her incredibly nervous and she heaved the case and carrier into the boot with an almighty sigh of relief.

She drove at once to her own bank and parked outside.

It too was closed for lunch. She contemplated trotting off for a bite to eat but the idea of leaving all that hard currency in the boot of a parked car was too much for Polly and she stayed at the wheel, smoking cigarettes and eyeing every innocent citizen who passed along the pavement as if he were Al Capone, until the bank opened its doors again.

In spite of the fact that Polly had had an account there for years, a large sum of cash tipped from a briefcase and a canvas sack was, perhaps justifiably, regarded with suspicion. The manager was summoned from a meeting upstairs and it was only on his recommendation that the deposit was finally accepted. But that was not an end of it. Government regulations demanded accurate records of all financial transactions and Polly, fuming, was forced to fritter away another hour while an aged female clerk noted down a welter of nonsensical details then painstakingly transferred them to a Treasury form that Polly had to sign before her passbook and identity card were returned and she was, as it were, free to leave; too late to catch Dougie before the children came home from school.

Her headache had become worse during the course of the day and she was tormented by a raging thirst. She could hardly see straight enough to walk along the pavement, let alone drive out to Blackstone Farm. She staggered to Cooper's snack bar in St Vincent Street and ordered tea and a sandwich, which she consumed hunched on a stool by the window while the sky clouded over and a fine drizzling rain began to fall.

At five o'clock, riding the first wave of rush-hour traffic, she left Glasgow.

At just on six, in fading daylight, she reached the end of the Blackstone Farm track where to her horror she found her way barred by three trucks, a police vehicle, and a very tall man in a tweed jacket who was leaning on the bonnet of a low-slung sports car and who, when Polly braked to a halt, sauntered up to the Wolseley, nodded amiably and said, 'Mrs Manone? Mrs Dominic Manone? Ah yes, I've been expecting you.'

'Don't you have a name?' said Polly.

'He won't tell you,' Dougie said. 'He's one o' them secret

service Johnnies. He arrived with the Mine Disposal squad, so my guess is he's Navy.'

'Is that true?' Polly asked.

'In the right direction,' Marzipan told her.

'You're not a bomb disposal expert, though?'

'No, I caught the call by pure chance.'

'I know who you are,' said Polly. 'You're Christy Cameron's controller.'

'I'm your controller too, Mrs Manone.'

'Where are the children?' Polly asked.

'Bernard's driven the girls an' Margaret an' Lizzie into Breslin,' Dougie answered. 'The girls were upset. Margaret thought it would be best if they weren't here when the bomb went up. They've gone for ice cream.'

'And Angus?'

The stranger answered. 'He's sheltering behind the stables with Petty Officer Mirrilees. I thought we should allow him to stay to watch the fireworks as a reward for his prompt action.'

'Angus found the bomb?'

'Mine actually, a parachute mine. His sisters stumbled on it, apparently, but it was the boy who had the sense to report it to Giffard, who duly reported it to Peabody, who, in turn, telephoned us.'

They were huddled in falling rain behind the farmhouse, Dougie, the stranger and she. She could see nothing of the ratings from the Mine Disposal unit. The mine, so the stranger informed her, was snagged in a tree about sixty yards from the edge of the wood, about seven hundred yards from the stable-barn. The blast range of a parachute mine was calculated at four hundred yards but the Navy boys were taking no chances. If they couldn't bring it down safely they would detonate it with rifle fire once the Garscadden Road had been closed and the wood sealed off.

'You said that you were expecting me,' Polly said. 'Why?'

'Because Blackstone Farm belongs to your husband.'

'It belongs to me,' Dougie put in. 'It's mine, nobody else's.'

'Perhaps,' Marzipan agreed, 'but you're really only Manone's caretaker. I suspect he signed the farm over to you to look after because there's something of value here that he couldn't risk being found.'

'Fairy tales,' said Dougie, sullenly.

Marzipan turned to Polly. 'I presume that Cameron has told you that you're leaving for Lisbon tomorrow night. Is that why you're here? To collect whatever it is that your husband told you to collect?'

The intelligence officer, Polly realised, had outsmarted them. If it hadn't been for the parachute mine, however, he might have been content to let matters take their course. The appearance of the mine had obviously rattled him and he had hurried to the farm to ensure that Dominic's plan was not disrupted.

She looked up at him, at the moisture clinging to his eyebrows and the fringe of tight fair curls that protruded from under his cap, at hazy blue eyes that didn't seem to be looking at anything in particular.

She said, 'You know all about me, don't you?'

'Quite a bit, yes.'

'My brother-in-law supplied you with all the sordid details, I suppose. Between them Kenny MacGregor and Christy Cameron have – what's the phrase? – stitched me up good and proper.'

'Mrs Manone,' said the officer, quietly, 'I think you already realise that you were stitched up, as you put it, the day you married Dominic Manone. You mustn't blame Cameron or Inspector MacGregor for what's happened, nor must you blame me. I'm not here to pass judgement; I'm here to help.'

'Why did you have to involve my family?'

'Family? If you mean Giffard—'

'I mean my sister Babs.'

'That wasn't my idea.' Marzipan glanced up at the sky. 'Light's fading. If they're going to send in a sharp-shooter they'd better be quick about it.' He stepped away from Polly and leaned his shoulders against the damp stonework of the cottage wall. 'What have you done with the money, Mrs Manone?'

'What money?'

'The forty thousand pounds you withdrew from the private account to pay Giffard off?' He seemed totally unconcerned about what was going on in the wood and had ceased listening for the explosion that would signify that the mine had been safely detonated. 'Or is it part of your husband's devious scheme to make us *believe* he's paying Giffard off.'

'Nobody's payin' me for anythin',' Dougie said. 'I haven't a bloody clue what you're talkin' about.'

'Where is it?' the officer said.

'Where's what?' said Dougie.

'The package Dominic Manone left with you?' Marzipan said. 'The diamonds Manone bought with counterfeit money in September 'thirty-nine and squirreled away somewhere on the farm.'

'Diamonds?' Polly said.

'Bloody diamonds!' Dougie exclaimed. 'Hah! You're dreamin', man.'

'You're obliged to give them to Mrs Manone, so why don't you just tell us where they are or, better yet, go fetch them?' said Marzipan.

The headache had vanished. She was alert and alive again. For too many months she had lived with the fear that what Dom had buried on Blackstone had been the murdered body of her father. Now doubt on that score lightened her spirit and brought her out from the shadow of complicity.

Diamonds: yes, diamonds were exactly the sort of thing that Dominic would buy with counterfeit money. She should have known better than to doubt Dominic. The deal he had cut with the Americans involved diamonds, not cash, for diamonds would neither rot nor rust nor be affected by fluctuations on foreign exchange markets. The forty thousand pounds she'd collected from Fin Hughes was Dominic's nest-egg to start him up again when the war finally ended and he returned unblemished from America, when he came marching home to Manor Park once more.

'Oh dear,' said Marzipan. 'You're not going to be difficult, Giffard, are you? Come on, where have you hidden them?'

'I haven't hidden nothin',' said Dougie, defiantly.

Marzipan drew in a deep breath. 'Why did you buy a pig?'

'T' keep the kiddies amused.'

'Didn't you buy it before the children arrived?'

'What if I did? Everybody was buyin' pigs t' fatten up.'

'But you haven't had it slaughtered, have you?'

'The boy dotes on that pig.'

'If I were given the task of hiding a potful of diamonds,' Marzipan said, 'I might consider hiding them where no one is liable to want to look. In a pigsty, for example, in the shed in the pigsty perhaps. You wouldn't be the first person to think of hiding valuables among the pigs.'

'There's nothin' hid anywhere,' Dougie said.

'Standard search procedure,' Marzipan said, 'would involve taking the farmhouse apart room by room and digging up the floor in the stable. Standard search procedure would allow me to have the pig – clearly a dangerous animal – shot so that we might search—'

'All right, y' bugger,' Dougie capitulated.

'All right?' said Marzipan.

'I'll get your bloody diamonds for you.'

'Are they really buried under the pig trough, Dougie?' Polly asked.

'Where the hell else would they be?' said Dougie just as shots rang out in the woods and, half a minute later, the parachute mine exploded with a flash that lit up the sky.

Babs opened the front door.

'Christy!' she said, 'What are you doing here?'

'Looking for Polly.'

'She isn't here.'

'Have you any idea where she might have gotten to?'

'None at all. Sorry.'

April came running from the lounge. She still wore her coat and had been struggling to unlace her shoes when the doorbell rang. It was a little after half-past six and Babs had only just returned from the Millses' house with April.

'Christy, Christy, you come back.' April threw herself into his arms. He caught her deftly and gave her a hug, then carried her over the threshold into the hallway and, following Babs, into the kitchen.

'How long has Polly been gone?' Babs asked.

'All day.'

'Didn't she tell you where she was going?'

'Nope,' Christy said. 'She took the car.'

'She probably had business to attend to,' Babs said, 'or she may have gone out to the farm.'

Christy seated himself on a chair with April on his knee. He unbuttoned her coat and slipped it off then held her while she made another attempt on the recalcitrant shoelaces.

'We're leaving tomorrow night,' Christy said.

'Leaving? Both of you?'

'Yeah, sailing for Lisbon to meet with Manone.'

Babs blew out her cheeks and whistled. 'Won't that be a wee tad awkward?' she said.

'Why should it be awkward?'

'Well, Polly's still his wife an' you're . . . you know what I mean.' She filled the kettle at the tap in the sink, placed it on the stove and lit the gas. 'Are you runnin' away with Polly? Have you come to tell me you're not comin' back?'

'I don't know what'll happen out there,' Christy said.

'Portugal,' Babs said, 'isn't in the war. You could stay in Portugal.'

'It isn't that simple, Babs.'

'You love her, don't you?'

'Love who?' said April, glancing up from her shoes.

'Auntie Polly,' Babs said.

'Auntie Polly's not here,' said April. 'I love Auntie Polly too.'

Kneeling, Babs slipped off her daughter's shoes and gently took her down from Christy's lap. 'Go into the lounge and play for a bit, honey.'

April nodded. 'You're not going away, Christy?'

'Not just yet.'

'Are you stayin' with us again?'

He shook his head. 'I'll come see you before I go, though. Okay?'

'Okay,' said April and ran off into the lounge.

Babs leaned her elbows on the table top and looked straight into Christy's eyes. 'You didn't answer my question.'

'I can't,' he said. 'I don't know whether I love her or not. It hardly matters. She's going one way, I guess, and I'm going the other.'

'What do you mean?'

'They're not gonna let me go,' Christy said.

'They're goin' to arrest you? What for?'

He laughed. The gold tooth that she had once found

unusual and appealing glinted for a moment. He said, 'No, they're not gonna arrest me, Babs, but they are gonna put pressure on me to work for them.'

'Who, work for who?'

'One of the new intelligence services.'

'Then you really will be a spy.'

'Seems like it,' said Christy.

'Is that what you want?'

'I don't know what I want.'

'You didn't want me, though, did you?'

'You're wrong there,' Christy said. 'I did want you.'

'Yeah, but only because you hadn't met Polly.'

'You were married, Babs, and I'm not that much of a—'

'I'm not married now.' Babs lifted herself up and, resting on her hands, smiled. 'Oh, don't panic. I'm not goin' to embarrass you by making a pass. You're far too nice for this job, Mr Cameron. You'll make an absolutely lousy spy, you know.'

'What about Manone? Will he make a lousy spy too?'

'Dom? God, no! Dom's a natural double-crosser. Do you think they'll send him to Italy?'

Christy shrugged. 'Maybe.'

'I don't blame the Italians for what happened to Jackie, you know. I don't even blame the Germans – well, maybe I do, some of them,' Babs said. 'Funny, I used to have this – this *thing* about foreigners; distrust I suppose you'd call it. Didn't like them 'cause I didn't know them. Always liked Americans, though, always fancied Americans.'

'What about spies?' said Christy. 'How do you feel about spies?'

'I thought you only got to be a spy when they dropped you behind enemy lines on a parachute. Shows what I know, eh? I never imagined I'd ever meet up with a guy who was cut out to be a spy, just a guy, a sort of ordinary American guy who takes photographs for a livin' an' who thought I looked cute standing in the rain in Cyprus Street.'

'Real cute,' said Christy.

'I'll miss you,' Babs said.

'Maybe I'll come back some day.'

'Some day,' Babs said, 'when the war's over.'

'Assuming we win, of course,' said Christy.

'Yes, assuming we win,' said Babs.

It didn't take the Mine Disposal squad long to pack up and leave but Petty Officer Mirrilees, who had a boy of his own at home, spared a few minutes to escort Angus down to the wood to let him sniff the astringent aroma of high explosive and gawp at the crater before he brought him back to the farmhouse.

By that time Dougie had put on rubber boots, had waded through the mud in Ron's enclosure and, with the pig butting and nuzzling his backside, had man-handled away the stout wooden trough by the shed, had lifted away a single paving stone and brought from beneath it a package wrapped in oilskin and sealed with black insulating tape.

Leaning on the fence, Polly watched Dougie replace the trough and slop mud around to hide the fact that it had been moved. He lifted the package, carried it to the fence and handed it to her. The package was heavy, the oilskin cold and clammy and smelling of earth.

Dougie wiped his hands on his trousers, clambered over the fence and snatched the package back from her. She had never seen him look so mean.

'If you're takin' it away,' he said, 'I'll be needin' a receipt.'

'A receipt?' Marzipan let out a bellow of laughter. 'My God! Don't tell me you expect a receipt for stolen property, mere possession of which could see you arrested.'

'I don't think it's stolen property,' Dougie said.

'Don't you know?'

'Keep it safe, Dom told me. That's what I've done.'

'Well,' said Marzipan, 'if it isn't stolen property it's certainly property purchased with counterfeit cash. Quite a witty touch, actually. I assume Manone intended to retrieve his hoard one day?'

'Search me,' said Dougie. 'I'll still want a receipt.'

'Perhaps,' Polly said, 'we should open the package before we jump to conclusions. For all we know there's nothing inside but pig manure.'

Marzipan hooted again. 'Forty thousand pounds worth of pig manure. Oh, yes, that would be typical of Manone, wouldn't it? Come along, let's go inside and open the damned thing.' Putting an arm around Dougie's shoulder he steered him round the corner and into the farmhouse while Polly followed on.

Newspapers were spread on the kitchen table. Dougie cut away the insulating tape with a sharp knife and unwound the oilskin covering just before the Petty Officer delivered Angus to the door.

The boy came running into the kitchen.

'What a bang,' he crowed. 'You should see the hole, Dougie. It's miles deep. Uprooted all the trees. Blew away the rooks' nests, too, an' there's a dead squirrel hanging . . .' Confronted by Polly and the stranger he became cagey. 'What's up now? What's that? Is that another bomb?'

'Will I take him upstairs?' Polly asked.

'No need,' Marzipan answered. 'Let him stay.'

Angus approached the table and stood by his Aunt Polly's side and watched Dougie slide the big glass preserving jar from its oilskin wrapping. The jar was sealed with a spring clip, the rubber edges protected by yet more tape. The walls of the jar were moist as if the contents were sweating and all Polly could make out was an icy grey mass, like slush.

Dougie cut the tape, released the clip and pulled off the lid.

He tipped the jar and trickled the contents on to the newspaper.

If Polly had expected glittering gemstones all cut and perfectly polished like the diamonds she had admired in jewellery store windows, she was disappointed.

Angus glanced up at his aunt. 'What is that stuff?'

'Diamonds,' Polly said, 'I think.'

'Diamonds! They're not diamonds,' said Angus.

'Ah, but they are, young man,' Marzipan told him. 'Industrial diamonds, uncut and unpolished but highly valuable nonetheless. Look at them, three, four, five carat stones, worth a fortune in the right hands.'

'Are they yours, Dougie?' Angus asked.

'Naw, they belong to your Uncle Dominic,' said Dougie. 'Aunt Polly's taking them to him. They're for the war effort.'

Unmoved by the appearance of a small fortune in gemstones on Miss Dawlish's table, Angus nodded. Compared to discovering a live German mine in the woods, diamonds were nothing to get excited about. He watched the stranger run his fingers through the stones, sifting and weighing them.

'Are they genuine?' said Polly.

'Oh yes, I'm sure they are,' Marzipan said.

'Worth how much?'

'Much more than forty thousand pounds,' said Marzipan.

'Will that be enough?' said Polly.

'More than enough,' said Marzipan. 'Clever chap, your husband. It appears he's contrived to deliver on his promise without spending one penny of his own money. I assume you have the forty thousand snugly tucked away in your bank account, Mrs Manone – forty thousand that I and my associates are supposed to believe went on the purchase of this little lot?'

'I don't think I'm going to answer that question,' said Polly.

'Very wise of you,' the officer said. 'And, to be candid, I don't think I'm going to pursue it. As far as I'm concerned Manone has delivered what he promised the Americans and that's an end of it. The rest is up to you.'

'How do we get the diamonds past Customs?' said Polly.

'Customs won't be a problem,' said Marzipan. 'One reason we're sending you to Portugal in a convoy ship is because the Portuguese police are more vigilant at airports and our friends in the American embassy aren't entirely omnipotent. We British do have a little leeway on the docks, however. We'll be able to slip you through without official involvement. The ambassador wants no part of it, you see. He doesn't much care for treading on thin ice.'

'Thin ice,' said Polly. 'Is that what you call it?'

'What's Dom goin' to do with this stuff?' Dougie said. 'He's not givin' it to the Americans out the goodness o' his heart.'

'Trade,' said Marzipan. 'He's going to trade.'

'In Lisbon?' Dougie said.

'Lisbon, Spain, Italy,' the officer said. 'The diamonds will be his calling card, a means of proving that he's no more honest than anyone else. Once he's accepted as a dealer then the Americans can safely use him as a go-between.'

'For how long?' said Dougie.

Marzipan shrugged. 'For as long as it takes.'

He ran his hands over the stones once more, stroking them as he might stroke a cat, then he began to scoop them carefully back into the jar.

'What,' said Polly, 'do you think you're doing?'

'Taking them away.'

'Oh no, you're not,' Polly told him. 'They're mine.'

'They're not anyone's at this precise moment,' Marzipan said. 'You'll get them back, every last carat, on Friday evening after you board. What's wrong, Mrs Manone, don't you trust me?'

'Trust you! I don't even know your name.'

'McGonagall,' Marzipan said. 'William Henry McGonagall.'

'You're kiddin',' Dougie said.

'Of course I am,' said Marzipan.

It was late now, very late, and there was no light in the upstairs room. They lay together in the big bed listening to the wind drone through the holes and fissures that the raids had left in the fabric of the solid old house that Carlo Manone had purchased almost forty years ago.

Polly clung to Christy, pressing her breasts against his chest, twining her legs with his. They were both naked and slick with the sweat of lovemaking but the tension between them had not been relieved. She wanted him to make love to her again, to so stun her with sex that her fears would be carried away on a tide not of love but exhaustion.

He felt big beside her, bearlike. She stroked him, softly at first then, digging her hand into his hair, pulled him to her and kissed him with desperate passion. She was still wet, sore and swollen with need of him, of someone, anyone who would calm the myriad little anxieties that throbbed and tingled in her head.

When he rolled away from her, though, she experienced no great ache of disappointment and when, fumbling, he switched on the lamp by the bedside and sat up, she was more relieved than not.

'Listen to that wind,' Christy said. 'I sure hope it calms down before we strike out into the Firth tomorrow night.'

He lit two cigarettes.

Polly kissed his shoulder, and sat up.

Sweat dried on her neck, on her breasts. Her fears had eased slightly now that there was a light in the room. She accepted a cigarette, drew in smoke and lay back against the crumpled pillows.

'Are you scared?' Polly asked.

'Sure I am,' Christy answered. 'I'm a lousy sailor. I get sick on boats.'

The wind flailed at loose slates on the roof and rain drummed on the boarded windows. Polly could hear the drip of a ceiling leak, the *pat-pat-pat* of droplets falling somewhere just beyond the bedroom door. She would have to deal with the mess when she returned from Lisbon unless, that is, another crop of German bombs took it all away and left nothing but ruins.

She had lingered long enough at the farm to say goodbye to Bernard and Mammy and help tuck her nieces into bed, and had driven home very slowly with headlights dipped, navigating more by instinct than by her senses.

Christy had been waiting for her in the kitchen, a pan of stew bubbling on the electric plate. He had used up every last scrap of food and had opened the very last bottle of Italian wine. They had eaten supper in the parlour, seated on the carpet before the fire, had eaten and drunk wine and talked of what had happened that day and what would happen tomorrow, sharing the little secrets that each had kept from the other until now.

'I don't know what sort of sailor I am,' Polly said. 'I'm not like you, darling. I'm not a traveller. I've never been abroad.'

'You could have picked a better time to start.'

'That's true.'

'At least it'll be warm in Lisbon.'

'How warm?'

'Like summer,' Christy said.

'I'll pack accordingly.'

'Yeah.'

'Summer things.'

'Yeah.'

'I have a passport, you know, a proper one. Fin got it for me.'

He nodded as if he knew that already and retreated into an uncharacteristic silence. Polly felt no compunction to cheer him up.

She said, 'The officer's going to pack the diamonds into two bottles of Scotch and make sure they're properly sealed. We'll be given them as soon as we're on board the *Tantallon Castle*, then it'll be up to us to keep them safe until we hand them over to Dominic.'

'If they don't wind up on the ocean bed,' said Christy.

'That's morbid,' Polly said. 'Stop it.'

'Imagine all the stuff that's down there already, all the gold, all the silver, all the cash-boxes and jewels . . .'

'Stop, darling, please.'

He glanced at her. 'So you are afraid of drowning?'

'No,' Polly said. 'I'm not.'

'What are you afraid of then?'

'Meeting my husband again,' she said.

A late-evening sun had broken out from beneath the rain cloud and spilled a prophetic trail of fire across the Firth. The tallest tenements in the coastal town caught the slant of sunlight and stood stark against a tar-black sky. The wind had backed to the north-west and even from the road you could see vessels bucking and angry waves punching against the shore. Seven cargo ships would leave the Clyde as soon as night fell. Three were moored at the quayside taking on fuel, the others rode at anchor in the deep-water channel.

Babs had packed lemonade and biscuits in case April got hungry but her daughter was too excited to be interested in food. She sat on Christy's knee in the rear seat of the Wolseley, her nose pressed to the window glass, and stared at the ships, the seagulls and the hurrying waves, and uttered small cooing sounds as if the trip had been arranged just to please and amaze her. Now and then she would turn her head, purse her lips and frown at Christy as if she couldn't understand why he too was not astonished by the textures of the world.

Polly occupied the passenger seat. She had given the wheel to Babs, who was a much better driver than she was and would be required to find her way back from Greenock in the dark. She watched Babs covertly out of the corner of her eye, envying her middle sister's confidence and resilience. Separated from three of her children, obliged to work every day, even losing her husband had failed to drag Babs down. It hadn't occurred to Polly before that for all her tough talk Babs harboured no cynicism and that the life she had chosen was the life that she, Polly, had deliberately renounced. Loving and being loved had not been enough for her, and none of the men who'd loved her, not even Fin, had given her what she sought, not excitement, not variety, but a nameless, shameless need to punish herself just for being Frank Conway's daughter.

'Wish I was going to Portugal,' Babs said.

'It's not a holiday, you know.'

'Beats catchin' the tram to Cyprus Street every morning.'

'I thought you liked your job?'

'It's all right,' Babs said. 'Keeps me out of mischief, I suppose.'

'I wouldn't like to work for him,' Polly said.

'Who?'

'The fellow with the glasses, at the funeral.'

'Archie? Archie's all right.' Babs drove on into the heart of Greenock and the walls of shipyards and warehouses closed about them. 'I quite like Archie, actually, now I've got to know him.'

'He's a boy, just a boy,' said Polly.

She was making conversation mainly to allay her anxiety. Behind her she could hear Christy chatting to April who, now that the canyon walls of industry and commerce had closed off the view, had become bored.

'Archie's older than he looks,' Babs said. 'He's only a couple of years younger than I am, in fact.'

'Did he tell you that? If he did, I'd take it with a pinch of salt.'

'I looked up his employment file,' said Babs. 'Employment files never lie, at least not often. He worked in the Co-op warehouse as a clerk for five years to save enough to put himself through university. He's a teacher, or was until the war came along. Did I tell you that?'

Polly had no interest in Archie Harding or her sister's defence of the man. April wasn't alone in finding the town oppressive. It smelled of the sea, of grease and petrol fumes, horse manure and burned dinners, of beer from quayside pubs and fat frying in fish supper shops.

'Where exactly are we going, by the way?' said Babs.

Stirring himself, Christy said, 'Look for a gate on the right with a navy patrol on guard. It's just past the next turn, I think. Got it?'

'Yep,' said Babs and, fisting the wheel, swung the big car up to the gate and braked.

Two sailors came forward.

They didn't really look like sailors.

They had webbing belts cinched around their waists, wore puttees over black boots, and steel helmets. One of them carried a rifle.

Behind them in the window of the guardhouse Polly could see the tall figure of the plainclothes officer whom Christy referred to as Marzipan.

She rolled down the window and said, 'I'm Mrs Manone. Mr Cameron and I are expected, I believe.'

'Yes, ma'am,' said one of the sailors. 'You have baggage?'

'In the boot.'

One of the sailors, the one without the rifle, disappeared and a moment later Polly heard the boot being opened.

She said, 'Can't we take the car on to the quay?'

'No, ma'am. Listed personnel only.'

Polly turned to Babs. 'This is it then.'

'This is what?' said Babs. 'Goodbye?'

Christy got out of the car, April clinging to him.

Through the maze of low buildings and tall cranes the ship was visible – the *Tantallon Castle*, fully laden with coal and making ready to sail. Deck officers were visible on the rail and the patch of grey hull that Polly could make out between the sheds had dirty water pouring down it from a drain high up on the side. She knew nothing of ships, nothing at all, but moored at the quay the *Tantallon Castle* looked big and solid enough to withstand anything the Germans could throw at it.

She watched Christy kiss April on the cheek. Heard the boot lid slam. Felt vibrations shake the car. Saw the pathetic pile of luggage that Christy and she had brought with them lying on the edge of the pavement.

Marzipan came out of the guardhouse and stood on the cobbles, smoking a cigarette, watching through the gate.

'All right,' Polly said, brusquely.

She kissed Babs, fumbled for the door handle and got out.

The wind caught her, almost spun her round.

She braced herself, legs apart, and clutched her hat with one hand.

Christy came around the bonnet and lowered April into the front seat. He leaned over the child and spoke to Babs, spoke softly, then, with a hand on her shoulder, kissed her on the mouth, backed out, and carefully closed the door.

The sailor with the rifle unlocked the gate.

'This way, ma'am, please.'

'What about our luggage?'

'We'll see that it's stowed aboard, don't worry.'

She looked at the gate, at the ship, at Marzipan waiting by the guardhouse – then at the car. For a split second she was tempted to give up, to let Dominic down as she had let him down so often in the past, to yank open the door of the Wolseley, jump in and yell at Babs to take her home.

She could see her sister's face through the windscreen, a strange tearful little smile compressing her lips.

Babs waved.

Polly waved back.

Christy took her arm.

She turned away from the motorcar and let him lead her through the gate while Babs, her duty done, reversed the Wolseley out on to the main road and swiftly, all too swiftly, drove away.

April

19

The weather that Sunday could have gone either way. Pearly cloud covered the hills and sifted down into the valley of the Clyde, drifting and wavering in the windless morning air. Dougie, out planting leeks, thought that the mist would thicken into rain and insisted that the children take their rain-coats to church, but by the time they returned from Breslin, accompanied not only by Miss Dawlish but by Bernard and Lizzie too, the sun had broken through and Babs and April arrived off the lunch-time bus to find the farm bathed in pale sunshine.

As soon as they'd been fed, the girls wandered off into the big field in front of the house to look for buttercups under Angus's watchful eye. He was very attentive to his sisters now, to April especially, for the praise that had been heaped upon him – much to June's chagrin – for his prompt action down in the woods had reminded him of his role as 'the man' in the family. Babs, in fact, was very proud of her son now that he had quietened down and even at age ten he seemed in some ways more sensible and mature than his father had ever been.

The adults were still in the kitchen, still seated around the table drinking tea and smoking, when Angus reappeared in the doorway.

'Mum?'

'Yes, honey.'

'There's a man out there.'

'A man?' said Miss Dawlioh.

'Where are the girls?' said Bernard, making to rise.

'He says he knows you, Mum,' said Angus.

Puzzled, Babs followed Angus out into the yard.

'Where is he?'

'I told him it was private property,' said Angus, 'an' to wait at the gate. He's over there, see.'

Babs looked up and laughed.

'You know him?' said Angus

'Yeah, it's only Mr Harding from the office where I work.'

'Does he always dress like that?' said Angus.

'Fortunately not,' said Babs.

Angus's less than warm welcome had obviously daunted Archie Harding and he had stayed right where he was at the open gate at the turn of the track. He had one hip braced against the gate and one foot on the ground and the bicycle, like a centaur's legs, almost seemed to be part of him. He wore shorts, a ribbed sweater and a yellow sou'wester. Babs grinned and walked across the yard, Angus trailing some yards behind.

'With a boy like that,' said Archie, ruefully, 'you don't need a dog.'

'You're lucky he didn't bite you,' Babs said. 'Are those supposed to be shorts?'

Archie glanced down as if the garment in question had attached itself to him without his knowledge.

'Yes,' he said. 'From my days as a Boy Scout.'

'They're the longest shorts I've ever seen,' said Babs.

'I was taller in those days,' said Archie.

'What on earth are you doing here?'

'Just passing by.'

'You came especially to see me, didn't you?'

'Emphatically not,' said Archie. 'Hoy, you.'

'Me?' Angus mouthed, dabbing a finger to his chest.

'Yes, you with the hair – is that a pig I see over there?'

'What if it— Yes,' Angus said, remembering his manners. 'It's a pig. It's mine. I mean, I look after him.'

'Do you, indeed?' said Archie. 'Well, I just hope you haven't given him some daft name like Sydney or – let me see – like Ron.'

Angus's mouth popped open. 'How did you—' One eye screwed up with suspicion. 'Mum told you, didn't she?'

'If you think, young man, that your mother and I squander valuable man-hours discussing livestock then you're not as intelligent as you appear to be.'

'Pardon?' said Angus.

'Mr Harding,' Babs said, 'this is my son.'

'Ron?'

'Angus,' Angus shouted.

'Really!' said Archie. 'You look more like a Ron to me.'

'Oh, stop it,' said Babs softly. 'He's only a wee lad.'

'No, he's not,' said Archie. 'He's a big lad.'

'Now you're here,' Babs said, 'just passing, perhaps you'd better come and meet the rest of my children.'

'How many constitutes the rest?'

'Three girls,' said Babs. 'I've never asked you this before, Archie; do you like children?'

'I'm a teacher,' said Archie. 'Of course I don't like children.'

'Are you serious?'

'Perfectly.'

'Oh!'

'I much prefer pigs,' said Archie, loudly. 'However, since I seem to have strayed into what amounts to a zoo, I suppose I might as well pretend to be nice in the hope that you'll offer me a cup of milk or a dish of tea. You.' He pointed at Angus and swung a leg from the saddle. 'Fetch your sisters from yonder field and tell them not to bring me buttercups. I hate

buttercups. Remember that for future reference. Mr Harding
hates buttercups.'

'Mum?' said Angus.

'After which,' Archie went on, relentlessly, 'you may take
my steed – you may even ride my steed – to the stable, give
him a good rub down with an oily rag and a bag of hay.
Got that?'

'Yee-ees.'

'I take it you can ride a bicycle?'

'Yee-ees.'

'Then ride this one.' Archie lifted the boneshaker by the
crossbar and hoisted it over the gate. 'Come on, lad, take it
before I change my mind.'

Angus glanced at Babs, who nodded assent, then, still
slightly stunned by Mr Harding's gab, grasped the bicycle
by the handle-bars, wheeled it experimentally on to the grass
behind the stable-barn, eased himself up on to the saddle and
wobbled away into the field to fetch his sisters.

Babs and Archie watched the boy find balance and pedal
off.

Archie said, 'You don't mind me dropping in like this,
do you?'

'Course not,' said Babs. 'Now you're here I suppose you'd
better come and be introduced to the rest of the family.'

'In these shorts?'

'Better with,' said Babs, 'than without.'

Then, taking him by the arm, she led him towards the
farmhouse door.

It was, Kenny realised, the first time that Rosie and he had
walked out together since the war began. It felt very odd to
be strolling beside his wife along Great Western Road on
a fine mild Sunday afternoon, even odder to be pushing a
go-chair with a toddler strapped into it.

They were heading in the general direction of the Botanical Gardens but Kenny knew that they would never reach the Gardens, that somewhere along the way they would find a café, pop in for a cup of tea and a dish of ice cream then turn about and head for home. He didn't much care. He was happy not to be stuck in St Andrew's Street or diving about the city in pursuit of Irish bandits, meat-smugglers or would-be collaborators. Evidence of war was all around, of course. Shop windows were boarded up or sandbagged over, handsome sandstone tenements pitted with shrapnel, here and there a gap in the skyline, acres of waste ground heaped with debris to remind him that they were far from out of the woods.

Among the strollers were lots of servicemen, and lots of pretty girls taking a breather after a long week's work on an assembly line or in a packing plant. Different, the girls, more brazen but also more relaxed than they'd been eighteen months ago; they thought nothing of wearing trousers on a Sunday and clung to and even kissed their soldier boyfriends right there in broad daylight.

Kenny steered the go-chair with one hand and held Rosie's arm with the other, as if he were leading her into a charge room or a prison cell, the only kind of contact he was used to these days.

Chewing on a huge new dummy-tit flavoured with brown sugar, Davy had been a dynamo of restless activity for the first half-hour or so. Held in check by the chair's cross-straps, he had wriggled, chanted and pointed at interesting passers-by, especially those in uniform, and at the horse-carts and tram-cars that rattled past the pavement's edge. Then, gradually, his eyes had started to roll and he had grizzled a bit, the dummy had slipped from his mouth and hung on its wet ribbon on his chest. Rosie, cooing, had tucked the blanket round him and, sinking back, he had fallen asleep, oblivious at last to the passing show.

'How did yuh-you do it, Kenny?'

He had been thinking of other things and the question caught him unprepared. 'What? Do what?'

She altered her step, linked her arm with his and hugged him. Because of her handicap they faced each other and spoke like sweethearts new to the game of love.

'Find him for me?' Rosie said.

'I didn't find him for you, Rosie,' Kenny said. 'Polly found him.'

'You turned a buh-blind eye, though, didn't you?'

'So did Nelson.'

'Hoh! That's not an answer.'

'No, I suppose it isn't,' Kenny said.

She had been crafty, his Rosie, waiting until they were out of the house to raise the subject, waiting her best chance, ready to pounce only when he least expected it; if she hadn't been deaf she would have made a wonderful interrogator. He felt a sudden wave of love for his little deaf wife and all the turbulent emotions that had unsettled him during the past months drifted away.

He pulled her close and kissed her on the lips.

'Kuh-Kenny!' she said. 'What's that for?'

'Being a good girl.'

'A guh-good girl?'

'A bad girl then,' he said.

He had been sleeping in Fiona's bed in Fiona's room since Davy's arrival, but last night, just before he closed his eyes, Rosie had entered the room, had scampered across the carpet and slipped into bed beside him wearing nothing but a brassiere and pants. It hadn't taken him long to get those off for she had been eager, more than eager, to make love.

When he thought of it now, the unromantic nature of their whispered conversation had actually increased his ardour.

'Is Davy asleep?'

'Uh-huh.'

'Are you sure?'

'Yuh-yes.'

'What about his teeth?'

'Kenny, his teeth are fine.'

'Are you certain he won't waken?'

'Stop uh-asking silly questions.'

Then she had straddled his hips, pinned his arms behind his head and shut him up for good and all. It was still with him, the memory, the promise of that passionate hour in the darkness last night, and all the things, not just sex, that he'd missed in the months when he'd been holding their marriage together by the skin of its teeth had been suddenly restored.

Working in Merryweather's and the experience of life among the matrons had matured Rosie – the loss of the baby too – but now the time had come to begin again and the little boy in the pushchair was, Kenny supposed, a symbol of it. He saw a pattern here – he would, of course – a pattern that linked Babs to Polly, Polly to Rosie. But Polly's sense of ownership was quite different from Rosie's, tainted by a kind of selfishness that he, a male, would never be able to understand.

He braked the pushchair gently to a halt.

Rosie kneeled. He could see her knees beneath her skirt, her breasts pressing against the blouse, the line of her slender neck and her hair, still short, brushing her cheek. He was without desire, though, and without desire he loved her all the more. She tucked the blanket around Master Davy's toes and glanced up.

'Isn't this better?' Rosie asked.

And Kenny, smiling for once, was forced to agree that it was.

The voyage to Lisbon took eight days and from first to last

proved to be a nightmare. From the moment the *Tantallon Castle* steamed out of the Clyde and slapped into a moderate sea Christy was sick; no mere moaning and repining sort of sickness but a vile and violent retching so messy and painful that it threw him about his tiny cabin in the ship's mid-section. There was no doctor on board. The second mate did his best with various substances from the medicine chest but Christy's cameras remained in the bag and the drama of sailing with a British convoy went unrecorded.

Christy found no relief at anchor in Milford Haven. The sea there was steeper than ever and even Polly suffered a queasiness that kept her on deck, breathing deeply and huddled inside a huge oilskin jacket that one of the crew had found for her. She had a cabin to herself, a narrow cubicle that reminded her a little of the larder back home except that the larder back home wasn't constantly pitching and rolling. Even when she dug herself into the bedclothes in the high-sided bunk and clung on with both hands it seemed that she might be tossed out at any moment and go sliding across the floor to ram into a bulkhead or the rattling, brass-handled door.

Manfully, though, she clawed her way to the galley to cadge hot tea for Christy, tea which soon wound up, like everything else, swilling across the floor of his cabin. Manfully, too, she presented herself for meals and managed to force down a few mouthfuls of whatever was on offer and, as it were, keep her end up with the officers.

Christy and she were the only passengers and provided light relief for the crew. At first Polly thought the seamen cruel to mock poor Christy for his lack of sea legs but after her stomach settled and she began to feel at home both below and above deck, she also teased her prostrate lover and relayed colourful tales of his predicament to interested parties.

The bridge and engine room were out of bounds but the

other parts of the ship were open to her and she spent a great deal of each day leaning on the rail watching the convoy ships jockeying to keep station, which was no easy thing to do, apparently. There was one attack from the air soon after the convoy left harbour. Although Polly was sent below for her own protection, she could hear the chatter of the Lewis gun and feel the shudder through the plating. The *Tantallon Castle*'s starboard mid-ship accommodation was riddled with machine-gun holes but there were no casualties and emergency repairs were soon effected. One ship in the formation lost its bridge and navigational equipment to an aerial torpedo and had to limp back to Milford Haven unaccompanied.

In spite of several alarms the convoy escaped attack by U-boats and was still complete when the *Tantallon Castle* peeled away well before dawn and, in an empty sea, steered a course for the mouth of the Tagus and the long, safe, neutral quays of Lisbon.

'Well, dearest,' said Bernard, 'I think we'll be able to move home soon.'

'Oh!' Lizzie said, with a distinct lack of enthusiasm. 'How soon?'

'Ten days or thereabouts,' said Bernard. 'What's wrong? Don't you want to get back to your own house?'

'Our house.'

'Yes,' Bernard said. 'Our house.'

'What if there's another air raid?'

'We'll be safe enough in the shelter, and if we're damaged again I'm sure Polly won't mind if we come back here.'

'It isn't up to Polly,' said Lizzie, 'not now she's gone.'

'Is that what's biting you?' said Bernard. 'Are you worried about Polly?'

'Aye,' Lizzie admitted. 'I am.'

'There's nothing we can do,' Bernard said. 'Anyway, she should be safe and sound in Lisbon by now, according to Dougie.'

'What does he know about sailing?'

'Dougie's well informed about most things.'

'Aye, but he can't see beyond the tip of his nose,' said Lizzie.

'Really? What makes you say that?'

'That Dawlish woman is after his money.'

'His money? Dougie doesn't have any money,' Bernard said.

'He has land,' said Lizzie. 'Isn't land as good as money in the bank?'

'It certainly will be,' said Bernard, 'after the war.'

'Huh,' said Lizzie. 'Will you listen to me, talkin' about land? I never thought when we were livin' in the Gorbals an' waitin' for the rent collector to turn up that I'd be friendly with a man who owned property.'

'I was the rent collector, remember?' Bernard said.

'So you were, so you were,' said Lizzie.

They were seated side by side on a bale of straw in the stable-barn in the twilight hour after supper. Bernard put an arm about her.

'You don't like Margaret Dawlish much, do you?' he asked.

'She's a good housekeeper, I'll say that for her,' Lizzie conceded, 'an' she seems fond enough of the children, but . . .'

'But?'

'She's just out for what she can get.'

'You can hardly hold that against her,' said Bernard. 'She's not sure what'll happen when the war ends, if Polly will want her back,' he paused, 'or if Polly will be here at all.'

He dropped the suggestion quietly into the conversation for

he was unsure how much Lizzie understood of the situation or how deeply Polly had dug herself into trouble, not with the lawyer or the American but with her husband, Dominic.

Whatever Lizzie thought of him, Dougie Giffard had his finger on the pulse and enough past experience of the Manones to realise that Dominic was sailing close to the wind. It was one thing to run local protection rackets and illegal street betting, to primp and preen down at the old Rowing Club and manage an import warehouse as a cover for selling stolen goods, quite another for Dominic to try to outwit the Intelligence services.

'Not come back?' said Lizzie. 'Why wouldn't she come back?'

'She might decide to settle in America to be with the children.'

'No,' Lizzie shook her head. 'No.'

'You can't deny that she misses them.'

Lizzie gave him a little push and disengaged herself. She stood up and brushed straw from her skirt, brushing and brushing as if to sweep away any suggestion that Polly might not return to Scotland.

Bernard pushed himself to his feet too.

He said, 'It's not . . . I mean, it's not settled or anything but you couldn't really blame her, Lizzie, if she wants to be with her family.'

'We're her family. I'm her family.'

'We're not, you know,' he said, 'not now.'

'Blood will always be thicker than water,' Lizzie said. 'Won't it?'

'Lizzie, Lizzie,' he said, 'the girls are grown up. They've set their own courses and there's precious little we can do about it.'

'Babs . . .'

'I know Jackie's only been dead for a wee while but he's

been gone for well over a year. The young man who came
to see her today—'

'Oh no,' said Lizzie. 'You don't think he's courting her,
do you?'

'Babs is a widow with four children. She's entitled to – well,
to look out for herself.'

'I used to think you cared for my girls,' Lizzie said. 'You
don't care at all. You only care about yourself.'

Her hands had fallen still. She didn't fold her arms in a
defiant attitude, though, but let them hang helplessly by
her sides.

Bernard felt a sudden wave of sympathy for his wife, for the
confusion that the war had caused and what it might cost her
in the long run. Young women risked losing their husbands,
older women risked losing their sons but what women of
Lizzie's age risked losing was all sense of purpose.

After the near-run thing with Evelyn Reeder – Lizzie would
never know how close he had come to betraying her – he had
finally found himself again. He had been wakened to the fact
that what he had was all he would ever get, war or no war, and
that his future and the future of the nation were so inextricably
bound up that they couldn't be separated. But how could he
possibly explain to Lizzie that the future belonged to Babs,
Rosie and Polly, and that wherever they might be, for better
or for worse, they would always be Lizzie Conway's girls.

'I care for you,' Bernard said. 'I'll always take care of
you.'

'God!' Lizzie said. 'Dear God! Is this what it's come down
to, that I need to be taken care of now like a baby or an
invalid?'

'No, no,' Bernard said. 'No, no, no.'

She raised a hand helplessly, and let it fall.

'See how bad it is?' she said. 'I don't even know where
Polly is.'

'Well, that's easily remedied,' Bernard said. 'We'll go and look at a map.'

'Dougie's map?'

'Yes,' said Bernard. 'Dougie's map.'

'Bernard, where *is* she?'

'Lisbon.'

'Where's that?'

'Portugal.'

'Is that near America?'

'Near enough,' said Bernard, and accompanied her down the wooden steps and out into the gathering darkness that filled the valley of the Clyde.

20

Soon after sunrise the morning mist turned golden and rising like a curtain revealed the rounded hills of Lisbon. Colour-washed houses with red tiled roofs clung to the terraces, and the impressive public buildings in the valley reminded Polly of great slabs of ice cream topped by meringue.

Sweet, that was how Lisbon struck her after drab old bomb-scarred Scotland. Lack of sleep, seasickness and the nagging anxieties of the voyage suddenly no longer seemed relevant. She could feel the sun on her back, smell the spicy odours of the docks and see ahead of her a city free of restrictions. She felt her spirits soar.

Christy tottered to the rail beside her. He had bathed and shaved but was still hollow-eyed and gaunt as a cadaver in his shabby old reefer jacket and roll-necked sweater. He didn't seem to fit somehow, didn't seem to belong in this gay and spacious city where there were no tanks, no rubble and no refugees.

Polly scanned the quays for sight of Dominic. She was no longer reluctant to meet her husband. Her luggage had been brought up, ready to be off-loaded. Wrapped in a bath towel in her blue suitcase were the two dumpy bottles of VAT 69 whisky that Marzipan had left in her cabin. She had scattered her frilliest things on top in the fond hope that the Portuguese Customs officers might be too modest to trifle with a lady's undergarments.

'Where's the stuff?' Christy asked.

'In my case.'

'The big case, the blue one?'

'Yes.'

'Who are you looking out for?'

'My husband.'

'He won't be there,' Christy said.

'Are you sure?'

'Sure I'm sure,' Christy said. 'He'll be hiding out.'

'Isn't Lisbon safe?'

'Depends who you're hiding from, I guess.'

'Are you going to tell Dominic about us?'

'Are you crazy?' Christy said. 'I don't want a bullet between the eyes.'

'That isn't Dom's style.'

'What is his style?'

'I don't know,' Polly said. 'It depends.'

'On how badly he needs you?'

'Yes.'

'If he only needs what you've got in that blue suitcase, Polly, what then?' Christy said. 'Do you really think he'll give us his blessing and Marzipan or some other guy in a tweed coat will whisk us off to live happily ever after?'

'I didn't say that.'

He still smelled faintly of sick and of something else, something intangible. In the fresh morning sunlight he looked not only unglamorous but almost unwholesome. She wondered what she had ever seen in him. It hadn't been love at all, hadn't been anything like love, only another manifestation of her need to have any man she fancied, especially Babs's man, Babs's exotic stranger. Whatever happened in Lisbon, whatever Dominic said or did, Christy and she were fated to kiss and part and go their separate ways.

'You have to tell him,' Christy said.

'I'll do nothing of the damned kind.'

'Even if it doesn't work out, I'll stand by you.'

'Is that what you told your Polish girl?'

'Jesus, Polly, that's harsh.'

'Yes,' she said. 'Yes, it is. I'm sorry.'

An ear-splitting wail from the *Tantallon Castle*'s whistle made her flinch. She stepped back and looked up at the funnel as wisps of brown smoke coiled across the bridge and spilled down on to the decking.

Christy leaned against her. 'I'm here if you need me,' he said. 'I'll always be here if you need me.'

'I'll remember,' Polly said and kissed him, just once, before Dominic reclaimed her.

Marzipan was true to his word. The Customs sheds were virtually deserted and Portuguese immigration officials seemed to have more urgent matters to attend to as Polly and Christy lugged their baggage down the gangway on to the quay. A little crowd of dock workers had gathered alongside the *Tantallon Castle* to admire the bullet holes in her hull. A jovial bunch, they conversed in French and broken English with the deck officers, who answered their questions courteously but with typically British phlegm.

Polly and Christy headed straight from the ship to the motorcar, a Mercedes, that was parked on the quay. Two uniformed police officers stood by the car chatting to a tall young man in a seersucker suit that seemed to have been painted on to his long limbs.

Catching sight of Christy, he raised an arm and called out, 'There you are, you old son of a gun. I thought they'd tossed you overboard.'

'Jamie!' Christy muttered. 'I might've known you wouldn't be far away.'

Setting down his bags, he hugged his brother and introduced Polly.

Jamie Cameron shook Polly's hand, his grip firm and friendly.

The policemen watched impassively.

'Where's my husband?' Polly asked.

'He's waiting for you at the Avenida Palace Hotel,' Jamie Cameron told her. 'We have one or two minor formalities to complete here, then we'll be on our way. I take it you haven't had breakfast?'

'Breakfast?' Christy pulled a face. 'I haven't eaten in a week.'

'You were never cut out to play Popeye, kiddo. You even got sick on the Staten Island ferry,' Jamie Cameron said. 'Look, all I need are your passports and thirty-day visas. I guess they're in apple-pie order?'

Polly slid her purse from her shoulder, fished out her passport and the documents that Marzipan had provided, handed them to Jamie Cameron, who handed them in turn to one of the policemen. The copper didn't seem in the least interested and the documents were returned with hardly a glance. He said something in Portuguese and Jamie laughed.

'What did he tell you?' Polly asked.

'He said that anyone so beautiful must be harmless,' Jamie told her.

Polly favoured the policeman with a smile and, a minute later, found herself seated in the back seat of the Mercedes. She watched Jamie and the policemen shake hands; no money, she noticed, changed hands. Christy stowed the luggage in the trunk and climbed in beside her. Jamie Cameron folded himself behind the steering wheel and started the engine.

The policemen bowed and waved like traffic cops and the car passed along the length of the dock, through a high wooden gate and out into the streets of Lisbon, heading, Polly assumed, for the Avenida Palace Hotel.

★   ★   ★

'Is it far?' Polly asked.

'Not far,' Jamie said, over his shoulder. 'It's hard by the railway station, the Estacão Central, which is also known as the Rossio.'

'Why is my husband staying in a railway hotel?'

'Mainly because the Avenida Palace has elevators, central heating, an excellent restaurant and beds not hewn out of granite,' Jamie told her. 'It also happens to be the number one spot in Lisbon if you're cookin' up a shady deal. Somerset Maugham couldn't have invented this place. Every sleazy type you can imagine drifts in and out of the bar. Austrian kids desperate to work in Hollywood, diplomats who've wriggled out from under the jackboot, gentlemen of fortune who can smell opportunity the way sharks smell blood. And women, rich women who can't get their hands on their funds and are looking to trade on the generosity of a male escort or two. Plus heaps of Americans who've lived in France for years and don't know how to get home again.'

'The Avenida, is that where you're billeted?' Christy asked.

'Not me, kiddo. I'm down the coast a ways in Cascais.'

'How come?' said Christy.

'The beach there is good, and you know how I like my morning swim.'

'Sure.' Christy glanced from the window, then said, 'I thought the British were playing nurse-maid to the Communist.'

'Nope,' said Jamie. 'I am.'

'US Naval Intelligence?' Christy said. 'Yeah, right!'

'I'm officially on shore leave,' said Jamie. 'Nuff said?'

'Nuff said,' said Christy.

In spite of the early hour the lobby of the Avenida Palace Hotel was crowded. Polly had never seen such a conglomeration of different nationalities. The broad staircase that angled up from the lobby swarmed with men and women and there were queues at the reception desk. Elevator doors opened and closed noisily. Porters in odd little cut-away vests darted about calling for Senhora This and Senhor That. Any notion she might have had of making a grand entrance vanished immediately. She was caught up in the tide and swept from the open doorway into the middle of the lobby before she could take her bearings.

She looked behind her, searching for Christy.

Her luggage had been ferried from the car at the pavement's edge and was being steered towards the elevators. Outlined against the brilliant light of the street, she noticed Jamie Cameron directing operations with eloquent gestures. For a secret agent he certainly made himself conspicuous but that, she thought, might be part of his disguise.

She waited where she was, jostled by strangers.

'Polly?' Dominic took her arm.

She turned on her heel and faced her husband.

'Bedlam,' he said. 'The Book of Exodus, minus Moses. Come with me.'

He held her by the arm, cupping her elbow.

She glanced over her shoulder, spotted Jamie Cameron heading for the elevators, Christy trailing after him. She wanted to call out, to let Christy know where she was, to keep herself safely positioned between the devil and the deep blue sea for just a little longer.

'He'll find you, never fear,' said Dominic. 'Meanwhile, we must give the captain time to do what he has to do.'

'Don't I have to register?'

'It's all been taken care of,' said Dominic.

'My room . . . ?'

'Our room, darling,' Dominic said. 'After all, we are still man and wife.'

★   ★   ★

The table was situated in a window corner protected by a Moorish screen. There were several such shoulder-high screens in evidence throughout the dining room. Behind them lurked elderly men in high, starched collars and morning suits, very stiff and formal, chomping on egg and steak and dabbing their moustaches with thick linen napkins while they received visits from faded women of a certain age or smooth-cheeked young men in expensive lounge suits.

'Who are they?' she asked.

'Bankers,' Dominic said.

'Jews?' Polly said.

Dominic's soft brown eyes never left her face. He looked different, leaner, his sallow complexion darkened by exposure to the sun.

'Certainly not Jews,' he said. 'Austrians for the most part, some French, a few Swiss. They claim to have access to confiscated bank accounts in German-controlled territories.'

'Do they?'

Dominic shrugged. 'Probably not. Some sort of note will be signed, promises made, accounts opened and the money . . .' he fanned his fingers, 'well, the money will vanish in a welter of paperwork and after a month or so the banker too will vanish and another white-haired crook in a claw-hammer jacket will appear and more desperate supplicants will throw themselves on his mercy.'

Thin slivers of white fish bathed in an egg sauce were on his plate. He toyed with them, breaking down the slivers into small flakes with a heavy silver fork.

He didn't eat, though, not one mouthful.

He said, 'Fin Hughes would make a killing here.'

'Fin, I think,' said Polly, 'is doing all right at home.'

'Did you do what I told you to do?'

She had eaten more than she'd eaten in months and drunk coffee that tasted like coffee. She glanced down into the street,

a broad avenue lined with café tables, at trams fitted with huge
cow-catchers nosing round the corner and vanishing behind
a plain brick wall that she fancied might be the gable of the
station. A waiter tapped a forefinger on the frame of the
screen and at Dominic's signal stepped round the screen and
removed the plates. He went away again, sliding sinuously
through the crowded tables.

Dominic poured coffee from a silver pot and lit a small
cigar.

He looked more like himself now, sipping coffee, smoking.

'Well, Polly,' he said, 'did you?'

'I put forty thousand pounds in my bank account,' she said.
'The other stuff is hidden in two whisky bottles in my blue
suitcase.'

'Which,' Dominic said, 'Jamie Cameron is checking out
right now.'

'Oh, is that what he's doing?'

'Of course.'

'Is he really going to marry our Patricia?'

'So he says.'

'Don't you believe him?'

'Patricia certainly believes him.'

'Is she in love with him?'

'Madly,' said Dominic, without a smile.

'The children will miss her.'

'I wondered when you were going to ask about the children.'
He slipped a hand into his vest pocket, brought out a sheaf of
photographs and placed it on the tablecloth. 'The children are
thriving. They're happy, that's the main thing.'

'Don't they miss me?'

'No, Polly, I don't think they do.'

'Why did you take them away? Were you punishing me?'

'Punishing you?' Dominic said. 'For what?'

It was on the tip of her tongue to say 'Tony' but she

still couldn't be sure if he knew about her affair with Tony Lombard or, for that matter, her fling with Fin Hughes, though fling was hardly the word for it. And Christy – she didn't dare confess that she had allowed the American into her bed.

She might offer excuses for Fin and Christy, might plead that he, Dominic, had run off with Patricia and had left her free to do as she wished but this was hardly the time or place to begin balancing accounts.

She said, 'You escaped, didn't you? You fled?'

'Under the circumstances,' Dominic said, 'I had very little choice.'

'Why didn't you tell me you were leaving? Didn't you trust me?'

'I'd no reason to trust you, Polly.'

'You trusted me to manage things at home, though. You went out of your way to arrange it so that I would do exactly as you wanted me to.'

'Not exactly, no,' Dominic said.

'Is it because I'm Frank Conway's daughter that you don't trust me?'

His eyes widened in surprise. He placed the cigar in an ashtray and watched smoke rise up towards the ceiling for a moment, then said, 'You aren't to blame for that any more than I'm to blame because my father's Carlo Manone. I gave you a chance, Polly. I gave you a choice, much the same sort of choice as I've had to make.'

'Choice? What choice is that?'

'To change.'

'To go straight?' She felt more comfortable challenging and teasing him as if he were just another chap and not her husband at all. 'Counterfeit banknotes wafting about Blackstone, a body or two buried in the woods and,' she lowered her voice, 'diamonds, a hundred thousand pounds worth of industrial diamonds purchased with fake money, salted away in a pig sty with only Dougie Giffard to look after them. Good God, Dominic, do you call that "going straight"? I certainly don't.'

'Clever, though,' he said, 'don't you think?'

'Too clever by half.'

He ground out the cigar, leaned over the table and took her hand. 'I'd like to claim that I could see it all coming, that when I cheated the Germans out of all that counterfeit cash I was motivated by patriotism, not self-interest. But you wouldn't believe me, Polly, would you?'

'You're right. I wouldn't believe you.'

'Well,' he said, 'I didn't see it coming, not the way it did. I love the way it's worked out, though, don't you?'

'How has it worked out?' said Polly.

'The money the Germans leaked into the system has blown back on them and will help, just a little, to bring the system down. I'm no more Communist than I am Fascist but I do know how to use people. That's my strength, Polly, my forte. I'm entirely untrustworthy. What better quality can you hope to find in a double agent?'

'Is that what you are, a spy?'

'I prefer to think of myself as a negotiator,' Dominic said. 'The Americans will make use of me for as long as they possibly can. If I prove my worth, when the war ends I'll be a villain no more. I'll be a hero, unsung and largely neglected to be sure, but a hero none the less.'

'And then what?'

'Then I'll go home.'

'Home?'

'To Scotland,' he said. 'To start up clean and fresh.'

'With my forty thousand pounds?'

'Precisely.' Dominic released her hands. He sat back. 'You haven't looked at the photographs yet, darling. Aren't you interested in the children?'

'Is that why you're doing all this, for the sake of the children?'

'Is there another reason?'

'Why *did* you take them away from me?'

'Because,' he said, 'if I'd left them behind, you wouldn't be here now. You'd have written me off, wiped me out of your life completely, wouldn't you?'

'Probably,' Polly admitted.

'I knew you wouldn't let them go.'

'What if you're wrong, Dominic?' Polly said.

'Wrong? Wrong about what?'

'What if I'm as relieved to be rid of the children as I am to be rid of you?'

'Then you wouldn't be here.'

'What if I came not because you asked me to,' she said carefully, 'but to please someone else?'

'Who? Fin? What's does he have—'

'Not Fin.'

Dominic shook his head, frowning. 'Cameron?'

Polly said nothing.

'Oh God,' he exclaimed, 'not Christy Cameron!'

'Perhaps you should have been a little more careful, Dominic, a little less devious and sure of yourself.' Polly lifted the sheaf of photographs and rose from the table. 'Now I'm going upstairs to bathe and change and lie down for a while,' she said. 'What time do they serve lunch?'

'Twelve or twelve thirty.'

'See you then,' she said and, pressing the photographs to her breast, made her way out through the dining room in search of a place to rest.

'Absenteeism,' Archie yelled into the telephone, 'isn't my responsibility. For God's sake, man, how do you expect me to be able to tell just by looking at them if they will or will not drag themselves out of bed of a morning? I agree that some *are* obvious candidates for the funny farm but the co-relationship between sheer inbred laziness and being a raving nutter has so far escaped me. Now hold on, just hold on: I'm not accusing *you* of being a nutter, Mr Macdonald, and, yes, I do realise that you have a factory to run, but . . .'

Babs paused in her typing and squinted at Archie through the half-open door of the office. She enjoyed watching Archie working himself up into a paroxysm of indignation. Experience told her that quite soon he would begin to wax sarcastic with Mr Macdonald, who managed a small asbestos factory on the far side of Renfrew and who, war or not, stubbornly refused to acknowledge the existence of unions or workers' councils. Four days was the average tenure of new employees, and several had even had the gall – or the gumption – to return to the Welfare Centre to register their complaints in person.

Archie stood up, pushed away his chair, turned his back and brought his voice down to a rasping whisper; always a bad sign.

Babs leaned over her Underwood, eavesdropping unashamedly.

'I will not,' Archie hissed, 'be talked to in this manner, sir. If you have a grouse about the quality of employees sent you by this office then I suggest you notify the Ministry of Labour who will, I've no doubt, be only too delighted to send round a team of Health and Safety inspectors to establish the facts behind complaints on both sides of the managerial divide.' He paused and raised a hand to heaven. 'No, Mr Macdonald, I said "managerial divide", which phrase, as far as I'm aware, does not imply a threat.'

'Excuse me.'

Babs had been so intent on listening to Archie that she hadn't heard the street door open. She swung round, bashing her elbow on the Underwood, and blinked up at the woman who stood before the desk.

'May I help you?' Babs asked, rubbing her elbow.

'Is he busy?' the woman said. 'Yes, I can see he's busy.'

She was just a little older than Mammy, Babs thought, and had a delicate, powdery style that Mammy had never acquired. Archie had a textbook phrase for the social type to which this woman belonged: middle-class aspirants Archie called them. It struck Babs that the classification might have been coined with just this woman in mind.

She couldn't imagine what the woman could possibly want in a recruitment office for she was clearly too genteel to undertake any sort of hard labour apart, perhaps, from flower arranging.

'I won't wait if he's busy,' the woman said.

'Perhaps I can be of assistance,' Babs suggested.

'I'll just leave him these, shall I?' the woman said. 'I'll just put them down here and you'll give them to him, won't you, dear?'

'Give him what?'

'He left his sandwiches, such a rush this morning, went off without them, too conscientious for his own good some-times.'

'San— Oh!' said Babs. 'Are you—'

'His mother, Archie's mother, yes, just an old fusspot, I suppose you'll think I am, but he gets so cross when he doesn't have a proper lunch.'

Babs stared at the neat greaseproof packet that Mrs Harding had placed on the desk before her. She could have sworn that an identical package was tucked into the pocket of Archie's overcoat in the cloakroom but she tactfully kept this information to herself.

The woman was still going on in a rushed little voice, so low and self-effacing that you had to strain to hear it, the sort of voice that would bore you to tears in no time. Babs was well aware that the sandwiches were only an excuse and that Mrs Harding had made the trip across the river not to ensure that her son and heir was properly nourished but to cast an eye on his female assistant.

Babs got to her feet and offered her hand.

'Why, Mrs Harding,' she said, laying on the treacle, 'it's a great pleasure to meet you. I've heard so much about you from Archie.'

'Have you, have you?' the woman said. 'And you are . . . ?'

You know bloody well who I am, Babs thought, and any second now you're going to take out your lorgnette, put me under the microscope and start asking all sorts of impertinent questions.

'Barbara Hallop.' Babs offered her hand again.

Mrs Harding closed both her gloved paws over it. 'The widow, yes, I'm so sorry for your loss, my dear, yes, it must be terribly hard to bear, losing a husband at your age, do you have children?'

'Only four,' Babs said.

Archie's filial instinct came into play. He straightened, growing taller. The hand that held the telephone tightened until the knuckles turned white. He kept talking, though, kept right on haranguing the manager of Resins & Asbestos as he swung round and, noble as a stag at bay, glowered out at Babs and his mother cosily holding hands and chatting like dear old mates. Then, in what seemed like slow motion, he extended his left hand, balled the fingers into a fist and punched down on the telephone cradle, cutting Macdonald off in mid-flow.

He laid the receiver on its back on the desk and, with a smile that would have made Dr Goebbels proud, advanced out of the office with arms wide spread.

'Mother,' he said, 'what an absolutely splendid surprise!'

*   *   *

The taxi-cab dropped them at the back of the Arsenal. They continued on foot up the Rua dos Remédios into the maze of lanes, and steep-stepped alleyways that made up the old Moorish quarter of the Alfama. They walked in single file on narrow pavements, Dominic leading and Christy bringing up the rear.

The old houses tucked back in secretive recesses blocked out the breeze from the Tagus, and it was hot now. Polly had chosen to wear a summer frock and cotton jacket. She was tempted to take off the jacket and carry it over her arm but Dominic wore a heavy black overcoat and Christy his reefer jacket and neither of them seemed to be feeling the heat.

She wondered if she was coming down with some vague inopportune malady that would defray the necessity of making decisions. She would, she thought, be perfectly happy propped up in bed in the airy high-ceilinged room in the Avenida Palace Hotel with Dominic or Christy bringing her cool drinks and fresh fruit, and bathing her forehead with a linen cloth.

Eight days at sea, and meeting Dominic again, had eroded her sense of reality and she felt as if she were drifting through the landscapes of a dream.

The blue sky was streaked with motionless wisps of cloud and slotted between the roofs of the houses she could glimpse the walls of an ancient Moorish citadel, the Castelo de São Jorge, high above. The tall buildings reminded her a little of the cluttered tenements of the Calcutta Road back home in Glasgow, except that they were draped with foliage and topped by flowering shrubs, and smelled not of beer and coal smoke but of sun-baked brick and spices.

There had been no sign of Jamie Cameron at lunch and Christy hadn't turned up until the meal was almost over.

Polly had seized the opportunity to give Dominic all the news from home. In turn he had told her about the children.

In fact she had spent the latter part of the morning kneeling in her room upstairs with the photographs spread out on the floor, struggling to recall what manner of mother she had been and why she had become so distanced from her children. She had never been able to see herself in them, to catch sight of her own childhood in those smug, scrubbed, scared little faces; nor did she find it even in the broad smiles and casual poses that Dominic's camera had caught, for the children in the snapshots seemed more like likeable strangers than her own flesh and blood.

What had passed between Jamie Cameron, Christy and Dominic in Christy's room in the Avenida Palace she neither knew nor cared. She was in Dominic's hands now. She would do just what Dominic told her to do.

Comical really, Polly thought, as she trudged up the steep stone steps, to realise that Mammy was at home fretting about hambones and mutton chops, that Rosie was focused on weaning an Irish foundling and Babs in finding jobs for misfits while she was about to meet with a man who might hold the fate of the Italian nation in his hands. It was all so fraudulent, so contrived, and yet, Polly thought, perhaps this is how agents and spies stumble into the game, nudged on not by pride and patriotism but by pettiness and petulance, by little bits of guilt and a great deal of greed; power too, she supposed, but unlike Dominic, she knew nothing of power or the damage it could cause.

'You sure you know where you're going?' Christy called out.

Dom glanced round. 'I'm looking for a red-painted wooden gate. The *pension*'s at the end of the garden behind it.'

'Haven't you been here before?' Polly asked.

'Only once, at night,' Dom answered.

'Maybe we should wait until it gets dark,' Christy suggested.

'Or ask someone,' said Polly.

They came to a halt at a corner. Broken cobbles, drains, a trickle of clear water, washing hung out to dry on iron balconies; the lane dived off downhill. Above the corner, though, it broadened out into something that was almost if not quite a street.

'You can't ask anyone,' said Christy. 'If you do then the Nazis might be able to trace our footsteps and track Emilio down. Right, Dominic?'

'That is a danger,' Dom agreed.

Polly had an almost irrepressible desire to laugh. Nobody in the street remotely resembled her concept of a Nazi. There were a few women pushing handcarts, one or two old men seated on chairs outside their shops, and near the top of the hill a rusty three-wheeled vehicle with chickens in wicker crates piled up behind the driver.

She said, 'What'll happen to Emilio if the Germans do find him?'

'They'll kill him,' Dominic said.

He kept his hands in his pockets, kneading a little bag of diamonds in each fist, clinging to them as if they were ballast.

What sort of racket could her husband hope to run in Portugal when he couldn't even find a boarding house with a red-painted gate? She looked uphill at a fat-armed woman, not unlike Mammy, hanging over the rail of a balcony, watching them. Was *she*, Polly wondered, in the pay of the Nazis? She was just on the point of calling out to the woman when a head appeared out of the plane of the wall. It was there and then it wasn't.

Polly blinked, unsure that she had seen anything at all.

She continued to stare along the line of the wall while the fat-armed woman leaned over the railing and unfurled a chequered tablecloth, flapping and shaking it with a snap of the wrists the way Mammy did with wet sheets.

Then the head was there again, the face of a girl.

'Does Emilio have a daughter?' Polly asked.

'How would I know?' said Dominic, irritably. 'I'm supposed to be a diamond merchant, not a damned census taker.'

This time the head did not disappear.

The face, a very pretty face, was twisted in an expression of urgency and a slender bare arm shot out and the hand on the end of the arm beckoned.

High above, the fat-armed woman spread the chequered cloth across the ironwork and shouted in guttural French, '*Ici, ici, vite, vite,*' and Polly, pushing Dominic before her, headed for the break in the plane of the wall and the red-painted gate that defended it.

'Do you want it?' Archie asked, pushing the plate towards her.

'God, no,' said Babs. 'I'm stuffed.'

'Well, waste not, want not,' said Archie, manfully tackling the last of the boiled ham sandwiches. 'The old bat knew perfectly well I'd brought my lunch with me. No, let me revise that ungenerous statement; she isn't an old bat, not really. Actually, she's just possessive. I mean I'm not supposed to realise how possessive she is. I'm supposed to be the archetypal spoiled-rotten son, fruit of her loins and apple of her eye, and just lap up all the attention in blissful ignorance of the fact that she's doing me irreparable psychological damage and rendering me totally incapable of ever being a tolerable husband.'

'She makes good sandwiches, though,' Babs said.

'She does, she does,' Archie conceded.

'She just came to have a squint at me, didn't she?'

'Old bat,' said Archie, ruefully.

'Is it true what she said?'

'Is what true?' said Archie, less ruefully.

Babs poked a forefinger into a clean handkerchief and carefully dabbed crumbs from the corners of her lips. 'About the picture?'

'Ah, the picture, yes,' said Archie. 'It's just that old thing from *Brockway's Weekly* that I happen to have lying around.'

'Framed?' said Babs. 'Hanging above your bed?'

'It's a very small room, Babs, a closet really, a hermit's cell.'

'I'm not the Virgin Mary, you know.'

Archie laughed then, being a mannerly young man, covered his mouth with his palm and chewed and swallowed before he spoke again.

'I'll bet you're not,' he said.

'You don't light candles, do you?'

'Candles? Oh, you mean under the— No, sorry, no candles. Been known to fire up the odd cigarette, if that counts.'

'It doesn't,' Babs said. 'It's candles, or nothing.'

'You're very demanding.'

'You don't know the half of it,' said Babs.

'I'm not sure I want to.'

'Liar,' Babs said. 'You do want to.'

He sighed, rubbed his nose with his wrist. 'Am I that transparent?'

''Fraid so, Mr Harding, 'fraid so.'

'Oh damn!' said Archie.

'Have you never had a girlfriend before?'

'Of course I have. Dozens – well, three.'

'But none of them were good enough for Mama?' Babs said.

'Actually, it turned out I wasn't good enough for them.'

'Mama didn't like them, in other words?'

'Mama didn't know about them.'

'She knows about me, though?' Babs said.

'Alas, yes, she does.'

'A world-weary old widow with four kids,' Babs said. 'The difference being that I'm not your girlfriend.'

'True,' said Archie.

Babs paused, then said, 'Archie, are we flirting?'

'I think we might be,' he admitted. 'On the other hand, it isn't right or proper for me to flirt with you while you're still in a period of mourning.'

'So I'm not the Virgin Mary, I'm Queen bloody Victoria?'

'You know what I mean,' said Archie.

'Aye, I do,' Babs said, 'and I appreciate it.'

'In addition to which,' said Archie, 'I wouldn't want to exploit the nature of our professional relationship.'

'Our what?'

'The fact that I'm the boss and you're merely my assistant.'

'Merely?' said Babs.

'Now you mention it, the statement is semantically inaccurate.'

'Glad to hear it,' Babs said. 'Are you finished?'

'Yes, thank you.'

She took away the plates and cups and carried them into the cloakroom, washed them under the tap and dried them on a tea-towel. She closed the door with her heel and studied her reflection in the flyblown mirror above the sink. She fished out a lipstick and touched up her lips, then carefully undid the top two buttons on her shirt. She hesitated, considered, refastened one of the buttons and went out into the reception area again.

Archie was still seated at her desk, his chin cupped in his hand.

'Archie?' Babs said.

'What?'

She placed a hand on his shoulder and leaned into him. She kissed him on the mouth, rubbing her lips against his

with a soft circular motion for a moment or two before she
pulled away.

'What,' Archie said, 'was that for?'

'For being a good boy,' Babs told him.

Then, seating herself at the Underwood, she rolled a clean
sheet of government paper into the machine while Archie
wandered into his office and quietly closed the door.

The Communist was nothing like Polly's image of a dashing
Italian freedom fighter. She had imagined a tall, bronzed,
hawk-featured man, a more robust version of Marzipan, in
fact, with brooding eyes and long black hair. Emilio had
almost no hair at all, only a few thin strands plastered to his
scalp. He was a rotund little chap no taller than she was. His
sandals barely touched the floor when he seated himself on
a worn horsehair sofa under the open window with the girl
stationed cross-legged at his feet.

The girl was young, not much more than twenty. She had
the manners of an English schoolgirl and a clipped, breathless
accent that to a Scottish ear made her seem both fey and
self-assured at one and the same time. She was dressed like
a tinker in a stained ankle-length cotton skirt and a grubby
blouse. Her shoes were a giveaway, though, very expensive
hand-stitched country brogues.

She was far from reticent about her origins and not in the
least ashamed of being the mistress of the fat little man on the
horsehair sofa. Within minutes of their arrival in the room in
the *pension*, Polly had learned that she was the daughter of
Sir Raphael Williams, a former British ambassador to Rome,
and that she, in her own words 'had gone to the bad in the
worst possible way'. She seemed proud of her fall from grace
and rather to Polly's disgust, stroked Emilio's fat thigh while
she served as interpreter and go-between.

The Italian had a voice like chocolate, thick, creamy and

seductive, quite at odds with his appearance. He ignored the girl and addressed himself to Dominic. Now and then, though, Polly caught him looking at her, looking not at but through her as if he could see all her hidden charms beneath the summer frock. She wasn't in the least flattered and if she'd had a little more command of Italian or French might have told him to keep his eyes to himself.

An old armchair, a kitchen chair, a bed, a wardrobe, a table, underclothing tossed in a corner, empty wine bottles propped on a shelf under the window, Emilio seated like a potentate on the sagging sofa with the girl at his feet, the light in the room honey-coloured and warm; small wonder that Polly felt as if she were caught up in a dream.

She wondered if this was how it was with crooks and spies and all those who lived beyond the law, if unreality eventually became the norm. If so, it would explain a great deal about her husband, her marriage and the loneliness that had driven her into the arms of other men. She was, perhaps, no better than the girl who was seated at the Communist's feet, a clever little fool who had got in over her head.

She heard Dominic say, 'No, I am not going to give you the diamonds.'

'You do not have the diamonds?'

'I do have the diamonds, but I am not going to give them to you.'

'That is very wise of you, Mr Manone,' the girl translated. 'I will, however, need to see that you are what you say you are and can do all that has been promised on your behalf.'

'Promised?' Dominic said.

'Promised by the Americans,' the girl said. 'Is it to keep the Americans informed that you have brought along one of them today?'

'This American,' Dominic said, 'is my courier. He is a journalist.'

'Ah! Journalist!' Emilio smiled and raised his hands. '*Bene, molto bene!*'

'His papers will enable him to travel to countries that are barred to you and me,' Dominic said. 'I brought him along to answer any questions you may have about the line of distribution.'

The girl hesitated, frowning. 'What's that?'

Dominic said, 'The channel, the road by which the money will be brought to you once Signor Emilio is back in Italy. Provided the Americans do not join in the conflict, this man – Signor Christy – will be able to reach you or your generals in Italy.'

'My generals?' Emilio said in English. 'No generals.'

'To the comrades who work for you,' Dom said.

Emilio did not respond. The girl swung her head and looked up at him, her grey eyes filled with anxiety, as if she feared that he might blame her for his lack of understanding. She stroked his thigh again, scratching at the material of his trousers with bitten fingernails.

Emilio continued to ignore her. He studied Polly once more but his look this time was calculating, not lascivious.

'This one?' he asked.

Nerves fluttered at the top of Polly's stomach, then the fluttering ceased and anger replaced it. She recalled the night, years ago, in the tenement in Lavender Court when one of Dominic's gang had threatened Rosie with an open razor and how Bernard had stood up to the thug, recalled too in a sudden, brilliant little flash, how her mother had beaten off creditors and layabouts; remembered suddenly that she had been Lizzie Conway's daughter long before she had been Dominic's wife.

'This one,' Polly heard herself say, 'is the wife.'

Emilio smirked and fluttered his eyelashes as if he could

see through a lot more than her summer frock and read every selfish, melancholy act that she had ever performed.

Polly got up from the chair and crossed to the sofa. She batted the girl's hand away and leaned towards the fat little Communist, leaned so close that her elbows brushed against his belly.

'This one,' Polly said, in the clear, well-modulated tone she used when addressing Rosie, 'is the one who buys the diamonds.'

'You government not give you the diamonds?' Emilio said.

'No,' Polly told him. 'I supplied the diamonds. Do you think, *signor*, that I am just a wife who sits at home and cooks supper for my husband?'

For an instant it seemed almost as if he intended to reach up and embrace Polly, but there was no warmth in his smile, no trace of amusement in his eyes. He did not like being challenged by a woman, that much was obvious.

He reverted to Italian and left it to the girl to translate.

'They do not mine diamonds in England.'

'No,' Polly said, 'but they do not mine diamonds in Germany either.'

'Do you have a source in Venezuela?'

'My source is not your concern. In England I have a source. I have a source that will keep you in bullets and explosives for years to come.'

'Hoh, she knows how to boast, your wife,' Emilio said.

'She isn't boasting,' Dominic said.

'Show him, Dominic,' Polly said. 'Give him the sample.'

Dominic took his hand from his overcoat pocket. The uncut stones were wrapped in an oilskin tobacco pouch. He unrolled it and spilled a few of the stones into the girl's cupped hands. Emilio leaned forward, peered at them. He knew no more about diamonds than she did, Polly guessed, and standing by Dominic's side, folded her arms smugly over her breast.

'How much is contained there, in dollars?' Emilio asked.

Polly answered, 'Five or six thousand dollars worth; in Deutschmarks or lire, much more.'

'I will take them,' Emilio said.

'No,' Dominic said. 'You'll take the money I give you, not the stones.'

'I can use the gemstones better.'

'Dominic,' Polly said, 'let's get out of here.'

'Pardon?' the girl said.

Polly said, 'He will take the stones and that's the last we'll see of him, and our profit will vanish into thin air. Tell him.'

The girl translated.

'Wrap them up again, Dominic,' Polly said. 'Wrap up our diamonds and we'll do business elsewhere. He's nothing, this man, nothing but a thief.'

Dominic caught the girl by the wrist before she could close her fist on the gemstones. He turned her hand around and caught the trickle of diamonds in the flap of the tobacco pouch. He even gave her hand a little shake to make sure that nothing remained. He rolled the pouch up and put it back in his pocket.

'Do you let your wife talk to me like that?' Emilio said.

'She told you only what I would tell you,' Dominic said. 'She is the one who takes the risks in England. She is the one who negotiates with the secret services to allow her to bring the stuff out. She is the one who handles the money. I have my father's friends to back me in America but my wife works alone.'

The girl spoke quickly, tripping over the words. She leaned on Emilio's knees now, looking up into his face, a face that had grown red in the past minute. The last trace of a patronising smile had gone. Polly expected him to hurl himself to his feet in rage but instead he rocked back and forth on the sofa like an old woman in mourning.

'Once I have established myself in Lisbon I'll sell to whoever pays me the best price,' Dominic said. 'I'm not obliged to honour my promises to the British Government. If the Germans outbid the Italians or the Italians outbid the French, I'll trade with them. How else am I going to make a decent profit?'

'You are no patriot,' Emilio said.

'I never said I was,' Dominic told him.

'What about this man, this American?' Emilio stabbed a finger in Christy's direction. 'He says nothing.'

'Me?' Christy said. 'I saw what happened to your guys in North Africa. I happen to think you're all chickens just begging to be plucked.' He stuck out a hand and waggled his fingers. 'I want my share, that's all. I don't care who pays me. I get a cut from Uncle Sam and another cut from Dominic on the profit he makes on the side. Nice, eh?'

'I thought I would have diamonds,' Emilio said.

'I know you did,' said Dominic. 'You thought wrong.'

Colour drained from the Italian's cheeks and the muscles around his mouth relaxed; he seemed satisfied, almost pleased with the exchange. Polly was tempted to glance at her husband but instinct told her that it was almost over, that the Communist had been convinced by their performance.

Emilio sat back, nodding. 'I will need money soon,' he said.

'How soon?'

'Three days, four.'

'All right,' Dominic said. 'Signor Christy will bring it to you. How much?'

'Three thousand.'

'Lire or dollars?' Christy asked.

'Dollars, American dollars.'

'I'll do what I can,' said Dominic. 'It might take me a little longer than four days, though. Are you safe here?'

'Safe?' Emilio said. 'Yes, I am safe.' He closed one eye, squinting. 'Am I safe with your hands, Signor Manone? That is the good question.'

'You're my money-box, Emilio,' Dominic said. 'Is that the good answer?'

And, not entirely to Polly's surprise, Emilio agreed that it was.

They reached the level streets behind the square of the Praça do Comercio in the full flush of the evening rush hour. Carts and trams, vans and motorcars flowed along the thoroughfare, and out on the river the ferryboats were thick as gulls on the Tagus's broad green back. A breeze had got up with the turn of the tide. Polly was glad of it for her lethargy had been replaced by tipsy, carefree excitement. Dominic's coolness and control had vanished as soon as he'd stepped out of the *pension*. He had unbuttoned his overcoat and flung it open and had walked with one arm about Polly's waist and one draped over Christy's shoulders as if, in the course of that afternoon, they had become boon companions.

They were looking for a bar to drink to their success in duping the Italian but the arcades around the square were shadowed now and the big, glittering shops that sold the most fashionable goods in Europe were putting up their metal shutters, and some of the lights that turned Lisbon into a fairyland after dark had already been switched on.

They loitered, uncertain, on the edge of the square.

The Mercedes slid sleekly out of traffic and stopped by them. Jamie Cameron rolled down the window and stuck his head out.

'Well,' he asked, 'did he bite?'

'He bit,' Dominic answered, laughing. 'Oh boy, did he bite.'

'I rather figured he would,' Jamie said, and then to everyone's consternation drove off again into the traffic without another word.

She lay on her back in the double bed in the darkened hotel room, knees raised and nightdress stretched across her thighs. She was too tense to sleep for now that her part in wooing the Communist was over she felt sure that Jamie Cameron would pack her on to another cargo boat and ship her off home just as soon as he possibly could.

She didn't want to go back to the mangled little mansion in Manor Park Avenue yet, to Fin's shabby office in Baltic Chambers and the shallow life she had been leading in Glasgow ever since Dominic had gone away.

The glimpse she'd had of an undercover war had thrilled her and that afternoon in the high, honey-coloured room in the Alfama, she'd felt as if she'd been playing a part she'd been born to play. Her life so far had been a series of roles directed by other people: the dutiful daughter, the loyal wife, sister, aunt and mother, lover to three very different men. She had grown so used to role-playing that she no longer knew quite who she was or to whom she owed allegiance – the nation, the family, her children, a husband who had used her, or a lover with whom she had fallen out of love.

She slid a hand down and cupped her stomach. The rise and fall of her breath and the heat of her body under the sheet were soothing, then she heard the door click open and Dominic enter the room.

'Polly, are you awake?'

'Yes.'

They had eaten dinner together, the three of them, in the crowded dining room on the ground floor. They had talked about Hitler and air raids, Poland and the desert war, about Babs and Rosie, about New York and the vast continent of North America where her children were happy and secure. They hadn't talked about the future, though, her future or anyone's future.

'Where have you been hiding?' Polly said.

'In the bar.'

'With Christy?'

'Yes.'

'Still talking about the war?'

'No,' Dominic said. 'Talking about you.'

She pressed her hand into her stomach and sat up.

He lingered by the door, separated from her by acres of brown carpet, his overcoat folded over his arm. He looked, she thought, like a hospital visitor, awkward and perhaps even a little embarrassed, unsure what to say. She reached up and switched on the lamp above the bed.

'What did Christy tell you?' she said.

'That you turned him down.'

'That I . . . what?'

Dominic shifted the overcoat from one arm to the other. 'He thinks you only took him in because he had a thing going with Babs.'

Polly leaned back against the bolster, hands above her head. All she needed to say now was 'Yes' and Dominic would believe her. Dominic had always wanted to believe her, to turn her lies into loyalty. He would believe her and come to bed, make love to her as if nothing had happened since the last time they had been together in the big gloomy room in Manor Park. What harm could there be in endorsing Christy's tactful lie? What harm would it do Babs now?

She linked her fingers together, high over her head.

'No,' she said. 'I took him in because I wanted him for myself.'

Far away, as in a dream, she heard accordion music, more Parisian than Portuguese; an exile, a refugee perhaps perched on a stool in a bar across the square or in a cold corner of the railway station, playing to assuage his loneliness.

'Do you know where Christy is right now?' Dominic said.

'No.'

'He's in a room three doors down the hall.'

'Is he?' Polly said.

'Do you want to go to him?' Dominic asked.

She unlocked her fingers and let herself fall forward, her back bowed, the light from the bed-lamp shining down on her. She rested her forehead against her knees and closed her eyes.

'I won't stop you,' Dominic said. 'I won't do anything to stop you.'

'I don't want to be with Christy.'

She raised herself up on her hands. He came to the foot of the bed and looked down at her. He wanted her as any man would want her but now there had to be something more, something that at least resembled love.

She said, 'I want to be here with you.'

'Why, Polly? Because I'm your last best option?'

'No, because you're my husband.'

It sounded too glib and banal to be anything other than a lie.

She scanned his face anxiously, fearful that he was about to tell her that their marriage was over, that vanity and fickleness had finally caught up with her and that her role as his wife and the mother of his children had been written out at last. She had sense enough to say nothing, though, to meekly await his decision, his forgiveness.

He tossed the overcoat to one side and seated himself on the bed.

'God, but you can be pretty stupid sometimes, Polly.'

'Thank you,' she said. 'Thank you very much.'

'Why do you think I brought you here?'

'You didn't bring me here, other people did that.'

'Wrong again, Poll,' he told her. 'I went to a great deal of trouble to bring you to Lisbon. Do you think it was easy negotiating with Jamie Cameron, squaring up to the US Intelligence services and the Immigration authorities when, as it were, I didn't have a leg to stand on?' He moved closer, his voice as soft as a whisper. 'If I'd come back to Scotland to fetch you, our Kenny would have had me locked up. Oh yes, there's quite enough outstanding in Kenny MacGregor's little black book to bring me to trial and probably convict me. He might be my brother-in-law but he's a copper first and foremost and he's never really forgiven me for getting away with murder out at Blackstone Farm.'

'Did you kill my father?'

'Of course I didn't kill your father. Your father took off, limped off, and that's the last any one of us has ever heard from him. Is that what you thought? That I was a murderer as well as a crook?'

'What are you doing here, Dominic; in Lisbon, I mean?'

'Making myself useful.'

'As a spy, as an agent of the United States Government?'

'My father's dying. He won't last much longer. When he goes, my brother will take over what's left of the racket in Philadelphia which, these days, is mainly a stranglehold on union labour, protection writ large. I want nothing to do with it, nothing. I'm sick of all the finagling. I'm sick of being known as Carlo Manone's heir apparent. Jamie Cameron's offered me a deal, a job if you like, and I've accepted it. As of now, Polly, I'm working for the Co-ordinator of Strategic Services, whatever the hell that means.'

'And Christy?'

'Christy too. We'll be working together here in Lisbon, at least for the next half-year or so.'

'Funding the Italian?'

'Making contacts, trading with the enemy, gathering whatever information we can about all sorts of things: Vichy France, Franco's manoeuvres to keep sweet with Hitler, the trade in arms that come pouring through so-called neutral ports, anything and everything that might serve the free world.'

'Do you want me to join you, to become a spy too?'

'No.' He shook his head. 'I want you to go to New York, settle on Staten Island and look after our kids. I want you there when I come home.'

'New York?' Polly said. 'I – I can't, Dominic. I can't abandon Mammy and my sisters. My home – our home's in Scotland, not America.'

'Not now, Polly. Your place is with me and with the children.'

'I thought they'd all but forgotten me?'

'They have,' Dominic said. 'And that isn't right, is it?'

'What about Patricia?'

'Oh, come September she'll marry Jamie Cameron and be gone.'

'Are you sure about that?' Polly said.

'As sure as one can be about anything.'

She leaned forward again, resting her brow against his thigh. He might have touched her then, stroked her hair, kissed the back of her neck, for her position was unconsciously submissive. But he was too shrewd to press her and sat quite still, his hands by his sides.

'What – what if you don't come back?' she murmured.

'Where else would I go?'

'I mean, if you . . . like Jackie?'

'Yes,' he said. 'That.'

She looked up, frowning. 'Is that what the money's for, the forty thousand pounds banked in Scotland? It's not to start a new life after the war, is it? It's insurance, Dominic, insurance in case you—'

'Protection,' he said. 'Yep, it's protection, darling, protection of a sort that my brother would never condone, would never understand. If anything happens to me then you and the children will be well taken care of.'

'And you brought me here . . .'

'All the way to Lisbon in the middle of a war, yes.'

'. . . just to con me into doing what *you* want, what *you* think's best, to convince me that you're a jolly good fellow with only my interests at heart?'

'No,' he said. 'I brought you here because I love you.'

'Dominic, I—'

He placed his forefinger against her lips. 'Ssshhh, you don't have to tell me anything. You don't have to say anything right now. Think about it, take your time, make up your mind, and when you do I'll be here.'

'Here? Where?'

'Right here,' he said, patting the bed. 'Beside you.'

'For now, you mean?'

'No,' he said. 'For always.'

21

'What's wrong, Mrs H.?' said Archie. 'You're not your usual jovial self this morning. Have I said something to offend you?'

'Lord, no,' Babs said. 'It's not you.'

'What then? Won't you tell me?'

'It's Easter.'

'It is,' said Archie, 'or will be soon; a time of rejoicing for all us Christians. The Lord is risen and all that. I always liked this time of year when I was teaching, and not just because we broke up for a holiday. Come to think of it, I liked all the festivals and fancy days. Hallowe'en, Christmas, Easter – they all had their special signs and symbols, their traditions. You could sense the excitement for weeks beforehand. For some of the kids anticipation was the best part of it, cutting out masks, making costumes, practising carols and drawing cards, painting hard-boiled eggs at Easter. Good fun all round.'

'Will you go back to teaching?'

'Absolutely,' Archie said. 'But you haven't answered my question.'

'I don't know what to do with my kids.'

'I see,' said Archie, nodding. 'Are they happy where they are?'

'Yeah, pretty much.'

'Then leave them there.'

'I miss them,' Babs said, ''specially at holiday time.'

'What did you do at Christmas?' Archie enquired.

Babs began to cry.

She was seated at the Underwood with all the paraphernalia of files, forms and envelopes spread about her. She reached into her purse, tugged out a handkerchief and dabbed her eyes.

'Sorry,' she said.

'Nowt to be sorry about,' said Archie. 'It's your husband, isn't it?'

'Yeah.' Babs swallowed her tears. 'It was just about the last thing we talked about before Jackie went overseas: the children, what I'd do with the kids at Christmas. I didn't realise I'd never see him again. I think it's just beginning to sink in. I mean, who am I gonna talk to now?'

'Talk to me, if you like.'

She looked up at him, smiled blearily, and said, 'If I can get a word in edgeways.'

Archie said, 'I'm going to put an arm about your shoulder, Mrs H. I'm warning you of my intention because I don't wish it to be misconstrued. Is that all right?'

'Fine,' Babs said. 'In fact, I wish you would.'

He pushed away a pile of folders, seated himself on the desk and put an arm about her. Babs cried some more. Archie said nothing until the little spasm eased and she let out a sigh. He tactfully removed his arm but remained seated on the desk, close to her.

'Have you heard from your sister?' he asked.

'Polly?'

'That's the one.'

'Not a word,' Babs said. 'Why?'

'Do you still have charge of her motorcar?'

'Yeah, it's parked in our drive.'

'If,' said Archie, 'I could pick up a few petrol coupons, you could stay over with the kids at the farm and motor back and forth to work during the Easter holiday. Would that help?'

'Petrol coupons?' Babs said. 'How would you . . . ?'

'I'm the manager of a government department engaged in vital war work,' said Archie, 'and I have unimaginable powers of persuasion, in case you hadn't noticed. I'll request a modest allocation of petrol coupons and by the time the powers that be discover that the department doesn't actually have a motorcar Easter will be long gone and we can start worrying about the summer vacation.'

'Archie, that's cheating.'

'I think I prefer to regard it as using the system to one's advantage.'

'And I thought you were a man of principle.'

'Hang principle!' said Archie. 'Would it help?'

'Would it ever!' said Babs.

Reading the newspapers from headlines to small ads on the walk back from school every morning had become a habit that Dougie couldn't break.

With every ugly twist in the unfolding tale of German aggression, however, he became more and more depressed. He imagined Polly Conway Manone dying of thirst in the desert or lying under a pile of rubble in the streets of Belgrade. Complete fantasy, of course; Polly was a thousand miles from North Africa and about the same, or further, from Yugoslavia. With all this useless geographical information packed away in his head, he still couldn't make sense of the war. Now, Rommel's *Afrika Korps* were snapping up all the desert towns that the British Army had taken from the Italians four or five months ago, Greece had been invaded and the Luftwaffe had blasted the undefended city of Belgrade. And as if all that wasn't bad enough, the Chancellor of the Exchequer had just increased income tax to ten shillings in the pound and Dougie's modest income had become more modest still.

During his 'lost years', when nothing mattered except

whisky and keeping the cat fed, he had lived without a
care in the world on the handouts that Dominic Manone
had provided. Now he had rejoined the community of sober
citizens, though, money loomed large once more. He didn't
want the children to leave Blackstone, and he didn't want to
lose Maggie Dawlish, but he knew that in time they would
go, all go, and he would be alone again, with just the cat, the
pig and the bottle for company.

He still had a few acres of land but regulations regarding the
sale of land had become so strict that he doubted if he would
be allowed to sell them. He'd have starved in the street before
he'd have stolen a single diamond from Dominic's hoard, of
course, but having the gemstones buried under Ron's trough
had been a comfort and he had felt like a traitor digging them
up and handing them over to the authorities, even though
that's what Dominic wanted him to do.

The stones had been delivered in a heavy brown-paper
parcel, together with handwritten instructions, about three
weeks after Dominic's disappearance.

Horse sense suggested that Dominic was safeguarding himself against a future in which banknotes might have no more
value than the German mark in the wake of the last Great War
and that if Dominic was making contingency plans, perhaps
he, Douglas Giffard, should do the same. Contingency plans?
God, what sort of plans could you possibly make when the
world was teetering on the brink of disaster? Now, with the
diamonds gone, and Polly too, he was thoroughly defenceless
and must take the future on trust just like everyone else.

Nose buried in the *Bulletin* he was halfway up the track
before he noticed Lizzie Peabody trotting towards him,
waving a beige envelope.

Dougie stopped dead in his tracks, the newspaper falling
from his hands. Polly, he thought; Polly drowned; Polly
blown out of the sky; Polly shot in the streets of Lisbon by

a German spy. For an instant he couldn't find the strength to make his legs work and stood stock-still while the big woman rushed towards him, waving the cablegram above her head.

'What?' Dougie roared. 'What's happened?'

'It's Polly.'

'Oh Christ, oh Jesus!'

Panting, Lizzie Peabody leaned forward, one hand on her knee, the other pressed to her chest. She wore a floral apron and house-slippers. Her stockings had slipped their moorings and were halfway down her legs.

'It – it's our Polly,' she gasped.

'Is she dead?'

'No, she's not dead. She's going to America.'

Shock and relief ran through Dougie like an electrical current. He wanted to weep, to laugh, to throw himself down on his knees and thank a God in whom he did not believe for sparing Lizzie Conway's daughter. Instead, he put a hand on Lizzie's shoulder, extracted the cable from her grasp and read it.

'She says she's going to the States to be with the children,' he said.

'An' I'll never see her again.'

'Course you will, Lizzie.'

'None o' us will ever see her again.'

'After the war—'

'After the war, after the war: I'm sick of hearing about "after the war",' Lizzie cried. 'Maybe I won't be here after the war. Maybe none o' us will.'

'Now, now,' Dougie said, 'you mustn't talk like that.'

'I'll talk any way I like,' Lizzie snapped. 'It's all very well for you, Dougie Giffard, you don't know what it's like to lose a daughter.'

He had been on the point of offering sympathy, but he was

hurt by the fact that she had forgotten that he had lost not a daughter but a wife and two small sons.

'Do you want me to fetch Bernard?' Dougie asked.

'Bernard'll be busy,' Lizzie answered.

She reached out and snatched the cable from him. She peered at the paper slips pasted to the form and stroked her fingers across them as if she thought there might be a hidden message, a secret code that the censors had somehow failed to detect.

She said, 'I want to go home.'

'All right,' said Dougie. 'We'll go home. A nice cup of tea will—'

'Home,' Lizzie said, 'to Knightswood.'

'I thought you liked it here?'

'I've come to the conclusion that it's not where I belong.'

'Course it is. You belong with your grandchildren.'

'They don't care about me.'

'For God's sake, Lizzie,' Dougie said, 'what's wrong with you? All this weepin' an' wailin' just because Polly's off to America to look after her children. You can't blame her for that.'

'She should have stayed here,' Lizzie said, 'with us.'

Then she set off back towards the farmhouse, leaving Dougie to gather up the pages of his newspaper and angrily follow on.

Bernard was quite phlegmatic about packing up and leaving Blackstone immediately after supper. He had grown accustomed to Lizzie's oscillating moods and whatever Lizzie might suppose to the contrary he was not unsympathetic. She was growing old, that was the long and short of it. Losing her children had hit her hard. She needed them to need her and the fact was that they no longer did.

She had grieved less for Jackie, whom she'd never liked,

than for Babs and was less than pleased now that Babs had attracted the attention of another, younger man. She had also been mightily annoyed to learn that Rosie had adopted a war orphan. Polly, though, had always been Lizzie's favourite because, Bernard suspected, Polly, like Lizzie in her heyday, had a mind of her own and a will of iron. Drape a woman in a ragged shawl and hang a mewling baby on her arm, Bernard thought, and she automatically becomes a heroine; wrap that woman's daughter in a Jaeger overcoat and send her off in an aeroplane to America and she immediately seems like a bitch. In other words, all the virtues that Lizzie had once displayed had become, in Polly, vices.

He could not for the life of him reconcile such conflicting attitudes. He was by nature conservative but there was enough flexibility left in him to understand what Polly and her sisters were about and to look past them to the generation of children they would raise and the values those children would inherit. He hoped he might live long enough to see not just an end to this terrible conflict but an end to pettiness, to spite and envy and all the class-ridden inhibitions that had marred his young manhood.

Angus lugged the suitcase down to the bus stop, skipping to keep up with Grandma.

'You're in an awful hurry, Gran,' he said.

'We don't want to miss the last bus.'

'Couldn't you have waited till the morning?'

'Grandpa Bernard has work to go to in the morning.'

'Is it the noise?' Angus said. 'I can keep the girls quiet, if you like.'

'It's not the noise.'

'Is it the smells then. If you stayed, you'd get used to them.'

'It's not the smells either,' Lizzie told him.

Grandpa Bernard had already reached the gate, suitcase in

one hand, a big soft bundle knotted with string in the other. Dougie, sulking, had stayed in the farmhouse and the girls and Miss Dawlish had waved goodbye from the window.

'I don't see why you have to go,' Angus swung the suitcase from one hand to the other and scuttled up behind the woman. 'Don't you like us any more?'

She stopped so abruptly that Angus almost ran into her broad backside. Carefully she put down her shopping bag. There were fresh eggs in it and a bottle of milk and she didn't want them to break or spill. She peered down at her grandson. She didn't have to peer far for Angus was almost, if not quite, as tall as she was and in a couple of years would be standing shoulder to shoulder with Bernard. She inspected him as if he were some weird creature she'd never seen before and she didn't know whether to be afraid of him or not.

Angus was going to say, 'It's me, Gran, just me,' but her eyes looked funny, her mouth was all pulled down and the expression on her face was more than just a scowl.

'Of course I like you, Angus,' Lizzie said. 'It's – it's not you, or the girls.'

'Is it because Auntie Polly's not comin' back?'

It was, she knew, the sort of question to which she should give a proper answer but she was just a stupid old woman who had raised three ungrateful daughters. She didn't know what she was doing stalking off in the huff but more and more she found herself doing things that the old Lizzie Conway would never have done, not in a million years. She had been too dependent on her daughters, had given too much of herself to them, and now there was nothing left.

'Auntie Polly's going to live in America,' Lizzie said.

'With Mr Cameron?' Angus asked.

Lizzie reared back as if her grandson had struck her. It

hadn't occurred to her that Stuart and Ishbel might have no part in Polly's plans, that it was the American, not the children, who had lured Polly away.

'She's goin' to look after your cousins,' she said.

'That's all right then,' Angus said.

'What's all right?' said Lizzie, frowning.

'I thought it was just us you were fed up with.'

She gave a little *tut* at her selfish disregard for her grand-children's feelings, and said, 'You'll understand when you're older, Angus.'

'It's not our fault Auntie Polly's gone away.' He shrugged and lifted the heavy suitcase once more. 'I mean, at least she'll come back some day.'

She looked at the half-grown boy and felt a pang of guilt at her heartlessness. Most of the ills she had suffered throughout her life had been of her own making but this poor lad had lost his father through no fault of his own.

'Angus,' she called out.

He went on, ignoring her now, leaning against the weight of her laden suitcase, struggling with it, endeavouring to be a man. Lizzie ran after him, not caring about the eggs or the milk. She caught him by the shoulder just as he reached the gate. Bernard was across the road at the bus halt, seated on the other suitcase, smoking a cigarette.

'Angus?'

'What?' he said grumpily.

She got down stiffly on her knees and put her arms about him, the shopping bag still in her hand. There was no grace in the manner of it but the intention was clear enough even to a ten-year-old.

'I'm sorry,' Lizzie said. 'I didn't mean it.'

'Mean what?'

'What I said about Auntie Polly, about you.'

He was embarrassed by the display of sentiment but was

not so truculent as to pull away, and after a moment gave her a pat on the back, as if to say that he forgave her.

From across the road beyond the gate Bernard shouted, 'Better hurry, Lizzie. I think the bus is just about due.'

'Dear God!' Lizzie exclaimed, reverting to the flustered state that marked grandmothers off from their grandsons. 'Oh dear God, I'm stuck.'

She tried to unlock her arthritic knees, to force them to unbend, but impatience caused her to keel over and topple on to her back. She lay on the grass by the side of the track with her heels higher than her head and heard Angus laugh, a long, growling half-suppressed chuckle.

Lizzie laughed too, giggling like a girl at her undignified position.

'Here, Gran,' said Angus, grinning broadly. 'Take my hand.'

'Both hands, son,' she said, still giggling. 'You'll need both hands,' and, throwing her weight on Angus's arms, let him hoist her to her feet once more.

In later years Polly would look back on the days she spent with Dominic in the sunny streets of Lisbon as the beginning of the middle part of her life.

Even at the time she was aware that the decision she had made there was not only important but permanent, that by agreeing to take over the running of the house on Staten Island – a house she had never seen – and become a proper mother to her children – children who had all but forgotten her – she was assuming responsibilities of a different order from those that had plagued her in Glasgow. She knew that she wouldn't be permitted to return to Lisbon, would be obliged to relinquish her hold on Dominic and learn to do what so many women across the globe were doing – to wait and worry and pray that her man would return to her unharmed.

During Easter week, she saw little of Christy and nothing at all of Jamie Cameron. The brothers had gone round the coast to Cascais, to a house on the beach that Jamie had rented for the summer and within which the first batch of recruits to the Office of Strategic Services, Christy and Dominic among them, would be trained, briefed and sent out to do their dirty work in Spain, France and the northern parts of Italy.

Emilio and his young English mistress were, it seemed, only small pieces in a puzzle whose parts had yet to be put together. Whisky bottles filled with industrial diamonds would be exchanged for packets of dollar bills and in due course dollar bills would be converted into arms and, in some vague future time, far beyond Polly's ken, the arms would be turned against the enemies of freedom, and those who abhorred the tyranny of small-minded, megalomaniac dictators would rise up and bring down the evil regimes from within.

It was not, Dominic explained, the dream of the old Colonials, those builders of the British Empire who had staked a claim to half the world by imposing law and order with rifle butts and bayonets. The American dream was more generous and compassionate and sometimes misguided, but a thing of good heart and valiant spirit none the less, and he for one was happy to be aligned with it, now and in the future.

He walked hand in hand with Polly around shady squares under a hot indigo sky, through churches cool and modern and cathedrals dark with the weight of centuries. They drank coffee at café tables, ate in the Imperium or one of the many restaurants that served lobsters and langoustines fresh from the sea. They made love eagerly in the middle of the afternoon and again in the glittering darkness of the night.

Dominic wooed her like a lover. He spoiled and pampered her almost as if she deserved it. And not once did he mention Tony or Fin or Christy Cameron or ask what they had meant to her, if they had meant anything at all. Once Polly agreed to become his wife again the rest, as far as Dominic was concerned, was a little piece of history buried in the debris of the past. It was not forgiveness but forgetfulness that Dominic offered and on those terms Polly was willing to do what was asked of her, to fly from a guilty past into a future that held no promises and no iron-clad guarantees.

After the processions and festivals of Easter week the city assumed a solemn mood. Dominic went down to Cascais and Polly was left alone. She spent most of the afternoon dozing in bed, listening to the sounds from the square, the bells and bands and, she thought, a pilgrim chanting from very far away; a far cry from dour old Glasgow's church parades and sober Sabbath silences.

On his return, just before dinner, Dom's mood, like that of the city, had changed and Polly realised that the fun and games were over and the serious business of spying was about to begin. He told her that Emilio was clamouring for money and that Jamie was angry because the officials in Washington were stamping their feet about establishing a fund for the Italian. She had the impression that Emilio had been at Cascais too and that very soon Dom intended to take matters into his own hands by leaking small lots of diamonds on to the underground market.

At the window table, bathed in candlelight, the Manones might appear to be an elegant, well-off couple spending a few weeks in the sun but Polly was well aware that there had been gossip and considerable speculation among the sinister guests who propped up the bar or conducted business meetings at the breakfast table. She sensed that eyes were upon them, sliding sidelong glances, and that whispers hung in the air, like Dominic's cigar smoke.

'You'll be leaving first thing tomorrow morning,' Dominic said without preamble. 'We've found you a ticket for the Clipper. Damned lucky to get it. It's practically impossible to get on a plane unless you're on official business. Jamie pulled a few strings. You'll be in New York in half a day. It's a fair haul from Richmond to the airport, though, so I'll cable Patricia to bring the car – and the children – out to the airfield to meet you.'

'When will I see you again?'

'God knows!' said Dominic. 'It might be sooner than either of us imagine, though, if America decides to enter the war.'

'Do you think that will happen?'

'I doubt it,' Dominic said. 'Not yet.'

'And if America doesn't enter the war?'

He shrugged. 'I don't know.'

'Will you write to me? Will that be allowed?'

'Of course.'

'And will I be able to write back?'

'It might be safer not to, at least for a while.'

Polly said, 'What will happen when the diamonds run out?'

'By that time,' Dominic said, 'the back door route into Italy should be open and established and I'll be moved on.'

'Moved on where?'

'I have no earthly idea.'

'You're enjoying all this skulduggery, aren't you?'

'I would be,' Dominic said, 'if it weren't so grim.'

'It is, isn't it?' Polly said. 'Grim, I mean?'

'You'll be quite safe in Richmond, on the Island.'

'I wasn't thinking about me,' said Polly. 'I was thinking about you and Christy, and all the others who'll be involved in whatever it is you're doing.'

'Don't fret about us; think about the Jews,' Dom said. 'The horror stories leaking out of Poland and Czechoslovakia, out of France and Germany, are deeply worrying.'

'Christy told me about Warsaw.'

Dominic nodded again. 'Yes, he was there at the beginning, but damned few of us know what's going on inside the conquered countries now. All we have to go on are rumours, terrible rumours.'

'Is that why you're committing yourself at last by signing up to a cause?'

'I suppose it might be,' Dominic admitted. 'However, since I don't want to demolish all your illusions in one fell swoop, darling, please continue to think of me as a selfish wee bugger who's just out for all he can get.'

'Ah yes,' Polly said. 'That's more like the chap I know.'

'And love?'

'And love,' said Polly.

There was no telephone in the bedroom. She wakened in the half-light to the sound of knocking on the bedroom door. She turned over, stretched out her arm and found only emptiness beside her. She sat up and looked around but there was no sign of Dominic.

The knocking continued, accompanied by an anxious voice calling out in broken English: 'Senhora, Senhora Manone, it is the time for you to be rising.'

'Yes,' Polly answered. 'I am – rising.'

'The gentleman – in room – below the stairs – he waits.'

'Yes, yes, thank you,' Polly said.

She had packed the blue suitcase and laid it out with her hand luggage by the shoe-rack near the door. The case and all the smaller bags, save one, had been removed. She wondered vaguely if this was one last attentive gesture by Jamie Cameron or unusual efficiency on the part of the management. Dom's suits still hung in the closet and his shoes were lined up on the rack, and in the bathroom a few yards down the hallway she caught the tang of the astringent lotion with which he dabbed his cheeks after shaving.

She bathed, brushed her teeth and combed her hair as quickly as possible. She didn't feel alert enough yet to be excited at the prospect of a long aeroplane journey to a brand-new country. She had made love to her husband for what had seemed like hours last night and her exhaustion at that early hour was almost insurmountable.

She returned to her room and dressed in the clothes that she had laid out, popped her nightdress and toilet things into the one remaining bag and, with the bag on her shoulder and her coat on her arm, went downstairs to find Dominic.

Christy was waiting for her in the dining room. He was standing by the table at the window.

The room was almost deserted. Three or four waiters were setting tables. A severe-looking man of about Christy's age was eating alone at a corner table and another chap, hardly more than a boy, was drinking coffee and trying to hide behind a copy of a Portuguese newspaper.

Polly carried her bag to the window table.

Coffee pot and a basket of bread rolls were set out on the cloth.

Christy pulled out a chair for her.

He said, 'We'll have to be quick.'

'Where's Dominic?'

Christy sat opposite her, poured coffee, selected a bread roll and put it on her plate. 'He couldn't make it.'

'Couldn't make it?'

'He sent me instead.'

'I see,' Polly said. 'He will be at the aerodrome, though, won't he?'

'I guess not,' Christy said. 'Eat, and let's get out of here, please.'

'Where is Dom? Is he in trouble?'

'Jamie needed him at Cascais.'

'You're lying,' Polly said.

'Yeah, I'm lying,' Christy said. 'Eat.'

She didn't eat, though. She drank coffee and took a few

puffs of the cigarette Christy lit for her. He looked different this morning, less ramshackle. He had discarded the sweater and reefer jacket and wore a soft linen jacket over an open-necked shirt. He had shaved and put a little pomade on his unruly hair and looked younger, she thought. She felt a twinge of regret for all that had happened between them, for all that might have been, a melancholy little echo of the loving time before Dominic had taken command of her life again.

She knew that there would be no more Christys, no more Fins or Tonys, that sexual adventures and betrayals must be left behind, shaken off along with the velvet grip of her family back in Glasgow.

'Got your passport?' Christy said.

'Yes, it's in my purse.'

He took a long envelope from his pocket and pressed it into her hand.

'One Clipper ticket, one-way,' he said. 'One permit of entry into the United States, signed by a consular officer. One hundred and fifty US dollars in case of emergency. Patricia will meet you at the other end. She'll tell you what to do and show you the ropes.'

'Why did Dominic send you?' Polly asked.

'He's not dumb, your husband.'

'What do you mean?'

'He knows I love you – or did.'

'So it's just another of his damned romantic gestures.'

'Yeah,' Christy said. 'He thought maybe it would be nice to say goodbye.'

'Won't you come to New York for the wedding?'

'Wedding?'

'Patricia's wedding to your brother,' Polly said.

'Oh, sure,' Christy said. 'The wedding.'

'He is going to marry her, isn't he?'

'I guess,' Christy said. 'Yeah, yeah, he'll marry her.'

'In September?'

'Whenever he can,' Christy said.

'So I'll see you in September?'

'Polly . . .'

She nodded.

She didn't need to be told that they might never meet again. She stubbed out the cigarette, finished the coffee in her cup, and got to her feet.

'All set?' Christy said.

'All set,' said Polly, and followed him out to the taxi-cab that would carry her out to the airfield and the first sad, happy step to her new life far away.

The girls had lugged Davy off into the field in front of the farmhouse. They swung him between them vigorously and now and then let him drop to the ground and rolled him over, tickling him without mercy to make him laugh.

If May and June were much taken with the latest addition to the family, April was enchanted. She followed the wee chap around as if she couldn't believe her luck in having a new cousin to play with as well as a grown-up brother; a boy to look after as well as one to look after her. The moment May and June stepped back, she sank to her knees and nuzzled her face into Davy's, administering kisses in a manner more maternal than flirtatious.

Davy, of course, loved all the attention and had no fear of the boisterous girls. Only now and then, in the midst of a swing or a tickling, would he thrust May or June roughly aside, look towards the gate where Rosie and Babs were chatting and yell, 'Ma, Ma, Ma,' until Rosie broke off her conversation, waved and called out, 'I'm huh-here, darlin'. Muh-mummy's here,' then, reassured, he would topple back on to the grass and encourage the girls to attack him again.

Angus and Archie Harding were in the field too, practising

acrobatic tricks on Archie's old bicycle, which had arrived roped to the roof of Auntie Polly's motorcar. Since Auntie Polly had gone to stay in America, the motorcar was theirs now. Provided Mr Harding could scrounge enough petrol coupons to keep it running Mum and April would stay at the farm for the holidays and Mum would drive across the river to work every day.

Angus was pleased that his mother and little sister were staying at Blackstone. He was even more pleased to have the big black motorcar sitting in the yard and, though he wasn't quite ready to admit it yet, to have Mr Harding dropping in to insult him and to teach him how to ride a bicycle backwards without using your hands.

If his dad had been daring on the Excelsior Manxman, his dad had also been, in that capacity, rather remote. There was something about the old boneshaker that Mr Harding had given him that made it, and Mr Harding, seem more approachable, particularly as Mr Harding was willing to attempt all sorts of tricks that Mum, let alone Miss Dawlish, condemned as dangerous, like riding up a plank of wood hanging from the rusty fence to see if you could land without falling off. Angus often fell off, but so did Mr Harding. The pair of them looked like a couple of tinkers after half an hour of practice and Miss Dawlish would have slobbered them both with iodine and slapped on sticking plasters if Mr Harding hadn't told her that a man must bear his scars bravely and, under his breath, back turned, had suggested that Miss Dawlish go chase herself.

Dougie had come out of the house and had watched their antics for ten minutes or so but when Mr Harding had suggested that he give it a go too, Dougie had beaten a hasty retreat to the vegetable patch.

'That boy's going to buh-break his neck,' Rosie said. 'Aren't you going to tuh-tell your chap to be careful?'

'Nope,' Babs said, contentedly.

'Is he giving you something?'

'Petrol coupons,' said Babs.

'I don't mean puh-petrol coupons.'

'I know what you mean, Rosie, and I'm not going to dignify the question by giving an answer. Mr Harding and I are friends and colleagues, that's all.'

'He's not hanging round just because you're his cuh-colleague,' Rosie said. 'He wuh-wants something.'

'Course he does,' Babs said. 'He wants to marry me.'

'What! Has he asked you already?'

'Not yet,' Babs said. 'But he will when the time's ripe.'

'When will that be?'

'When the kids have got used to him.'

'And when he asks you, if ever he does, what'll you say?'

'Are you kiddin'?' Babs said. 'I'll say "yes" like a shot.'

'Have you forgotten about Juh-Jackie already?'

'No,' Babs said. 'I'll never forget my Jackie.'

'Bet you will,' said Rosie, 'once you've guh-got a new man in your bed.'

Babs shook her head and sighed. 'To think,' she said, 'that you were once Mammy's prized possession, her sweet, wee innocent girl.'

'I've changed,' said Rosie.

'I know you have. We all have.'

'It's the wuh-war.'

'Probably,' Babs said.

She watched April stick a buttercup in Davy MacGregor's ear and give him a kiss to make up for her clumsiness.

May and June were gathering buttercups too but there was something less than charming about the way her older daughters went about it, not plucking the flowers but ripping them up by the roots and tossing them at poor, chuckling Davy. She would, she knew, have trouble with that pair, just as Mammy in her day had had trouble with Polly and her.

Now, with Polly gone, it was Rosie who had taken the bit between her teeth and, a new baby notwithstanding, had experienced a little more of real life than was good for her. Kenny would keep Rosie in check, though, for Kenny was a good man too.

Babs said, 'I wonder where she is right now?'

'Mammy? She's at huh-home in Knightswood cooking the dinner, I expect,' Rosie said. 'I wish she'd stayed. I wanted her to see Davy.'

'She's doesn't approve,' Babs said.

'Doesn't approve of Davy?'

'Doesn't approve of any of us,' Babs said. 'I think she feels she's let us down, or maybe that we've let her down.'

'That's duh-daft,' Rosie said. 'As if we'd ever let Mammy down.'

'Well, bringing up kids is worse than a marriage,' Babs said. 'You bring them into the world not knowing whether they'll turn out for better or worse.'

'Which was it for us?' Rosie asked.

'Both,' Babs said. 'Neither. Oh, I don't know. It just sort of . . . *is*, I suppose. Anyway, I wasn't thinking about us.'

'Uh-huh, you muh-mean Polly. She'll fall on her feet,' Rosie said. 'Our Polly always falls on her feet.'

'Funny how things work out,' Babs said.

'What is that supposed to mean?'

'If Christy and Polly hadn't . . . Oh, never mind.'

'He wasn't for you, Babs,' Rosie said. 'Did you sleep with him?'

'Nope.'

'Don't you wish you had?'

'Nope.'

The sisters were silent for a moment, each occupied with

her own thoughts, none of which were very profound. They watched Archie balance the boneshaker on the plank, holding pose perfectly, then dip and shoot down on to the ground and, with a whoop, swerve round to face Angus.

'*Voilà!*' he shouted. 'What do you think of that, prune-face?'

'Not bad,' said Angus, grudgingly.

'Not bad! It was brilliant,' Archie said.

'Okay,' said Angus, 'now it's my turn.'

'Be my guest,' said Archie, and handed the bicycle over the fence.

The girls, and Davy, had gone quiet.

They were lying on their tummies on the grass, peering at some small insect that had had the temerity to crawl out from among the buttercup roots. Davy had his bum in the air and April had an arm about his waist.

'Peaceful,' said Rosie.

'Make the most of it,' Babs said. 'It won't last.'

'Nuh-no,' said Rosie. 'It never does, does it?' just as the gang among the buttercups broke into shrieks and howls and fled from the threat of the invisible bug and Angus, poised on the bicycle on the plank, held out both arms and shouted, 'Mum, Mum, look at me, Mum,' and nose-dived into the grass.